Safe

Frances Galleymore

ORION

Copyright © 1996 Frances Galleymore

All rights reserved

The right of Frances Galleymore to be identified as the author
of this work has been asserted by her in accordance with
the Copyright, Designs and Patents Act 1988

First published in Great Britain in 1996 by Orion
An imprint of Orion Books Ltd
Orion House, 5 Upper St Martin's Lane, London WC2H 9EA

A CIP catalogue record for this book is available
from the British Library

ISBN 1 85797 764 5 (cased)
ISBN 0 75280 145 7 (trade paperback)

Typeset at The Spartan Press Ltd,
Lymington, Hants
Printed in Great Britain by
Clays Ltd, St Ives plc.

The characters in this novel are fictitious. Any resemblance
to real persons, living or dead, is coincidental.

Safe

Safe is dedicated to
every woman who has ever been attacked

Her face, close beneath his in the sifting light, was sharp with need. A sense of power flooded through him and mingled with the tenderness as he stroked her, seeing that longing. She was his father's wife, and within his power. That was the crazy, anachronistic truth: she was kind of possessed, by the man who had spawned then disowned him for so many years – by the man he could destroy. He knew such a darkness inside his own heart, poisoning it. He kissed her, hungry for the magic that could drive out the pain, and the evil. She could do that, always, for him.

I

She never felt safe.

In the city, she lived with several million strangers and did the things that people warn about. Travelling alone at night, she took the Underground, choosing the fuller carriages. In London streets, she followed police advice and walked against the flow of traffic, aware of anyone close by. She carried an alarm on the key-ring in her pocket, charted a course by the lights from shops, avoiding shadows.

It was not quite logical, her fear of strangers. The cause – she tried not to think about but kept it buried – surfaced only at the darkest edges of her memory. Since that time, she had trained as an actor and was often searching for work. The flat she shared was a basement, where she slept alone with the window locked. In the dark, that piercing shape would glint past her eyes and press against her throat, cold on the skin. If she moved, life would end. Then she would start awake, and the terror kept her from sleeping again.

She was determined to overcome her past, but struggled to live normally, full of unease. That was, until now. Harry had changed everything.

Harry was like no one she had ever known closely before. He was successful and substantial in every way, tall, and powerful from fitness training. He told her she could rely on him, and proved it constantly, through the whirlwind days and nights of their affair.

Harry dissuaded her from going out alone. At first he would

send his car to collect her, but soon they spent all their time together. He was with her, and he did not leave. She felt at peace in the discretion and quietness of his surroundings, the restaurants, his penthouse eyrie by the Thames. Because he had been famous, there was the visibility – extending slightly now to her – but it didn't matter. She revelled in the cocoon of his protection, and of privilege, but it was not only those things that she cared about. It was Harry. He was clever and know-ledgeable, tender and charming, and so firmly in control of things. When she was with him, she felt that she had a right to live, unafraid.

When Harry had to visit the States, he asked her to go with him and, of course, she went. She loved him and felt lucky, and it was only meant to be for a week.

No one expected them to marry.

SEEN IN TOWN . . .

British actor Harry Glass, *Will Vengeance* star of the seven-ties. Glass, 56, is visiting for the network launch of his true crime series, *Cry Murder*. He introduces each drama on screen, so is this a comeback? 'I never stopped making movies,' says Glass. 'It is simply a change of role, to pro-ducer.'

Stories from his hell-raiser years still pop up – some say the actor got confused with the part. Does Glass miss the old high life? 'I lived in the fast track then,' he admits. 'Now my company, Topnotch, produces successful shows and life is different.'

Glass is honeymooning with his third bride, blonde Karen Kincaid, 28, an up-and-coming Shakespearian thesp. The couple met six weeks ago, in their native London. Where, Glass assures me, he is busy making more international movies.

'Our hotel is a giant wish machine, it's a magic town,' Karen said, and Harry laughed.

Looking down, she glimpsed the vast foyer with florist and pharmacy, jewellery and clothing stores. The restaurant, where they were having brunch, was built of towering glass. Waterfalls tumbled down the side of each chrome staircase, Perspex-channelled, and walls of mirror multiplied them into infinity. Harry and herself, his friends Leonie and Bill. Countless figures repeating, wherever she looked. She looked a lot, with pleasure: it made her feel she belonged with him.

'Karen in Wonderland.' Harry smiled, indulgent. 'It's her first trip.'

She touched his arm, her fingers meeting the fine stuff of his sleeve. The jacket was a colour he often wore, lighter than his grey eyes, darker than the thick, silver hair which curled endearingly. 'I still can't quite believe what we've done.'

'But don't you just know when a thing feels right? Impulsive, hey – and why not?' Leonie raised her glass of Buck's fizz. 'Congratulations.'

The four of them touched glasses. 'Good to see Harry settled,' agreed Bill. 'Of course,' he joked, 'The guy's a real pro, he'll do anything for PR.'

Harry said, 'I first saw her on stage, in a fringe production of Ibsen. I'd been asked to look at the lead actor, but I couldn't take my eyes off Karen, she was so lovely.'

'Harry came backstage, and asked me out. He swept me off my feet, that night – everything was about Harry after that.'

'Lucky man,' commented Bill.

'These guys are nuts about each other. Romantic, huh?' Leonie turned from her husband, as their food arrived.

'You should see the reviews of her Cordelia in *Lear*,' Harry told them. 'Rave notices! Darling, is that all right? It doesn't look hot.'

Karen took a forkful of scrambled eggs. 'I don't mind – it's good.'

Harry had signalled the head waiter to their table. 'This meal is cold. You can't possibly expect my wife to eat cold egg.'

'I'm sorry, sir.'

'We would like it freshly cooked, very hot – and fast.'

'Yes, Mr Glass.' He hurried off with the plate.

After an awkward moment, the other three began to eat. Karen watched them hungrily. Harry always looked after her well, he was attentive and considerate, but sometimes she wished he'd let her decide. He was used to taking charge. 'Everyone knows who you are over here. In England, we don't like success. We slay our heroes.'

'You should move here,' Leonie suggested. 'You'd both do great things, and with those looks, Karen would soon find work.'

'Oh, shall we, Harry?'

'I've a stack of projects lined up at home.'

'You must come back soon.' Leonie, blade-thin, slid a morsel of seafood between scarlet lips, perfect teeth. 'Harry's big reputation, it all started here.'

'Do you know those movies?' Bill asked. 'Of course, they were before your time.'

'They're on TV and video,' Harry said. 'We must watch them together, sweetheart.'

'Could we get the videos here? Do let's.'

'They're splatterfests. Will was a psycho,' Leonie warned. 'But they were mega.'

Bill added, 'If we're talking here of Harry's big reputation, he got into some famous fights, during those years.'

'Those stories were hype, the media took it over. People in the street or in bars would recognize me, pick a fight. So the stories kept escalating.'

Karen flew to his defence. 'Poor Harry. Having strangers jump on you because of a part you played.'

The head waiter brought her new dish, steaming hot. 'Enjoy your meal, Ms Glass.'

She ate, ravenously. The others had finished, and Leonie was pushing away her untouched plate of bread and butter. 'No wonder you're so slim,' Harry complimented her. He poured their coffee from a silver pot, answering questions from Bill about his production schedule.

Karen watched Harry. He was popular, well known, established. Could she live up to him? She was learning to fit into his world, to belong with Harry, who had given her everything – security and affection, a future. If he guessed at her self-doubt, or at the extent of poverty and survivalism in her life, he gave no hint of it. He was a very English gentleman, often surprising her.

'You getting into bed with Al?' Bill was asking Harry.

'Now Karen's wondering who Al is,' Leonie noticed, laughing. 'Hey, no more film talk, guys. So you've got a few more days here?'

'We go back on Wednesday,' Karen said. 'Harry's got a couple more days in the studio.'

'I'm recording trailers. I've asked Raima to look after Karen and take her shopping.'

Leonie was giving Harry a strange, censorious look. She turned to Karen and said, kindly, 'If we weren't so frantic at the magazine, I'd love to shop with you myself.'

'That would've been fun, I'm sorry we can't.'

'Karen will have a wonderful time,' Harry said, firmly. 'Raima will know exactly how to spend a fortune's worth of my money. She knows my taste, she'll know where to go. They'll have a whale of a time together.'

Raima was younger than most of Harry's friends, and she sizzled with a sharp, confident glamour. Since they had all met up at a party, Harry had arranged their girls' day out. Waiting in the Green Bar, Karen tried to feel pleased.

Twenty minutes late, Raima arrived in a cloud of scent, air kissing, hyper. 'The car was horribly late, darling. Let's go.'

Briefly they were outside, where the day was overcast, raw and blustery. Then into the overheated limo, to glassed-off roars of traffic as they crawled and snarled along the grid. Soon they were browsing in Fifth Avenue, in the hot, bright interiors of boutiques, and big stores packed with jostling customers.

Raima sifted briskly through rails of glittering prizes. Selecting outfits, she held up each against Karen, steering her towards the mirror. 'Harry would adore this! Those English rose looks are pretty, but these would give more definition.'

Who would they define? The other woman was very tall, striking with dark, glossy hair and voracious features. Karen felt mousy, her slight build and fair colouring eclipsed. These structured clothes seemed alien, locking her stiffly away, so she was restricted, brazen and false. She would be acting a role in them. At home she wore jeans and sweaters, was rarely on show except in costume on stage. A new life lay ahead. Might it really be so different?

She wouldn't waste Harry's money, buying things she didn't want. She tried on dozens of outfits and eventually chose a black pantsuit, to wear anywhere. Raima bought, for herself, a Gucci dress that set off her exotic looks.

As they had lunch, picking at giant hot salads, Raima asked, 'Have you always worn your hair that way, hanging down?'

'I like it long. So it can be dressed, instead of having to wear a costume wig, for working,' Karen explained.

'That college style does nothing for you. I've got this genius who'd know what to do with it.'

'Harry likes it this way.'

After a moment, Raima drawled, 'This is all new to you.'

Karen blushed, melting with embarrassment: she must seem out of her depth. She decided to misunderstand. 'It's my first time in New York. Las Vegas, too. It's exciting! I'd like to see more of Manhattan.'

'There won't be time. Harry's instructions are to raid all the best boutiques.'

'Let's play hookey,' she suggested, then saw that they wouldn't. 'How long have you known him?'

'We're old friends. He's always visited.'

Karen's training had taught her to study people, their mannerisms. She noticed Raima's precision as she sipped mineral water, refilling the tall, iced glass. Her nails were long, painted a plum colour. Two platinum rings decorated the smooth, unworked hands. Everything had to be the best, and the world – or some wealthy man – owed her a living. Was

Raima divorced, or being kept by someone? Did women still live that way? She was being paid for by Harry, right now, on holiday. She felt a sudden longing to be in her old life, working at her craft.

'I suppose Nora knows all about you?' Raima broke in, and must have seen her blank look. 'Didn't Harry tell you he's got a sister? She's his only relative. Of course, she lives in Canada, but I'm surprised she didn't go to your wedding.'

'It was very spur of the moment.'

'You're real strangers to each other.' Raima smiled slightly, watchfully.

'We both know how we feel.' Karen's voice sounded sturdy. She hoped it didn't betray her thoughts, the panic that was starting to rise. Raima knew more about Harry than she did, and must think he had made a bad choice. Raima herself looked more the kind of woman that someone like Harry might want, sophisticated and sure of herself.

Had they been lovers? Would she want to know if they had? Harry was exactly twice her age. Those twenty-eight years seemed a lifetime to her. Years she could never really understand, decades of living, loving other people. He'd had two wives before her. Maybe there had been lots of women? The thought made her feel lonely. She was so used to being with him, she was missing him already.

They went on, to a big store. Maybe it was Bloomingdale's: afterwards, she could never remember. Huge and noisy, it was crowded with afternoon shoppers, and everything anyone could ever want. Displayed like a feast of desire, this was life on a plate, delectably arranged. Raima wanted to look at scarves. Soon they were in a world of rainbows, draped, cascading, entwined. Meandering slowly between banks of cashmere and silk, chiffon and chenille, that softened to the hand and stretched the eye with dancing patterns, Karen lost Raima.

She realized, later, just how badly she'd wanted to escape. But her first reaction, looking round and seeing she was alone in the crowds, was surprise. She had left Raima at that wall of paisley, swirling silks. Or had it been at that other rack, or in another

7

direction? She was here somewhere. Karen dodged through shoppers, past stands and counters, barriers of flimsy cloth. At any moment she would see the tall figure in the plum wool coat, expertly sifting merchandise.

Strangers surrounded her. She had wandered too far, got hidden from view. Raima would think she'd walked further on into the store, she should go that way, or stay where she was. Karen took a few steps, then stopped. She stood still in the milling, humming, eager honeypot.

The processed air, white lights oppressed her. She could tell someone, or find the store's office, go there. They would put out a message. Maybe there was a Meeting Point. Or Raima would tell the staff, her name would be called over the speaker, and they would get together again. But when had she last felt the wind through her hair, the solid ground propelling her feet, a freedom to go wherever she liked? She had been guided, monitored and advised for ages.

Glancing around quickly, hoping now that she wouldn't be seen, Karen headed for the exit doors. There, caution and effort fell away like shackles. Perhaps Raima had wanted to escape from her, too. She laughed aloud, and skipped out to the sidewalk. The streets of Manhattan, unknown and pounding with life, stretched all around. The afternoon was cold with gusts of fine rain, and she raised her face to breathe real air, leaving behind all the well-heated interiors, their modulation.

She started to walk. Silver buildings sheered into the sky, towering so high they seemed to lean inwards and meet. They were giant glaciers, and along their foot people tumbled in torrents: she was borne into them, and on. They pulsed with temperament, ran with noisy human grit.

This city had a topcoat, glossy and gleaming, and a dark underbelly, half hidden from the casual eye. Desperation and violence, misfortune: in the crazed eyes of an addict staggering on the sidewalk, or a drunk who shouted incoherent anger. She wasn't afraid but felt safe, even having no guide or map, and was too impatient – running now, with energy – to pause and read the signs. She wasn't alone, but was a part of everything.

Harry's charmed bubble of safety, spreading out wherever she went, had set her free.

Between the blocks, tracing the geometric streets, she crossed a square to join spectators. Skaters were whirling on a floor below, floodlit, brilliant in a tide of swooping, gliding colours. She felt the euphoria in their flight, her body tingled with exhilaration, eyes marvelling at patterns forming and transforming, endless, fast. They were vivid and primary, while overhead young trees, black and leafless, were spun about with delicate lights of silver-gold. If only Harry was here to see.

The lights were coming on because the afternoon was darkening. It was late. She must have walked for hours, Harry would soon be back, and nobody knew where she was.

Just before it started to rain, she found a cab. It was five seventeen. She was about twenty blocks from their hotel, unlikely to make it back before Harry arrived. Suppose Raima had been concerned? She should have got assistance from the store, not slipped away. The traffic was thickening. Spangled lights of white and red drew shimmering paths in the wet. Rush hour was turning into static hour: the cab scarcely moved. Trapped in vibrating rumbles, plumes of exhaust, honks and shouts, everyone was heading for somewhere different. The grid simmered with argument.

It would be quicker to walk. Paying the cabbie, she set off among seething pedestrians, was almost swept down a drain-like flow to the subway. Holding on to a barrier, she edged past. The subway might be faster but she didn't know the system and could get lost, and Harry would be appalled at her travelling that way.

Impossible to walk freely among these aggressive crowds, umbrellas and bags. If she was a bit late, surely it shouldn't matter? She would make an adventure of her walk, a joke of her anticlimactic attempt to return. The rain fell heavily, gluing her hair and running down her neck, seeping round her ankles and feet. Perhaps she should have stayed in the taxi. But there were the lights of the hotel ahead, portico with carpet, uniformed doorman looking slightly incredulous. Karen crossed the lobby to reception.

Harry was back. It was a quarter to six. She headed quickly for the elevator.

'Ms Kincaid? Excuse me.' A woman, smart in a pinstripe suit, approached eagerly. 'I've an interview with your husband, and I've been waiting an hour. Shena Saville.'

'Does Harry know you're here?'

'I haven't let him forget.' The journalist was edgy. 'We fixed this with him two weeks back. I'll come up, OK?'

Had Harry really been back an hour? He was supposed to stay in the studio till five. 'You'd better wait. I'm sorry. I'll remind him you're waiting.'

Shena Saville looked her in the eye. 'I need this. It's important.' And she paced back towards her sofa.

Whisked up to the twenty-eighth floor, deposited in the softly carpeted corridor, Karen went into 2814. The first things she saw were a dozen glossy carriers from Saks, Bloomingdale's, boutiques on Madison and Fifth Avenue. In front of the leather-topped desk, Harry was sitting with a drink in his hand, staring at her.

'Harry, darling – sorry I'm late. I've seen the whole town. Listen, there's someone down in the lobby –' She stopped because as she got nearer she could see that Harry was very angry.

'Where the hell have you been, the entire afternoon?' He looked at her coldly. 'I told you to stay with Raima and buy clothes. Instead you took yourself off – to where?'

'We – got separated. So I went for a walk.'

'I searched all over for you.' Raima's voice cut across. She was standing stiffly by one of the tall windows. 'The store put out a message, but you weren't there. I called up Harry and he left his recording session –'

'I've had people searching for hours. You went for a walk, leaving me not knowing what you were doing. I had to leave the studio. Why didn't you call? I would've sent a car. Or you could've got a cab back, at least. Instead you vanish all afternoon, and – look at you.'

'Harry, I got caught in the rush hour. I ran back through the rain, because it was quicker – to be with you,' Karen said, shocked by his reaction.

Raima was stepping across the room to the door. 'Karen has come back perfectly safe and sound. I must go now. We'll talk later.' Quickly, she left.

Harry ignored her. 'So where did you go? You were missing for several hours.'

'I don't know where. I'd lost Raima and – just felt like walking. Harry, I need to get out of these clothes, have a shower.' She longed to escape, but he was between her and the bathroom.

'Am I supposed to believe that? You don't know where you went? In every city there are crazies, and streets where you should never walk. You could've been mugged, wandering alone.'

'I was careful. Nothing happened. I'm back, so can't we forget it? I did enjoy the city and felt happy.'

Harry's face was turning red; his features changed to venom, mouth a line of hate. She had never seen him in such a temper. Of course, he must know how she hadn't looked for Raima and hadn't got help at the store, how much she'd relished the taste of her individuality and strength. Happiness must have shown on her face as she walked in.

Harry turned away, and poured himself another drink. He sounded betrayed. 'I arranged it for you, with my friend. I went to that trouble, and also, in case it has escaped your notice, I financed everything. So did you think that you knew better?'

'Don't talk to me this way,' she broke in.

'Listen. I have told you, *never* wander on your own. Bad things can easily happen – you've no comprehension, no knowledge of the different districts. But you obviously prefer not to listen to what I say, the minute my back is turned.' He looked at her again, clearly disappointed. 'I did expect a little gratitude.'

If this angry stranger would disappear, Harry could return and everything be as before. She felt ashamed. He would never love her again, now he had seen that she wasn't worth it. 'Harry, I'm sorry. You must've been worried. It was inconsiderate, not to come straight back.' His face was unresponsive, and she felt close to tears.

The phone rang. Harry exclaimed with irritation, picking it up. 'Yes? I'm busy . . . No, I can't. If she wants to go away . . . I can't say. Possibly tomorrow. And I don't want to be bothered again tonight.' He put down the phone. 'Damned journos! She's nobody, they're fobbing me off.' Then he stepped towards her. Tracing the wetness on her cheeks, his voice grew kind. 'You're crying? But you're safe now, with me.'

She whispered, 'Please don't shut me out.'

'Don't cry.'

She stood mute. If Harry stopped loving her, she wouldn't survive − not now. He was beginning to breathe heavy, brandy-fumed breaths. 'You will learn, poor darling. You have so much to learn. Let me teach you.'

Harry was guiding her towards the kingsize bed, sliding down her jeans and briefs. He unzipped his fly, climbing on top of her. 'I want you with me all the time, I love you,' he panted, trying to prise her open, to stuff his half-erect cock inside. She could hear his words, but couldn't take in their meaning. Her body felt cold, closed and dry. He pushed and shoved his way in, and she gritted her teeth. She couldn't ask him to stop, she felt so bad about letting him down, after all he had done for her, after he'd chosen her. It didn't last very long. Eventually he came, and subsided his weight.

'I adore making love to you. I couldn't bear it if you got harmed in any way.' He murmured softly, 'You are mine, completely, and I am yours. You will always be my princess.'

He fell into a doze, and he was heavy. She shifted a leg slightly, careful not to disturb him. Knowing he still wanted her − that was like balm. She was grateful that sex between them was undemanding, since anything more would be difficult for her. But she had started to notice how people around Harry, although admiring him, never seemed at ease. Were, maybe, a bit afraid of him. His manner could be harsh, and she was beginning to feel tentative in his company.

She must learn not to disappoint him. For years she had lived in fear of men, but Harry had plucked her out of that old life, had offered his protection and shown he cared. She had kept one or two secrets about her past, things she had meant to tell him then wasn't able to confide. Guiltily she told herself that what he never learned could never harm them. She would make up for silence by being a perfect wife.

In the morning, she was relieved to see tenderness in his eyes. 'Our last twenty-four hours here. Will you still love me in England, Harry?'

'Darling child, if you only knew how much. Now, don't detain me. I've to get to the studio, and since you were extremely wayward yesterday, there's an hour's recording to make up. If I haven't started a technician's strike by leaving early.' He slid out of bed.

'I'll order breakfast. Shall we have a full cooked English breakfast, to get reacclimatized? Harry – can we eat it in bed?'

'Such appetite!' He chuckled. 'Why not? Go ahead.'

Karen ordered, and Harry showered. She lay back on the soft pillows, waiting for him and breakfast. She felt happy. Her eye wandered to the boutique carriers, unopened. Inside were a dozen smart outfits, tried on yesterday. Raima must have gone back to buy them. Why had she? What difference would it have made – what could Harry have said or done – if they had both returned almost empty-handed?

There it was: his expensive, masculine fragrance. She looked round and saw Harry draped in a towel, watching her. He padded across the carpet, chose a carrier and drew out layers of tissue, a sheer black chiffon frock. 'Givenchy? Marvellous. Will you try these on for me?' Could she possibly live in Raima's clothes? A knock at the door saved Karen from replying, and she organized the breakfast trolley. 'I'll send a car to collect you,' Harry decided. 'So we can get lunch together.'

'Oh,' she agreed. 'That'll be great.'

He caressed her hair. 'Darling heart, you will let me dress you? I want to spend a lot of money on you, on quality. I want to dress you because you can look so stunning.'

The phone rang, and Harry reached out to answer it. The caller must be some long-lost friend, for his voice sank to intimacy and promise. 'Of course we must meet,' he said, charmingly. 'You're downstairs? Let's do breakfast. I'll see you in the Blue Room, in five minutes. Looking forward to meeting you . . . Mm. 'Bye.' He hung up, jumped off the bed. 'Needs must, when the devil drives.'

'Who was that?' Karen asked in surprise. 'Was that – Shena Saville?'

Harry was getting dressed with care, in denim shirt and pale trousers, blue casual jacket. 'Don't mind, darling? I need the publicity, don't we all.'

She gestured towards the laden trolley. 'But what about *our* breakfast?'

'Dear heart, it's all on expenses. Must rush. I'll call you. I'll send a car.'

When he had gone she, too, abandoned the bacon and sausages, tomatoes and mushrooms, the neat triangles of crustless toast, marmalade, coffee and orange juice. She couldn't go out because Harry would call and expect her to be there. What would she do all morning? She lazed a while, wallowed among scented oils, bath essence and moisturisers, then un-packed the pristine garments to try them on. She felt curious, knowing their power to create the new: a self for the wearer, a persona for the outside world. When she looked in the mirror, Karen smiled. She had become a glittering creature, parodic of Raima. If she wore these, might Harry get the joke?

To try out the new Karen, she sat at the desk and dialled England, London, her own home. The phone rang and she pictured it, on the bare floorboards or frayed Mexican rug, in a decrepit armchair or on the tea chest that served as a table. Then the machine clicked on, with Poppy's breathless tones. 'Karen and Poppy are out. Poppy's gone to the Rent Office and will be back. Karen's gone to the States. If it's about work, please call the Vicky Hedges Agency . . .'

'It's me!' Karen sang out. 'I've missed you. We're coming home tomorrow – of course, we'll be at Harry's place. So much to tell you, babe! See you.'

Replacing the receiver, she sank back. A nostalgia swept her, for the madcap Poppy, their chaotic, hand-to-mouth existence in that poky basement. Times together, nights with friends and days of frenetic opportunism, hope and ambition . . . Karen got up, went to the wall of the walk-in wardrobe to look at the few possessions she had brought from England.

They were no longer there: her favourite jeans, long black sweater, the fake-fur tigerskin she adored and had found in Portobello market. She began to search everywhere, in wardrobes, drawers and suitcases. Could Harry have got rid of them? They had been hers for years. They were all she had that was familiar.

How could he be so insensitive? As Raima had said, they knew little about each other. She had felt rapturously displaced, agreeing to marry him in all the rashness of transit, among the new. Their real relationship was waiting until tomorrow. She had blurred, remembered impressions of Harry's life back home, his friends there. Could she fit in? Everyone who knew them would be astonished.

Poppy had gone silent with shock when Karen broke the news by phone. Then, shrieking with excitement, interrogated her for details. 'Wow, that's safe – brilliant! You get to the Big Apple, then you hook the famous film star and get the *deliriously* exciting new life. Bitch! I'll never speak to you again.' And it was true, Harry was a catch. He was romantic, and very generous: he wanted the best for her.

He was right. She should not look back, but only forwards to their future. The deliriously exciting new life. This was her environment now. Secure, with an army of people between herself and harm. On the desk stood the red roses her new husband had bought, and a photo of them, radiantly together at a gala dinner. Her only problem, her biggest decision in life, was which outfit to meet him in. Whether, perhaps, to start varnishing her nails. Except they were all bitten to the quick.

She whiled away the morning until the car arrived. It was white, long and sleek, with a uniformed driver. In her new pantsuit and cape, she sat and watched Manhattan glide by beyond the smoked windows. Then into the television studios, briefly waiting in a comfortable reception. Harry appeared, handsome and beaming, greeting her as if they had been parted for ages. She was so proud of him as they kissed.

Neither had any idea that for the past two days, they had been followed by a stalker carrying a gun.

His name was Damien Calvino, and he had been hunting them since the night flight brought him in. He was young, tall in a black, scuffed leather coat, jet hair corkscrewing over his eyes, hollow cheeks unshaven. For two days, he had prowled invisibly through Manhattan. No one gave him a thought unless they saw those eyes, burning and crazed with hatred.

The gun swung, cold and heavy, in his hip pocket. Using it was the only thing he still lived for. Outside the TV Center, knots of people were stopping, looking for stars. He had to get ordinary, check his thoughts, just stopping, too, to wait for someone. Crowds. Jostled, pressed by people: and so much pressure inside him, explosive. Those ugly mugs, munching, gaping, blank. So alive that he hated them, reminders of loss, death . . . Bitten by cold, he got immobilized and could feel nothing, like now.

Until he saw her. A white Lincoln, drawn up at the studio, her stepping out. For a second, he wasn't sure. She had changed fast, since the press photos. Dressed to kill, in threads costing thousands of dollars. A spoiled rich bitch, half her husband's age, smiling at the driver. No cares, a lifetime ahead. The cruelty of that.

People shifting away from him. Got to chill out. And the limo was moving off. She'd gone in the building. He'd never talk his way in, he was beyond that, a bum. If he tried it, they'd call the cops. Wait. Wait for ever, if you've got to.

Suddenly there he was again, arm in arm with Virgin Bambi. Albert Harold Sharp. Born 24 March 1940, at Bermondsey, East London, England. A.k.a. Harry Glass, famed and loaded, seventies icon.

Staggering forward, ripped by hatred, grasping the Beretta in his pocket, he saw it happen. Aiming the gun at that broad back, squeezing the trigger, hearing explosions, seeing blood. Glass falling, lying crumpled on the sidewalk. But too many people got in his way, he was buffeted and shoved off course, unsure of the ground, short circuits blinding him inside. Then he glimpsed them, disappearing into some smart eatery, shepherded to deep seclusion.

Waiting, again. He needed to eat. Bought a hot dog at a street stall. Gagged on it, that soft white dough, the pink-grey flesh, its worm of red.

When they came out, flushed and cheerful, it was his lucky day, they walked. He slipped back, although if either had turned and seen him, they would never have known who he was. Through the remnants of the afternoon, using the crowds, tourists and shoppers as a screen, a sort of intimacy began. He was watching Glass, and the way he treated the girl. Kept looking at her, kind of worshipping, real courteous; and the girl was close to Damien's own age, his sister's age. Tracking, intent and clever, for a while he almost forgot.

Until in the early evening, heading down Lexington and to Broadway, he lost them. He couldn't believe it, hunting, cursing aloud, around each junction and in every foyer.

It was the last chance, tonight. He owed it to her, had vowed it to her. There had been no flowers on her grave except his own, no memorial, a pauper's funeral. *Angel.* Her face flew into his vision. He would never see her again, had laid her to rest inside the cold earth. And Harry Glass had killed her.

They would be back tonight, had gone to some show. Damien walked forty blocks to their hotel. From almost opposite he watched that bright expanse of entrance with its flower tubs and long green canopy, and the burly, uniformed security. It was starting to rain, cars swished by. When they stopped, he strained to see. He had turned up his collar and the legs of his jeans clung. His fingers felt again for the gun, snug. He had practised. From the moment he found her, he knew what he must do. Luca had left the gun for this purpose, the old man had suspected what might happen.

When the taxi drew up, he tensed. Saw Glass's silver head emerge, his body shielded by the yellow cab. Leaping out of the dark, he kamikazied across the street. Horns blared, cars swerved. *Now!* Glass was turning towards the revolving doors, the girl following, in the way. He stopped on the sidewalk ten yards off, legs braced, hand closing, drawing the gun, each second unfurling slow.

'*You – stop!*' Security, hand snaking to his holster – and Glass, the girl, screened by that big figure while the doors turned, revolved, taking them in. He ran, hurtling into shadow, throwing himself through the traffic, round a corner, into crowds and down the subway. Rasping breath, among the noise. Invisible, now.

He had been seen, and maybe the gun. They'd think he was a thief or a crazy, but he couldn't go back. Was it over?

Damien rested. He took the subway one stop, came up into the black, wet night with its streaming lights, ephemeral, past. Lost chances. He was filled with loss, until he felt the rush of hatred again.

Green for go: Walk. He would follow them to Europe and settle the score.

2

On landing at Heathrow they were met by Martin, Harry's aide. 'Welcome home.' He smiled, then turned stiffly to include Karen.

Had Harry told Martin, or left him to hear about their wedding? 'Thanks, Martin. We had delays at Kennedy, we're tired.'

'Hop in, I'll do the bags.' He had opened both doors of the Jaguar, front and rear. 'Have I got things to tell you, Harry.'

Karen slid into the back, into soft, palest leather, safe as a womb. Harry was getting in the front, saying, 'I need an update.' They glided on to the motorway, between fields, through cluttered suburbs. London was a muddle of narrow streets and little roofs, lights flicking on. Listening to the murmur of voices in front, she saw their heads turn together, the fair and the silver, exchanging a look. They had been close for years. Martin was always polite but remote towards her. Perhaps she had been one of a string of girlfriends. Until now.

'You must take things easy,' he was saying. They were approaching Docklands, the Thames rippling prettily with lights. Ahead lay Pipers Wharf, its converted warehouses, courtyards and shops. Then the Jaguar slid down a ramp and concrete enclosed them, white fluorescence, pits of shadow. Hard chrome snouts, glittering snarls lined their route as they eased towards Harry's bay. Doors slammed, sounds exploding, magnified.

In the security lobby Harry introduced her to a guard on duty before the lift whisked them up to the penthouse. Loft living,

Harry called it. The vast, split-level apartment was an expanse of white carpet and pale wood. Wide windows gazed, over a half-glassed terrace, across the Thames, and pillars studded the space. Wall lights illuminated long glass tables and giant sofas, shelf dividers and a tall, slender tree. Even after weeks in New York, his home still awed her.

Harry was glancing around, his eye lighting on objects. 'Drink, darling? Then I must look at the horrors that've built up in my absence.'

Martin poured drinks. 'We expected you back last week. Alice has put out the urgent stuff, I'll show you. Then I expect you'd like a bite to eat.'

'That would be marvellous. Hungry, darling? We won't be long.'

Martin went with Harry to his office. Karen hovered, swirled the ice in her vodka and tonic, then crossed to the kitchen. It was steel state-of-the-art, all gadgets and dials, switches and timers. No food lay in sight, but an array of empty surfaces. Instruments hung from a row of hooks, above a butchers' block and a rack of knives.

A footstep behind: she whirled round in strange alarm. It was only Martin, with his closed expression and careful manner. 'Did you want something?'

She had no reason to feel nervous of him. 'All this high-tech equipment, I've no idea how to use it. This, for example, looks lethal – what is it?'

'Those are for the rotisserie. Harry likes a variety of cuisine, and – yes – he has nothing but the best.'

The phrase hung between them in a silence. Martin thought she wasn't good enough for Harry, that's why he was unfriendly, cool towards her. Careful with him as he was with her, she ventured, 'You must show me how to use everything.'

He was taking containers from the man-sized fridge. 'I can if you like,' he answered eventually. 'But Harry's used to my cooking, and to me looking after him.'

'I'm sure you do a very good job. But I'll want to cook sometimes, now this is my home. I'm sure you understand.'

Martin said nothing; his back spoke volumes. He went about preparing salad in a deliberate, fastidious way. She asked, 'Harry has a secretary – I've seen her a few times. When does she come in?'

'Mornings, nine till twelve. And there's the maid, each afternoon – but you don't need to bother about any of that. The place runs like clockwork. It has to – Harry's a very busy man.'

How would she fit into these lives? The kitchen was clearly Martin's concern, and the office Alice's; the domestic arrangements Martin's, with the maid. Karen went out, up the blond wood stairs, past other doors to the big bedroom she would share with Harry. It was pale blue, with two walls of storage and a view upriver.

Their luggage was waiting and she clicked open one of Harry's cases. Carefully, many hours ago, she had wrapped and lined the folds of each garment with tissue, as he had taught her. She unfolded one of his jackets, and opened the wardrobes. Shirts, trousers and jackets hung in sharply pressed rows, graded by colour – white through dove grey, tones of blue deepening to navy – and by weight. The more substantial suits were hung towards the corner, and country clothes had a section of their own. Dozens of drawers were neatly stocked with underpants, socks and ties, each folded small.

This time she didn't hear him but felt Martin's presence, then caught his fleeting expression of dismay. So she was supposed to leave Harry's unpacking, for him. 'I was just wondering where everything lives.'

'Those will go straight to the dry-cleaning service,' he answered. 'Shall I do the same for your clothes?'

'They haven't been worn,' she blurted out, then blushed scarlet. He would know anyway – everything she had was brand new, bought by Harry. If only there was something she had already owned and paid for.

Martin seemed not to notice her confusion. 'This side's yours, but I can do the bags. Harry's waiting downstairs.'

'Of course, I'll go straight down.' She stumbled out, with a smile she knew was horribly false.

They ate, the two of them, salmon pâté and rocket salad with small crusty rolls, at the long table. Harry was solicitous. 'Is it nice being here? You must ask anything you need to know.'

'I'm not quite used to it, your beautiful home.' She toyed with the silver cutlery, drank from a wine-glass so fine perhaps it was crystal. When they were alone together, her ignorance never seemed to matter so much. She touched his hand. They would be all right: they were committed now and would grow closer every day. 'It's a bit hard to see what I'm going to do here. You're well looked after.'

'You're the only companion I want, sweetheart. The others are employees.'

'I know. And we'll have times alone together.'

'Life is very simple here. And when we go to the weekend place, it's even simpler.'

Martin removed their plates. They ate cheese, and Harry had brandy. When Martin retreated to the kitchen, she took Harry's hand mischievously. 'Let's go out to the terrace,' she whispered. 'You can finish your drink and we can be private.'

Harry allowed her to tow him on to the terrace. They leaned on the parapet, gazing across the Thames at the city night. Lights drew paths of silver to them. Opposite, the flats were a yellow honeycomb, a silent hive of unknown lives. The sky above held clusters of tiny lights. 'So many stars!' she marvelled, until Harry roared with laughter. Parts of the clusters were moving, carving slow arcs.

'Those are planes, circling the City Airport. Funny one, I adore being with you! We'll see Europe this summer – you'll come and join me.'

'That would be great. I've no work, though I could get lucky.'

With sudden attention he asked, 'Would you still want to act?'

'Whenever there's the chance,' she told him. Harry didn't answer. They had never discussed the future, everything had happened too fast. She looked up at him and they hugged, his warm, solid masculinity enclosing her. He was powerful, protective. 'Harry? Let's be deliriously happy together.'

He began to kiss her. Martin, from the doorway, said, 'Harry – it's Robert.'

'Yes, let's,' Harry murmured in her ear. Unhurriedly he turned to take the phone. He began to discuss a contract, and Martin handed him a document.

Annoyed, Karen said quietly, 'It's after ten thirty.'

Equally quietly, Martin admonished her, 'Whatever time it happens to be, you don't refuse a call from your lawyer.'

Did Martin despise or hate her as if they were rival wives? He was too polite, ready with comments that she felt as criticism. She watched him in all his importance of activity, that handsome face, the well-tuned body waiting for Harry's command. It seemed he loved to serve, and was proud of his special relationship.

In Harry's crowded, busy life, she felt the sudden loss of real contact. Exploring the health club and the shops and cafés of the Wharf development, she thought how the outer world was beyond reach. Harry needed the car, and there seemed a lack of other transport. Surrounded by luxury, she was stranded and isolated. Pride forbade her asking Harry for money. He wouldn't understand her wanting to leave such comfort, and he might not help.

The second day, she paced the apartment alone. Outside, the light was fading and the river flowed silver as a police launch sliced through silently. The door of Harry's office stood ajar. Pushing it experimentally, she went in and saw a hymn to technology, phones and fax, computers and printers, copiers and files. There were desks for Martin and Alice; and Harry's, the least burdened with paper, elegant wood with olive leather. His desk held pens and a row of old-fashioned ink-bottles, scripts in a stack, two phones. Its tall chair was of buttoned, matching leather.

Karen sat in Harry's chair. She swivelled it, surveying the office, his minions' sweatshop areas, the Thames and a panorama of London. It felt like being a god. Did Harry feel as if he was God?

At a sound close behind, she leaped up guiltily. A cracking noise added to the whirs and clicks. Paper was tonguing out of the fax. She had upset the pens, the inks: bottles lay spilled over the desk and a steel trolley. Glass fragments, and a pool of red ink, stained the precious tufts of pale beige carpet.

She stared at the growing patch of scarlet, as if it was spilled blood, then fell to her knees, ripped off her sweater and stuffed it over the ink. Scarlet soaked through white cashmere, arterial, permanent, turning it into a used bandage. She shouldn't have done that. It was too late now. Mopping, heart in mouth, at the edges of the stain, big as a human head and still spreading, slowly now.

Oh, God. What would they decide about her now? Running to the laundry room, scouring through the cleaning cupboard. What was the right thing – detergent or soap? Or salt, maybe, as if to take out red wine? There were stain removers for oil, various foods, lipstick. None that mentioned ink. She ran back to the office – suppose Harry and Martin were to return? – and knelt again to pick out bits of glass with scarlet, guilty fingers. Scrubbed at the incriminating patch.

It paled slightly, the tufts looking flattened, tired. The ink was drying into the fabric. Tomorrow the maid would be in at two and might know how to remove the ink. Or maybe she could get to the dry cleaners, in the morning, and ask.

She couldn't tell them. It would confirm everything Martin thought of her, and that Harry, by some kind of osmosis, seemed to be thinking too. Harry would fly into one of his rages, and she couldn't let that happen again. Beside the desk stood the trolley, with volumes of *Spotlight* and other directories. By shifting it forward twelve inches and moving the wastepaper basket, the stain could be nearly hidden. Would anyone notice?

The white cashmere sweater, drenched with scarlet: he had chosen that for her. Listening for the lift, she stepped out to the landing and checked the lights. Nervous, red-handed, she fed the sweater into the garbage disposal. Back in the laundry room, she scrubbed at her hands with scourer, bleach and pumice, until they appeared innocent.

Karen sat staring at the river. Harry would hate her, he would never love her again. But that was stupid: it had been just an accident, anyone could have an accident. But she should never have been in Harry's office, he had made it clear she was to have nothing to do with his work. And he loved his possessions, those carefully chosen symbols of success. He would love that beautiful oriental carpeting.

She picked up a phone and dialled, was relieved to hear Poppy's greeting. 'It's me,' Karen said, woe in her voice.

'Hey, babe! You're back, in the lap of star-studded luxury. Yeh?'

'I suppose. Poppy, I feel lonely.'

A cackle of laughter. 'Are you whingeing? I'll trade places. Did you see that pic of you both in the *Daily Mirror*? It's all so sexy. What d'you mean, lonely?'

'I miss you. Are you getting someone else to share?'

'We had a final notice for the phone, and the Electricity sent a ghastly legal thing so I'll have to. Gawd, is that the time? I'm meeting Caspar – must fly.'

'I've got to see you – and to sort things out. Tomorrow?'

'Make it lunchtime. Great . . . see ya!'

Karen felt a surge of pleasure. She was dying to talk and relax, be her old self. How would she get to Camden? The Docklands Light Railway wasn't too far away. She had a few uncashed travellers' cheques, and there was a bank in the next building.

Then she heard a voice from Harry's office. Not a machine but Martin – he was in there, talking on one of the phones. He must have come in, through the living room, while she was speaking to Poppy. How silent he was, and creepy. How long might he have been there?

'Any plans for today, darling?'

Karen glanced swiftly from Harry to Martin spreading marmalade on toast. 'I'm going to see Poppy, and to pack up my things.'

'Your clothes or furniture?' Harry raised his eyebrows. 'Sweetheart, I scarcely think so.'

'Poppy needs to find someone else to share, she needs the space.'

Martin said, 'Camden, that's near the BBC.'

'I've to be at Portland Place later,' Harry explained. 'Anglo Road is on our way so we can lend a hand.'

She wanted time alone to catch up with Poppy, and to rescue treasured bits and pieces. 'I don't want to waste your morning, and there's the train.'

'I'd never dream of letting you go by train. I want to be with you, every moment we can. We'll leave in ten minutes.'

Karen said nothing. If Harry and Martin came with her, they were less likely to see the damaged carpet before the maid arrived. For a moment, she imagined telling him. Lightly, even amusingly so he would mind less: alone and missing him, she had sat down in his chair and, like an idiot, happened to blunder into . . . But she could not. She was afraid of his ridicule, and rejection. From the car she phoned Poppy, who was not fond of mornings and took a while to answer, squawking at the news that they were both on their way.

The Jaguar glided over the potholes and litter of Anglo Road, where the meters were taken and so were the yellow lines. Martin double-parked by a battered Ford. He peered up the street to where a gang of boys, outside the council estate, were staring back with nonchalant interest. 'I'll stay with the motor, yes?'

Karen said, 'Harry, you could just drop me off.'

'Don't be silly. Martin will wait for us.'

She felt ashamed because it looked more awful than she remembered. Someone had dumped a mattress over the railings, the steps were strewn with litter. Cyclamen paint had peeled from the door, and the place stank of tomcat. Then Poppy stood beaming, shawled in a blanket, with her red hair wild. Karen flew to hug her. 'Poppy, you're just the same, and it's been ages.'

'You look fantastic, wow – will you still speak to me?' When

Poppy turned to Harry, she was suddenly shy. 'Hello. Sorry, it's an icebox, the electricity's cut off. Sort of expecting that, weren't we? Dark, too. I'll light candles. That'll keep us warm, ha, ha.'

Harry had visited only once, and now Karen saw her home through his eyes. It was short-term housing, unrepaired although they had lived there for years. Wires hung loose and ceilings had fallen, revealing wooden slats. The walls were tacked with posters and scarves to hide the damp. She saw the junk, the mess, the poverty. The sofa was a futon, and male clothes lay around, distressed jeans and sweater, boots caked in mud. Karen cleared a space for Harry to sit. 'Like a coffee, darling?'

'Caspar and I were celebrating,' Poppy chattered on, nervously. 'He's got a part in *Casualty*. Fantastic, eh?'

'That's a prominent series.' Harry sat gingerly on the futon. 'What's the part?'

'Well, it's a walk-on. Although he'll have one leg in plaster so he doesn't actually walk. But it gets him off waiting at tables. It's so hard, you know, to get anything. I haven't worked for . . . a while.'

Harry looked at Poppy appraisingly, returning her admiration with interest. 'It's hard to see how any casting director could overlook you, Poppy. Perhaps you haven't been up for the right jobs. Tell me what you've done. I'm casting six films,' he mentioned casually, then turned to Karen. 'Yes, sweetheart, to that coffee.'

Karen smiled slightly to herself, putting on the kettle and listening from the kitchen. Did Harry intend to help Poppy? Her friend was agog with hope and premature gratitude. As she took in the cups, Poppy said, 'Karen, you've married the bee's knees. Is there a brother – a twin, please?'

'If I were twins,' Harry replied gravely, 'you'd be taken.'

Poppy laughed. 'I want to know about Las Vegas. Did you go to one of those chapels? Did you gamble?'

Harry said thoughtfully, 'We're both gambling, to some extent.'

'Oh, whatever does he mean?' Poppy asked.

Her bedroom door opened, and her boyfriend Caspar, naked, came hurrying out towards his clothes. 'Oh, hi . . . folks.' He stared sleepily in surprise then, slightly abashed, retreated to wrap himself in a sheet.

Getting up, Harry said, 'Martin's waiting, we must move.' He hadn't touched his coffee. Karen saw too late: the cup bore a hairline crack.

Her bedroom was exactly as she had left it. Harry watched, questioning why she needed to take this or that, as she dismantled her old life. She had been mostly happy here. Now her furniture would have to remain or be thrown out. There was one old suitcase, another borrowed from Poppy, and two black plastic sacks, to carry the stuff from her whole lifetime.

'What are these?' Harry asked, spilling out the contents of a cupboard.

'They're from my tour of East Africa.' She picked up her drum, checking it was undamaged. 'With the National Theatre, with Gus Mackintyre.'

'Really? What were you doing?'

'It was improvization, drawing on national mythology, and wildlife.'

'Were you a hyena? Or an elephant?'

'I played lots of creatures and spirits. There was quite a buzz about that tour.'

'Not a lot of hisses or roars, brays or laughs? Honestly, darling, where are you planning to store all this?'

'I'll find somewhere.' Karen felt stubborn, angry with Harry. It was as if he thought her life had been valueless until they had met. Or was he insecure? She had never thought of him as jealous before. Soon her room was stripped and left empty. 'Sorry I have to rush off,' she told Poppy. 'I'll bring your suitcase back next week. And we need to talk bills.'

'That ghastly summons thing –'

Harry broke in, smoothly. 'Why don't you tell Martin we're ready? You could keep an eye on the car while he fetches things.'

Poppy came rushing after her. 'Wait, Karen. I bumped into Andrew Carter last week, he asked what you're doing. He asked if you'd done any telly.'

'Poppy! You didn't say I hadn't?'

'Of course not. I referred him to our esteemed agent.'

How fantastic it would feel to be working again. 'Maybe I'll call him. D'you think I should? He directed the Ibsen.'

'He was probably making conversation,' Harry said. 'Andrew and I are old friends. He started in film, and was some kind of runner when we made *Will Die*.'

'Wow, that's such a classic!' Poppy glowed at him. 'I'd love to hear about it all. I mean, if you ever have time.'

They stowed the luggage, she said goodbye, and Martin negotiated the one-way system. Harry took her hand. 'You're very quiet. Poor darling, what a sadly deprived lifestyle. It always was, I think, wasn't it? I promise you won't ever have to play a hyena again.' Karen glanced at him, deciding to say nothing. It was her closest companion now, this feeling of being ashamed. 'I settled up for you,' he went on. 'I gave her extra, so you won't ever need to go back, or return that old suitcase.'

She thanked him, burning inside. She would visit Poppy but not tell him. Harry was Sir Galahad – generous, courageous, and in thrall to his own bloated vanity as he carried her off. He said, 'Let's screen my movies soon, shall we? I can't believe you've never seen them. Here I am – the BBC. Martin will take you straight home with your rubbish bags.'

It took her breath away. She began to retort angrily, 'They're not rubbish –'

'Karen, I was referring to the container not the contents. You're being difficult. Please be in a better mood by the time I return.' He vanished up the steps of Broadcasting House.

Martin drove her back in silence. What would happen if she asked to be dropped off at a cinema, or taken to friends in Stepney? She didn't have the confidence, right now, and there was the carpet to deal with. When Martin went out again, Karen ran upstairs towards the sound of hoovering.

'I'm Mrs Glass. Do you understand English?' The maid looked alarmed at being spoken to, as Karen beckoned her down to the office. To her horror, the trolley had been pushed back: the stain of ink roared out, a vulgar flowering of old blood against that delicate, oriental beige. It was hideous, violent. The maid gave a cry, gesturing as if to ward off evil.

Karen showed her the ink-bottles and imitated washing away. 'Please. Can you make it good again? Please.'

The woman stared at the stain, stricken. Then she brushed past, out to the laundry room. Karen started to follow. Would she know how to remove the ink without damaging the carpet or its dye? Who could have found it, pushing things back to where they had been?

The phone rang, and she picked it up. 'Hello?'

The voice was a woman's, muffled in some way. 'That must be Karen. Mrs Harry Glass III? I know it's you.'

'Yes. Who's that?'

'Congratulations.' The hoarse whisper was intimate, confiding. 'You got him, Karen. Now, what's he like?'

Her mouth had gone dry. 'I don't know who you are. And I'm going to hang up.'

'Don't do that,' the voice rasped. 'You wouldn't be interested in me. But there's something you need to know. So listen. The others . . . Did you think you're only the third wife? You should ask him about them, Karen. Ask him what happened.'

The phone clicked off.

The screaming filling the sky came from seagulls whirling free, scattering silver from a pale sun. Damien Calvino stood on the edge of the world, it seemed. The English Channel was grey, empty except for a smudge near the horizon, some kind of battleship, and a bright ferry furrowing across. Here the rocks ended, giving way to a lower, deserted coastal path. At their ending, Harry Glass's weekend house, a cluster of whitened stone and tile, had been built around a lighthouse.

Someone was coming out of it. Slight, in dark jacket and jeans, a travel bag over one shoulder. Walking up the drive, she

30

paused at the gate before it opened. She was a youngish woman, black-haired.

Damien scrambled down the dunes. Was she an employee, maybe local? She was passing his hired Escort on the corner, setting off down the coast road. Ahead of her lay a flat heath, with a golf course on the other side. The road led nowhere, surely, except into the nearest town. He trailed her in the car, keeping some way behind, then pulled in ahead and lowered the window. She came alongside.

'Hi.' He took off his shades. 'It's a long walk. Like a ride?' She was weighing him up, and he smiled. 'It's OK. I'm not some killer on the loose. I'm a visitor, and would like the company.'

'OK, thanks.'

'Want to throw that bag in the back?'

'I'm only going to the station – along this road.'

Not local, then. Where did the trains go from this coast? She had a heavy, preoccupied manner, and didn't seem happy. Her cropped hair looked badly dyed, her clothes were old and her boots scuffed. She didn't care about herself, maybe was poor. He touched the gas, set off. 'So where are you heading?'

She took out a black pack of Death cigarettes, offered him one. Damien shook his head. 'London,' she said, lighting up from a Zippo. 'And you?'

'London.' He sparkled more at her because she wasn't responding. 'Great. You know the route?'

'OK. I'll get us there.'

So she had been here before. 'You're from London? My name's Damien, by the way.'

She looked at him intently, then glanced away. 'I'm Viv. You look Italian or something.'

'You're partly right. I'm from Chicago, over here to see Europe.' They drove in silence a while. 'I was down by the dunes on that beautiful shoreline. Didn't I see you,' he asked, casually, 'coming out of that amazing kind of a tower house?'

Viv didn't answer. Then she sighed, and said flatly, 'That's right.'

'What is it – a lighthouse, or some naval defence?'

'It's nothing, only a house.'

'But quite a house, yeah? Must be some view. Who lives there?'

'Nobody.' She stubbed out her cigarette. 'Not now, not often. It's a holiday home, owned by some geezer who used to be a film star. Harry Glass.'

His heart jumped at the confirmation, even though he didn't need it. He knew about the Keep from a photo feature that he had read and re-read. Now he whistled, in a long, low sound of surprised admiration. 'You know Harry Glass, Viv?'

Almost reluctantly, she said, 'My brother works for him.'

'That must be interesting, if you get to hear about things. You know him well?'

'Harry's not a star any more. He's turned producer, and makes telly series now.'

'He was one of the greats.' She made a face, said nothing, and he tried again. 'Where does he live the rest of the time – leaving that spectacular house empty?'

'He travels. They're just back from America. He has a London pad. Why're you so interested?'

'Just – he was so big, a legend back home.' He shrugged. 'Seventies nostalgia, you know.'

'I see, you're starstruck.' She seemed amused.

Damien drove her all the way to North London, where she lived over a shop on Crouch End Broadway. He turned the conversation to her, flattered her. She stayed cool and didn't ask him in. Then, before he drove on to his bed-and-breakfast in Pimlico, he got her number.

When Damien called her, two days later, she sounded pleased: that made things a whole lot easier. He wanted information – facts, addresses, times and schedules – and he needed access to Harry Glass. Right from the beginning, meeting Viv, he had known he would do whatever it took to get her help. Glass had a home in London, but where?

They talked a while before he asked her out. 'You can buy

supper if you like,' she agreed, without much of a pause. 'But it'll have to be tonight.'

He was getting used to the way she never explained herself. 'I'll come by and pick you up. Say, at eight?'

It was as easy as that.

Viv wanted to go to the World Café round the corner, she said she liked the atmosphere. It was busy, filling up fast. He got them a table, overlooking the street and an old church. 'Pretty, isn't it? And they do the best ever beers, from all over the world.'

She was different, with a new, high energy, as if she wanted something. Her hair was gelled, and she wore a black shirt, a man's. It was partly undone and when she moved, her pale skin flashed at him. They ordered, then she asked, 'Been seeing a lot of London, have you?'

With a shrug he told her, 'It's not so great on your own.'

'There's the rest of Europe, too,' she reminded him, slightly mocking.

'There is. It's good to see you again. You're looking sharp.'

She said nothing, but he caught, flying across the smile on her face, a cynicism. It was only there for a moment, but he recognized it. This babe hated herself. She only seemed tough. She was like Angel, that way. 'Really,' he insisted, and felt a moment of conscience. 'What do you do, Viv? Got a career?'

'Come off it. I used to do some temping when I had to. I don't know why people work. You have a job?'

'I've been studying. This is a vacation.'

'I see. If you're partly Italian,' she asked, suddenly changing the subject, 'what's the other part?'

'A lot of Irish,' Damien explained, 'because of our grand-mother, Bridie – she raised us.'

Viv exhaled smoke above him. 'So when you go back to Chicago, who's there?'

The sudden depression took him by surprise, sealing him into leaden isolation. 'Oh,' he managed to say, 'no one much.'

Their food arrived then but she ignored it and leaned towards him. 'What is it?'

'Nothing.'

'Tell me.'

The armour of rage had deserted him. He had to look away.

'You've got a brother, or sister?'

'She died. Last month. It was heroin.' And he heard himself saying, 'She was murdered.'

Viv's voice was shocked. 'You mean by dealers or what? You know who did it?'

He had said way too much already. 'Why're you so interested?' he snarled, in a welcome return of anger.

She got off his case, then, and after a while they retrieved the evening. But he couldn't get her to talk about Harry Glass. 'Ask me another time, will you, Damien? He's a boring subject to me, you know.' So she wanted to meet up again. OK. He had all the time in the world.

But Viv was in a hurry. As soon as they had finished their meal, she said, 'Come on, let's go.' She took his hand, walking round to her place. Together they went in, not even talking about it, up two flights of stairs. She had one barely furnished room, but it didn't look as if anyone really lived there. Her bag of clothes lay spilled half over the floor, and a cooker and sink stood in a corner. Nets hung at the window, traffic thundered past. The single bed was covered with a flowered duvet, and she led him straight to it.

He had planned for this to happen, thinking it was the only way to get close enough, to learn what he needed to. But somehow, by now, it was feeling all wrong. In a minute she was undressing him, placing his hands on her small, firm breasts, covering him with quick kisses. He reached for the buttons of her shirt. 'No,' she said, pulling away from him. 'Not that. This,' and helped him to unpeel her leggings. Her body was undernourished, the white skin stretched over her pelvic bones; her bush was ginger, soft fur. He felt unease. What were they doing – why this? Who was she, anyway? They were both casualties, looking for a rush and short-term oblivion. He wasn't too sure about it because she looked vulnerable, and he was using her. When her kisses moved down his body, freeing him enough, he drew back to look at her.

Damien said softly, 'Hey, Viv? Talk to me. Is this what you want, really?'

A pain of rejection, then anger lit her eyes. Without answering she pinched him, nipping his thigh, so he drew his breath sharply, furious. Her hand closed over his prick, expertly. For an instant, he was unwilling. Then his body responded, on automatic. He was dialled to sex, hardening, throbbing. OK, she wanted it. And he craved oblivion, the more the greater. He took her the way she wanted, from behind, fucking her fast and growling into her ear, about his need, her power over him. That was when her rhythmic, throaty little sounds built and broke. He ejaculated. Fierce pleasure, a tide of relief: huge tension was flowing out from his limbs. They curled up together, still saying nothing, to drift asleep.

He woke during the small hours because the depression had locked around him again. Loneliness, cold, although his skin was touching hers. What was she thinking? He could tell she was awake, keeping very still, her pale face averted. She was a strange girl, scrawny and needy. She seemed to have nothing. What did matter to her?

By just not leaving, the next day or the next, he stayed on a while at Viv's apartment. Ennui enveloped them. She might be anorexic, he thought, she needed feeding up. So he took her shopping, and they cooked – hearty pastas, nourishing soups. After a couple of days, they collected his things from the B-and-B. It was maybe a kind of loose affection: she didn't want sex now, he had served his purpose. But he felt a wish to see her nurtured, and smiling more often.

And, of course, they talked a lot. Damien told her about Angel's death, nothing much, just the way it had been. The way she had looked when he found her that morning. How he had had to watch through the years before. How he couldn't help or stop her going wrong. Viv wanted to know about Bridie and Luca, first-generation immigrants raising two grandchildren alone. Then she got free with information about Harry Glass. He was learning a lot.

What would Viv say if she knew why he was there, what

Harry Glass meant to him? He had never even met the guy.

Harry was screening his first big success, *Will Die*, and fast-forwarding through the bits where he didn't appear. Why would Karen want to see the other actors? 'This scene – watch me in this next scene!'

'Harry, my darling, d'you ever wonder if you're the tiniest bit megalomaniacal?' Karen laughed. She felt happy. Martin had gone out and she and Harry were sprawled on one of the huge sofas, giggling and applauding his dated police-action movie. Harry was a breathtakingly handsome young English detective, seconded to New York.

'It's an occupational hazard,' he admitted cheerfully. 'Watch this – pow! You've no idea the number of takes, getting that.'

Despite his protests, she kept hiding her eyes. Will Vengeance was vindictive, blowing away people who annoyed him. His favourite weapon was a Beaumont Adams revolver. Harry had kept the piece, starting his collection of arms.

'I'm not in this sequence,' he muttered, fast-forwarding again.

'How could you stand it?' she asked. 'All the glamour, the money, the popularity.' Then, more seriously, 'Did you make a lot of enemies?'

He shot her a glance, as if she had said something odd, then snapped his attention back to the screen. 'Everyone was sick with me,' he agreed, then clapped like a delighted small boy, as his character despatched an unfortunate bystander.

Of course he had made enemies. It was in the nature of such success – colossal, luminary, as his had been – to stir envy, hatred, degrees of obsession. And, years later, he still had enemies. Three days had passed since the anonymous call. Without mentioning it to him, Karen's first reaction had been panic. Someone knew all about them, and had managed to get hold of their number. That someone had sounded intimate, seemed to know her and to guess at the haziness of her knowledge about Harry's previous marriages.

He had never volunteered much and she had felt warned off, respecting his privacy. But she knew, from what others had told her, that the caller was wrong and just trying to alarm her. Some jealous fan maybe, with an imagined grudge. She wouldn't bother Harry about it. Except that the caller had their number, could call again, and just might have their address. She ought to say something.

'Harry,' she asked, when the blood-soaked screen had faded. 'Is there anyone who might want me to think you're some kind of Henry the Eighth?'

She told him about the call, making light of it. Harry questioned her closely. 'What a malicious pack of lies! There are all sorts of people out there, envying us. It was a spite call. You didn't take it seriously?'

'Of course not. I thought – one of your fans. But I was a bit shaken, at first.'

He looked sad, saying wryly, 'To be widowed once is a misfortune. Twice would be carelessness. Jacqueline, my first, is now Lady Harbinson. As for the second . . . D'you want to hear this boring history, Karen?'

She wanted to know, and Harry must have seen it in her face. His own expression darkened and he looked away. 'Tanya was a deeply disturbed neurotic. She was also an alcoholic. It was against all judgement that I married her. I loved her too much. I was trying to help.'

'What happened, Harry?'

'An accident. She used to do suicide gestures – small overdoses, shallow cuts to the wrist – you know? It was to torture me. I'd given her so much, and Tanya was very twisted. She would spend her days lying in bed, and she drank. Imagine what it was like for me. On that occasion, she miscalculated. She was expecting the housekeeper to find her, but the housekeeper had flu and didn't come.'

Karen felt chilled. 'She died by mistake? Where were you?'

'Working in LA. She wanted to give me a bad time, that's all. She was a cruel bitch.' His voice was venomous. 'You'd understand, if you'd met her. I got over it, I never took her seriously.' He added sharply, 'Of course, she did hurt me. Remembering these things is difficult.'

Was that why he seemed so callous, about a woman who had killed herself? She hadn't meant to die, and Harry must feel guilty. He had been away, unable to stop her, and now he was protecting himself.

Harry took her hands in his, searching her face. Karen could think of nothing to say. Appalled by his coldness, she longed to believe in his warmth. 'Darling,' he said. 'We're so lucky. I love you, and everyone can see. That's why you're a target for nuisance calls. Am I suddenly sinister, deadly by association, as you've been told? Sweetheart, if you're home alone, don't answer.'

'But there'll be calls from my agent, and friends —'

'We can give you messages. I won't allow that unpleasantness. Now I must get ready – Martin will be back, with Robert.'

'Harry,' she asked suddenly, as he turned away, 'when we go to Sussex at the weekend, could Martin stay here?'

'But, my dear, why ever do you suggest that? He's perfectly civil towards you, I hope?'

'Oh, yes. But . . . he seems to be wherever we go. Like a shadow. Could it be just us?'

'What on earth do you mean? I rely on Martin for everything. He would be most put out, after all these years. I can't remember a time . . . What are you trying to do?'

'Just to be with you, now that we're —' She stopped, seeing his expression.

'You don't have to remind me of our position together. But I do expect you to respect my needs. I need Martin with me, and you will have to get on with him. I can't allow him to be upset. That is the end of the matter,' he said firmly, as the apartment door opened.

The lawyer was shown into Harry's office. At least the maid had magicked the stain from the carpet. Karen felt furious with Harry. Why couldn't they talk, decide things together? It was as if he didn't see her as a person, she was for decoration. But that was hardly Martin's fault. She followed him to the kitchen and watched him roll out pastry. 'I expect you've seen all Harry's movies?'

'A hundred times. Harry was always the star to me.'

That was interesting. How old was Martin? Easily thirty-something, although he looked younger with that soft, unlined skin. 'When you were a boy?'

Martin glanced at her. 'He was *the* hero, for teenage boys. A role model, a rebel. Most parents didn't approve.'

'He shocked people? So where did you live, when you were a kid?'

'The south coast.' He was slicing apples, wafer thin.

'Oh. Near to the Keep?'

'Not too near.'

'You got to work for your hero. How exciting! What were you doing before that?'

'Was there life before Harry?' Martin gave her the ghost of a smile, then the conversation was over.

She joined Harry and Robert Bellman for drinks. The lawyer was Harry's contemporary, portly in a three-piece suit. 'Robert's my right arm.' Harry introduced them. 'We go back years. I couldn't be setting up Artemis, all my new ventures, without him.'

Robert Bellman said, as if she wasn't there, 'She's very pretty. You must get her into that photo-session.'

'I might if she's good.' To Karen he added, 'My sister Nora rang. She's coming over from Canada, for an education conference in Europe, and she'll join us at the weekend.'

'How nice.'

'Has Karen seen the Keep? Remarkable home of a remarkable man – you must be proud. It's part of the national heritage. As is Harry, of course.' Robert raised his glass. 'God bless the new venture. May you and Al have a glittering future.' They drank, and he added, 'If you haven't met him, my dear, I'm sure that you will.'

Harry drew himself up tall in his chair. His features metamorphosed, becoming eagle-like, the brows drawn inwards and downwards. The lower half of his face swelled with petulance. The voice he spoke in was not his, but slightly reedy. 'Do you seriously mean to tell me you don't know who I am, Mrs Glass? Do you expect me to believe that?'

Robert laughed, and Martin applauded. Karen felt terror, inexplicable. She was trembling, the skin was prickling on the nape of her neck, the backs of her hands. She stared at Harry: a brilliant mimic, he could capture the exact tones and timing of anyone he had ever heard. The glass she held was sliding from her numb, slippery fingers. It fell to the table, and cracked in two. 'Oh dear,' said Robert into the silence.

'It's a precarious existence,' Harry remarked drily, 'being precious Venetian, or any other kind of glass, when my wife happens to be around.'

'I'm sorry,' she said, scarcely able to push out the words. She had known that voice from somewhere – somewhere terrible. Who was it? She took a deep breath, hoping Harry would explain and hoping he wouldn't because she felt so afraid.

He went on, 'She throws ink over my carpets, too, then never owns up. I've been waiting for some small apology, but not a bit of it. She's gorgeous, but also many other things – including *stupid*.'

Robert laughed at Harry's joke. Karen blushed scarlet. Martin called from the kitchen, 'Harry – phone call. Want to take it in the office?'

Harry picked up his desk phone. 'Harry Glass.'

A pause, then a surprised, 'Harry. It's Andrew Carter.'

'Good God. Andrew! Must be how many years? How are you?'

'Fine, and you? Congratulations on *Cry Murder*. That's doing well?'

'It's hot in the States, yes. I hear you're doing some television these days.'

'I'm about to start on a four-parter. Great scripts – the BBC are very keen. Actually, I wanted to speak to Karen.'

Harry sat down. 'I'm afraid she's not here. What was it about?'

'I directed her at Stratford East. I've always remembered Karen. Such emotional power when she's given the right role. I know she hasn't done telly, but there's a small part that's made for her. We're very keen to see her.'

'I'm so sorry, I'm afraid Karen doesn't want to work, not now.'

There was a pause. 'I had a call from her agent. Vicky said that Karen would be interested.'

'She's changed her mind. Sorry, Andrew. We just got married, you know.'

'Of course, I know. But . . . Tell Karen I called about it. Get her to ring me anyway, would you?'

'I'll give her your message, soon as she gets in. Andrew, we must have a drink some time.'

'We must do that. 'Bye then, Harry.'

Harry replaced the phone, straightening it carefully on the olive green leather. The reproduction desk had come from Harrods last year, as had the carpet. He was a man of considerable means, and was prepared to share everything he possessed. All he asked in return was her presence and respect.

Perhaps it was a bit megalomaniacal, what he had just done. But was he really asking much, expecting her to stay at his side? She should not waste her days with nobodies, not now. She was not a good actress and she must stop chasing her dreams, for her own sake.

In the beginning, he hadn't really noticed how exasperating she could be. Karen was inclined to sulk and withdraw, and to question his judgement. A pity. Such a stunning girl.

Quietly, he opened the office door. He wanted to watch Robert admiring her. She was a lovely girl, a goddess. Those legs. That cloud of hair, and the sweetest face. He worshipped her. She'd had a poor life, all the wrong friends and influences. Now she was his wife he could help her to change, get rid of the flaws. After all he had spent on her, she would do as he needed.

Robert looked up and saw him. 'Is all well?'

'Just slight panics about our casting session,' Harry replied easily. 'I've sorted them out. Now, do let's find out what those delicious aromas might be. Hungry, darling?'

3

Harry Glass is my father. Still Damien hadn't said it, not to Viv or anyone.

What was a father? What could Harry have been? The model for what a man might become? The strong companion, who never was. Fathers took their sons about, let them know how things went. They were a source and a presence, who left an inheritance. But Harry was an absence, seething with explosive questions.

Damien felt consumed by hunger, aching to know the man he had missed, who had never seen or acknowledged him. The man who had destroyed his family; hearing that prosecution all his life, now he needed the defence. Who was Harry Glass? He interrogated Viv. She never asked why, but sated the craving. Grasping her bits of information, he tried to pin them to what he knew, to make up a person, to understand.

Glass was rich and admired, and lived in fortresses. His London home was impregnable, spiky with guards and security. The guy didn't want to be approached – hell, he'd known that – but did demand to be recognized. All that star stuff. Image conscious, working out every day, hiring a trainer and dietician. Then, he married women who looked like daughters. He'd just started on the third, and they all knew what she wanted.

Harry never had any kids, Viv told him.

'My brother Martin, he's a slave. Harry's got this charisma. But if he thinks you're not under his control, you couldn't have a dirtier enemy. What does he do? Find your soft parts – and does he enjoy turning the knife.'

'You're not too big a fan, Viv.'

'I worked for him once, secretarial. Not for long – I enjoy my freedom. And I've no reason to respect Harry Glass.'

He felt tempted to tell her everything. Who he was and . . . What could he say?

In this unknown city in a strange country, time was passing in dislocation. The traffic's pulse beat from the street below; windows, greased like wrapping paper, sealed him in. Days flicked by in measured bars of light, dust motes caught tumbling. He was trapped in a web of conflicted emotion. Twenty-five years in the wilderness, raised to hate Harry: his father had had horns and a tail from the start. Now that he had learned so much, Harry was no longer a symbol. What Viv told him confirmed, but confused; now he knew what the man liked for breakfast.

He had to confront him, declare himself. Then what? He had left the gun back home, and something else with it. Certainty. It had seemed so clear, meant to happen, when he had been out of his head from grief. All the times he and Angel used to talk, as far back as he could remember. Bridie's and Luca's accusations. Harry's refusal to acknowledge them as his, even failing to respond when Angel wrote and asked to meet. His mother's suicide, all those years ago, because of the way she had been treated.

'What am I doing here?' he wondered aloud.

'You're on holiday, to get over your sister dying. You should talk about that.'

So he did, and Viv was a good listener. They were nearly always together, except the times she went out and didn't want him along.

When she left him alone, he paced the small studio, his tall rangy body confined, his head a turmoil of contradictions. He was the survivor of his family, he owed them. But doubt and dread were holding him back. And so many feelings, things he had never felt before. This hunger, and longing: a need to see what his father's eyes might say when they finally met. He needed to be recognized.

Damien tore open a pack of Viv's cigarettes, lit one. He gazed down from the window, on to the Broadway's crowds. No use trying to reach Harry in town: that security was designed to keep him out. It would have to be on the coast. He needed to know when Glass next visited, and Viv could surely find out from her brother.

Where was Viv? She had been gone half an hour.

Viv had almost given up when she saw the silver juggernaut inching round the corner of Crouch Hill. It stopped with a long, airy hiss. Her cousin Joe jumped down from the driver's cab, bullet-headed in a number-two cut, and swaggered across. His jeans and T-shirt were tight, stretched over his beefy torso; cap sleeves showed off the tattoos down his arms. Punching her lightly on the shoulder, he sat down with awkward grace at the pavement table.

'You're bloody late, I've been here ages. And if you leave that there, it'll get moved on pretty swift.'

'Have I lost my touch with the meter maids?'

'So what're you having? I'll have another Anchor Steam.'

He ordered two. 'You're back out in the cold again,' he said, not as a question, so that Viv pulled a face which was wry and dark. 'Nothing will change. How long are you going to waste yourself?'

'Look at you,' she retorted. 'Just small-time, thieving and wandering.' Then wistfully, 'Where are you off to?'

'Brussels, Bremen, Hamburg. With one or two select gigs *en route*. Come for the ride.'

'Not this time. Is it worth the risk?'

'You bet. I'm too smart to get caught.' He drank his beer. 'Listen, Viv, get real. We've only one life, and you could do stuff.' Then he saw the way she was smiling.

'What would you say if I said I'm seeing someone?' Viv sipped her beer. 'He's waiting for me right now.' She preened for a minute, so Joe would notice the hair, the clothes she'd put on to make him see.

'You levelling with me?'

She nodded. 'It isn't what you think, though. And you'll never guess. He's a Yank, pretending to be a tourist – it's so funny, he's convinced I believe that.'

'And what? Who is he?'

'He's only our Harry's long-lost son.' And she burst out laughing at Joe's incredulous expression.

'You're having me on.'

'Would I? About anything quite so – interesting? Damien. He's not too enamoured of . . .' And she stopped because Joe was looking so strange. 'Hey. What?'

'Does Martin know?'

'What d'you think?' Scornful, she drained her pint. 'Right now,' she went on bitterly, 'Martin's extra thrilled. He's thrilled to pieces, at driving down to the seaside with his bucket and spade, and his poncy Mr Glass.'

The Jaguar slid through the electronic gate and up the shingle track. Someone had once planted a garden here. Karen saw stunted oaks, wind-blasted firs and, sheltered behind stone walls, clumps of spiky grass and spiny, silver-leafed acanthus. The Keep was a white, low cluster of stone, spreading out from the tower at its centre.

Nora Sharp, sitting beside her, patted Karen's hand. 'It's a genuine old fake. Has he told you? A wealthy trader wanted a lighthouse. There was nothing in the right location, so he built this.'

'It's excellent repro.' Harry pointed. 'See the lamp room at the top?'

'There's no great headland. It doesn't make sense, here.'

Martin laughed, drawing up at the door. 'It made a lot of sense. There are cellars cut into the rock, connected by secret passages. The marshes were famous for smuggling.'

'Look, here's Christine, and everything's just the same as last year.' Nora went on, 'The housekeeper lives out, but she's obliging and loyal.'

Harry was greeted with quiet delight. Christine was a salt-dried woman of around sixty, and her status in the community must come from his celebrity. 'Mr Glass, such a time since we saw you. You look fit and well.'

'Wonderful to be back, a tonic just to see the place. Let me introduce my wife. Christine saves our lives here on a regular basis. It's all looking splendidly well kept, and the garden.'

'The fire's going in the sitting room, it should be warmed through. I expect you'd like tea?'

The house was solid stone and dark inside, with a tangy chill. Stairs wound up in a spiral from the hall, and doors led off. Karen glimpsed the kitchen, and a round living room overlooking the sea. The stone of the hall gave way to wooden parquet flooring, almost black, and a smell of furniture polish. She exclaimed at the view, the antiquity. Nora was sorting the tea trolley. 'Is the arthritis a little better, Christine?'

'Mustn't complain. DCI Hargreaves rang about the fête. You're not going to let us down this year? It's next weekend.'

'I promise to be there. I'll call Colin. Could we ask them to lunch?' Harry checked with Martin.

'Tomorrow's pretty full. That journalist's here from ten.'

'You've come for a rest, Albert. Did I just call you Albert, Harry? You see,' Nora dimpled at Karen, 'I still think of him as my little brother.'

'Nora's my anchor — keeps my feet on the ground.' Harry laughed. 'Very well, I'm outvoted. I'll ask Colin to pop round later.'

The Chief Inspector came for supper, prepared by Christine, cooked by Martin. He was a big man, a contemporary of Harry, with thinned grey hair and a conservative manner.

'This is DCI Colin Hargreaves. Karen.'

'Welcome to Brigsea. Harry is an old and valued friend of mine, and of the community. I trust, in time, we'll all become friends.'

Hargreaves' eyes were cool, as if he had already prejudged her privately. Was it because she was much younger than her husband? 'I hope we will,' she said, heart sinking. They were all her parents' generation, and fluttering round Harry, puffing up the self-importance that made him so impossible. Out of place, she sat listening dutifully to a conversation that bored her. They would all be thinking her dull.

Karen understood how much Harry missed fame. Here, he was a great whale among minnows, drinking in the adulation. He would do the honours for the charity fête, and Colin Hargreaves would speed up permission for a new garage.

When Hargreaves had left, she climbed the winding stairs with Harry. They had scarcely spoken to each other all day. He lived behind a veil of others: nights were their time alone together, and the time she felt most lonely. Their bedroom was round, with a balcony overlooking the sea. It was low-ceilinged, with grey stone walls and heavy dark wooden beams and floor. In blue silk pyjamas, Harry climbed into his four-poster bed. 'What a long day, sweetheart. Goodnight.'

Tentatively, she reached out to him. 'Harry. Could we talk?'

'After you sat there being so dumb all evening? Now's the time for sleep, my dear.'

So dumb. Yes, she felt stupid with him now, unappreciated and unloved. In public, he was adoring – only she felt the growing barbs of condescension, his constant small put-downs. Harry's affection was strictly conditional. He had chosen her for some unknown reason. Perhaps she had only seemed worth caring for at first. Did she love him, with his breathtaking egocentricity and, almost, his cruelty? It seemed that neither was the person the other had thought.

She lay listening to his breathing, as he fell asleep. Then, to the rhythmic sighing of the sea. It was either the waves, or pulses, pounding insistently inside her own body. She felt brimming, close to overflowing with longings she couldn't quite name: perhaps for real affection, for contact, or sex. With Harry, sex meant his brief self-pleasuring. He was selfish, complacent or unaware of her. She had never known good love-making, anything tender that moved her, had never been orgasmic, and she was only vaguely aware of what might be possible. Her sexuality was hidden behind a wall of fear, the cause of which she didn't want to remember, the half-forgotten trauma that had frozen her. She had known, or suspected, that with Harry there would be no fulfilment. She had chosen him out of a greater need, for the sense of safety against being, ever again, attacked. Reminding herself of all those reasons, uneasily Karen fell to sleep.

In the morning, Harry's interviewer turned up. Hal Jones was better known for his biographies of John Osborne and Ted Hughes than for pieces on actors. This was to be for a series in the *Sunday Times* about the daily lives of the famous. As two professionals, Harry and Hal quickly bonded, retiring to the lamp room.

Karen and Nora went for a walk, up a path that led over the rocky promontory. It was a bright day, becoming windy. Their view of the coast stretched out while the sea gazed quietly, mirroring a pale blue sky. Distantly there huddled a town, with seaside promenade and pier. Nearer, on sand revealed by the tide, three lost-looking tourists, staggering and dazed by the spring sun, were imprinting trails.

Nora looked back towards the shrunken house and garden, a low-lying expanse of fields, marshland beyond. 'See those horses in the field? You can hire them from Friar Farm, past the village. Do you ride?'

'Yes, I can.' Karen remembered holidays with a better-off schoolfriend, sharing her pony. 'Where's the village?'

'A few miles inland, you can't see it from here. Harry has a boat – a small rowing tub. There's an inlet, hidden from here. Bit of private beach, good for swimming, and the chalet – no one ever uses that.' She finished her brisk inventory. 'So, are you going to be happy here?'

Karen stared at Harry's sister, almost blurted out that she expected to be with Harry, in London or travelling. 'It's beautiful,' she replied instead. Then she realized: they had lived here, the other wives. While Harry stayed in the city, doing whatever he did, Jacqueline, and then Tanya, had lived at the Keep.

As they walked on, Nora questioned her in a friendly voice.

She was sharp-eyed as a ferret. 'Are you a country girl? Where were you raised?'

'In Dartford. My father was a stonemason.'

Nora shot her a surprised, interrogating look. 'Harry never mentioned that. And are your parents still around?'

'They retired and emigrated, ten years ago. I've a much older brother, living near Sydney.'

'You don't seem like a working-class girl. You don't have any accent,' she added, after a moment.

'RADA saw to that. I'm one of those classless persons, the well-trained actor. Harry was raised in Bermondsey, wasn't he?'

Nora nodded. 'Our mother dedicated herself to making him very ambitious, a big success. She worshipped him. Her eldest son had died, you see – Harry was born as a replacement, and even given his name. He was really the youngest, and a sickly child, but he became totally driven.'

'I can tell he did.' Karen looked at Harry's sister. She was successful too, as an educational psychologist. 'I sometimes wonder why he wanted me,' she confessed, then wished she had not. The older woman was silent. She was wondering as well, now, why her brother had burdened himself with this awkward creature who couldn't talk to his friends. She would tell Harry his new wife was a misfit, and a mistake that he would best be rid of.

Nora said, 'You must see, my dear, the attraction. You are very young. And beautiful, soft and gentle – my brother worships you.'

'Harry doesn't want to know me. Only to boss me about,' she added, with a false lightness.

Nora stopped walking. 'Shall we sit down? I'm jet-lagged, and the grass is dry.'

Karen forged on, relieved at speaking out, not wanting to think about the effect. 'I can't be the way he wants. Anyone who's worked on stage is tough, independent. I'm not a clinging rose, not underneath. I'm a person.'

Nora's eyes were twinkling, but she looked sad. 'I can see that's all true. But listen. Didn't you choose Harry for his strength? I suspect you did, from what he's told me. So, let him be in control.'

'But—'

'Don't cross him,' Nora said sharply, as if it was a warning. 'Just play the game.'

It was clear. Spelled out. Harry had been born into, grown up in a society of males who never questioned their superiority. Women must agree with him, whatever they really thought. But her own generation was different. She felt, like a crushing weight, the intransigence of this older man: he who must be obeyed. She belonged to an age of equality and sharing.

'You only have to practise duplicity,' Nora went on. 'Then enjoy. It is quite a deal for someone – well, from your background. My brother had to make himself up to become Harry Glass. By his own efforts and talents, he's worth a few million.'

Karen felt shocked. She had been so naïve. This was why they were all so cautious with her, or suspicious – Martin, Robert Bellman, Colin Hargreaves – and why Nora was vetting her. She hadn't really thought about it. *A few million?*

'Shall we walk back?' Nora suggested. 'Harry is vulnerable as a public figure, and as a chap. He's had such misfortunes in his personal life.'

'With Tanya and Jacqueline? What went wrong?'

'The less said about them the better. I'm sure Harry's luck has changed, and you'll be very happy. I'm glad we've had this chance to talk. I hope you'll remember what I've said.'

As they went in through the garden, some instinct made Karen turn and look back. On a rise, twenty yards along the path the way they had come, someone was watching them or the Keep. He was almost silhouetted against the light sky, a tall man, standing in shadow. His clothes and hair were black. There was an intentness in his looking: he was so still, he seemed to pierce her. She shivered with presentiment and felt troubled, but did not know why. She stared, and he turned away, abruptly disappearing from sight. Slowly she trailed after Nora into the house.

The photographer arrived mid afternoon. Harry's sister was leaving already, sharing a taxi with Hal Jones, and continuing her journey to Vienna. Her visit had lasted twenty- four hours, and had clearly been to check on Harry's new mate. What had Nora made of her, the silences, the complaints about Harry? Now they would discuss her. She should never have said so much.

'Put on some make-up, and get changed, sweetheart. The photographer wants to start in the cellar.'

'I didn't bring anything else.'

'Why not? You can't be seen in those tatty things.'

'But I got this last year in a sale. It's by Ghost—'

'Somebody sewed the label on – their granny ran it up from curtains, I imagine. You look like a jumble sale.'

Listening to Nora had crystallized things: now it seemed that Harry was a hopeless case. It was no use pandering to him, and at the decision to stand up for herself, anger took hold. 'This is me – what I choose, what I like. Harry, stop undermining me.'

Harry stared, and Martin burst out, 'How dare you speak to Harry like that?'

'Don't you tell me what to do!' she exploded at him. 'You don't have that right, just because you're employed by us. Leave us alone for once.'

Karen saw Martin recoil, silenced. She caught a quick sight of Harry's thunderous expression as he stepped towards her. She shrank. The photographer appeared in the living-room doorway. 'I'll want plenty of exteriors, but let's have a go at the arms collection first.'

There was a short, tense silence. She saw that Martin had vanished. 'I think Harry's decided not to use me in this.'

'On the contrary.' Harry took her wrist in an iron grip and flashed his most charismatic smile at the photographer. 'Have you looked at the lamp room? Well, let's do the antiques.'

They went through the hall, to three steps leading down. A brass stand, filled with walking sticks, seemed to guard the cellar. The door was of steel, heavy and studded, with an old-fashioned, ornate lock. They started down the rough stone stairs and below lay a dungeon, carved from the oppressive rock. Its rooms were red-carpeted, walls draped with heraldic flags fluttering in a strange, icy draught. Iron grilles turned Harry's collection into a miniature Tower of London. There were stands, display cases of mahogany; the unearthly white light illuminated rows of implements of battle, guns and daggers and swords.

'It's a fabulous setting, but I suppose it's been used?' the photographer asked.

'Not recently.' Harry released his hold on Karen's arm. 'Like it, darling?'

Karen looked around at the weapons, proudly displayed. From a velvet lined case, she took up a dagger. She held it experimentally. Who had owned and used it? Who had died by it? Now, it was a beautiful object. She felt solid, strong. 'Where would you like me?' she asked, in a voice of honey. She had done some modelling in the past. Harry didn't know half of what she had done. She knew how to give them cheesecake smiles, breasts pushed forward, elbows closed to deepen her cleavage, knee turned, exposing the line of her thigh. She would give them exactly what they wanted. 'And how would you like me?'

Martin snapped home the fastening on Harry's weekend case, and sank down in the chair by the bedroom window.

They had been coming here together for years, but now that was spoiled. The whole weekend she had hung around so Harry did everything with her, and he never stopped talking about her. Harry was doting and fond, acting like a fool. His mind wasn't even properly on business, these days. There had been a few comments about that.

The girl was genuinely bimboid. What did Harry see in her? She had no conversation or sophistication, she was graceless in Harry's kind of company. She had no clue how to handle him. There was a certain satisfaction in watching that, the sheer disaster of it, because where would it end? And did she give a damn for him? For his money, sure: that was only human. Harry's wealth attracted and magnetized, like his fame. And he was inseparable from his things: they were him, almost. He had admired Harry too much, the first years. That had been fantasy. He had wanted to mean something to him, to be someone. Now this was the question: why did Harry have everything while all he ever had was Harry? He was not only rich, he was selfish, too. Then she pranced along from nowhere to bask in everything. What had she ever done to earn that? He felt eaten up by it.

They had been through so much. Loyal, he had stayed and worked his balls off. Sometimes, now, he was sick of running around – Harry wants this, Harry says that – co-ordinating, organizing, looking after. Anticipating what Harry would need, keeping tabs on each area of his complicated life, often he lay awake at night from stress. And when was he last given a free day? *Employed by?* She had hurled the words, they had flown straight into him, right inside. He was more than that! He never complained because it wasn't just a job, it never had been. He and Harry were special.

Or they had been. Almost mates, companions anyway. Now it was as if he counted for nothing, they were never even alone together. He had devoted his life to Harry, and had nothing else, only life with him. He felt sick, and it would serve Harry right if he did get sick. It was being at the bloody coast that did it, however much he tried to live in the present. The smell of the sea and the past came back.

There had always been girls around – young and impressed and malleable – wanting Harry, but Martin had never expected him to be fool enough to marry again, not for a third time. Then, Harry had never even told him, treated him like a dog, disregarding his feelings. He had probably felt more for Harry, and knew more about him, than anyone. He had seen him through the nearest thing to a scandal, after Tanya, and that had got hushed up. Now Harry's secret son by an American was sniffing around after him. A real time bomb, just ticking away. Harry was in for a big surprise, and soon.

Martin got up from the chair and went to check the windows. Turning, he caught a glimpse of his reflection in the tall mirror, his blue eyes and muscular frame. He smoothed the tweed of last year's jacket. Slightly long in the sleeves, as they always were, but not enough to need altering. It was a fine jacket, beautifully cut. Nothing but the best for Harry.

Karen appeared in the doorway. She hesitated there. 'Harry's wondering if we're ready to leave. Look, I'm sorry – about earlier.'

Surprised, Martin reasserted his guard. 'Let's think nothing of it,' he said, in his equable, distancing way. Glancing round the room, he picked up Harry's case with a show of cheerfulness. 'Right-oh. It's a couple of hours' drive back to town and we mustn't keep himself waiting, must we?'

On Monday, in the *Valour* production office, Karen read for the part that Andrew Carter wanted her to play. She was the eighth actor they had seen but the atmosphere was intense. The two men were watching the face of a young woman they could scarcely recognize. She had become their Bosnian refugee, in love with a war reporter. When she reached the end of the marked pages, nobody moved. Then Ivor Griffiths, a quiet, courteous man, broke the silence. 'Thank you.'

'That was very good.' Andrew shifted sideways in his chair, looked at his producer.

Karen came back to an awareness of the room. Had she passed or failed? She'd had to play it down, contain the feelings, internalize. Had she kept her voice low, her few gestures muted? They had been watching as if through a lens, magnifying, because this was for the camera's intimacy, and she was used to projecting from a stage. She wanted the part desperately, as if her life depended on this chance to prove herself, and become Maja, with all the power she knew was possible.

It was a miracle she had got to the meeting. Calling her agent routinely, she heard from Vicky about a phone message, never received. Could she read for Andrew this morning at the BBC? In a rush of excitement, Karen got the details then sneaked out from Pipers Wharf. There was no time for argument with Harry. She had cashed a travellers' cheque, taken the DLR then the Underground. On the way, she scraped her hair into a rubber band, psyched herself down to feel battle-wearied. She had arrived, just in time, as their morning was ending.

She was intent on winning the part, and poured out questions. Maja's strength was underscored with vulnerability, with experience. Since war broke out, she had seen family and friends killed, had lived with hunger and fear. There were no rules left for her.

Ivor asked about the work she had done with Andrew, her film training, and lack of camera experience. Tom Kovac and Sheila Morris were playing the leads; Simon Keane had been offered the war reporter. Karen had met Simon in rep, they worked well together. The locations included Hungary, and production started after Easter.

'We'd have to put her in a wig,' Ivor mused aloud.

'We could dye my hair – maybe brown?' she offered, eagerly.

Andrew gave a protesting laugh. 'Karen, I'm so glad your availability is OK. We're keen, and we'll let you know. Tomorrow, I'd think.'

She thanked them. Full of hope, she left the TV centre. It was a gem of a role, small but brilliant, and the competition was mega. If she got this, there might be more television. Then she would have more freedom.

Travelling back on the Underground, deep inside all its grubby sobriety, Karen felt euphoria. It must happen. The part was exactly right for her. She changed lines at Bank, beaming at work-stained City faces, purely happy, vivid with confidence. The DLR, gleamingly clean, launched smoothly overground in the direction of Harry's apartment.

Anxiety struck when she glanced at her watch. It was almost two. She had been gone for four hours with no word. Of course she should have left a note, or called and made up some story. She had been keeping a long-standing appointment, maybe. Not wanting to bother Harry, she had just slipped away. He need not know about the meeting unless or until she was offered the job. But he would make a scene about her absence.

Harry was at lunch, she remembered now, with a new business partner. She had heard Alice confirm it this morning. Suppose she went to the restaurant, joining them for coffee? Then he would be charming for his new associate and he might forget to be angry later. At West India Quay she got off, started to walk towards Canary Wharf. Towering glass and steel, virgin concrete, money surrounded her. The restaurant was on the next corner; they had tried it out last week.

Then she saw Harry just yards ahead, walking away from her towards the car. Martin was going to open the door. With Harry, deep in conversation, and wearing an almost identical suit, was a man she recognized. She knew him at once, Alistair Quentin. Even the back of his head, from this distance, although she had not seen him for years.

Karen stopped dead. Realization swept over her. This was the man that Harry called Al. The owner of the voice to which she hadn't been able to put a name. Those years of forgetfulness, deliberate mists of amnesia . . . Because she had never wanted to set eyes on him again. Now they were at the car. At any moment one of them could look up and see her, and she would have to join them.

Darting away, she ran through the expensive concrete desert, office towers, empty squares. Harry's new business partner! He would be around. They would have to entertain, be entertained. There was no way she could escape him any more. When she stopped, she was shaking all over, her legs giving way. She needed to scream, needed to hide herself. He had done that, Alistair Quentin: taught her to be deeply ashamed, to try to be invisible – unless in another's identity.

She sat down on a bench inside a square. A fountain was falling by rows of coloured, nodding flowers. Her hands were fisted in her lap. She drank in troughs of air and spoke out loud into empty, pale sunlight. Talking to nobody, like anyone else driven to despair. 'It's him that should be ashamed. Quentin. He should be running away from me.'

She had called him Quentin from the first time they met because he preferred it to Alistair. He was in his thirties, affluent, restless. He had been born with old money, she supposed. He had never had to question himself or make much effort, and he wore the look of someone bored. He had an advertising agency, but wanted to move into films. All this Karen learned within a week of starting at Mabey's.

At eighteen she was newly out of school, and at college in London, ambitious and dirt-poor. Her elderly parents had never known how to offer guidance, and now they had flown to the other side of the world. She was free – and rebellious. The new life was exciting, and expensive. Like Poppy, Karen had to work at nights. Mabey's was a media hangout, infiltrated by businessmen, famous for its resting actresses and models. The new manager, Sybil, was running a less known business, providing escorts. It wasn't prostitution, Poppy said, though some of the girls made their own arrangements. Fascinating, Karen thought. Fun.

Everything was fun. It all lay ahead: happiness, fame and fortune. They were all convinced of brilliant futures. That confidence and trust had got them this far. Days at RADA were dedicated to hard work, while nights at Mabey's revealed glimpses of worlds unknown to her. She was gauche, experimenting, and learning about her power of sexual attraction.

Quentin noticed her, when she wore the silver sheath dress. It belonged to Poppy's old flatmate, had reached Karen by circuitous sharing. That evening, surrounded by more sophisticated women, she was flattered at Quentin's attention. He complimented her, and made her feel special. She needed to feel wanted or desired but, if she was honest, she didn't much like him then.

He asked her out to dinner. Karen told an outraged Poppy, 'He reminds me of a fish, and he's old – it's the expression in his eyes.'

'Then don't look at his eyes! He'll take you somewhere fantastic and posh, you'll get proper food. How can you say no to a decent meal?'

'D'you think he's married?'

'You don't fancy him so just go out with him.'

She told Quentin yes. She dressed up for the evening, enjoying looking older and more sophisticated than she was.

When she met and talked with him alone, she liked him better, felt impressed. The evening was full of treats, wildly civilized after what she was used to. She was easily persuaded to drink rather a lot – large gin and tonic, shared bottle of wine, small potent liqueur – until the room spun hazily, pleasurably. Quentin was good company and practised small kindnesses. Producers and directors glittered like gold dust through his conversation. Romain was a friend, and Quentin was part financing his new film. Leo Romain, one of the most talented directors around! Now she was really impressed. It was naked ambition time: she would give her eye-teeth for the chance to meet him.

Quentin placed a sweaty hand over her hand. 'You look adorable,' he said, fish-eyes slithering over her breasts. Should she draw away, make an excuse, or enjoy being wanted? What would Poppy do?

She smiled. 'It's been great talking to you, but I've got to get home. For someone who phones every night at eleven. He'll wonder where I am.'

It was a lie, and she expected Quentin to ask, 'Is that your boyfriend?' But he just stroked her hand, asking if she'd like anything else. He signalled for the bill, which must have been astronomical, and he paid by card. 'It seems a pity to break up the evening. My place is nearby in Cadogan Square. We could have a nightcap and you could call your friend. It's almost eleven, anyway.'

'I'm sorry, but I have to get home.'

She was careful with men, knowing it wasn't usually her they cared about. It was only her looks and sexuality, the way the molecules of her face and body were arranged. She got a lot of hassle and was inexperienced, although not a virgin. There had been a boyfriend at sixth-form college, until he went away to Leeds University. When men desired her, she wanted that feeling of being wanted but her power scared as well as excited her.

When Quentin, driving her home, put a hand on her thigh, she froze. His palm was hot and clammy through the fabric. He removed it briefly to deal with corners then it plopped on to her again, like a soft, sinister leech. What could she say? Please excuse me, but I find you physically repellent. He had been kind. She did not want to offend. It was only his hand on her leg, for God's sake.

It seemed a long way back to East Ham, where she was sharing with Poppy. They pulled up and Karen thanked Quentin for the evening, for being such good company. She avoided his lunge towards her and slipped out of the car.

'Where did you go? What did you have? Has he got contacts?' Poppy shrieked. 'Why didn't you ask him in? I could've disappeared discreetly.'

Karen hooted. 'You? Discreet? He's a groper. But he's working with – he's financing – *Leo Romain*!'

Quentin didn't come to Mabey's for a couple of weeks, and that was unusual. Karen found herself looking out for him, feeling disappointed. Might he have been offended? He had treated her well and she had been silly, obviously running away like that. All she had to do was explain, with the excuse of a fictitious boyfriend, that she would like to be just friends.

When he came in, she saw there had been nothing wrong. He was friendly, they talked for much of the evening. She still found him unattractive, although she wished that might some-how change. And he had clearly got the message. But she felt proud of having his attention. He was influential, powerful even. And he mentioned, casually, that he was going to Romain's home for dinner next Sunday. Maybe she would like to accompany him?

Karen had never felt more torn. Immediately, seeing her hesitation, he began to lose interest. 'It's up to you, I thought it might help. I'll need to know tonight.' Quentin moved off to greet a glamorous redhead, who was soon falling all over him.

Dinner with Leo Romain. What could be the harm? He was

casting his new film, she had read it in the trade press. The other girls, envious and generous, donated a scarlet Aisha dress and a decent handbag. Karen knew she looked good.

She assumed Romain lived somewhere like Quentin, in Chelsea maybe. But they drove out of town, north and then east, until they were passing through a forest, along lonely lanes.

'Where does Romain live?' she asked, hoping her words sounded light.

'They prefer a quiet life, as you'll see.'

The car slid silently through the gathering dark. There were no houses here. 'What a long way out! Are you abducting me?' she joked, with a little laugh.

'Of course I am,' he joked back. 'It's the only thing to do with a girl like you.'

Karen's heart was thumping with fear. She knew so little about him. Was she in danger? When he slowed for the next corner, should she open the door, throw herself out? Then what? There were no people around. She felt like his prisoner, and they were heading away from human contact.

She forced herself to think clearly: play along, keep calm, don't make him angry. Deciding on a plan, she waited until they were nearing a crossroads, there were lights shining through the trees. 'Quentin. I'm not well, stop the car.'

'Here's Romain's house,' he answered, glancing at her. And there really was a mansion, detached and standing in acres of woodland. They drew up at the side. Lights were on, from inside the house. Such welcoming lights, she felt giddy with relief. She had been mistaken. She laughed out loud, and followed Quentin. He was carrying champagne. 'Come on, let's surprise them.'

They were going in the side door. He had a key. *Because the house was empty.* He ushered her in. The sensation of emptiness flooded her. If she screamed, there was no one to hear. And what might happen if she made him angry?

In the empty kitchen, he picked up two glasses. They went into a barn–like living room. A phone stood on a side table. Where was she? And suppose she might be mistaken about him?

'Where are they, Romain and his wife?'

Quentin, loosening the wire cage, slid the cork expertly, silently from the bottle and poured two glasses. He handed her one. 'Darling, do stop pretending to be a silly little juvenile.'

She threw the glass at him, and lunged towards the door. Abruptly she was thrown to the floor, face in the carpet, body crushed under his fat weight. When she twisted her head round, her eyes met the glittering stem of a broken champagne flute. Then she felt it, cold against her throat.

'Just be good, now.'

She blanked out, and froze into paralysis. It wasn't happening. This sick person was only a nightmare: she would wake up.

'Look at that dress. All come on, and then fuck off. Bitch! You want it, all right, you want it like this. All you cunts, disgusting, dirty, teasing cunts – never mess around with me again!'

He was grappling with a fish on a slab. Then he cut into her, piercing her closed, frightened vagina, slicing her open with his cock. Sensation returning. Stubble, abrasive, and hairiness, and his smell of stale cheese, rank sweat. A tomato-faced, monstrous white grub, programmed to destroy. He pumped in hatred and violence, flooded her with poison. When he had done, he was still.

She lay locked, but still alive so far. Cut into more than one piece, like an experiment at school, but still alive. He had tried to annihilate her, make her into nothing. But she was living in a different form. *No one will ever know who I am.* After a while, she started to laugh and cry.

'Don't be ridiculous,' Quentin said. 'That's what happens if you play hard to get. Cigarette? You make it obvious you're panting for it, then play silly buggers with me. So don't be difficult now. You're a little fool and I hope I've taught you a lesson. Working in a tarts' parlour, and the acting business – pretending to be a professional virgin. Listen,' he added, a bit later, 'be careful what you say. I could make things extremely awkward for you unless you're a good girl.'

★

From the bench, Karen looked up and saw rising around her the pale, empty buildings of Canary Wharf. New order, emptiness, and suits.

After the rape, she could not feel safe alone or with strangers, or with men she knew. Unable to trust or relate, she couldn't sleep for nightmares, couldn't eat because her body felt invaded. She thought about suicide.

With Poppy she went to the police, but two days had passed. There was no evidence, nothing could be proved. She had gone out with Quentin, and juries believed that rape was committed by strangers in alleys. Quentin was respectable, establishment. She had not been a virgin. She would be tried and might be judged because of her work, looks and age, her working-class background. The police were sorry but a conviction was too unlikely.

Then she kept a shield around her sexuality. Lonely, she had tried to take lovers but couldn't get close. They never stayed. Not until Harry, the refuge and release of his caring, his wanting to look after her.

Avoiding Quentin, she had heard what he was doing, dabbling in films, entering television, rising in the ranks of the BBC. Two years ago he had left to enter independent production. Now he and Harry had set up Artemis and were celebrating development deals.

Alistair Quentin, and Harry. They had always moved in the same circles, had probably known each other for years. He was just the person Harry would choose for a business partner. He had old money and a family name. Harry would envy and covet both, and could only buy them by association. Was there even something similar? Might Harry and Quentin be somehow alike? She shied away from that disloyal thought, much too frightening to pursue. Harry could have no idea of what Quentin was really like.

But she knew. He had cost her the life that she should have had, and she could never forget, never forgive.

4

The Brigsea Fête and Fayre was held, as usual, at Friar Farm. Marquees had sprouted, with a children's funfair, stalls and competitions, and a big, roped-off arena for displays. The crowds were thickening, milling in hot brightness, pressed under overcast gloom, warmed by sun again. Weekenders mingled with the locals. Teenagers were gathering, looking for action, while families took a day out. Trippers and tourists were arriving for Easter, with cameras, macs and extra sweaters.

People in the crowd noticed him because he couldn't imitate their meanderings. There was a rush to the ropes as the brass band marched out, the loudspeaker announced a sheepdog display. Among mothers and fathers carrying babies, towing toddlers with balloons, Damien felt like the devil's ambassador.

From among the crowd, he had watched Harry open the fête, and listened to his witty speech. The people here all admired Harry Glass. His name brought a glow into their lives and he was asked for his autograph. These people felt favoured because he was here.

None of them knew about his own existence. His, or Angel's. Was Harry even aware that his daughter was dead? Perhaps he had succeeded in completely forgetting them. Was that really possible?

He was going to be reminded, faced with the past.

The fête was a fund-raiser for good causes. Harry was surrounded by women of his own generation, stout organizers, energetic and capable, while he held the hand of his young wife.

They still looked ill-matched, like in New York. After the opening they had retreated inside the official tent until someone brought folding chairs. Then they all settled outside the tent flaps with cups of tea.

From a few yards away, Damien pretended to study the events programme. He was watching the way Harry drew people in, how the fascination was spun. The man had a seductive charm, used like a weapon. The loudspeaker was asking for quiet while Mr Trevor Williams worked with Bess and Lassie. From outside the tent came little bursts of laughter, jokes and gossip. He wanted to hear what Harry said. He was right beside them now. At any second he would get noticed.

One of the women, tall and grey-haired, glanced at her watch. 'Are you going to judge the jams and preserves, Harry? They'll all be assembling, hopefully.'

'Joan thinks I need sweetening up.' Harry smiled at his wife. 'Still, rather jam today than garden vegetables. Perhaps I'll leave those to Karen. Mm, darling?'

'Karen, you must let me show you what we've managed to get growing, salt and gales notwithstanding. Tea, tomorrow?'

'How kind, Mrs Hargreaves. I'm sure we'd love to, wouldn't we, Harry?'

'Call me Joan. Shall we say four? Now, Harry, off to that jam session.'

'We'll make it a joint effort. Come on, sweetheart.'

Karen took Harry's arm, and they strolled away from the tent. Damien began to follow alongside. His heart was jumping, his throat felt dry, as he stepped in front of them. They both paused, they had to. With a shock, looking straight at Harry, Damien found himself gazing into Angel's grey eyes. He drew a deep breath. 'Hello, Harry. Maybe you and I could talk.'

'Don't tell me – you're a reporter.'

After a moment Damien answered, 'How did you know?' He hazarded a guess, certain he would be challenged. '*Brigsea Gazette*. Damien C.' Was it possible that Harry never got the photo Angel had sent of them? Wow, he thought, in the next minute: I'm really talking with my dad. He really believes I'm a

Brit reporter, called Damien, with my accent? 'I'm doing a journal piece, maybe you can give me a quote.'

There it was: a flicker of unease jerking across Harry's smooth, flawless expression. Even in the flesh, in daylight, his face had the expensive, carefully tended look of English lawns, while his manner was pure old-fashioned squirearchy. Only his eyes had started to wriggle. 'Well now, Mr C, what is it you would like to ask me? Not that I can promise to answer. I normally grant interviews on a somewhat more formal basis.' He raised a hand, smiled a greeting to someone in the crowd.

Karen said suddenly, 'But you don't have to do this, Harry.'

'Darling, I know that I don't. But it's all for such good causes, every year. Fire away, Mr C, but any interview must include my wife, Karen.'

Damien ignored the girl. 'You're such a generous man, Harry. Well known for it,' he drawled. 'But, don't you see, I know so much about you already. And it hasn't always been this way – not at all.'

There was a pause. 'That's hardly a question.' Harry smiled pleasantly, before the smile switched off. 'Chicago, isn't it? You think I don't know?'

A burst of scattered applause from the ringside, settling into quiet concentration again. A man approached, proffering his programme. 'It's for my son, he grew up on *Will Vengeance*.'

'What's his name?' Harry signed with a flourish, a smile.

The man retreated. People were standing around looking at Harry, they were trying not to stare at him. 'Yeah, I grew up there.' He heard his life summed up in the phrase, and watched Harry taking it in. His mother's jet eyes, and gypsy hair, his age. He saw the clear, veiled recognition. Only none of it felt like he had imagined.

'Harry,' Karen asked, 'what the hell's going on?'

'Where? Exactly.' Harry drilled the words.

'You must remember. Did you get the picture Angel sent?'

A woman hurried up to Harry. 'There you are. They're all ready for you. It's this way. Oh, I'm sorry.' She stepped back, noticing Damien. 'I interrupted your conversation.'

'That's OK. I'll come along with my father – while he judges the jellies, is that right? I'm Damien, by the way. I'm Harry's son.'

Harry said slowly, 'Yes. This is Damien, who's been living in America.' He felt ill, from the shock of the boy's abrupt appearance, the way he had just . . . But nobody must see, so he added lightly, 'He's been getting his education over there.' He saw Karen's astonishment. She had to catch on and back him up, pretend she already knew.

Christine was saying, wonderingly, 'Why, Mr Glass, you are a dark horse. How many years have we known you?' She asked Damien, 'You've never even come to the Keep.'

'I've been there. But you and I didn't get to meet.'

The show must go on, and nobody guess what he was feeling. 'The jams! How is your sweet tooth, Damien? Come along, everybody.'

As they headed towards the table of jam-pots, Harry caught a fleeting admiration on the face of his unknown son. The boy had expected him to crumble, had turned up like this deliberately.

I'm made of tougher stuff than that, he thought, greeting the little knot of jam-makers who had come to meet him. There was humour, there were smiles and pleasantries. It was outrageous. How could his own son do this to him? Producing a bombshell in public, designed to embarrass him, to undermine his position and his image.

Harry could scarcely taste the jams, they were all paper. He found a few wisecracks for people to remember and treasure. He used wine-tasting terms, since he had the reputation of a connoisseur. Karen, then Damien, must taste each preserve with him. He wanted a vote. He wanted family unity.

In this bizarre situation – held to ransom as he felt – looking at the boy he caught some similarity. To himself – and to that grasping, unstable woman. He could never have made her his legal wife. He had been on the brink of success, and she had exerted emotional blackmail of the most ruthless kind. She had tried to hang on but he had asserted his right to freedom, escaping her.

Why had the boy turned up like this? How dare he! Now everyone would know about that whole episode, so long ago. He had to accept that the secrecy was over. He would have to make the best of things. But that disturbing familiarity – like seeing a ghost. 'Could I possibly beg a small glass of water?'

'Darling, you're very pale. Are you all right?'

'It must be the heat,' Harry said, weakly. He had to get out of here, couldn't keep on with this. Staggering slightly, hearing cries from people, he clutched at the trestle of jams, then subsided slowly to his knees. In Karen's arms, he rolled to the grass. Voices of alarm surrounded them, with advice and suggestions.

'Loosen his clothes, his collar.'

'Has he fainted? Is there an ambulance here?'

'Dr Greene's in the crowd, I saw him. We'll put out an announcement. Joan, go and tell them.'

Harry came round. 'No, please. I don't need the ambulance. Felt a little faint, that's all. Could you possibly fetch my driver from the car park? I'd like to go home.'

'But we must get the doctor,' Christine said.

'Please don't make an announcement. It upsets people and there's no need.'

'Darling. Are you quite sure you'll be all right?'

'Yes, sweetheart. Just help me up. I'll be well looked after, you see, by my family. And here comes Martin.' Thank God the British press paid him less attention, now he no longer acted. There was a chance the whole affair might be contained, handled right. 'I want to go home. Where's my car?'

'Just here, Harry. I've brought it close.'

'This is my son, Damien. He's studying in America, to be a doctor. Martin, my assistant.' Somehow Martin appeared completely unsurprised at this news, before taking charge in his calm, cheerful way. Harry leaned gratefully on his arm. 'I'd like to sit with Karen.'

'You did insist on coming.' Martin told the concerned onlookers, 'Harry's been overworking a bit, jetting around.'

68

'You must have Dr Greene call today. We'll tell him if you don't,' was Christine's parting shot.

Harry said in a brave voice, 'The jam wasn't that bad, really not.' He got into the car.

Karen glanced at the crowd, taking her cue. 'Yes, don't worry, he only needs to rest.'

Martin said to Harry's son, who was standing uncertainly among them, 'You hop in the front with me, Damien. OK?'

Damien got in. It was an XJ12, smooth as flying. They left the fairground and its curious faces. The loudspeaker drone faded, with the tinny music from waltzer and merry-go-round, as the Jag nosed into narrow, dark lanes, between banks and hedges, under trees that met overhead, through their tunnels torn with fragments of sky. Still no one spoke.

This is my son. Four words of acknowledgement, leaving him broken up inside, unable to speak for the lump in his throat. Until Harry had done his dying swan, ducking away from it all. Underneath his anger, he admired his father's presence of mind, play-acting. He had everyone taken in. Or maybe Harry was sick? The guy had just got a really big shock. He looked white and that couldn't be pretence. Suppose he had a heart attack? Harry's collapse was his fault.

From the back seat, he heard, 'How're you feeling? Would you like more air?'

'I'm all right, sweetheart, just . . .'

Glancing back to check on Harry, Damien saw his stepmother take hold of his hand. Martin was asking, 'Where've you been staying?' He was easy, as if they had been friends for years.

There was no way Martin could know that he had been staying at his sister's. 'In London. At a friend's place.'

'London is where Harry's based, you know. Have you been over here for long?'

'Not too long. Everything's pretty new to me.' He felt glad of Martin's interest, even if he was just being courteous. His father had asked him nothing, not yet anyway. The situation was pretty weird right now, like being kidnapped by three strangers.

69

But having found Harry he wasn't about to let him slip away – not till he'd told him things and heard what he had to say.

They swept round a bend and the sea lay before them, long and narrow and pale as a scar. Marshes purred past and rocks loomed ahead, the stretch of dunes, and the tall gates to his father's house. Martin opened them electronically, the car cruised up the drive. The Keep's round tower was blackened by clouds. A rich man's folly, he supposed, an Alcatraz for vacation times. English eccentricity, usefully newsworthy, maybe? He didn't seem to spend much time here.

As they went in, Harry brushed off reminders to call the doctor and seemed suddenly to revive. He was all charm and welcome, playing host. 'Would you like to see around? Martin, perhaps some tea?'

'Not outside, it's looking like rain,' Martin said. 'In the lamp room?'

'An excellent idea. Come through, Damien. Perhaps it would amuse you to see around – I have several antique collections. Are you interested in weapons, in guns perhaps?'

Damien smiled grimly at the irony. 'I don't think so.'

Harry began to unreel a pitch as they went through the house, as if property was what they were about. Following in silence, he heard details of history, of value. It was like listening to a guide and he took in little, gathering an impression of age, dark wood and bare stone, the crooked stairs. He was meant to be impressed. All his life he had been shut out from places where Harry lived, locked out from his enviable existence. How the hell could he admire it now? The memories were too bad. His family, back home, had been so poor.

They climbed the tower to a glass room filled with plants. The view stretched on every side, grey sea ahead, miles of common land behind. The house stood pressed in open isolation. And how alone he felt, with Harry trying to win his admiration. 'This was the lamp room, for signs and warnings. Of course, the whole thing is stunningly good old repro – this was never actually functional.'

Just like us, Damien almost said. Like us, as father and son.

'A seriously fine view, isn't it?' As he shrugged in reply, Harry pursued, 'This is only my weekend home. How did you know I was connected with Brigsea?'

'I heard things about you. We both read stuff, over the years.' The bitterness welled up. 'You wanted to forget about us but we were never going to forget you.'

Harry looked startled. Karen said, from the doorway, 'How can you talk to your own father like that?'

She was really beautiful, and really mad at him. He felt an urge to break her smug delicacy, her presumptions. Who was she, this bitch? If she wasn't here – if she and the other babes had never hung around – then perhaps he would count for something: Harry might have wanted their relationship. 'Exactly because he is my father!' he shot back at her. 'That gives me every right to come here, say what I want.'

'It does not – you're incredibly selfish and arrogant. And when Harry isn't well.'

'You don't know a thing, so shut up – darling. Harry doesn't know what I've come to tell him.'

'I'm beginning to get some idea.' Harry looked furious. 'First, you don't insult my wife. This is her home. Second, it was in the poorest possible taste that you chose to make your appearance in the midst of a public function. If we are to speak, you will show respect and consideration. I might even have expected some thanks from you and your sister. I've been supporting and educating you both.'

Damien almost felt pity for him. Almost, but not quite. He said quietly, 'You don't even know, Harry? Angel is dead.'

His father seemed to freeze. 'What did you say?'

'Angel's dead. She pumped herself full of heroin.'

'Angeline? She can't be. I would've heard. The lawyers . . .' Harry trailed off into silence. He sat down on a wicker chair, his face shattered. 'Is it true?'

How sweet, Damien thought savagely: the grieving parent. Who never gave a damn. 'Yes. She's dead.'

Martin had come in with a tea tray, and put it down. He stood looking worriedly at Harry, the man who had everything but neglected his own kids. 'Are you OK?'

'Oh, Martin. Some very upsetting news. Perhaps I could talk with Damien alone. All right, Karen, sweetheart?' She was reluctant to leave them alone, he could see.

Harry waited, then said, 'Angeline, was she really on heroin?'

'Both of your kids were no-hope junkies. You wonder why?' He saw Harry's questioning look. 'Oh, I got off it – finally. Angel's sort of been cured, too, hasn't she?' Harry winced as Damien ploughed on. 'I don't get it. How could you chuck us away, out of your life? As if we were nothing.'

'But I gave you an allowance –'

'We had a relationship with your lawyers till we were each twenty-one. While you told the papers you didn't have any kids. After Mom died, while I was still a baby, why didn't you want us then? To make some kind of contact?'

Harry answered heavily, 'You don't understand, Damien, about your mother's parents. They already had care of you. I did the best I could. What did you want? To be the star's kid in Hollywood? Really?'

'To be any man's kid. You left a gap, and it's permanent. No one's ever known about us, or Mom – were you that ashamed? Angel, she grew up feeling rejected. Your daughter never knew you. She had no self-respect. I found her that morning. It should've been you, lying there.'

'You were raised to hate me. That's what happened, isn't it?'

Damien leaned against the wall and saw her there. *Angel . . .* He had loved her more than anyone. They had been close. She lay waxen, and smaller, crumpled in her old T-shirt and jeans among tangled bedding. Her life was gone, her future wasted. He remembered all of that long road, relived it for her there and then, through deprivation to despair. He had been unable to stop her, to prevent this. He had failed her.

There was a sudden clattering on the glass all around. Rain was drumming at them, translucent blood streaming at the windows, running down. 'I wanted to have nothing to do with you. Until I found her. Yes, we were raised to hate you.'

72

'Luca and Bridie poisoned your mind. It had nothing to do with the truth. Don't you want to know what happened?'

Damien sat down opposite in a chair with a patchwork cushion. Harry began, as if telling a story. 'Carla's parents, from different cultures, had made a courageous move to the States. Programmes existed to aid them as immigrants, and they were given every assistance. But Luca never mastered the language and that limited employment. Bridie, as a child in Northern Ireland, had witnessed acts of violence. Those poor people, never adjusting, poured all their hopes into Carla. Your mother was a troubled girl when I met her.'

'So you gave her two kids then abandoned us all. Why?'

'Try to understand, that was not my choice. She was an ambitious starlet, and very neurotic. Determined to get me at any cost.'

Had Harry not wanted them from the start? Did that make things better or worse? 'All the years we were growing up, you never wanted to see us?'

'Of course I did!' Harry exclaimed. 'I wanted you to live with me. But I met resistance from your grandparents. They were going to keep you and turn your minds against me.'

'While you were busy getting famous and rich, having girls around. Kids would've spoiled things, yeah?'

'I was not to blame. My letters were returned unopened. When I tried to visit, I was kept out.'

'I never knew that.' But was it true? No one had ever said so.

'If Angeline became damaged, it was because of her mother's final, selfish gesture. Her instability made things impossible. I tried to do the best for you, I paid all the bills. It cost me plenty and I received no thanks – until this, Damien. I needn't have helped, she had no proof of paternity. But one day, when you're a doctor and making good money, then you'll thank me.'

They stared at each other, across a world of misunderstanding. How strange. Harry believed he was still at medical school.

Suddenly the rain stopped. The sun had come out, sheeting through the windows, blindingly bright so he had to turn away. The sea sparkled under a washed blue sky. What kind of a country was this? 'Money,' said Damien. 'You thought money was what we wanted, in place of a parent?' Was he being fair? The thought made him angrier. He didn't want Harry's point of view. He wanted to destroy this vain, destructive monster.

Shrugging off his jacket, he pushed up his left sleeve, above the elbow. The old needle tracks leaped out from the skin, in that merciless light. 'How could I study? How could they not find out? There was nowhere to go but down. I've a police record, Harry.'

Harry looked away, his face disgusted. 'You're blaming me? You let me down, Damien.' He added slowly, 'And Angeline, too. Didn't you? She would've looked to you for an example.'

Yes: secretly he blamed himself. If he had never tried stuff, way back in his teens, then Angel might never have followed. By the time he found out about her, it was too late. Suddenly he felt stiflingly hot, in this glass room. He stood abruptly, almost violently, his chair clattering against the safety rail. 'I need to get out of here.'

'Let's go out into the garden. I can tell you more about Carla,' Harry went on, as they started down the winding stone stairs. 'I want you to understand, it could never have worked with your mother.'

The house was silent, chill with shadow as they went through. Outside the day was glittering, the sun hot, grass and bushes spangled with raindrops, the scent of wet earth rising. His senses felt sharp, with a new, hyper-reality. It was like drugs. Was this some kind of happiness? He hadn't come here seeking to be happy.

Harry led him along a gravel path that circled the house. Damien said, matter-of-factly, 'You were getting to be a star. You must've been caught up in that so you dumped her.' He wanted to hear it wasn't true.

'I told Carla, right from the start, not to get too attached. So much was at stake. She tricked me. The first time I thought it was an accident, until she refused the abortion. We parted – I continued to pay for everything. By the time she had you on the

74

way, I certainly wasn't living with her. She could be damn persuasive – but not that persuasive.'

'OK,' Damien answered, after a minute. 'But once we were a fact? I can sort of see why you denied our existence to the media. But Angel tried twice to contact you and you never responded. That crippled my sister. What would it have cost you – five minutes to answer, to thank her for the photo?'

'Damien, I never had anything from her. No photograph.'

'It was sent care of the lawyers. We had no address for you.'

'I never received it, I promise. I had no notion there was any problem. I wish you had let me know.'

'What would you have done? Paid for the clinic? It was you that she needed.'

'I had no idea, believe me. What else could I have done at the time? I couldn't tear you and Angeline away from your grandparents – you'd been indoctrinated against me from the start. Or away from your country, your home town, the schools. It would have meant an ugly, damaging legal battle.'

I'm being sucked in, Damien thought. Harry was good with words, and he was getting to him. 'That would've been bad for your image,' he snarled.

'It would have been bad for you. I don't believe you wanted to grow up in the public eye, towed from place to place by nannies. A clean break seemed best.'

'Maybe you were wrong. The "clean break" looked a helluva lot like neglect from where we were, over the years.'

Harry gazed away from him, across the garden. 'I can only ask you to forgive me for poor judgement. My motives were good. I know you don't believe that, yet. You're a fine young man, strong and intelligent, well educated. And now you're here. Let's make up for the past and have a future. Yes?'

Did Harry really think he could claim him now, as a right? Like hell he could! Damien said nothing but scowled past Harry into the bright day. Karen was approaching with a tall, grey-haired guy who looked like authority, walked like a cop. He and Harry greeted each other warmly.

'Colin. Nice of you to come.'

'You're looking recovered. Everyone was concerned. What happened?'

'Never touch the non-local fish, mm? I'm fine now. I'm a very proud dad – this is my son, Damien.'

He's just saying that, it's political, Damien told himself quickly. He shook hands – unbelievably, given his record back home – with the senior British police officer, as they were introduced. Detective Chief Inspector Hargreaves wasn't looking too surprised. They must all have been talking about him. 'He looks like you, Harry.'

'A little like me, perhaps.'

'Your father's been hiding you away from us, Damien, in a mysterious way. Why is that?'

Damien could feel Harry holding his breath, waiting for what he would say in reply. He could make things look bad for him, if he wanted to. But . . . *I'm a very proud dad*. Whether he'd meant that or not – and it was designed to soften him up – it had the strangest effect on him. He couldn't say anything, but gave a crooked smile. Something was pricking his eyes.

'Damien's been in the States, training hard to be a doctor. I shall try to persuade him to study over here so we can be closer.'

Karen was staring at him. He must have been a shock to Dad's little bride. As if she read his thoughts, or sensed his pleasure at her new exclusion, abruptly she turned away from him. 'Colin says the fête's been a big success.'

'We had a good turnout – all come to see you, Harry. Seriously, thanks for doing the business. Joan's looking forward to seeing you tomorrow. Are you coming too, Damien? I hope we'll see more of you.'

'If the studies allow,' he answered, neutrally.

'And Karen, of course.' Hargreaves looked at her, coolness edging his voice. 'I suppose you'll be stuck in London, now? Anyway, congratulations on the new job.'

'Thank you,' Karen said. She had told Joan, hoping Harry would hear about it while people were around and he was distracted. But she wished he didn't have to know. At any minute, he might flip over into rage.

'See you tomorrow.' Colin Hargreaves went off across the garden.

Harry said, in a controlled way, 'Darling. Is there something you haven't told me?'

She answered quickly, defensively, 'I just called Vicky at home – she's been away. It's a new series for the BBC. The part's small but good, so of course I said yes.'

'You didn't think to ask me, first?'

'Harry, I knew you'd be happy. It's what I've needed. The director's Andrew Carter –'

'Didn't he want to see you first?'

'I did see him,' she admitted. 'I didn't mention it, because . . . Oh, we're all so superstitious. I was afraid of jinxing my chances.' She knew Harry didn't want her to work but whose life was it? Guilty, defiantly, she added, 'Sheila Morris is in it. There's some filming in Hungary –'

'You're intending to be away? For how long? Am I allowed to know? Who is the male lead?'

'Tom Kovac. And Simon Keane.'

'I've never heard of Simon Keane. He must be an unknown.'

'Aren't you pleased for me?' she cajoled, lightly demanding. When he didn't answer, she said to Damien, 'Harry is pleased, really. I've been praying for this because it's months since I worked.'

They began walking back to the house, the three of them. 'Who's producing?' Harry asked.

'Ivor Griffiths.'

He laughed, as if relieved. 'I've known him for years, we've worked together. He's been owing me a favour and must've heard about us.'

How like Harry, to think she was offered the part because of him. Karen reminded herself of working with Andrew before. He was a good director and she was sure of her own talent. Harry must accept her acting. She had got to regain her identity, and value.

It had been a long, eventful afternoon. Now suddenly it was evening, chill. A premature dusk of clouds had gathered, creeping in from the sea. Martin lit the fire, and served an early supper. As they sat around the oak table, to any observer they might have looked like a family.

Karen wondered about Damien, this proud, intense man, who seemed so bitter. He was almost her own age, a stepson she had never known existed. The more she tried to welcome him now, the more he seemed to hate her – for no reason she could think of. Perhaps he hated everyone. When she looked at Harry's son, or when he was near, some sense of danger jangled through her.

Harry was asking Damien what he'd like to do tomorrow. They could go out for the day, he must stay the weekend, then return to London with them. In the middle of displaying his film stills, Harry remarked to Martin, 'Karen is going off travelling, by the way, with Tom Kovac and a troupe of wannabes. Did you know?' She met Martin's surprised look. Pretending not to have heard Harry's sarcasm, she told them about her schedule and the trip to Hungary.

They were locked in a struggle, quiet and concealed. 'I didn't want to show you up,' Harry told her, as they were going to bed. 'But, really. As if you need to work, now I'm looking after you. What have they offered?'

'It isn't much. But I do need the part.'

'I want you with me. How can you go off to waste time on such a trivial thing? Why do you think I picked you up from nowhere?'

'As if I were a thing – to be picked up!'

'You never had a hope as an actress. If you were to have any success, it would've happened. Face the fact, their offer is charity.'

Karen drew a sharp breath. Could he destroy, in a sentence, everything she had ever achieved? They were about to fight, mortally, and she had to stop it. 'Damien's in the next room,' she said. Yes, he could undermine her confidence like no one else. She understood why, and felt strong. She must work again, and they must learn to support each other. Perhaps she should have told him earlier about the meeting. She felt bowed by the weight of things she couldn't tell Harry: about Quentin, the bad time in her past that she had so dreaded re-emerging. They must learn to talk together, there was no alternative. 'Tell me about Damien. How did it happen that you lost contact? I thought you had no children. Had you really disowned them?'

'Certainly not. I poured thousands of pounds every year into bringing up those two. And they could've contacted me any time. Whereas I had to stay out of touch because of their grandparents' custody order.'

'Why did you let them have custody, Harry?'

He examined his nails and began to file one. 'You know how it is, when you get a once-in-a-lifetime chance of success. Carla was a dreadful woman, a ball-shredder.'

'I hope Damien doesn't remind you of her too much. Does he?'

After a minute Harry put away the file and turned out the light. 'He's so tall, adult. Karen, perhaps I've had my day. Is everything over now for me?'

Surprised, touched by his appeal, she answered, 'Of course not. That's such nonsense. You're in your prime, and your son will do you credit.'

'I certainly doubt that. He informs me he's been a drug addict. I haven't wanted to ask but he has some kind of a criminal record.'

She felt no surprise. The aura of wildness surrounding Damien had suggested criminality. He was difficult, dangerous even. And, she admitted to herself, in the secrecy of darkness, he was also magnetically attractive. How could he be both? But he was.

With any luck, he would not stay around but would go back to America.

Damien woke early to the sound of rain and, from miles away, the ringing of church bells. Sunday morning. Nothing was familiar. He opened his eyes to a beamed ceiling, gnarled stone

79

walls, paisley curtains. He was in a guest room in his father's house. His whole world had changed, and perhaps his future, too.

He took a shower, put on yesterday's clothes, and went downstairs with a feeling of adventure. A radio was playing, and music flooded the kitchen. Martin was alone there. 'Good morning, you're up before anyone else. Did you sleep well?'

Damien nodded. The other man was cleaning the Aga. 'I didn't expect Harry to live this way.'

'He doesn't. We pretend to be country people here. This beauty does the best cooking in the world – that is, allowing for the chef. What would you like for breakfast? I could grill you something – sausage, bacon, mushrooms?'

They settled on bacon and eggs, and while he was cooking, Martin described Harry's London loft. 'Quite a life of luxury there – does that fit your pictures better? Sit down and make yourself at home.'

Why was Martin acting so cute towards him? If he knew that he'd screwed his sister, he wouldn't be so friendly. All the developments of the past weeks were making Damien feel disoriented, light-headed. He was Harry's son and heir. He had been accepted. How bizarre. He devoured breakfast, with two mugs of coffee, and listened to Martin.

The rain had stopped and he decided to go for a walk. Outside was silent except for the gulls, and raindrops falling from gutters and roofs. He walked around the house and through the sodden garden to a wooden jetty, and a boatshed which was locked. Steps led to the empty beach where the tide was out. Damien headed along a strip of sand, across a wide inlet, towards the rocks.

There was so much sky, a dizzying amount of space. A city child, he found his mind travelling to holidays and summer camp, seasons out of ordinary time. Small pools and rivulets splashed underfoot, with a crunch of shingle and shells, and seaweed lay in shining ribbons. From a breakwater he gazed at the calm expanse of sea. This could be his everyday life, if he wanted. Amazing. He couldn't take it in, not everything that was implied, not yet.

Later, he walked back to the Keep. Everyone was up now,

and Martin was cooking beef for their lunch. It was Easter Sunday. Harry had returned from jogging. Karen was unpacking vegetables, brought by the housekeeper. It seemed a peaceful, domestic scene, in a ready-made family home. All he had to do was fit in, like a cuckoo.

Harry told Karen she must go alone to the Hargreaves' and make their excuses. She didn't look too thrilled, and Damien enjoyed an ignoble triumph. He felt greedy for Harry's attention, and for something else he couldn't name. Fetching his jacket, he followed his father to the garage. He reached out a hand to touch that fantastical, shining wing of the Jaguar XJ12. Without thinking, he had walked around to its right side.

'Want to drive?' Harry asked carelessly, and tossed him the keys.

Did he? The Jag was quality out of this world, but he'd never driven on the left and never in a right-hand drive. 'Sure,' Damien said, determined not to thank him. Why shouldn't Harry's toys be his to enjoy? He had a birthright.

'Let's go down the coast, maybe stop for a drink.'

The Jaguar practically soared into space. They flashed past the fields where, just yesterday, the Fête and Fayre had been held. The fairground had vanished, leaving a sea of debris and churned mud. They sped out along the open coast road. He was someone in a movie, a hero or villain, and he wanted to do a hundred miles an hour. Surely Harry would tell him to slow down?

Harry said nothing. Incredible. He could do as he liked. Somewhere further on Damien slowed of his own accord, because driving this was a dream – at any speed. 'Pretty good, mm?' remarked Harry.

'It's OK.'

They parked overlooking the sea. Yesterday he would have driven Harry, with his smart set of wheels, straight off the quayside into the deep. Had things really changed? Could they change in just one night?

It was a pretty harbour and the pub was crammed with rich old yachtsmen. They drank pints. Harry talked knowingly about the yachts lined up, as far as the eye could see, in the marina.

'You have a sailboat, Harry?'

'I used to. But time is a problem.'

'What's in the boatshed, locked up?'

'A rowing tub with a motor – it's nothing. D'you like boats? My new partner, Al, he's into sailing, he'll take you out. Come to that, I could always buy something for you.' Harry was smiling slightly, surely joking.

'I'm more into cars,' Damien answered, cool. How far would Harry go to buy his loyalty? I could get to be a real brat, he thought. 'And while I'm here, I'd like to see Europe.'

'That's easy,' his father said at once. 'We're filming this summer, in France and Italy, and I have to keep an eye on things.'

'Don't you have to be on location all the time?'

'My line producer does the day-to-day sweat. You're interested? I could introduce you to people. Have you been over here before?' Damien shook his head. 'Then there's a lot to see. You will come back to town with us, tomorrow?'

'I'll let you know, tomorrow.' It was just to keep his space, a choice. 'Can we move on? This place is . . .' It was giving him the creeps – not the place but the situation. He felt precarious, with unfamiliar feelings, and almost wished he had never approached his father. As they walked back to the car, Harry said, 'Why didn't you come years ago, Damien? But no matter. We'll have such times together. Won't we?'

Damien slammed the Jag door, and something tumbled from a shelf in front. It was a scarlet scarf, patterned with white, the kind of thing Angel might have worn. It must belong to his stepmother.

He turned on the ignition. Harry picked up the scarf, and folded it small. 'Unforgivable,' he said softly. 'She took that job behind my back. There's some chap, it seems, who she wants to spend our first summer with instead of me. Never trust a woman, Damien. Never believe one word of what they say, once they've got you, or you could be hurt.'

5

Damien would stay at Pipers Wharf for a few nights, then disappear. A lifetime of anger was like a fire gone underground: it could not be put out. Small quarrels were extinguished before they could flare up. And Harry's pretence of acceptance, with his peace-offerings, covered an old rage.

Harry was afraid of humiliating exposure. What did a father do with a son who was six feet tall, twentysomething, visiting for the first time? He was trying to fit Damien into the fabric of a settled life, taking him about, to outfitters, around car show-rooms. He learned which friends and associates had least curiosity, asked no questions. Coming to terms with Damien, he felt the weight of history, mortality, his eventual replacement. How could his son do this to him?

Early in the mornings, Harry would wake and slip away. He would be first at the health club, working out and lifting weights, sweating off pounds, and sometimes Damien joined him. Karen had no time now, not even for swimming. She had no time for him.

Karen felt happy to be working again. It was a good part in a prestige series, with actors she respected. Friends said every-thing would change now, with her face being seen, her name known. Best of all she was earning, regaining independence and becoming herself again. Karen Kincaid, from nowhere, with only an acting talent plus determination. She threw herself into the part, needing to know the background, what it was like to be Maja. She was working with a dialogue coach, rethinking technique, studying actors she admired. Time was short and she was focused.

The first morning of rehearsals she had arrived late. Harry had said he would take her there himself. Was he accepting her working, at last? The rehearsal rooms were a long way off, and the traffic would be heavy. It was kind, but she said she couldn't put him through that. A minicab, or the Underground, would be quicker.

Harry insisted: she must arrive in style, in his car, with himself driving. To please him, she agreed. That morning, the office calm was shattered by Harry's shouting, and at ten past nine, Alice walked out in tears. This had happened before. His secretary, devoted to Harry, was his favourite punchbag if things went wrong. She always returned the next day.

Karen, anxious and ready to leave, dialled a cab.

'Damn it, what's that for? I said I'd take you and I will. Don't you desert me too!'

Karen said, 'I have to go now.'

For the next hour and a half, crawling through bottlenecks of traffic, Harry recited a list of her faults and inadequacies, the ways in which she had let him down. She cared only for herself and advancing her career. Things were difficult right now, she was failing him, he was disappointed. Terrified of being late, she gave up countering what he said. Her mind was a turmoil of conflicting responsibilities and a downward spiralling sense of herself: worthless, selfish, ungrateful, disloyal. A precarious confidence, slowly built up, subsided with every word. She understood – he felt threatened by her working, and with other men – but his put-downs were reducing her. She tried to concentrate on the route. Where they?

'Harry? Why've you turned off the flyover?'

They were trapped in the snarling, fuming, edging-so-slowly wall-to-wall cars of Shepherds Bush, its one-way jams. Where was Acton? 'Karen. I do know my way around.' Had he done it on purpose? He was complaining about her lack of trust, not relying on him, and how that made him feel.

She glanced at her watch. 'Harry, shut up and drive. Concentrate – it's almost eleven.'

That was way out of order. Harry jerked the car to an angry stop, turned off its engine. He was almost speechless. 'If you think I'll listen to that, when all I'm doing is helping, then think again and cope without me.' He got out of the car and strode off.

Karen slipped into the driving seat. She knew the right direction. It might be quicker through the side-streets, she might still get there on time. Then she saw that Harry had taken the key. She abandoned the Jag, right there in the middle of Uxbridge Road, to protesting horns and shouts. She started to run. A cab was drawing in ahead, setting down its fare. Karen leaped in and gave the address, begged the driver to perform a miracle.

She arrived seven minutes late, flustered and nervous. Let it go, she told herself. You're here now so calm down, be professional. You know nothing about Maja yet: be empty.

Karen had been shaky, that first morning. The others had film experience and she must learn from them. Taking the train in the next day, she tried to put Harry out of her mind. Burying herself inside Maja felt like a way of saving herself. They were working in a room laid out with tapes and poles. Reinterpreting the script, she broke up her preconceptions and formed relationships with the other actors, their characters starting to mesh with hers.

The producer came in, consulted with Andrew, then they had notes. Time was the master, and rehearsal a luxury. Andrew knew how to get good work from her. They talked character, motivation. Maja was a damaged but very strong woman. Trampled by man's inhumanity, she had witnessed slaughter, experienced rape. She was beyond being able to love and trust, Karen suggested. None of the cast had lived through war. It was a feat of the collective imagination to understand the consequence of so much fear.

Vicky phoned and asked if Harry was still opposed to her working. How had that news reached her agent? Perhaps she should have confided it from the beginning, but acting roles were only won through cut-throat competition. The drama series was a big-budget investment, and she would have been crazy to talk about Harry's attitude.

'He wasn't keen at first but he's fine about it now,' she said. Vicky told her the director was pleased with her work, she had met him at a function.

Harry did seem to have accepted things. Some charm had crept back into the relationship, his manner had a double-sided acquiescence. He questioned her each evening. Was she having a good time? Where had she gone for lunch, and with whom? How did she spend her long breaks? Was she enjoying her scenes with Keane? Weren't they rather intimate scenes, he suggested, glancing through the scripts.

She talked about the bonding process of the group, how they all went about together. It was some of the hardest work she had ever done, with everything moving on so fast. Would Harry tell her about film technique? She wanted to involve him. He had been checking up on her, calling the rehearsal rooms. From the way he looked her up and down each morning, she felt he was judging her sexuality, how she might get noticed by the people she was with every day. She tried to reassure him, but his possessiveness annoyed her.

At least Harry had Damien around, sometimes staying. Karen felt guilty, and glad of her absences. Guilty because she saw less of Harry, and glad to escape the presence of Damien.

He disturbed her so. Contradictory and intense, between sunny pleasure one minute and hatred the next, he had a strange, instant route to getting under her skin. She could not possibly be any kind of mother to him, yet she should try to be. While her body leaped into sexual arousal when he walked in the room.

He was almost her age, like herself an outsider. Did Damien hold some key to a better understanding of Harry? She didn't dare get close enough to find out. So mesmerised was she, by his eyes and dark, turbulent chemistry, by his voice. She kept her distance, noticing how much he resented her and how he flaunted any closeness with Harry, as if he had to compete with her.

★

Damien watched a pleasure boat, laden with trippers, carving purposefully up the Thames. It slowed, bobbing on the wind-chopped surface, and the faint tones of a speaker filtered across its slapping wake. Had they come to stare at the Wharf, home to the rich and famous, with their cameras and binoculars? He stared back, through narrowed eyes, and sipped his beer.

'They want an eyeful of these new developments,' said Martin, sitting down beside him. 'With all the cash that's been poured in.'

He could see the glittering spine of Canary Wharf, rising out of building sites that littered the area with their cranes, earth movers, scaffolding. Harry lived in a desert of money and mud, and sounds of construction rang, clear and hollow, along the Thames embankment each day.

Martin was diligently sorting papers. 'Must look crazy to you Yanks – our national politics of envy.'

'Preferring failure?' He gave a little whoop. 'Hey, Harry's decided I'm to keep the sports car I tried out.'

'That's nice of him.'

'Is it so I'll hang about? Or so I'll get the hell out of his life? You don't need to answer. Martin, you want a ride? I'm a stranger here. Show me around – tomorrow, maybe?'

Martin smiled, then his face clouded with disappointment. 'I can't, not till next week. I have to be away this weekend.'

Unbelievable. Harry's assistant had seemed to be always on call, having no life. 'He's given you a weekend off? I hope you'll go somewhere good.'

'No, I'm not,' Martin said quickly. 'My sister's moving house, I'm lending her a hand.'

That was a bigger surprise. Viv, moving? Damien had got used to staying odd nights with Viv, in her small rented studio apartment. He had been there a few days ago, and she had said nothing about leaving. They were friends, and she would want him to know where she was, surely? When he had finally told her he was Harry's son, Viv just said she'd guessed as much – no one would be so hung up on Glass unless it was personal.

'Why don't you take Karen?' Martin suggested. 'She'll be here and Harry's got meetings.'

'I don't think so.' That was the last thing he would do. He wasn't sure why he felt so mad at Karen, except that she was somehow an obstruction to his being with Harry. His feelings about his father were so mixed up – did he really want what seemed to be offered? Looking in the mirror, Damien scarcely recognized what he saw. There were the new threads, a haircut, and a hard, sharp look he'd never had before – not even at the toughest of times. He couldn't feel comfortable, and he wanted to make a distance. Harry had destroyed his family. Even if his actions had been innocent, he had those effects. Damien could never forget that history; it burned inside him.

Wanting to see Viv, he set off in the new scarlet MGF he had just been given. London lumbered with buses and trucks, juggernauts. Low and fast, with featherlight steering, he could have made the distance under their axles. He headed up Crouch Hill, among sudden crowds, and there was Viv coming out from a store. She looked easy, happy. Damien hooted. She turned but didn't know the car, not at first.

'This is mine. Come for a ride.'

She jumped in at once. 'Wow. How much?'

'Neat, huh? Oh, sixteen K plus.'

'Really nice. Big Dad is coming across. Let's take it on the motorway.'

He drove through the outer suburbs on to the open road. 'It really goes,' Viv purred, admiringly. 'It's your kind of motor. Here – all I can give you is a bunch of grapes.'

They spat the pips from the open-topped car. Disgusting. Childish. 'Martin said he's helping you move house.'

Viv laughed. Then she explained, 'Oh, I hate London for the summer. I always get out.'

'Where're you heading?'

'Anywhere – I like to roam around. Maybe I'll go to the coast, who knows?'

'Just like that?' There had been nothing, really, between them. Some kind of desperation, that first time, then nothing else. It was just an encounter. Still, he was surprised by how easily she could have disappeared – maybe never seeing him again – after they had talked so much, staying together.

'I'm sure we'll meet again. We've got my brother in common, haven't we? I'm off this evening. Damien, you could stay in my room if you want. The rent's paid till Monday.'

He didn't feel like going back to Pipers Wharf for a day or two. 'OK, I might.'

'How're things? How's Harry?'

When Damien thought of his father now, what came to mind was Harry's obsession with Karen. The moody martyrdom and flashes of rage. 'Harry's not too hot. He thinks his girl bride is giving him the runaround.'

'And is she?' asked Viv, in an interested way.

Damien shrugged. 'Maybe she's up for it.'

Looking at her watch, Viv said, 'Turn off here, I've got to get back. If she did, I wouldn't blame her at all.'

Karen was obsessed with Maja. Everything she saw and heard seemed to be about the character. She was looking for the inner conflicts, to breathe life into Maja. A refugee, she was a young woman like any other, full of the same hopes, fears and longings. What did she believe she wanted? And, underneath that, what did she really want? Ideas came to her all the time for Maja's bearing, her small mannerisms and voice.

Late on Friday the PA phoned. Asked to come in tomorrow, Karen remembered she had a coaching session. It was unusual, going for notes on a Saturday.

In the production office, no one would meet her eye. She sensed at once that something was wrong. The secretary went out, and Andrew began awkwardly, 'I don't know how to say this.'

'It can't be too unexpected,' Ivor said in his kind, courteous way. 'We know you've been under strain. And, after very careful consideration, I'm afraid we must let you go.'

'What did you say?' Everything solid and real seemed to be sliding away: the floor and chair, the room, these two strange faces, with stranger words. 'Let me go?' She was smiling, in rictus, lungs frozen.

'I'm afraid we can't go ahead with you.'

'But . . . you were pleased?'

Andrew said, 'I am. Unfortunately—'

'Unfortunately, you've no experience,' Ivor interrupted.

'But you knew that!' How could they do this when she had worked well, Andrew said so? It didn't make sense.

'I've spoken with Vicky. You'll be paid in full.'

'That's crazy,' she managed to say. 'You're happy, but – replacing me?'

'Someone's taking over, from Monday,' Ivor said cautiously. 'We're sorry.'

'But why?'

'You've seemed rather stressed since rehearsals began. We can't risk the production.'

She shook her head, unable to believe it. They clearly wished the meeting was over. Then she realized why they were so uncomfortable, and couldn't give a proper reason. Harry knew them both, Ivor was a colleague of his. 'Harry's been making a fuss. Hasn't he?'

That upset them. Their friendliness evaporated. Andrew said, 'We know about the drinking and the pills. Look how tired and shaky you are some mornings. We've every sympathy, but –'

'What on earth has he said? I don't drink! I don't take pills. Andrew – you know I wouldn't lie? I'd never let you down.'

There was a strained silence. They didn't believe her. Had Harry really said she was having problems?

'We can't take risks, you must understand.'

'I'm not a risk. Talk to my doctor. Keep me on, please. Harry can't—'

'It's too late. We can't afford to get into the area of domestic discord,' Ivor said sharply. 'I must say, Harry's most concerned. He wants to look after you and your best interests.'

'Like hell he does!' Karen stood abruptly, furious. 'Harry wants to stop my career, to make me dependent. How could you believe that stuff? Or perhaps you don't believe it. Yes, he's a powerful man. If you can't stand up to him, I can't work with you.'

She swept out. Fury carried her through the building, out from reception. She would not break down but swallowed back a sea of feelings. She must go straight to Harry, confront him. But, no, she needed time first. Time to think it through and reach some kind of calm. To make a decision, perhaps.

It was as if, with a handful of words, he had killed part of her. Karen Kincaid: her invented self, an ambitious achiever who got respect. The one who had a future, despite her past. Where was that person now? How would she work again, ever do more than follow as Harry's shadow? He seemed to have won. Her professional reputation had been built over years, but if Andrew thought her unreliable then everyone would.

How could Harry have done it, this secret sabotage? Suppose she had never found out but thought it had been her own inability? She had resolved to make things work between them but, wandering blindly through the streets, Karen thought she could not return to Harry now. She could not become his possession, controlled by him. She bought a Tube ticket, riding through the city's dark, rushing underworld, among the busy and the unbelonging.

It was Saturday midday, and Camden High Street was a solid, shifting crowd. The market stalls were stuffed with ethnic imports, leather, and cheap bead jewellery. She had grown weighted by Harry's years, and now the bustle, competing pitches, the smell of takeouts and frying spices brought back her previous life. She pushed slowly through the noise and crush, among the junkies, drunks and thieves, mingling with the visitors. Had she only wanted Harry because she was afraid? But she had cared for him in many different ways. He had displayed such kindness, and she had admired his worldliness and achievements, and the way he took charge. Now that had gone too far.

Poppy and Caspar were on the roof, and Karen called up to them from the street. The key was still hidden by the door. She went in through the chaotic basement, climbed the house stairs, then a rickety chair set on the landing. Through the skylight, the patch of asphalt was the same refuge among sooty bricks walls, slates and chimneys, satellite dishes. Below, a siren began to whoop. Beyond the black racks of fire escapes, a train trundled on a bridge over mean backyards, grimy streets.

'Hey, babe. Where's Harry? Have you left him?'

'Why did it take me so long?' Karen sank on to their sunbed of duvets.

'You're joking? Nobody could leave Mr Bee's Knees.'

She told them what had happened. They were shocked. Poppy said, 'But did he know it would turn out that way? Did he think you wouldn't want to work? He's a catch. If I had Harry—'

Before she could go on, Caspar had pushed her over and they wrestled, in fits of giggles, until Poppy gasped for mercy. 'You wouldn't last with an older guy, Poppy – too much mouth.'

'Mm – and don't you just love it?' She pouted, suggestive. 'Listen, Karen, you go and lay down the law. You can't leave – all that money, the fame, the lifestyle! Even if it has made you drop your friends.'

How could she explain that Harry didn't want her friendships to continue? He had been sweet to Poppy, before paying her off. 'Forget that. Life should be fun, with acting and kindness.'

'Poor little rich kid,' Caspar sympathized. 'Anyone fancy an Indian? I'm starving. I'll phone.'

When he had gone, Poppy asked, 'Couldn't you really sit back and eat lotuses? You'd never have to worry again.'

'Never is a long time. Harry and I are not a good thing, he destroys my confidence. Such underhand tactics – why couldn't we talk it through? And his friends are hideous.'

'All of them?'

'They're patronizing snobs. Especially . . . Harry's got a new partner. Guess who that is, who he's chosen to work with?' She looked bleakly at Poppy's serene non-comprehension. 'Alistair Quentin.'

Poppy looked horrified. 'You're having me on.'

'They're both independent producers. Harry wants what Quentin can give him – a brand of respectability. Ironic, isn't it?'

'But surely . . . Haven't you said anything to Harry?'

Karen laughed shortly. 'You don't understand, babe. I couldn't possibly or I'd never hear the last of it.'

'Oh, surely, if you just tell him . . .?' They heard Caspar under the skylight, the chair scraping. Karen shook her head, warningly. She had never told anyone else about Quentin. 'But you won't have to see him,' Poppy continued in a neutral way, as Caspar emerged through the roof.

'Who won't she have to see? They said ten minutes. Anyone got any money?'

Karen remembered. 'I've still got the advance from that job.'

'How come you and Harry don't talk?' Poppy asked.

'He thinks I'm questioning his judgement if we do – and perhaps I am. But I can't confide in him.'

'It sounds feudal. Like being a servant in the Middle Ages. I suppose he wants you to serve his middle age. Anyway,' Poppy urged, 'you sort him out.'

'I'm going to.'

'Why not stay the weekend? He'll miss you. When you go back he'll listen.'

Through the day and evening she gradually relaxed, and decided to sleep for one night in her old room. It was empty of any sign that she had ever lived there. Caspar's boxes and bags stood around. For a while she lay on the mattress, surprised by the poverty and richness of her old life. Then she sat cross-legged, listening to the sounds of traffic, cats, a burglar alarm.

She had been away so long, so much had happened. Harry was on her mind, a question she would have to answer, and her anger had grown overlaid with determination. They must talk. He must understand and respect her need for a life. Otherwise they would have to part.

He must have guessed by now that she had found out what he had done. Tomorrow she would make some rules. But now she felt too uneasy to sleep. She decided it would be better if she was there when he woke. She would go back and sleep in the spare room. In the morning she would confront him and tell him how outraged she felt: they would talk.

In the small hours she dressed, then called for a cab. She scribbled a note to Poppy and Caspar and slipped out quietly into the street.

Harry had expected Karen to return, newly unemployed, hours ago. He had been ready to console and offer again the protection she wanted.

At six in the evening, he had given himself a double brandy. It had been a bad day, full of problems he didn't want on his mind. *Cry Murder* was about to start production, but he had doubts about two of the key people. Worse, the negotiations on Artemis were becoming protracted. He had signed projects for development, but the company still only existed as a letter of intent. Perhaps he had jumped the gun.

Where was she? Karen had sneaked behind his back to get that job and she deserved to lose it. He would not be made a fool of. In the past week he had seen her, dressed provocatively, set off each day with a new glow about her, then at night she would be on the phone. Karen had become evasive and sly. He recognized those signs.

He picked at the cold meat supper that Martin had left. Cold comfort. After years of cosseting and fame, he was not cut out for being left alone. The more you gave the less you were valued, or so it seemed. Grievance was niggling, spreading through him. Martin had gone off to his sister. And Damien? The boy had swooped on his life, intent on demolition. Mollified and kitted out with clothes, with a very expensive new car, he disappeared without a word whenever he chose.

Harry was getting drunk. He had missed the gym today, had lost the will to work out. Karen wouldn't care if he kept himself fit and healthy. That place was full of young men, their easy, grace-filled strength. He no longer received respect, the defer- ence he was due. There had been incidents with receptionists there, about the change in locker numbers, and even his charge card.

He tasted his bitterness. When you gave anything to women they became greedy and demanding. They had all abused him. How was he to have known she just wanted to further her acting career? She had never said so. She had wanted his money and had used his name.

It was three in the morning. Across the Thames, nearly all the lights of the flats had gone out, leaving a stale, reheated night. The little slut could not have shouted it out more loudly than this. She was making him a laughing stock. Unsteadily he came in from the terrace, set down the almost empty bottle. That face, that body of hers would not leave him in peace. He saw her spread on the sheets of an unknown bed, young limbs tangled with young limbs.

A fool, he had chosen her. So foolishly, he loved her. And now she must do as he wished, she must be there for him.

He looked up at a small sound. The apartment door, opening – and there was Karen creeping in stealthily, with guilt written all over her.

Karen closed the door. She was shocked to see him awake, still dressed in crumpled shirt and trousers, tie dragged loose. His face wore a blurred, raddled look. 'Harry. Why are you still up?'

He smiled oddly. 'So you decided to creep back. I won't ask what you've been doing, all day and night.'

She felt a surge of strength, almost of relief: they would talk now and get it over. 'I went to stay with my old friends, Poppy and Caspar. And you know why, Harry.'

A sneer twisted his features. 'You must think I'm a fool. Was it the penniless, little boy actor that no one's heard of? Or Queen Carter? My guess is the little scruff. Like unto like, my darling. It does not take long to revert to sleazy type.'

Fury swept over her. She had expected some remorse, some shame from him, but he was still attacking her. 'How can you say these things? I know what you did, what you told Ivor Griffiths.'

'Don't try to divert me.' Harry rounded on her. 'Slut! Anyone can see, all they have to do is look. But looking's not enough for you, is it? Staying out all night, like an alley cat. Why did you crawl back?'

She laughed, it sounded closer to howling. 'Yes, why did I? What a mistake, when you think so little of me.' She turned to the apartment door but Harry was there in an instant, flinging it shut again. Imprisoning, fixing her with his eyes.

'You will explain. Where you have been.'

A new fear of him battled with her anger. 'I lost the part after you persuaded them I was unreliable. I didn't want to come back here after that. I went to talk things over with Poppy.'

'And Caspar,' he prodded, with a small, tight smile.

'Call them, if you don't believe me.' Where was Martin? she thought wildly. Why doesn't he come? Surely he had heard the door slam, Harry shouting. 'Why on earth would I want an affair? Is it because you don't love me, you're afraid someone else might?'

To her relief Harry backed off, moving away from her. She dodged across the arid living expanse, its shadows and light pools, towards the big blind windows that reflected them.

'Karen, you're quite mistaken. I haven't talked to Ivor about you. I've been too busy discussing a new project, which he and I might develop together.'

Ivor would need that, so he had done what Harry wanted. She said, 'They told me they knew I was drinking and taking pills. I couldn't convince them it wasn't true. That was you, Harry. Nobody else would've spoiled my chances like that.'

'You're paranoid. Haven't you realized they were unhappy with your acting? Everyone has tried so hard to be kind. My dear, you're a lousy actress and we have all tried to tell you. It's time to leave those dreams behind – surely you can see?'

Karen thought of the work she had done across the years. The awards, and rewards, for dedication, the reviews, the requests to work with her. Harry had talked proudly of her talent – until they were married. Her anger welled up again. She said slowly, 'It isn't the acting that I'll be leaving behind. Haven't I as much right to a life as you?'

'I gave you a life – but you're not even grateful.'

'I'm suppose to tag along as Martin's shadow?'

'Martin isn't here, and you weren't here. God knows where you've been. Now you've the nerve to be difficult. Don't try to come between Martin and myself. At least he's loyal.'

She looked at him, at the rigid, bellicose set of his features, the bulldog stance. He was hopping mad, just like her. None of what she had to say was going to change things. They were fundamentally opposed. Harry was like a small child, forcing what he wanted, by any means and at any cost. But, physically, he was not a child. She must check her own anger and hurt, try to find a calmness between them. 'Harry, we can't go on this way.'

'I've given you everything in my power. It's rather better than you're used to, in that slum with insalubrious people. Why is it too much to expect,' he asked bitterly, 'that you should be here for me?'

'The things you say make me feel so bad, Harry, that I need other people—'

'I know what you've been up to – making a fool of me. Some way of saying thanks. You've no taste, Karen. No style. There is something tawdry about you, the way you've lived, that grasping, selfish nature. Unable to give, to make one compromise, in return for all you've received. You can't even bear to be at home for me. What a common little girl! I should've noticed, no one wanted you. I should've known what you were after. What possessed me?'

'So I'm selfish, common and – a little girl. I won't listen to you attack me or mock my background any longer. We did love—'

'I could not care for you.'

'Would you be happier if I slit my wrists, after all you've said?'

'That would rid us all of a cheap, lying tart – who comes expensive. No one would mourn, we would sing and dance. There is too much scum cluttering the world. This is all my fault, for taking pity, trying to drag you out of the gutter. The gutter is the only place you belong. I've watched you every day, luridly sexy in those tight, cheap clothes, going to meet your lover—'

'Harry, there is no one else.'

'Disappearing off, at every opportunity. I know that PA, she's told me everything. Every evening, hours on the phone. Why do I finish up with bitches, neurotics – sly, stupid women, who take advantage of me? You're beyond help. I should have left you to rot.'

'Harry, the things you say and do are destroying us, they've changed my feelings for you. I don't see how I can stay.'

He stopped pacing and stood still. 'It's all you wanted, isn't it? To take my name and money, then run.'

'No. But how could I trust you now?'

'You don't care at all.'

'I don't know if I could care again.' She saw he was listening, quietly at last. 'You have got to stop undermining, sabotaging me. I'm a person, Harry. And I never signed up to be one of your servants. I will act and if you can't accept it—'

'Then what?'

'Then we must part.'

Harry laughed suddenly. She couldn't bear the look in his eyes – the venom and violence. He veered towards her. 'Slut! Betraying me!' She began to dart away, but he lunged at her, punching her left breast, then her stomach. She doubled over, screaming, and staggered back against the furniture, trying to escape, to run. When Harry grabbed her, she fell, her body electric with terror. She lay, curled up, covering her head with hands and arms as he rained kicks at her.

'Dirty bitch! You will not leave. You will do what I say!' The kicking stopped. She listened to his ranting. There was silence, then she heard him muttering, and something being dragged across the carpet. She was too frightened to open her eyes, or move. 'You made me do that,' Harry said. And, after a while, 'Are you going to lie there all night, Karen? Stop pretending or I'll get annoyed again. I said, get up.'

Her pulses were storming alarm, her flesh felt tattered. She wanted to kill him. Dragging open her eyes, she saw Harry standing by the window. He was watching her, with a righteous expression. 'Come on,' he said. 'Get up. Don't be so dramatic. Karen?' And he started towards her.

'Don't come near me. Don't you dare touch me!' She unfolded cardboard limbs.

Harry looked offended. 'Don't be silly. You insulted me. No one should put up with that.' He had taken her arm, his grip sucking her along to the sofa. 'You just don't understand how I've felt, what it's been like for me. You've never obeyed me for long.'

'You're right.' She was cold, shaking from shock. 'I really don't understand.'

'And that's why it happened. You will understand now, won't you? It's been beyond endurance.'

'What has?' she asked, from between chattering teeth.

'The way you've shown me up. First to Raima. And my sister – when the *Sunday Times* came? Your behaviour was dreadful. My colleagues – Ivor, Andrew. What are they supposed to think when my wife openly flouts my wishes? You must see my position.'

Had he said possession or position? He was possessed, and so was she. She felt confused, guilty. She was an unbearable person, who didn't understand him: he was constantly embarrassed by her. And she felt grateful because he had stopped hitting her. Harry was saying, in a magnanimous voice, 'You're very young – it's not too surprising you don't understand the anguish you cause. You've offered nothing but opposition, I've tried to forgive you.'

She heard the sorrow in his words, then their meaning. He had tried to forgive her? She was guilty, in the wrong, beginning to doubt her own perception. But that was outrageous. He was trying to turn things round. What Harry wanted was power, control over her. He was violent and she must leave. Every instinct screamed at her to leave, while her body throbbed with terror, cringed away from the memory of those fists, the kicks. Fear was paralysing. But she must escape, now.

She had raised her hands to cover her face, her expression, despair. Her skin shrank, shrivelling away from his skin as he took down her hands, and nausea welled through her. Blood was running from cuts on her hands; they felt as if she had inflicted violence. 'Darling, if only you hadn't made all those dreadful, unforgivable accusations,' he said, while she sat mute. Did he feel any remorse, responsibility? She was all damage. There was pain in her stomach, breasts, and her head: her heart and mind were not hers. Was he still Harry, the one she had vowed to stay with?

She had longed for them to be alone together. Now they had been. Where was Martin? The vast luxury apartment held a stillness, that quality of silence when no one was around. If only she had noticed when she walked in. If she had said nothing, been circumspect, might that have made a difference? He asked, 'What're you thinking?'

'About Martin,' she answered, after a minute. 'Just, where he is.'

Harry turned her hands over, fixing her with sharp eyes. 'Martin decided to go away,' he said, matter-of-factly. Then, 'If you were ever to tell anyone, about tonight, you would regret that very much indeed. Do you understand?'

'I understand,' she whispered. Cowed. Like a cow. To be used, or slaughtered, because he saw himself as a superior species and her keeper.

'Good. Sweetheart,' Harry laughed suddenly, 'do lighten up. Please – enough of that dour face. All you have to do is be a good girl – then we can be happy again, I promise. We were happy and will be again.'

She looked out to where dawn was spreading across the river, and the city's buildings stood solemn in silhouette. How could she get away from him? When he turned his attention from her, if he believed they'd got over this, then she would run away. Her head was throbbing, she couldn't think straight.

Harry was kissing her right hand, then her left. 'Poor little Karen, let me kiss these better. Come – Martin keeps first aid in the kitchen.'

On her invisible rope, she followed. Among the stainless-steel racks and knives, Harry sat her down and, very gently, dissolved away the tattered red ribbons of her hands. 'I've been beside myself with worry,' he told her. 'There's such a large element of financial risk, in production. There've been very worrying things happening.'

'You could have told me, Harry.'

'You were too busy to listen. You made things worse.'

Did he expect her to apologize? She stayed silent, and after a while he went on, 'But you knew how I felt about the boy turning up. So upsetting. He was suddenly around, you were not. Then you provoked me.'

Again, she said nothing. It seemed the safer course. After tonight, she knew, she could never feel safe with Harry again. As the Elastoplast covered the backs of her hands, she recognized the irony. She had seen in Harry a refuge, a protector against a dangerous world, and she had fallen in love with that false image. The shield had turned into a weapon and attacked.

He was putting his arms about her, drawing her close, saying tenderly, 'It's because we're so special together. No one else can give me what I need. You must know how much I adore you.'

She was shaking from fear of him, shame and exhaustion. She drew back. 'Harry. You'll never do that again.'

'Of course not. Nothing so bad could happen to us again – not now.' He held her gently. 'You're all the world to me. I could never let you go.'

He would never let her go but could not let her be. He was offering warmth and kindness now, the affection that she craved. As her feelings welled and broke into tears, he patted her. She was a puzzled, stupid pet, being forgiven some grave misdemeanour during training. She felt quite desperate for his approval, as if that could save her life.

'You're sad now, but tomorrow we'll be happy again. You'll see.'

She would never again risk being herself with him: he could not tolerate the genuine. From now on, her acting would be for Harry. She was crying from loss – of a hope for understanding, the possibility of love, the trust she had tried to place in him. And he thought they would get over it.

They went upstairs to bed, drawing down the blinds. Harry held her. For a while Karen felt his body slackening into sleep. She lay very still, trying to calm her thoughts, her complete confusion. Later, when Harry slipped quietly out of bed, she breathed shallowly, feigning sleep until he had gone. She would leave him as soon as she could.

6

The beach chalet, perched on the rocks above the inlet, looked as if nobody ever went there. Its wood had been weathered by the harsh, salt winters, and its blue paint whitened by summer sun. On this lonely stretch of the shore, it stood separate from the other huts and the beach café. There was no one to notice that it was lived in now.

Viv was listening to her Walkman as she swept sand off the verandah's dried, misshapen planks, down over the rocks. She stopped a minute, to look out. Right now, the great sheet of sky was serene, with soft puffs of cloud drifting slowly, high overhead. Further out towards the horizon, clouds had layered up into a mackerel effect. What did that mean? She should know by now. Perhaps Martin knew. And that sea: a still, low tide, shimmering as if it was made of spun light. Deceptive. A sea of secrets.

From pillar to post, she thought. But it was good to be back, with everything just as it had been. The blackout curtains, folded where she had left them in the drawer, were hanging from their hooks again. Her rucksack, stuffed with all her possessions, lay open in the corner. It was home.

Viv filled the kettle, switched it on, then sat on the steps. She took cigarettes from her pocket, lit one. It was Sunday morning. Out on the public beach, near the shore, the sand stretched gleaming wet and ribbed, holed by rocks, seamed by breakwaters. People were walking, insects crossing. There had been no sign of anyone from the Keep. Would Martin come, before they all went back tonight?

She had to put up with the grudging nature of his small concessions – when she could be near, when he needed her – but nothing could ever change that last weekend. Amsterdam, the two of them. The trip had been her reward for a favour done, services rendered. He always kept his side of a bargain with her. It had been almost like the early days, and she had the memories, the snapshots inside her head. The last track of the tape ended, and her mind wound on like snatches of songs.

Martin couldn't live without her, she knew that. One day he would wake up and see that it was true.

Martin arranged the potatoes, already parboiled and drained, around the minted leg of lamb. He basted it all, replaced the roasting tin on the Aga's top shelf and set the timer. He had a good hour to sort the car. It was hard, these days, finding anyone who would do things right. Some old dust had collected in corners of the dashboard and fittings, and if he looked now, he would probably find other signs of a slapdash attitude.

He took the Jaguar out of the garage on to the drive, then fetched the box of cloths and brushes kept for the job. The interior wasn't too bad, really, but still it annoyed him. He wanted it immaculate for tonight's drive home, the week ahead. Saturday's *Times*, a chocolate wrapper from an ashtray, leaflets fallen out of a magazine, those had all gone straight into the garbage.

How could anyone do an imperfect job on such a machine? It hummed with money and quality. If he was honest, it had a lot more class than its owner. The car seemed like his: he drove, and he looked after it.

Then he saw Harry walking back up the drive, his face flushed, jogging suit darkened with patches of sweat. He straightened up. 'Good run?'

'Not bad.'

'Karen didn't go with you?' Martin kept his tone light.

'I'm out of favour, the lady is not being kind. Do you understand women, Martin?'

'I'm much better with cars.'

'How sensible. They can be very mean. And, eventually, it gets to one.'

'She should show respect. Don't let her neglect you, Harry. This beauty's been left in a right pickle. I'm going to change your valeting service.'

'What would I do without you to look after me?'

Harry turned towards the house, the kitchen, and Martin followed. He had heard a few things, enough to guess what was going on. As if he hadn't seen it coming from the start. During the past thirty years, everyone knew that young women had changed, but Harry had not changed and he would not be disobeyed. Was it going to end in another scandal and cover-up?

'I can always tell when you're worrying,' he said, and poured a glass of sparkling mineral water, slightly chilled. 'But I'm not so sure if it's about her.' Martin knew a lot about Harry's affairs, enough to know when he was taking risks, possibly making mistakes. Over-committing to loans, investing in dreams, his mind not concentrated. Harry was sailing close to the wind. 'Best talk some sense into him, while you're both relaxing. Has Al still got his yacht?'

'It's at Brighton Marina.' Harry nodded. 'But he's got children and wives. Complicated.'

'Ask them all down here. It's the best way.'

'I'll think about that.' Harry turned as Damien strolled in. 'Good morning. Or should I say good afternoon? Would you care for a pre-lunch drink? I must shower, after my run.'

'Hi, Harry.' Damien slid easily, gracefully into the chair at the head of the long table as his father went out.

Martin put on some coffee, then started the baby carrots and mange-tout. 'You slept well.'

'Catching up. What is it with him?'

'People always sleep here, it's the air. Your father, he's got some business to sort out.' When he had first seen Damien, he had been like some young desperado, piratical. Now, already, he seemed made for Harry's kind of life. Relaxed and at ease, looking good. Like someone destined for inheritance. If Harry hadn't remarried, Damien would be in line for a lot of money.

He must have thought about that; he must resent his step-mother. Neither of them would ever want to ask about the will because Harry was suspicious of people's motives, and it would remind him of mortality.

Martin poured coffee. Black, no sugar, the way Damien liked it.

Damien joined the lunch ritual, slightly familiar to him by now. Sunday morning in the country. He was staying with these people, but he didn't belong, didn't understand what was going on with them. The coolness with Harry was mutual: he could think of a dozen reasons why a successful, self-made English-man might not rate a son like him. He felt defiant and free to rebel.

He had grown sickened by his own brattishness. He had got to find some self-respect. The new MGF sports, staying in its parking spot for most of last week, seemed a really tacky payback now. Why milk Harry, acting spoiled? It had been easy to do: the great car, grand apartment, the kudos of being introduced around to everyone as Harry Glass's son. He could take that or leave it because, in the end, it all meant nothing.

What was wrong with him, that he couldn't love his father – had even wanted to kill the guy? There were other things, too, like the way he used Martin's sister. Only some kind of monster could do all that, be so alienated, lacking in ordinary feeling. He was unable to love. He was bad. Nobody – and not Harry for sure – could ever replace the family he had tried to avenge. It was as if he lost his own humanity, the morning he found Angel dead.

Harry was slavering over his wife and she was treating him like nothing. On the surface Karen and Harry seemed OK, but he could sense how cold she was underneath. Had they just fallen out, or did she really hate her husband? He remembered Viv hinting that Karen had married for money. It looked like she was regretting it now.

As they lunched overlooking the sea, he thought how there was a loss of spirit about Karen, as if she was in retreat, pretending. The girl was really unhappy. Why, when she had everything?

'That looks marvellous,' exclaimed Harry, as Martin brought in the fruit crumble. 'But Karen doesn't like custard.'

'It doesn't matter,' she said.

'But of course it matters. Do we have cream, Martin?'

'There's some yoghurt, I'll fetch that.'

'I'm not hungry, I couldn't eat any more.'

'But, Karen, you've hardly touched Martin's wonderful lunch. You can't possibly not have any of his crumble.'

'That looks very good, Martin. Could I have just a little?'

'You seem rather peaky, my darling. Slightly washed out. We shall get such a good nap together, this afternoon.'

As Harry covered her hand with his, Karen froze visibly. Then she put down her spoon, positioning it casually to hide the food she had left, and turned to Harry. 'That was a long run you had, this morning. You need to rest, but I'm afraid I'd only keep you awake. So I'm going to – take the boat out, and see you later.'

After a moment Harry pointed out, 'It's low tide.'

Damien looked from his father to his stepmother. 'The tide's half-way. Martin and I could give you a hand with getting the boat out, if you like.'

'Yes. Yes, please.'

He glimpsed Harry's anger at him, and felt glad. Tight-lipped and cool, Harry gave in. 'Very well. But I'd like you back here by four, if that isn't too much to ask.'

They went out through the garden to the boathouse, where the twelve-foot blue dinghy, the *Hope*, was set on trailer wheels. It rolled over the jetty to the small slipway, fairly easily across the sand to the water's edge. As they went further from the house, and from Harry, Karen's mood seemed to lighten. She confessed, 'I don't know how to – drive it. I don't know a thing about boats.'

Her pretext was transparent as his own. She wanted to get away from Harry, while he just wanted to fight with him. 'You don't exactly drive them. I'm told you steer them through the water somehow.' That was misleading, because he knew about boats from vacations back home. He felt full of mischief, solemnly following Martin's instructions as they fitted the outboard, then dragged the dinghy out beyond the shallows. Martin grasped the gunwale, to steady it. Climbing in, Damien turned and reached out to Karen.

Standing in the waves, she took his hand. He was too aware of that contact as she clambered over the side, jumping into the hull. Her suddenness sent the little boat rocking out of control. It tipped them both sideways, throwing them off balance, and instinctively he put out his arms to steady her. She stumbled, close. For a moment he felt her, half naked, against him. He held her, then held her away from him, aware of nothing but the shock of demand in his own body. Then, of the boat's lurching, easing, becoming stable again. She was stepping back. Martin was climbing between them.

Damien glanced at Karen, then away. Hell. Did she have any idea? Dad's wife, he thought. She's Dad's wife.

'Lesson one,' Martin was saying, starting the engine. 'Never move your weight around too abruptly.'

'OK,' she said, sunnily, sitting down in the prow. She looked like a figurehead of an angel. Happy, lit by adventure and gazing out to sea, shading her eyes to watch the gulls wheeling above the shore. Damien looked away. He had been staring at her for maybe the last five minutes. She wasn't staring at him, and why should she?

'Let's go along that bit of coast,' she suggested.

'We'll go further out, first. There are some rocks and a drift.' Martin steered into the tide and they bobbed through rolling waves. It was cooler and windy, with flying spray, until he turned, slowing, to motor parallel with the strip of beach. Here the channel was busy with ferries and small craft, as they neared a resort, and the dinghy drifted sideways, slowed by the drag of undercurrents. Ahead lay a steep pebble beach, covered with a bright patchwork of tourists. The promenade had a pier and hotels, a funfair with tinny music, and the wail of a ride: there were shrieks and screams, as Martin cut the stuttering engine.

Damien glanced at Karen. 'Not too like your world, your beach. Is it?'

'That isn't my world – and it's Harry's beach. I like things that remind me . . . Candy floss and hook-a-duck. Ghost rides.'

'Seafronts – those sound like cries of despair to me,' Martin said.

Karen asked, 'Which town was it, where you were a kid?'

'Bournemouth. My mother ran a bed-and-breakfast. She made sacrifices, to send me to boarding school.'

'Just she and you?' Karen sounded sympathetic.

'She was busy, and didn't have much time,' answered Martin.

Did no one have fathers any more? Sons were left searching, confused. Damien felt that lack, in his own irresponsibility, his violent last resorts of ego standing in for protective strength. It seemed that Martin had adopted a fantasy parent, dressing in Harry's clothes and trying to become him. 'We're almost the same,' Damien said, and he answered Martin's surprised look, 'My grandparents raised me.'

Martin turned away and stared at the shore with its pleasure machines. 'Harry scarcely compares. Come off it, Damien – you're the luckiest chap, don't you know that?' He restarted the engine with a jolt, and they began in a desultory, meandering way to tour the seafront with its flotilla of pedalos.

On an impulse, Damien said, 'I met your sister. In London.' The words drifted off on the wind as if he hadn't said them, but his heart had begun to beat fast – some sense of risk, something he didn't understand – and it demanded a response. Martin's face was hidden, he was concentrating as a ferry approached. 'I gave her a lift home – it was sheer coincidence. Didn't Viv ever tell you about me?'

Martin answered cheerfully, 'Fancy that, then. She never tells me anything, little Vivvie. Who ought to settle down.' The ferry rolled out its bobbing wake, and he turned their craft bow in to it. 'My watch has stopped. Got the time, Karen?'

She looked at her gold wristwatch, on its slender bracelet studded with diamonds, just the kind of thing to go sailing in. Her voice was reluctant. 'It's twenty-five to four.'

'We'd better head for home.'

'I'll take us back.' Damien stood up, and took the tiller from a surprised Martin. 'And if we're late, *mea culpa*.'

Martin moved aside. Steering them out to sea in a wide circle, Damien opened the throttle and sent the little boat speeding across the waves. They troughed into walls of water, skimmed the air, ploughed almost under, surfed again on arcs of spray. From the prow, Karen twisted to look back at him. Her eyes were shining, her hair flying, mouth wide open in an excited cry.

She loves danger, he thought. She longs for danger.

'Hey,' Martin cautioned, gripping the side, 'don't break her up.'

Damien slowed, motored prosaically back towards the shore. They were almost level with the Keep; its round tower and cluster of roofs dominated the horizon as they approached. A silence had fallen over them until Karen said to Martin, 'Tanya lived here, didn't she? You must've known her.'

He was dismissive. 'I scarcely met her.'

'You were working for Harry, weren't you?'

'In London – I was his assistant there. She hardly ever came up to town. Christine looked after her here.'

'Why was that?'

'Perhaps she preferred the country.' Martin shrugged, as if bored by her questions.

'She died here, on her own.' Karen's voice was sharp.

'It was an accident,' he said brusquely. 'Tragic or not, depending on your point of view. Frankly, she asked for it.'

Karen looked furious, and Damien watched her bite back a retort. She wasn't going to answer. 'This was Harry's second wife?' he drawled. 'She was real popular, then.'

'She was a trial, by all accounts,' Martin answered. 'Hysterical, depressive, couldn't mix with people. I met her towards the end, when I started with him.'

Damien asked slowly, 'They would've divorced? If she hadn't – what, swallowed the pills?'

Martin gave him a hard look. 'None of that was made public.

Harry needs protecting. Anyway, it's old news.' His voice lightened a little. 'There he is, waiting on the jetty. I'm sure we're later home than he wanted.'

They were ten minutes late. Damien apologized, and Harry brushed him aside. 'So you haven't all sailed away, forgetting to inform me? Sweetheart, there is such a glow to your cheeks. Now, come. Share a tiny portion of your company with me before we're obliged to drive back.' He linked arms with Karen, leading her away.

Watching them go together through the garden, and out of sight, Damien felt oppressed. The empty sky, the great ocean, the very clean salt, holiday air could not wash away memories of loss. They lay open, raw, and unexplained. And he needed to find out the truth.

'Oh, you did give me a turn! Appearing from nowhere, like that. I thought you went back with the others, last night.'

Damien gave Christine his most winning, contrite smile, picking up the broom that she had dropped. 'I'm real sorry, I never meant to alarm you. OK? We should've told you, I decided to stay on. And here you are with all this clearing up. Can I help?'

'I couldn't allow that. What would Mr Glass say?'

'He wouldn't know so he couldn't say a word.' The kettle on the sideboard was sending out steam, and Damien laid the broom handle against the wall. 'Take a break and talk with me.'

'Well, it is ten twenty.' She bustled about, making tea and fetching biscuits, hesitating over which china to use, while he got her talking. The housekeeper must be in her sixties, devoted and loyal. What wouldn't she do for Harry?

'You must know my dad a whole lot better than I do, Christine. All those years. You've seen him through good and bad times. Maybe you could fill in the gaps for me?' She looked surprised. 'I really need to know things, and who else has been around so much as you?'

She said sympathetically, 'You did miss out, by all accounts. And him being famous, too.'

Given the chance, she loved to gossip. Gradually Damien steered the conversation around. 'My mother died when I was still a baby.' He ignored the embarrassment sweeping the housekeeper's face. 'Then, I only heard things. I had a stepmother, Tanya, who I never met.'

Christine hesitated, fractionally. 'Well,' she launched out, at last, 'you never missed a thing, dear. That one was no better than she ought. Been around. Not the right girl for Mr Glass. We all thought that when he brought her home.'

'They were not the happiest of couples?'

'What that poor man had to put up with, I can't say. Spoiled and lazy, she never went out, nor lifted a finger. And — temperament. Not helped by the fact we were putting out a crateful of empties, every week, all hers. The man was a saint, if you ask me.'

'She became a recluse, before — her accident?'

'It wasn't my fault, and it wasn't his — not Mr Glass. I had the flu very bad. My son Joe delivered a note, saying I couldn't go in to keep an eye on her.' She pointed, dramatically. 'The note was still there, on that kitchen doormat, when they found her cold the next day. A sea of troubles, that girl.' She brightened, pouring more tea. 'The first wife, now she was much better. It's a pity — you never met Jacqueline, did you? She's Lady Harbinson now. There were pictures of her last year in *Country Homes*. It was all about Jacqueline's lovely house.'

'Have you kept that magazine?'

'Well, of course. I keep everything about Mr Glass, and Jacqueline was a lovely girl. I've got two scrapbooks, full of him.' She smiled at Damien. 'Now, I know what you're going to ask. Yes, I could bring them in for you.'

'Tomorrow? Not sure if I'll be here tomorrow, Christine. Hey, you ever got a ride in a sports car before?'

She looked horrified, and by the very idea of him calling at her home. Then, she was persuadable. The housekeeper lived in a small terrace cottage east of the village, with her grown-up son. The living room was tiny, cramped. It must be Joe Taylor — ginger-haired and mean-looking — in that colour snapshot over the mantelpiece. Beside it stood, in pride of place and silver-framed, a publicity still of Harry, years ago.

'Mr Glass gave me that portrait, signed by him. "It's for the first fifteen years of working for me," he said. The first fifteen years – I like that. Here we are, my collection from the newspapers. You will take proper care of them, won't you?'

'I'll guard them with my life,' he promised. 'You'll have them back tomorrow.'

He returned to the Keep, then looked at what he had been given. All of Harry's more recent, post-Hollywood life was here, in two bulging scrapbooks with worn covers. The cuttings, yellowed and fragile, were from tabloids and popular magazines, sprinkled with photos of the father he had never known. Slowly, he turned the thickly pasted pages. Something fell out. It was fresh and glossy, a three-page spread. *Lady Jacqueline Harbinson's Tranquil Manor.*

Jacqueline, he read, lived just outside a Hampshire village with her stockbroker husband and two young sons. A high-born Englishwoman, living the comfortable life she might expect. There was no mention that this must be her second marriage. The photos were of artfully sculpted gardens, a mellowed, eighteenth-century brick manor house. Designer interiors. Designer couple, posing with scrubbed children, horses and Labradors. Jacqueline looked the part, through and through. Where had Harry fitted in? Was he a secret of her girlhood?

He leafed back through the scrapbook. There was little about Tanya, until the accounts of her death. Her pictures were baffling in their contradiction. She was smiling, lively and bewitching. In reproductions of family snaps her face had grown sombre, her stance subdued. After she died, Harry gave copious interviews, generous with photos of himself, the grieving star of *Will Vengeance* fame. The news coverage was more conflicting in tone, from the discovery of Tanya's body up to the inquest. Then it seemed the press had lost interest when a Princess Diana story broke.

Tanya had not left any note and had no reason to kill herself.

She died from a mix of diazepam with alcohol, and it could have been accidental. It had all happened just as the housekeeper had said, except for some unexpected details. Harry 'had returned from business talks in Los Angeles' the previous day. He had been at the Keep but, unaware that his wife had taken an overdose, he had left alone for London.

Damien got up, crossed the living room and looked out. Evening was drawing in, streaked with the gathered black of clouds. The wind was gusting and roaring, sending waves to crash in an angry, constant white thunder on to the rocks.

Tanya had lived alone in this place. But it seemed wrong, how she had died alone. According to the estimated times, Harry could have known that she had swallowed the sleeping pills. He could even, possibly, have got the housekeeper's message, read and replaced it, and then gone. If Christine had suspected anything, perhaps she might have covered for him, protecting Harry's image?

The marriage had been over, by all accounts. That way, there would be no alimony. There could be no later, bitter recriminations against him in public. And nothing could ever be proved.

Surely Harry would never have left Tanya to die. He could not have known what she was doing. Or had he?

'Mr Glass, a corner table was not specified in your booking. As you can see, we're rather full.'

'That is perfectly outrageous. My assistant would never book a table surrounded by through traffic.'

'I'm sorry, sir. Perhaps—'

'Do you know who I am? I would like to speak to the manager.'

'I'll see what we can do. One moment, please.'

Harry tapped his fingers testily on the bar top. 'It's appalling. Why should we be inconvenienced? Martin always makes certain of a corner table. I will not be overlooked, nor overhead.'

Karen gazed intently at her expensive shoes and at the highly glazed terracotta of the floor. She had learned to be wary with him. If she remembered fear at all times, then she could silence any comment beyond agreement. Out of the corner of her eye, she watched an anonymous couple being moved. The best corner table in the trattoria, overlooking an exclusive Thames harbour, was being tidied and reset for Harry. She was sure they didn't know who he was – the management here was young, and Harry no longer famous – but he was imposing and bullying enough to get his way.

They were seated. Harry was satisfied, but not for long. 'What is this?' he spluttered, over the mineral water. 'I specifically asked for Perrier, which this certainly is not.' Karen listened to a lecture on mineral water. She ordered rocket salad, followed by fillet of sole. 'But, my darling,' said Harry, pleasantly, 'the wild salmon is a far better choice. And you don't really want that rabbit food. My wife will have asparagus to start, then the salmon. I will also have the asparagus, followed by mustard steak. Extremely rare, almost breathing in fact.' He leaned forward. 'You must have only the very best. I do adore you so, my darling.' He touched her hand, its heavy rings, intricate gold chains, the eternity timepiece he had picked for her. She was weighted and shackled by his gifts, as he courted her again in his own way. 'And you do care for me too, I know that.'

Karen kept her expression rigidly bright, neutral, because Harry must not glimpse the loathing she felt. It was ten days since he had attacked her. The purple bruises had faded to yellow, while the memory of that night stayed livid, inside. She was at risk, living with him. Instinct told her it would be even more dangerous to leave Harry Glass while he remained obsessed with her. Trapped, she was waiting for the chance to escape.

Between Mondays and Fridays she lived cautiously inside his gilded London cage. He was busy with French and Italian productions, and the apartment was filled with people coming and going for meetings. She had to be there and not go out without his agreement. She could shop sometimes – at Harrods and Harvey Nichols, where Harry had accounts – but only if Martin escorted her. If she went to the cloakroom, Martin would wait outside the door. She did not argue. She would not risk getting hit again, but was biding her time. If she was there, with no interests beyond him, then Harry was not violent. Karen kept her thoughts and feelings to herself, practising suspended animation, in the paralysis of fear.

She was trapped, but she would get free.

On weekday evenings she was displayed at media functions and dinner parties. Afterwards, unless she had been lively enough, in private Harry would become enraged by what he called her dourness and her misery. She must be seen to be happy with her husband – while she hated his hypocrisy, the false popularity he contrived, the way he manipulated others. He insisted on adulation, and intimidated, even damaged the reputation of anyone who failed him. People played along with Harry. He was establishment approved and had been put forward for an OBE, for services to British film.

'Harry deserves baubles, he's such a remarkable chap,' gushed Ann Bellman, the lawyer's wife. 'Robert tells me he started out with nothing. What an achiever, you must be terribly proud.'

Terribly proud, or terrified? She could not say to the other wives. Her role was to mix with them, to fit in with talk of domestic management, holidays, shopping, recipes, children. She studied how to act the part. These women hid their real selves, doused their sexuality, twittered banalities, and that seemed to keep their marriages going.

Often, she thought about Damien. He was staying away from Harry, it seemed, and she didn't know whether to be glad. When Harry wasn't around, if she shut her eyes she could remember Damien, holding her close in the boat. Karen felt the strength of his body and the warmth in the touch of his skin, exploding her senses into a spiral of confusion. Then, she shrank away from the memory of her own response, the treachery of her body. She could not want a man again – she could never trust male physicality. And he was no good. She dismissed him, too, by association: like father, like son.

There must be something terribly wrong with her. How could she want him, of all people?

★

On Friday morning, Damien drove west on the A259, along the south coast. His mind was on Jacqueline's magazine interview. He craved to know about his mother Carla: of Harry's past three women, only Jacqueline was still alive.

Yet he delayed in finding her and stopped for lunch outside Petersfield before he studied the map. The village of Framwell was easy to find, and a farm worker directed him. Framwell Manor lay behind a white gate. Rhododendrons screened the house until the drive widened and he drew in under a chestnut tree.

Damien got out of the car. Instantly, the afternoon quiet was shattered as two black Labradors bounded towards him, barking excitedly. He paused while the dogs circled, performing their ritual warnings.

'Jasper! Blackberry!' The dogs crouched, sniffing the air around him. He recognized Jacqueline at once, although her hair was hidden under a scarf and she was wearing gardening trousers. She called from a distance, 'Can we help you?'

Did she see him as a threat? He was a stranger, young and scruffy. I am dangerous, Damien reminded himself, with a wry smile. He had intended to say he was a journalist, maybe writing a book about Harry. Looking at Jacqueline now, he sensed that he would be sent away. 'My name's Damien Calvino. I'm the son of Harry Glass and Carla.'

An odd flicker cracked across the composure of Jacqueline's face. Disbelief and suspicion mingled, then were banished. She had long buried her first husband, that was clear. She asked, 'And why are you calling on me?'

'We never got to meet.' He stepped nearer, so she could see that he and Harry had similarities. She didn't retreat.

'It's years since Harry Glass and I parted.'

'Hell, I know it's a long time. You must think me bad-mannered. I would've called, but you're not listed.'

'There is a postal service.'

He said quickly, 'I'm just visiting from the States. Lady Jacqueline, can I talk with you?'

She didn't refuse. She had an appointment in twenty minutes, but they could talk briefly. They went into her house, into a sunlit drawing room. 'Do sit down.' She disappeared, and from somewhere further inside a sound of vacuuming stopped.

Damien looked about him. The room was pleasantly English, mellow and relaxed. The windows looked out on to curving lawns. Vases of blooms softened the room, and family photos were arranged on a table behind a gleaming piano.

Jacqueline returned, followed by a woman with a tea tray. She had changed her clothes, performed a two-minute transformation, and her hair was combed into a clip at the nape of her neck. He felt crass beside her. Had this woman really been with Harry? She had been the replacement after his years with Carla.

Jacqueline handed him a fragile teacup. 'I can see you're his son.'

'I was raised in the States, and never met him till a month back.'

'There's nothing I can tell you that your father couldn't.'

He wanted to shout it out: *You're the one who destroyed my mother. When she heard about you, she killed herself. What did you think?* What did Harry say about it? He imagined Jacqueline's response, the shutter that would come down between them. 'I read a few things,' he said. 'You met in Scotland, then joined him in Hollywood – and had a sudden wedding. Yeah?' He remembered that her father had been publicly outraged, and this woman, like Carla, had married against opposition. Surely she must have loved Harry, so what had gone wrong? He couldn't ask. He was inhibited by her Englishness, the steel inside the porcelain.

'That all seemed frightfully romantic,' Jacqueline allowed, with a small smile. 'I was twenty-one. Of course I grew up, while Hollywood remained as it was.'

'And Harry, he made it. How, exactly?'

Jacqueline sounded vague. 'Harry starred in two commercially successful films. He directed himself in a third – which bombed, as they say. I returned to England before that. Harry came back for a while, and we divorced – as quietly as possible. More tea?'

He held out his cup. She seemed to feel no warmth, nor bitterness. It was uncanny, and she was beginning to unnerve him. Casually he said, 'Harry took a second wife. A few years later she died from an overdose.'

'I've no information about that, we had no further contact.'

'You must've seen the newspapers. Didn't they ask you for interviews?'

Her voice rose abruptly. 'I would never dream of speaking to reporters, and I had nothing more to do with him.'

It was the first and only hint of nervousness. He asked quickly, 'But you must've known about my mother's suicide when you became Mrs Glass?'

'I knew about you and your sister. But Harry . . . There was nothing I could do. And now I'm afraid I have to go out.'

Damien stood and held out his hand. 'Thank you for talking with me.'

She smiled. 'I hope I've cleared up any questions about your family. Now, why not put the past behind you? If this is your first visit to England, I'm sure there's a great deal to see and do. Goodbye.'

He turned the car and set off slowly the way he had come. His mother was everyone's secret, she was closed to him. Harry had left Carla to marry across the English class barrier. Perhaps he had wanted to become more credible. And perhaps he had resented Jacqueline. All these years later, she knew better than to talk to the press, or even her own stepson. She had been unnaturally silent, out of a residual loyalty, or residual fear.

It was fear. He recognized it in Karen.

Damien put his foot on the gas. Would she be at the Keep this evening, with the others? When he had first met her, he saw her as some kind of a fake. Now she looked like the latest in a line of Harry's disasters.

There was going to be a houseparty, Martin had said. Some business partner of Harry's, with his wife and kids for the weekend. So she would be there. He wanted to see her, way too much. He slowed deliberately, to meander back along the country road.

★

Karen picked up the phone, which had gone on ringing shrilly while Harry and Martin were outside on the patio. 'Hello.'

Immediately, she wished she had left it. There was the listening silence, down the line. The breathing, the wait that went on too long for it to be any wrong number. *Bitch*, she thought, suddenly remembering that earlier call, the rush of fear, the lasting anxieties; then her looking at Harry in a new way. But something kept her holding on now, bridging the silence. 'Who's that?'

'Hello, Karen.' It was a man's voice, this time. Muffled, like the woman's had been, and with the vestige of a rough accent she couldn't define.

She felt electric with tension, small sharp impulses pricking her hands and scalp. 'What do you want?'

'Not too lucky with women, is he?' said the voice. 'You did ask him, didn't you? Reckon he didn't tell you the half of it, though.'

There was some sound in the background, behind the voice. A rhythmic thudding. Rock music, perhaps, in another room, or machinery working. She listened intently. She would keep him talking until she had some clue to where the call was from. 'Why are you telling me this?'

'Because I'm your friend, Karen. We're on your side.'

The distant noise faded. 'If you tell me who you are, then I might listen.'

'Oh, but you are listening.' The man laughed. 'And you did ask him. They die, somehow, they've a habit of it. And you know what? You're the next, Karen.'

She heard the clatter of the receiver replaced at the other end. Quietly she put down the phone and took a breath. Her palms were sweating, the skin crawling at the back of her neck. Who could it be, having both Harry's private numbers, in Sussex as well as London? How could they know these rare times when she was alone in the house or apartment? It could not be coincidence, not twice.

This time, she would say nothing to Harry. Before, she had wondered who would want to frighten her. Now another, more sinister idea occurred. What if the calls were genuine warnings, from people trying to keep her out of danger? 'I want to leave,' she murmured softly, to the silent, cradled telephone. 'But if he came after me, could it get worse?'

She heard another sound, of a car approaching up the gravel drive. It was Damien, or their visitors. She stared out of the living-room window, but could see nothing beyond the broad sweep of garden, the beach below and a small patch of driveway, empty except for Martin walking towards the house.

'Karen! Our guests are here, come and greet them.' It was Harry, calling through the hall from the front door.

She went out into the luminous evening. Harry, at the top of the steps, took her arm in a gesture of solidarity. They began to descend together, almost formally, towards a blue Range Rover which had just parked. A woman in a white summer dress was climbing from it, waving towards them, before she began to extract small children from the back.

The driver's door swung open and a fat man in shorts got out, slammed it shut. 'We had a good run, we made good time,' he called, seeming not to recognize her.

It was Alistair Quentin.

7

Karen stayed very still, her mind and body racing. He had seen her.

Surrounded by his young family, Quentin looked startlingly normal. She expected him to cringe with shame, seeing her. Instead, he smiled across, friendly and affable, towards Harry and herself. It was as if the memory of him, which had poisoned her life over the years, had been only some nightmare.

She recognized something else in that smile. It was complicity. He believed she would remain silent, he just assumed it. She stared into his smug red face. His eyes were hidden behind wire spectacles, pear-shaped, the colour of gunmetal. Quentin bent to pick up a toddler, who was tugging at his leg. He held his son like an alibi.

Harry was sweeping forward from the steps. 'Al, welcome. Amanda, darling, you look absolutely stunning.'

'This baby has been crying for the entire journey,' Amanda told him. 'She's only just fallen asleep, now we've arrived.'

Harry peered at the baby. 'But she's awfully pretty. Do come and meet Karen. Amanda – and Alistair.'

What was she going to do? Play along and pretend? She was almost too angry to speak. 'But we've met before.'

Uncertainty flickered across his confident expression, and she gloried in it. Then he wrinkled his brow. 'Now, where could that have been? Of course. You were – possibly under-age, working in that bar. What was it called? M something . . .'

'I don't remember,' she replied.

'How extraordinary,' Harry broke in, with a strained casualness. 'You worked in a bar, sweetheart? Were you researching for one of your roles?'

'That's right. Shall we go inside? It's windy, and the baby's waking.'

'Jeremy, come to Mummy now.' Amanda took the toddler's hand, and turned to Martin. 'I suspect that the offspring need drinks. Alistair can take the bags up for you.'

'I'm sure the charming Mrs Glass will show me to our quarters.' Quentin gave a small, gallant bow, before locking the car and picking up their luggage.

Damien's things had gone from the big guest room. Karen pulled the door closed behind the two of them, so fast she almost struck Quentin with it. He set down the bags, and she turned on him. 'What a pathetic low-life you are!'

'I could make things frightfully unpleasant for you,' he said smoothly.

'I've heard that before. Don't forget, I filed charges against you.'

'Which were promptly dropped.' He went on, 'This is such a silly old story, it's hardly my fault that you acted so badly afterwards. Aren't you worried? Whatever would your husband think, of you being a scrubber?'

'Liar! Does your wife know she's married to a shit?'

'Amanda is a very sensible girl. As I trust you will, somehow, attempt to be. A weekend isn't long, and we'll go off in the boat tomorrow. As it happens, there's rather a lot at stake.' He glanced at her, thoughtfully. 'Obviously you don't tell Harry about your past relationships. How much does he tell you about business?'

She stared. There was something he was afraid of, this slimy little toad. If only she could work out what it was. 'How can you call that a relationship? Abduction and rape of a teenager? How sick! I suppose no woman would go near you, any other way. I hope you rot in *hell*. And enjoy your stay with us,' she added, in air-hostessy tones, opening the door to go downstairs.

Without another word, Quentin followed her. There she tried

123

to lose him among the others, for the weekend and for a lifetime. The nightmare had returned, but it was real. Her heart, her flesh carried their own memories, clamouring with repulsion against his nearness, loud in their knowledge. Afraid now, she filled with imaginings. He might decide to tell Harry his version of events. She should never have mentioned any connection between them. Harry had grown intensely curious, and Quentin was entertaining himself with that curiosity. He had injured her, and he had to seem right. What else might he do, to look and feel better, now?

She became falsely spirited, playing up to Harry's desire to show her off. They had drinks in the lamp room, overlooking a turbulent sea. The baby was put to bed by Amanda, the little boy was read stories by his father. How could a man who had attacked a woman be responsible with a child? Or was she being unfair? Could he really have believed that she was for sale, and had no rights?

As they went down for dinner, Martin warned Harry, 'I caught the forecast, and it's gale force seven.'

'In that case,' said Amanda, 'I'll be caring for the children here tomorrow.'

'Seven – is that all?' Harry sounded robust. 'You won't cry off our trip because of that, Al?'

'It would be a little rough,' he answered, easily. 'We couldn't take the children – and what about your delightful wife?'

'Karen can keep Amanda company.'

'Oh, but doesn't she want to come? I had rather hoped to see more of Karen.' He gave her his lizard smile. 'Aren't you going to come?'

'My wife does what I say,' Harry replied shortly, for her. 'But Damien might enjoy the trip, if he makes it back from wherever he's gone.'

'Let's not be deterred by a puff of breeze. We used to slip across and around the Med before the offspring put the kibosh on things. That made a decent little tour.'

'I'll settle for the Isle of Wight,' Harry told him. 'And a chance to talk some business.'

Business was not mentioned again until after dinner. Taking refuge in her role, Karen was brightly solicitous, anticipating need, smoothing conversation. It was a game – they were divided by gender – and she could escape Quentin's remarks by concentrating on his wife. Amanda, pale and sharp-boned, had left fashion journalism some years before. Simmering with discontent, she seemed almost resigned, until she talked about her former job and came alive.

A ten-year-old brandy was poured, Martin made coffee, and they settled around the log fire. It was a vision of harmony, full of no such thing. Harry was trying to turn the evening into something celebratory. Big projects and starry names, numbers full of zeros tripped off his tongue in silver monologue, punctuated by Quentin's small questions, words of agreement. Eventually, Amanda stood up. 'If you'll forgive me, I'm the one who'll be getting up in the night then starting my day at five.'

'Is there anything you need?' Karen asked.

Quentin said, reassuringly, 'You get your beauty sleep, please do.'

'Thank you,' she replied, snappy.

'Poor old Amanda,' laughed Quentin, when she had gone off to bed. 'I think she rues the day that she decided a family was the thing.'

Reluctant to leave Harry alone with Quentin, Karen pretended to listen to music. She had never been able to confide in him and now it was too late. She watched from the sofa, across a room twining with curls of smoke from twin cigars. They were so alike – in height and build, in attitudes – and both were dressed in grey with navy. But Quentin wore certainty while Harry, in his company, became a pretender trying too hard. Sliding off the headset, she overheard phrases. 'The Castle development . . . Needs discussion, with Agnew and Bellman. After all, neither of us . . . History, and all that.'

If Quentin decided to say anything to Harry, there was nothing she could do to prevent him. She rose to her feet. 'I seem to be getting rather a headache.'

'Oh, poor you. Do I get a kiss?'

Karen bent to kiss his thin, muscular lips, which suddenly reminded her of Quentin's force. Harry patted her bottom possessively. He came to bed soon after, switched on the lamp and tried to wake her. She feigned sleep, unnaturally heavy. Later she heard a car purr up the drive. That must be Damien's. The wind, still rising, rocked their room, high above an angry sea. The dawn was red. She fell asleep, and woke to find Harry shaking her again. 'The others are up, we're leaving in a minute.'

Memory returned. 'I've got a migraine,' she told him, acting.

'Suddenly, she gets a migraine. The first, the only weekend I ask you to do anything, to entertain a little.' She struggled to sit up, face the day. 'And it has nothing to do, I suppose, with your hostility towards my partner? You've never told me anything about your past. How well did you know him, anyway?'

'Hardly at all. There's nothing to tell,' she heard herself say quickly. 'Listen to that gale.'

'I'll get Al to tell me. And, by the way, I would prefer you not to wear my extremely expensive Piaget wristwatch when we're down here roughing it. Didn't you know, those things are for town?'

'I'm sorry. Are you really going yachting in this weather?'

'I'll ask Martin to put that in the safe. I'm not made of money. Of course we're going, I told you we were.'

From the stairway, she saw Quentin out on the drive already, with a circle of onlookers. He was shifting equipment – fluorescent suits and polythene bags – from his car to Harry's for the run up to Brighton Marina. She went down slowly to join them all there, wishing for invisibility: even the baby was hiding her face in her mother's coat, against the destructive force of the day.

Amanda said, 'If it's bad, I want you to turn back, please. Alistair, think of the children. You'll be here tomorrow afternoon? We leave at four thirty.'

'You see what I have to put up with?' said Quentin. Then, to his children, 'Jeremy, Jessica, I hope you'll be good trinkets.'

'You're not coming, then?' Harry asked his son.

Damien straightened up from stowing the bags in the Jaguar.

'I'm not the best of sailors, don't want to hold you back.' Walking round the side of the car, he saw Karen. 'Hi,' he said.

Karen felt the rush of attraction and turned away quickly, awkwardly.

Quentin had caught their glance. He was examining her closely, looking her up and down, with a sneering expression. *I'll get Al to tell me . . .* Suddenly she could not bear to stand there any longer. Harry and Quentin would be together for two days, they would talk, and she knew what Harry would be told. She could not stand by and wait for it to happen, for Harry's reactions.

They were all clustered around the car. Karen slipped away through the silver bushes, across the side of the garden. As soon as she was safely out of sight, she began to run – through the rushing, whirlwind morning, down to the empty expanse of beach. As if, were she to run far and fast enough, none of them would ever catch her, or see her again.

Damien heard Al Quentin say drily, 'Your wife wishes us *bon voyage*, and regrets she couldn't stay to see us off.'

'She was here just a moment ago,' said Harry, looking round in surprise.

'Here one minute, gone the next. Actresses!'

'She doesn't want you to go in these conditions,' Amanda suggested.

Harry picked up his shoulder bag and portable phone. 'Well, Martin. We'll be back tomorrow afternoon.' He slid behind the driving wheel.

With a wink – so fast that it could have been an illusion – Quentin murmured, 'She always did it for money, and that's all.'

Damien stared. 'What did you say?'

His father's partner leaned towards him, eyes crawling with malice behind his spectacles. 'Gorgeous piece of crumpet. But do you think your daddy knows he's married a slag from a well-known knocking shop?' He laughed, then got into the car. 'Off we go, Harry. 'Bye, children!' With a fanfare from the horn, they swept off down the drive, pausing as the automatic gates swung open.

At once, Martin began shepherding Amanda back towards the shelter of the house. 'I expect Karen's making coffee. Let's get these children thawed out.'

Damien stood, buffeted by the wind. What had Quentin meant? Had it been some kind of joke? He had seen Karen hurry away across the garden and she had looked upset. He hesitated, then turned to follow the way she had gone, until he reached the jetty. From there, he could see that the beach lay empty in both directions, but from the foot of the steps faint indentations led out across the sand. He went down. The white rollers crashed, throwing spray that licked and foamed, swallowing the tracks as they zigzagged to the ocean's edge. Struggling to stand upright, or to move at all, he progressed like a crab along by the rocks.

She was half a mile further on. Pockets of calm lay in the folds of rock, and there he saw Karen, crouched, sheltering. The jagged slabs gleamed, like misshapen, neglected graves. Closer, he saw that her hair was snakes, her face clenched. Shoved away from her by the gale, he found his lips were too frozen to speak, until effort pushed like anger inside him. 'What the hell are you doing?'

She yelled back, 'Did Harry send you? Did he tell you to get me?'

'They've gone, until late tomorrow. You think I'm some kind of a puppet?'

'I've had enough, I want to be alone.'

Let her want. Crouching beside her, out of the storm, he watched. The roaring sea, its moving walls of water blackened by dark fists of cloud, dashed in white fury at their feet, again and again. She shouted something, snatched away by the gale.

He looked up to where she was looking. The sky was a thickened mass of gulls. The air that battered them against the earth had become a joyride for the flock of wheeling birds. They were hovering, surfing the air, falling like stones then soaring, wings patterning a light, fast dance. Their necks were outstretched, feet dangling in parody, beaks split open. Faintly, he heard their mocking shrieks.

Karen jumped abruptly to her feet. She whirled, and snatched up both his hands in hers, which were cold like steel. As if she had caught the seagulls' mood, she was suddenly laughing. 'Let's go back, then.'

They began to run, they had no choice. The force of the wind that had pushed him back propelled them now. It tore at their clothes, sculpting cloth to the shape of their bodies. She danced across the sand, tugging him with her. He marvelled at the changes in her – away from Harry, extraordinary – her strength, that happiness. Now they were weaving across the beach, hands clasped, like witches summoning demons. He was breathless and desiring, shocked by his sense of her power. The sky grew blacker, closing in, and they ran under driving rain, hit by a squall.

'The chalet – come on!' He was led, scrambling up the slope of beach, slithering over wet rocks. They pulled, tugged each other along, and came to the blue beach-hut. Thudding up the steps, Damien pushed the door and it swung open. Inside was gloomy, close. The storm was muffled as the door banged shut. He had dropped her hand running up the steps, and now she brushed beside him, so near that his senses filled with her. Then he grew aware of the scent of old wood, and some kind of spirit or oil. His eyes adjusted, his hearing filtered back to clarity.

'Look, it's full of things.'

At first he thought it was just trash lying around, bundles of rags in corners of the floor, until he saw the jacket hanging from a hook. A pair of boots stood in a corner, and curtains, sewn from black stuff, hung from bamboo rods. Beside the cooker was a box of stores, and a black rucksack, somehow familiar. 'A visitor,' Damien said softly.

'It's all organized, someone's squatting. And they might come back.'

'This is Harry's land, right? Martin would be mad, if he knew. They won't come back, not now in this rain.'

She became quiet, and Damien cursed himself for mentioning Harry. He sat, catching his breath, on the faded matting. The hut was alien now, lived in by an unknown person, while those old clothes seemed more familiar by the minute. Or were they just reminding him of his old life, back home? 'I've lived like this,' he told her. 'With nothing – but in the city, in Chicago.'

He caught the gleam of her eyes, intent. 'So have I. Until recently.'

'You? Never.' He didn't believe her.

'How do you think actors live? There's never money, nothing stable in that life. Not until you get lucky.'

'So, you got lucky, landing Harry. OK.' His voice was harsh, because she had been bought, it was true. She was rich and cosseted, in a loveless tie, and unhappiness was justice, then. He saw his father with her – saw them naked together, contrasted and incongruous. Disgust filled Damien, and he let it show in his face.

She flared up at him. 'How stupid, how ignorant you are – just like him!'

'Why else would you marry someone you hate?'

Without answering, Karen searched his face. Then she looked down at her hands. 'I did care for Harry. It – began very well.'

Damien laughed, with an ugly, violent sound. They were so close, it ripped them apart. 'That guy, Quentin – you've known him before. Haven't you?'

She shot back at him quickly, 'No. Why are you asking?'

'He sure believes that he knows you. Before you met Harry, he kind of said. Did you work as a call girl?'

Karen stared at him, utterly scornful. 'What gives you the right,' she demanded, 'to ask me a question like that?' She snatched open the door, turned to say, 'I've told you what I was. That man is my enemy – for his own reasons. And you believed him? My God. So that's what you think of me.'

She didn't know whether to laugh or cry. It seemed the past had the power to reach out, touching everything, painting it a darker shade. Damn him! The wind shrieked, snatching words, folding her double, sending her back towards the lighthouse a hundred yards ahead. The rain had stormed itself out, and the raw, soaked morning stretched like an empty heart. Pulseless, bloodless. She hated him.

His footsteps grated across the shingle bar. She scrambled faster up the slope, couldn't even get away from him. 'Karen. Will you wait!'

'Go to hell.' He was beside her, staggering as the stones fell away, catching hold of her arm, breathless. She twisted away from his grasp, in fury. 'Let go of me!'

'Don't you treat me like this, like shit! Just *listen* to me, damn it. I've talked to Jacqueline.'

Karen stopped, looked at him. There was a hunger in his eyes: she saw it, and something turned over inside her. She drew a deep breath. 'Do you mean Harry's first wife? Why on earth did you?'

'I was thinking of you. And my mother, killing herself. Jacqueline was embarrassed, I guess. She's a lady, but tight as a clam.'

The others died . . . But Jacqueline was alive, thriving, and out of Harry's class. That would carry a lot of clout with him, the man from nowhere, whose other wives were nowhere women. The anonymous calls, the people making them – was this something they didn't know?

Damien had been thinking about her. She looked at him, at the craving in his eyes, and the hard, fine planes of his face. A wild man, his hair like a raven's wing, tumbling. He was all mixed up, untogether as she had turned out to be. They were both out of balance and hostage to events, dangerously propellable. That magnetism: a drug, a powerful poison in the end. She felt torn in her heart. Her senses and mind were at war. She wanted so much to kiss his mouth.

What was it that attracted her to the bad in men? She must break that to survive. Why him? Damien was standing close, braced against the wind, shielding his eyes as he stared across the beach, towards the ocean. He pointed. 'Look, there's something down by that breakwater. Can you see it?'

She saw that some clothes lay slumped against the wood barrier, half-way down where it stretched to the sea. A mound of brightly coloured women's clothes in blue, green with a stripe of orange. A scarf, perhaps? Until with a jolt, she realized: it was a woman's body. Something small and white was flapping out from it. A hand that was waving or moving in the gale.

Before she could answer, Damien strode away across the beach, towards the thing. Slowly, she began to follow. When he was ten yards from it, he turned to call back. 'It's OK, I guess.'

She went near. They were just old nets from fishing boats, cast adrift and caught in a tangle on the posts. Except something was trapped inside that brilliant nylon mesh. The white form of a bird, a seagull that seemed to be struggling to get free. Karen knelt quickly. 'But it's alive. Oh, the poor thing.'

Damien bent to unravel the nets, unfolding them carefully until the wind whipped their edges from his hands. The gull lay still, its feathers fluttering. Its great yellow beak was stretched wide, ready for attack. A wing flapped forward, into the unforgiving sand. The wing was broken. It must have died so recently. She watched, eyes stinging with sudden tears, and Damien lifted the bird and cradled it against his jacket, so gently it might have been still living. She reached out and touched the white feathers, softly, heart breaking for it.

You are mine, completely. Harry's words came to her, clearly as if they had just been spoken aloud. She thought she understood. How could he possess any other person until their own spirit had gone? Until they were dead. She thought of the gulls and saw them whirling, soaring.

'You're crying? Hey, don't be sad. It had a great life, think of that. Riding the wind, owning the ocean? Hell, that any of us were so free. Even for a real short lifespan, I would trade for that. Karen. What?'

'I can't bear that it's dead.' She hid her face: it was his tenderness that she could not bear. Karen felt, too late to stop him, Damien's arms go round her. She leaned against him until she was cried out. From his stillness, his fingers woven in her hair, she knew that if they moved – if she only raised her head and looked at him – then they would kiss. Not moving, they stood hypnotised. Space and time receded, and between that dark, blinding cloud and the deafening, demonic sea, awareness faded. There was only the supple skin of his leather jacket, clasped under her palms; the heat and bone of his face, bent against her cheek. She never knew how long it was, he became her world.

She had to keep clear of him and forget that powerful attraction. Karen broke away, stumbling from the suddenness. The gale tore into each of them, slashing, gnawing, separate. Now she felt calm inside. They were impossible. 'Harry would never forgive us,' she said, looking directly into his eyes. 'If we neglect his house guest, the way we are.'

Damien nodded, his hands finding his jacket pockets.

They were careful, after that – not to touch, or go too near, not to look at each other – in case they were drawn in again. Or was he rejecting her once more: Harry's wife, who disliked him but stayed for the money? Perhaps he did see her that way. Still she knew, sensed, how much he wanted her. Damien was distant now, turned away from her. 'You go back in,' he said, not as a suggestion. 'I'm going to bury this, where the tide comes in.'

Karen was happy to ignore him, to deny the danger. She had gone for a run, she told Martin and Amanda, finding them with the children in the kitchen. She had no idea where Damien might have gone. It was as if, by saying that, she could undo time and make herself safer. While Harry was absent, she would enjoy the weekend. If she concentrated, she could do that – or else the weight of anxieties, swilling underneath, would break and flood, fill her with panic. She must forget what might be happening now, on Quentin's yacht, somewhere between the Sussex coast and the Isle of Wight.

Amanda said, 'It's so crazy to be out in this.' They followed her gaze, through the security of glass, to the racing ranks of jagged cloud, the huge breakers far out, smashing into spray. 'It was a dare, really. Like a couple of schoolboys.'

They were marooned there, besieged together in the house by the wind. She could not be that close to him, not all day. 'Why don't we go, too? To Brighton, I mean,' Karen suggested. 'There are the shops, and entertainments indoors for Jeremy. It would be fun.'

She had meant the two of them and the children, but Damien, then Martin decided to come along. Still, in the back of the Range Rover, she could chat with Amanda sitting beside her, while Jeremy and Jessica distracted them. A pair of green wellies slid over the floor, large-sized. Quentin's.

Amanda had met Quentin nine years ago, Karen learned. The wedding, four years later, had coincided with his step up to power in the corridors of the BBC. Amanda was thirty now. Most weekends she took charge of her husband's three adolescent daughters by his previous wife. Even with a nanny in London, her life was a barrage of people with tantrums and temperaments. She seemed exhausted, brittle, and a good choice for Quentin. She might complain, but would not leave.

What would she say, if she knew her husband had raped a teenager? With so much invested in him – in his respectability, and responsibility – perhaps she would still find a way of seeing him as right.

They spent the day in Brighton and lunched in a Regency restaurant. On the beach, kids raced up and down the shingle, playing Canute with the giant waves. In the shops and marine entertainments, couples held hands. Karen was looking after Amanda, helping with the children. All day, following along with Martin, Damien found himself watching her too much. He fantasized being with her, dining at Wheeler's, sleeping in one of the seafront's tall, candy-coloured hotels with the wrought-iron balconies. For all her great looks, something was missing. She had a cool, passive sensuality: he wanted to feel her fire, to burn.

Drawn along on her string of attraction, he kept missing what Martin said to him. He would feel the other man's gaze, and know he had been caught staring at her again. If Martin noticed, he might imply something to Harry. The last thing Damien wanted now was more trouble with Dad. He kept turning his attention to Martin, being friendly: he tried to rebuild anger against Karen, in his mind.

They arrived back at the lighthouse, and the women went in ahead. Following through the gloom of the hall, they saw Jeremy playing with the walking sticks. Martin gave a whoop of alarm. 'Don't ever touch those! They're not toys.' The little boy's face crumpled in fright. He ran off to the kitchen, towards his mother, and they heard him beginning to cry. 'Oops,' said Martin. 'But if he plays with them, he could get considerably more than he bargained for.'

He drew out two sticks from the stand and handed one to Damien. It was of ordinary knotted wood with a silver knob, but curiously heavy. It was not for walking. Martin, giving a quick flick to his wrist, pulled the handle away and revealed that the stick was a sheath. From it he drew out a long, lethal, glittering blade.

'What the hell—' Damien exclaimed in surprise. He copied Martin's action with the humble stick he held: the rapier it concealed was slim and razor sharp. He gave a long, low whistle.

'Victorian swordsticks.' Graceful as a dancer, Martin made a slow, practised lunge with the weapon.

'Hey,' said Damien, uncertainly. One slip, one error of judgement, and that sword could eviscerate or take a man's head from his shoulders.

Martin was feinting, playing in a little mock fencing match, and smiling at his unease. 'I studied this at my fancy public school. Along with some other terribly useful life-enhancing skills.'

'These were part of Dickens's London, yeah? I wouldn't like to have been a thief, then.'

'They're nothing, compared with the other stuff in Harry's collection. Haven't you see it? Tell you what, I've got to stash something for Karen. Wait here. Or why don't you go on down?'

The heavy steel door had sturdy hinges, with a big lock and key, old-fashioned after the coded electronic security surrounding the house and garden. Damien went down a curve of roughly cut stone steps. He was descending into a central cavern, with caves leading off. The cellars had been hacked out, partly from the solid rock. They were cool and dry, oddly draughty. Stark white light flooded the private museum. Pistols and rifles, swords and daggers were arranged in rows, hung over the walls, displayed on stands and locked in cabinets. 'How bizarre,' he said, as Martin scuffed down the steps behind him.

'It's the envy of other collectors. Now, let me put this into safe keeping, so to speak.' On a ledge in the rock, Martin laid the diamond-encrusted watch that Karen had worn. He reached up, grasped a heavy breastplate and lifted it down from the wall. Behind the armour, a combination safe lay hidden, set flush in the rock. 'Clever, mm? Harry doesn't trust banks too much. This is his equivalent of stashing it under the mattress.'

He opened the safe and, from among the papers and boxes inside, drew out a silver-embossed jewellery chest. In it were trays of ornate pieces fashioned in gold: emeralds and sapphires, diamonds and pearls flashed brilliantly. Damien stared. 'Is all that Karen's?'

'Not yet,' Martin answered, ambiguous. 'Most of this stuff belonged to Mrs Harry Glass II. He never sold anything. It's all beautifully crafted, and some is very valuable.' He caressed the jewels, lovingly, then put everything back in its place.

Damien looked around idly. 'A treasure trove, almost under the sea. How poetic. But why does he keep all this other trash?' The weapons seemed ugly to him, and some of the collection was really suspect. Among smugglers' pistols, axeheads and cutlasses lay Native American artefacts: a pair of women's small moccasins, faded and stained, and a buckskin revolver holster with beadwork.

'This trash, as you call it, is worth a bit. Some of these little items could fetch a couple of thousand. The Burmese Dha, the Malay Kris. The jewelled small-daggers collection in that display case. Those are early nineteenth-century.'

'Yeah?' Damien drawled, refusing to get caught up in that

enthusiasm. 'How much is Dad worth, I wonder?' Then he laughed, in case Martin took him seriously.

'It's his insurance policy. Bermondsey style.'

'And does he come and look at them, or what does he do?'

'I think Harry's rather bored by it now. He used to go to all the auctions, to bid – he was fanatical. Now he just likes things kept in good order. It's useful for visiting journalists, and so on.'

In a dim alcove were cleaning stuffs, and among them, metal polishes and leather soap, bottles of spirit and paraffin. Damien gave a last glance around. He shivered from the cold atmosphere, and the strange, dry wind that rustled whispering through these secret, subterranean rooms.

'So it's Mr Glass's son,' said a voice from the steps. He turned to see Christine, arms folded stoutly across her chest, beaming. 'And Martin. Here I was thinking, who's down there in his armoury, and whatever can they be up to?'

Karen woke early on Sunday morning, drowning in terrors, half remembered. Awake, she could tell herself the fears were groundless and start to cover them up again, to submerge them under a raft of action. The wind had fallen during the night, leaving a peculiar calm and an empty, suffocating sky where the dancing air had been. The distant sea lay like a window, breakable.

It was warm, almost hot. They took the children down to the beach and had a picnic – Amanda and herself, Martin with Damien – and built castles in the sand, dug moats with channels to the tide. The day was sunny, innocent. Hours passed slowly. Every minute, just under the surface, her thoughts prodded and tore holes in the calm, closed the great space of beach and sky, boiling up the sunlight into darkness. She could hardly breathe. What might Quentin be telling Harry? What would happen when they came back?

She would be safe until the Jaguar reappeared. Several times the phone had rung, with calls for Harry. She had jumped with alarm, thinking it was him. Every nerve screamed at her. At any minute, they would return.

It was three-thirty. The baby woke from her afternoon sleep and they had tea on the patio. They had all fallen silent for a while, but now Amanda wondered aloud if she might have to drive back alone. Martin was beginning to worry. He had tried calling Harry on the mobile, but found it was switched off. 'It's odd – Harry always keeps in pretty constant touch. There are all these messages waiting, building up for him.'

'It's peculiar that Alistair hasn't called, in two days.' Amanda frowned. 'I hope they're all right.'

Damien said, with a shrug, 'They've had a good time. They'll come rolling home, any minute.'

Four o'clock came. There was no sign of Harry or Quentin. Amanda was annoyed now. 'I wish he'd called to warn me. I'm going to have to drive all the way back to London, with two babies probably both screaming their heads off. On my own. It's typical, really.'

'You could stay the night,' Martin suggested. 'Or leave later, at least. They're bound to be back very soon.'

'Thank you, but that would disturb everyone's routine. I did warn Alistair he would have to make his own way home. Come along, Jeremy. You're going to have to be a very good boy.'

When Amanda and the children had left, there was nothing to do but wait. If there had been an accident to the boat, then it would have happened yesterday in the storm. The waters of the Solent were always so busy, surely nothing could go unnoticed for long? The coastguard, or the police, would have been in touch by now. Quentin and Harry were just late, and as long as they didn't come back, nothing bad could happen.

At almost seven, Martin wheeled a barbecue on to the patio, and lit the charcoal. A smell of searing skin filled the air, and lumps of raw, bloody flesh turned black. Karen felt sick. The evening was beautiful; luminous waves sighed in the twilight. A plane split the sky with a great white crack. Perhaps he would never come back. Perhaps they would all stay here.

Long after darkness had closed around the Keep, at a quarter to midnight, they heard a car. It crunched softly up the gravel. Karen followed Martin, hurrying to the front door. From the steps, through the pitch night, she saw the black car, with its twin beams, swing round into the house light. Harry was getting out from the driving seat, as Martin went to meet him. Where was Quentin? Then she realized. Harry was alone.

An instant of relief left her giddy, light-headed with certainty. It was all right. Quentin had gone off somewhere, and if he wasn't around then nothing might go wrong. The next moment, she filled with foreboding. Why had Harry returned on his own?

'Is all well?' Martin was asking.

Harry nodded shortly. He looked haggard and angry. 'The tide delayed us. It was a tough crossing, yesterday.' Passing Karen in the hall, he stared straight through her. 'Al Quentin took the Brighton to London train.'

He knew. She could sense already, a hardening in his attitude against her. He had heard everything, every lie that Quentin could dredge up. How could she have hoped otherwise? Harry was condemning her, she could feel it.

She said, 'You look exhausted, Harry. It would be better to stay here tonight.'

'We're going back. I want to leave in five minutes. I've an important meeting in the morning.' He took the brandy that Martin held for him and drank it quickly.

'Then I'll go and sort our bags.'

Karen escaped up the stairs. Blindly, clumsily, she gathered the things they had brought with them. He must let her go, back to her old life and old friends, as if they had never been together.

There was a knock at the door. It was Damien. 'I'll take the bags down for you.' He came into the bedroom towards her and the twin leather cases that waited, zipped and buckled. He touched her arm quickly, urgently. 'There's something wrong. What is it?'

She shook her head as if she didn't know, then looked up at him. 'Aren't you coming with us?'

'I'm to stay here. Harry's not in a mood for discussion.'

The Jaguar slid out from the Keep, wound through the lanes, illuminating tunnels of trees. She glanced across at Harry sitting beside her in the back. He was silent and fixed, his profile in darkness. She told herself he was just very tired. He had done too much and probably had not slept; he had business problems, financial concerns that she didn't know about. 'We were worried because you hadn't called. Martin couldn't get through to the mobile.'

'Were you worried about me? How very touching, Karen.'

She felt his smile, like a snarl. They were among lights, passing through towns, and she sat looking straight ahead, hands clasped. They didn't speak again. The car sped along the empty route, through a halogen hell of midnight suburbs, into a false dawn of city streets and office blocks. The silver-lit torch of Canary Wharf rose distantly. They picked a way forward, to the squat prison of Harry's home.

'Shall I drop you at the door?'

'Take us inside, Martin.'

Flanked by them both, she was their prisoner. The lift swept up, they were in the penthouse. While Martin gave Harry his messages, she vanished upstairs. She could never feel safe in his bed, but if she pretended to sleep then he might leave her alone. That had worked before, and he needed rest, after two long days at sea. Hurriedly Karen slipped out of her clothes. She found a long white cotton nightshirt and pulled it on, thinking too late how it resembled a shroud. Scrambling into bed, she buried herself under the feather duvet, craving unconsciousness. If only he would let her be.

Time passed. The bedroom flooded with light from over-head. She kept very still. If he spoke, she would not answer. Then, with one great forceful movement, the covers were ripped away and she lay exposed.

'Let me take a really good close look at this,' Harry said.

She smelled the brandy, thick on his breath. 'What are you doing? You woke me.' She sat up. His eyes were tiny, darting, in the reddened lumps of a maddened face. She shrank inside, but her voice was calm and bold. 'Harry, you're drunk. Just go to bed.'

It was as if she hadn't spoken. 'So innocent, such a good girl.

Decent and pure, I thought. Someone of her age. Now I see you in your true light! Soiled and dirty. Deceiving.'

She slid sideways quickly, and stood shivering with the empty bed between them. 'Listen to me, Harry. If Quentin has said anything to you, it's all lies. Because he wants to get back at us both, for whatever reasons of his own.'

'So what do you think my partner said, Karen? He can prove it, too. He knows people who knew my wife – *my wife* – and who enjoyed her favours, no doubt, in the previous life that she never saw fit to tell me about!'

He began to step around the bed. She was trapped. She forced words out. 'Listen – and don't you dare to insult me any more. I worked as a waitress, we all had to do jobs—'

'And what a job she did, by all accounts,' he sneered, his voice full of contempt. 'I never perceived any glimmer of technical expertise in the woman I had taken, on trust, as my spouse. I rather thought she didn't like it much. Was a little young and touchingly innocent. Now I think she was all used up – by half the City, half my colleagues!' He launched himself. His fist slammed into her ribs, sending her crashing into the wall. She screamed. Her head cracked on something sharp as she fell. Blood oozed on to her hand.

Harry was kneeling over her. He had picked up the onyx lamp and was holding it high. About to kill her. She shut her eyes and heard his whisper. 'Did you go with him, with Quentin? Is that what he was telling me?'

Her tongue seemed frozen with inhibition, struggling to move. 'No. He – forced me.'

The only sound was Harry's panting breath. She dared to look again and saw his rage, jaw twisted, eyes narrowed and disappearing. 'You cheated me.' His words were deadly quiet. He dropped the lamp. She felt him grasp the neckband of her nightdress.

'Was it like this?' With a sudden force, he tore the fabric. She began to struggle, to fight against his weight, as he fell on to her. The smell of his skin was sharp and rank, overlaid with expensive cologne. Repulsion lent her strength, propelled her muscles. Grappling against him, she freed herself to draw in air, to scream for her life until his hand grabbed her mouth, silenced it. Twisting sideways, she clamped her teeth over his fingers and heard him yell, short, sharp. His hands went around her neck, tightly squeezing. Breath, life was going out of her, exploding, scarlet. That persuading, pounding wave was pressuring, plunging her into unconsciousness.

8

Voices, soft. The sound of the sea in a shell, the surf, pulling and tugging her into awareness, life. The flood of memory that meant she was alive. Harry . . . He was at the bedroom door, talking. He was talking with Martin.

She tried to swallow: her throat filled with concrete, drying and swelling. Tearing breaths sucked through her body, washing her up. She needed to save her own life. Scrunched on the floor beside the bed, blood soaking the pearl fibres of carpet. Harry would be angry . . . the police. She needed help, someone to keep her alive. On wobbling limbs, up between bed and bedside cabinet, by the brass handles of drawers, levering to the top. Swaying, gasping for breath, she took up the phone. Lift the receiver – a woman's voice saying a surprised hello – dial 999. No ringing. No sound. That had all happened the wrong way round. The phone slithered sideways out of her hand, down to the floor, with the wrong kind of clanging sound.

The next moment Martin was there, replacing the telephone neatly where it lived. She was on hands and knees, dizzy.

'You'd better sit down. Where's this coming from? Somewhere on the scalp. Let me look.' Blood was trickling, in sticky lines down her cheek, she blinked it out from an eye. 'What did you do – say to him? Harry's got the world on his shoulders, didn't you know that? I heard you both. Amanda's on the line.'

She tried to speak, and croaked. Martin was pulling her blood-soaked hair apart. 'I think it's only a graze, shallow. Head wounds always bleed a lot. Can you see? Here, come and sit by the basin and I'll clean it up, have a better look.' He must have seen the questioning in her eyes. 'Yes, Amanda Quentin, calling at three in the morning. She thinks something may've happened to Al. He never got back from Brighton.'

Harry was there, calm and sober now. 'He probably decided to book into a hotel. Their domestic affairs are not our concern,' he said, pointedly. 'Karen, my dear. It's one thing to break up my possessions, and my glass collection, but it is quite another to break your own head.'

Now she could see, in the round mirror above the sink, her reddened hair and the red, angry swellings on her neck. Martin was swabbing with cotton wool, ice-cold water. 'She should really go to the hospital. A blow to the head – you never know.'

'Oh, surely not,' Harry answered, lightly. 'You feel all right, don't you, Karen? She fell and cracked her head on the bedpost.'

'You shouldn't be drinking.' Martin finished his mopping up and rinsed the pink water out of the sink. 'You've the Italians coming at ten, for heaven's sake.'

'Martin, don't fret on my behalf. Go back to bed, there's a good chap.'

The door closed on them, alone together, and Harry sat on the bed beside her. 'My God, you look terrible, darling.'

Dully, Karen stared at him. *She thinks something may've happened to Al. He never got back from Brighton.* She swallowed, through the lump of concrete. 'What happened?' she whispered.

'What happened?' Harry echoed, consideringly. 'I could tell you, if you really want to know.' For a moment he seemed almost amused, reading her. Then his tone switched to regret. 'If only you hadn't lied to me with silence. If you had considered me . . . This has been the most terrible revelation of my entire life. That you, of all people, could have cheated me.'

'I didn't mean to, Harry,' she whispered, watching him very carefully.

'I've been saddened by you. Disappointed, because I had trusted. I loved you, Karen. But you've destroyed it all, my great love. My voice has gone unsteady,' he noticed, with concern.

He's going to let me go, she thought. Quickly she lowered her eyes, in case he saw into her. Then Harry was patting her knee, dashing her hopes. 'Now you're in such a sorry state. Despite all you've done, I feel pity. You're young, and ignorant. I know you regret those deceptions. Now, you can't even speak,' he added with satisfaction. 'And yes. I could tell you what happened to Al Quentin.'

Harry smiled. In that smile, she saw it all. Quentin had told stories about her. He had hinted and goaded. Harry, probably drinking, had flown into one of his rages. The other man, shocked by that sudden change, wouldn't have stood a chance, alone at sea with no one to hear or intervene. Fury always gave Harry such strength. That, and the element of surprise . . . Perhaps Quentin didn't even have time to put up a fight, maybe he was quickly struck unconscious, then his body tipped overboard, taken by the tide. Had Harry paused to weight it down? Would he have made sure it might never be found? People often disappeared. No one could know the truth, she was only guessing. Karen shivered, and shut her eyes.

'Yes,' he said, softly. 'Yes, darling. You will never be troubled by that person again, I promise. Despite everything, I care for you – and I have proved how very much.'

'Of course,' Karen whispered, keeping her eyes shut.

'We will forget our little row tonight. We will forget, and I'll try to forgive. But that depends, my darling. Can you learn? I do wonder.'

'I'll do my best.'

'I believe you will. Perhaps things will improve.'

'Harry, do you have any aspirin?'

'Poor Karen. Here you are. What a dance you have led me. And now it's time for sleep.'

When she closed her eyes, she saw Quentin submerged beneath the waves and Harry's taunting smile. He was quite mad. He was a murderer and had tried to kill her. It was only a question of time. She must escape right now, and never come near him again. London was vast, anonymous. All she had to do was vanish into it. She would need her documents, which Harry kept locked in a personal file in his wardrobe, the key in his bedside cabinet. She would need to take her jewellery. The eternity watch, which would have fetched enough to live on, was still in the safe.

Damien flew into her mind. They were going to lose any chance of ever seeing each other again. She had to run at the first opportunity, and no one must have any hint of what she planned. They would forget each other because they had to.

Karen drifted asleep, and woke to the purr of a patrolling riverboat. It was early. Sounds, sensations of external comfort surrounded her: in the velvet silence, a sigh of air-conditioning readjusting itself, and a soft click of the lift as something was delivered for Harry. The Monday morning *Times*, milk and freshly squeezed orange juice, from the Pipers Wharf delicatessen. She opened her eyes to soft, pleasing light, but could hardly see because of the pain throbbing from her head and throat.

Harry was cosseting her, making up. He was pleased when he saw her wearing his gold jewellery: it was a sign of affection that he understood. He admired the pretty Liberty scarf she wound round her neck. When he went downstairs, Karen unlocked the hidden files. Her passport and birth certificate, driving licence and Social Security card, all fitted in an envelope which she sealed, in case he looked inside her bag. She had no cash, but the remaining travellers' cheques, worth almost two hundred pounds, still lay hidden in the zip compartment.

Acting ordinarily, she breakfasted. Harry was in a good mood, and turning his attention to his meeting. After the current *Cry Murder* production – starting to film in southern France – work would begin in Italy, on another true-crime drama. His Italian co-producers arrived at ten, and Harry went into action. 'Luigi, Marco – welcome. Come through, and Martin will take your coats. Lovely weather for ducks, don't you agree? This is my wife, Karen – she has laryngitis and can't speak, forgive her. My office is this way.'

They went in. Karen's heart was drumming so loudly she was surprised no one could hear it. Martin was making coffee. She planned, rehearsed in her mind exactly what she was about to do. If it went wrong, or if she was stopped on the way, that could cost her dearly. She thought of Quentin, underneath the sea. One wrong decision, some foolish words.

Ages passed, before Martin took in their coffee tray. From the top of the stairs, clutching her bag and rolled-up raincoat, Karen sped silently down, out of the apartment, closing its door softly, carefully. She ran to the lift and pressed the button. It was at ground level. A sudden thought struck her: where was Alice? She hadn't arrived yet. The lift was approaching, its indicator lights flashing up. Seven, eight. Was Harry's secretary inside? Would she be able to act calmly, convincingly? While, at any moment, Martin could come out from the meeting and decide to check on her.

The lift arrived, slid open. It was empty. If she met anyone on the way down, she must have a story. Except she couldn't speak. So, be casual. The little steel box lisped downwards imperceptibly. It had stopped. Why? Someone – two people in suits were getting in. Neighbours of the Wharf, not knowing each other. In the security lobby, past the guard. Act unconcerned. If Martin had discovered her missing, he or Harry would call straight down to security to stop her.

Nodding to the guard, she crossed the lobby to the outer door. Miraculously it operated, swept open, releasing. She was free, *free*. She wanted to dance, run, gather the arms of passers-by, cry and laugh with triumph. Soberly, quickly, she put on her mac and set off. It was raining, and the morning was ordinary, grey and practical. The taxis that passed were all taken. A train, then.

In the bank, she stood in line for the exchange counter. Minutes passed. If they discovered her gone, they would never think of looking here. Harry was busy with the Italians, important business. Surely he might even feel relief, when he realized she had left. Her papers were still in her maiden name, like the travellers' cheques. The marriage had been a brief mistake for them both. They would get over it. She recited, repeated these thoughts in her head, a mantra for safety, not to be too afraid.

One hundred and eighty pounds. Not much but enough for escape, to make a new start and vanish into anonymity. She took the crisp new notes, folded them. Her entry visa, for life.

'Hello, Karen.'

It was Alice. She had been queuing at another counter, her neat grey head familiar, not quite registering. Alice had seen her come in, collect the money. She was loyal, had worked for Harry for years. Suppose she alerted him, right away? They stared at each other, then Karen smiled and put a finger to her lips. 'Don't tell him. It's for a surprise for Harry.'

Alice whispered back, conspiratorial, 'I won't say a word.'

Karen walked off casually. As soon as she was out of sight, she ran, burying herself among the Monday-morning travellers. She must get out of the station fast: it was the most likely place to get stopped. A train drew in as she ran to the platform. She glanced back through the carriage window. She had not seen anyone following, but Alice might tell Martin about seeing her in the bank. Martin would guess at once why she had slipped out alone, why she needed money.

In the city, changing to the Northern Line, she phoned from the platform. Caspar had left a new answerphone message. It was half past ten, early for him and Poppy. Were they there but still asleep? She needed to talk, and work out what to do next: she would head for Anglo Road, although it couldn't be safe to stay. Would anywhere ever feel safe again? Among these hurrying crowds, merging, faceless, she could never be found, but then she couldn't walk for ever. And terror was not rational. She hurried towards her old home, that faded, peeling door to the basement flat, as if it was sanctuary.

No one answered when she knocked. The spare key had gone from its hiding place. How much time did she have?

'There's a message about those guarantees. Can you call the bank. And Matt, in France. It's important, he—' Martin broke off, as Alice came rushing out past him in tears. 'What's the matter?'

'Do you happen to have seen my wife?' Harry asked quietly,

silkily. 'Do you happen to have had a little chinwag with that tart, this morning, about her future plans – yes or no?'

'No, I thought she . . . I thought Karen might've gone back to bed – she looked pale. Why? Where is she?'

'You haven't seen her since breakfast, then? Wonderful! My entire staff, in some well-cocooned, overpaid daydream, have come up trumps again. Were you not aware that I had put that cheating slag into your charge, in your safe keeping? Especially after last night's little dramatic escapade, didn't it occur to you to keep an eye on her, even? Damn it, you let her walk out on me!'

After a silence, Martin asked, 'How can you know?'

'She has taken her papers. And was last seen gaily gathering cash at the local bank. You stupid, untrustworthy fool!'

'That isn't fair, you never told me to—'

Harry felt blind rage cut him. 'How dare you argue with me? You forget your place, and I will not tolerate this any more. I no longer require your services. Get out, and don't come back. Get out!'

Martin stared, then folded his arms, but his voice shook. 'Here you go again, blaming me. I don't know how that girl put up with you for so long. OK – don't worry, I'm going. And whatever will become of you, Harry?' He banged the office door shut behind him as he went out.

Harry was alone, pacing the luxurious, empty space between machines, the technology, half-completed work. Let them all scream for him, make their demands, add to the chaos. His business was heading for the rocks, anyway. Everything he had built up was slipping out of his control. No one would give him their support. The French film, looking abysmal suddenly. The Quentin débâcle . . .

That dirty little bitch. Betraying, making a double fool of him. She had run to her lover – or to a pimp. And he was wrenched inside by the thought of someone enjoying her, those honeyed favours, her youth. He should let her go – she was nothing but grief and trouble – but he could not. She had got him trapped, and the only solution to it all, by now, the only answer lay in her submission. That fucking vulnerability of hers

– how she paraded it! How that enraged him. She used it to get to him every time.

He opened the office door, which didn't seem to have been damaged by Martin's temper. Then he saw Martin himself, with his coat on, sitting on the furthest edge of the furthest sofa. He was wearing his closed expression: he was upset. I can't deal with this, Harry thought. They looked at each other in silence for some time.

Martin cleared his throat and asked, in an injured way, 'So what do you want me to do about it?'

A key was turning in the lock. Karen shrank back in the flat's narrow hallway: behind the frosted glass of the front door, a tall shadow loomed. She held her breath, hidden there, thinking too late that anyone could have found Poppy's spare key and be using it now. Even Harry.

He came in, unrecognizable at first against the light, and she sank back among the old bicycles. She began to laugh quietly, hysterically. 'Caspar. It's me, Karen.'

'Hi,' Caspar said, in mild surprise. 'What're you doing here? Hey, what happened?' He peered down at her, then flicked the light switch. It didn't work.

'Richard upstairs let me in. You don't mind?'

'What's wrong with your voice? Poppy's in Bournemouth, she got a job.' They went into the living room where Caspar cleared a chair. 'You look like a ghost. Hang on a sec.' He brought a glass of water from the kitchen. That ordinary kindness, reminding her of normal human contact, broke her up. For the moment she was safe, but as terror receded everything she had lived through welled up, vivid. 'Hey,' said Caspar. 'Tell.'

'It isn't the first time, but . . . Harry attacked me last night,' Karen whispered. She unwound the silk scarf from her neck.

'*Jesus*. Harry Glass did that? The guy must be nuts! What d'you mean, it's not the first time? Does Poppy know?'

'No. I was afraid if I ran he would find me and things get worse. But now . . . Harry may've already killed someone.'

Caspar's eyes grew wide. 'What d'you mean?'

'I'm the only person who suspects. Harry's partner has disappeared. They'd gone sailing, and no one's seen him since.'

Caspar, cross-legged on the floor, leaned towards her. 'You don't mean Alistair Quentin?' He whistled, long and low, with surprise. 'I read in the trade press, they've set up a company. But a lot of muddy water flowed under that bridge a few years back. You didn't hear? They fell out over a deal – Glass was the loser but they both kept quiet. Seems odd, them getting back together. Why did they?'

'Maybe everything else was right. Or it was meant to straighten the score. If people refused to work with anyone they'd quarrelled with, no films would ever get made.'

'That's true.' He grinned. 'Maybe your old man did lose his rag – with Alistair Quentin – with some good reason.'

For a moment, she was tempted to tell him the rest of it, about the rape, but she could not. Only Poppy knew, and the police, who hadn't been able to act. As if catching part of her thought, Caspar said, 'You must go to the fuzz. You've been beaten up, right? Whatever else, the bloke's a thug.'

'You know what they'd say? I'm his wife, it's a domestic. They wouldn't be able to do anything.'

'You can't know for sure. What've you got to lose?'

Only my life, she thought. 'It wouldn't stop him. Let me tell you some things. Harry's best friend, he *is* the police. And there's a question about his second wife's death but he got cleared of involvement. Harry's a kind of hero, you see. He's a success story, who smashed the class barrier, and he's up for an OBE. He'll probably get it because he knows people. So – thanks for the thought, but forget it.'

'Wow. What will you do?'

'Make a new life, somehow.'

'You've always been – I don't know. Together. Not like me or Poppy. Weren't you?' he asked, as she fell about laughing. It was croaky, hysterical laughter. She had felt so precarious, her life unstable for ten years. She must have put up such a good façade. She laughed, then cried, and Caspar hugged her until she grew calm. Then they talked about what to do.

'Glass knows this place, he might come looking. You need somewhere before tonight,' Caspar pointed out.

They thought of friends, and possible places, then called Poppy. She was rehearsing a summer season of *Mother Goose*, and Caspar was to join her in a week. Another friend, Filo, had got a part in the same panto. It was Poppy's idea that Karen should take over Filo's flat. 'You'll have to pay the rent. But if Harry looks for you he'd never think of searching Hackney, would he? You'll have to do something for money – or go to a lawyer?'

'Harry must never learn where I am. I don't want anything from him, just to be left alone.'

She would need a new identity and appearance. There had been no time to think about it, how to vanish entirely from Harry's orbit. It was almost one o'clock by now, and he had probably found out that she had run away. Karen shivered, remembered his obsessional nature and the promises he had made, always in the name of love. He would look for her. Anglo Road was probably where he would start. Quickly now, she got ready to go. She tied back her long, tell-tale blonde hair and hid it under a scarf of Poppy's.

They took a bus to Hackney. She felt almost safe with Caspar beside her – but, then, how would they know if they were being followed? Rain was falling steadily. The bus was crammed, steaming, with misted windows. She would rename herself and look different, become impossible to find. When they got off, the intensity of East End life seemed shocking. She was used to the careful, quiet loneliness of Harry's homes, but these streets were a noisy, crowded hotchpotch of making do and resilient spirit, cheerful or dour. They passed small shops and takeaways, bargain stores, the down-at-heel and the scruffy, among traffic and grime, reggae blasting from open windows and battered cars. By a street market, with stalls of vegetables, packs of meat, summer clothes and kitchenware, a narrow entrance led to a block of flats.

Up four flights, they found the studio which Filo was buying. It was simply furnished, had a kitchenette and tiny bathroom, a TV and phone. Karen closed its sturdy door, noticing the double lock. The window looked down on to the market, where a couple of guys on the corner were clearly selling drugs. Caspar said, 'I'm not sure you'll be OK here. It's pretty rough.'

In their own home, her husband had tried to strangle her. Drug dealers and street crime seemed like nothing. 'It feels fine here.'

'I'd never rest easy – and you're still married to a maniac. I can't leave you on your own.'

Caspar stayed for a week, sleeping on the spare mattress, going off each day to work out his notice at the Whistle Café in Islington. Karen's bruises faded, and she felt stronger. As a redhead called Sally she arranged to take over Caspar's job when he joined Poppy. It was a new life, of a kind. She had been used to poverty: now, for a while and in summertime, poverty felt a million times better than luxury with terror.

On her own, she would be coming home alone in the dark each night. But in all the bad things that had happened, her attacker had been known to her. Now she learned the facts. In the streets, men were more likely to get mugged, because they earned and carried more money, but the media preferred to publicise attacks on women. She had been safer than she had ever believed before she met Harry. Now, if he found her, she might never be safe again.

Walking in the dark, Karen practised independence. She was learning the street language and to read signals. Back in Filo's block, she started to make allies, and Caspar was staying for now. She began to understand how she had looked for strength in someone else, instead of in herself, and how that had left her weak.

Harry's old films were being reshown on ITV. How could she have got involved with him? There was a side to her that was unloved, self-hating, and confused bad treatment with caring. Somehow, she had sought out the misogynistic Harry – who was like his rival, Quentin, in the end – while feeling won over by his kindness and protectiveness. His money had made her feel safe, but wealth could not be a substitute for love. Harry had turned his success, and himself, into something god-like. He seemed to believe he was beyond morality.

She missed acting, and hoped to return to it. She called Vicky, her agent, told her how her marriage had failed: it was vital that Harry didn't learn where she was. For a while, she wouldn't seek work in theatre or television, but in voice-over and radio, which were less likely to reach Harry's attention. Vicky took her new phone number, and promised to talk to her radio colleague, Tim.

Every day something would remind Karen of Damien. An American spoke on the Underground, and she jumped, searched for him. A tall, dark-haired man walked past and she was drawn, as if to a magnet. She tried to make herself forget him. They could never meet again. For every reason, Damien was dangerous to her – and she knew little of his true nature. Remembering his gentleness, she distrusted it as she might have distrusted Harry's. Damien was too wild, too complex: he could turn out like his father. Still, she caught herself thinking about him.

She had spoken to Tim only twice since he had joined Vicky Hedges a year ago. When he called, she recognized his slight Manchester accent. He thought it possible he might be able to get her some work. It would take time to set up and, by the way, a small BBC royalty had come in. Could they have the new address?

Karen started to say where she was hiding. Then she hesitated. 'It'll be confidential, just for me,' Tim said.

She decided to get out of telling him, although she never knew quite why. It was just a sense of something not quite right. 'That's OK,' she answered cheerfully. 'Send it along to my old Camden address.'

'We'll need the new one,' he said. 'It'll be perfectly safe in my personal book.'

Why was he being so insistent? 'I'll probably be moving again,' Karen lied, and listened to the angry silence. The skin on the backs of her hands was beginning to crawl. 'Tim, what's the royalty for exactly?'

'Something you did, in . . . I haven't got it with me. Someone's buzzing the other line, I have to go.' He hung up. The empty line whined through her head, like the tracks of a train speeding towards her. Now she no longer wondered if Harry was trying to find her. To make sure, Karen called the agency and spoke to Tim. No, he said in surprise, he hadn't just rung although he had been meaning to.

It had been Harry.

Terror surged through her. Harry had got her number. Who could have given it to him? He had very nearly succeeded in tricking her. He could mimic anyone and could deceive other people into giving away her whereabouts.

She was Sally, living in Hackney where nobody knew her past. Surely it would be safe to stay? The phone number couldn't help Harry to get her address, and he hadn't revealed who he was. She wouldn't answer the phone again, but would check every contact, now she knew he was hunting for her.

Damien learned that Karen had run away. Nobody had come to the coast at the weekend. Then Harry's line producer in France, Matt Berkley, had called urgently, twice, trying to get hold of his boss. It seemed Harry had gone AWOL. During the week Christine cleaned the house, and on Friday she rang to find out Harry's plans.

'They've not made contact, I don't know what he's doing.'

'He won't be coming, then. Leaving you on your own, in that great place. It's a shame.'

At first, he felt glad to have time alone. He walked on the beach, where a thick sea mist covered ocean and shore, blanketing space, suspending reality. It was as if something was waiting to happen. Thinking about Karen and their walk together, he felt a strange pain begin to spread through him because she was no longer around.

On Tuesday, Matt called again. They were about to start shooting in the Cevennes. Harry would throw a million fits at the result if they just went ahead. The locations were wrong and they had permission problems. The director had started serious drinking. Where was Harry? No one was returning Matt's calls to London, he had left a dozen messages.

Damien called them at the Wharf. Might Karen answer? No one did, even during office hours, and he left two messages. Where could Harry be working from, he wondered. Eventually, at midnight, Martin rang back sounding pleased. No, Harry wasn't around and neither was Karen. She had walked, and Harry blamed him. 'Don't let on that I've told you. The man's in a state of nervous breakdown, and she's put the cap on it. He tried to fire me.'

'You're still working for him? And she –'

'Just call me Mr Scapegoat, Damien. She's vamoosed, could be anywhere, and he's spending all his time trying to trace her. Not good for business. He knows Matt's got problems on the French production. But does he care?'

Karen had gone. Disappointment washed through him. He tried to lift his voice, or spirits. At least she wasn't with Harry, and that was good, right? 'Why does he want her back? They weren't exactly getting along.'

Martin laughed. 'A good question, Damien. That's the funny thing about him – he loves her. He makes disastrous marriages, old Harry, but he does love them, in his way.'

'Maybe he won't find her,' Damien said.

'Oh, he'll find the girl. Harry has ways and means. It'll all go on, I've known him years. Listen, if you're finding life too solitary, why not come up to town?'

'I might. Let me know what happens.'

Damien put down the phone. After a while he got up, and went to the master bedroom. His stepmother's and his father's. There was the side of the bed she slept on, made up and waiting. There was nothing of hers, no sign of her in the entire house. It was as if she had never existed. Would he go to London? She wasn't there, and Harry would be.

He went out, walked to the jetty and along the beach. The mist had cleared away; now there was a half moon and stars, drifting wisps of cloud. The night sea was calm and flecked with silver. If they didn't trace her, if she didn't return to Harry, then he might not see her again, ever. Under the same planets, illusory stars, she could be anywhere at all.

From Islington's Upper Street, busy with Red Route traffic, Poppy ducked in through the doors of the Whistle Café. Karen, learning her routine at the tables, finished taking an order and went across to her, beaming. They hugged. 'Hey, babe. You look great.'

'Oh!' Poppy gave a shriek of laughter. 'We look like sisters! I can't believe your hair. Sally.'

'Yes, do try to be a bit discreet.' Karen grinned. 'Your old man's through the back. Good timing. I'll swear we're due a break.'

'This honest toil is a bit much, isn't it? And the cloak-and-dagger stuff – *assumed names*,' she stage-whispered dramatically. 'Necessary, huh?'

'I think so,' Karen answered, wondering if any of it was. Maybe, after that one attempt, Harry had come to his senses and given up. Perhaps it was time she stopped running and hiding? It was strange that there had been nothing in the media about Quentin's disappearance. Was it possible she had imagined everything and he was back home with his family, after all?

She glanced around at the customers, and Simon busy at the till. Half the stripped-wood tables were empty, and she showed Poppy into an alcove, screened by ferns. 'I'll tell Caspar, and ask if Celia can take over.'

'Get me a menu, then – Miss. Let's see you do your stuff.'

Poppy was back to collect more of her things, then take Caspar with her to Dorset. The seaside was the place to be, she said, but by the end of summer she might change her mind. Meanwhile, it was a laugh and they were getting paid. 'If we'd known what was going to happen, you might've been able to slum with us instead of here. How've things been?'

'I could get to miss the money,' Karen admitted, truthfully.

'But you don't want to go back to him? Listen, we didn't want to scare you . . . Caspar, tell her.'

Karen's heart jumped a beat. 'What?'

Caspar leaned across the table, his friendly expression grown serious. 'There was a guy hanging around, watching the house. Richard upstairs noticed him. He called the police, a patrol car came by – and the man vanished.'

'Probably someone hoping to break in,' Poppy said. 'And, anyway, he hasn't been back.'

'That could've been Martin, or even Harry. Except they already know I'm living somewhere else.' Karen told them about the phone call and Harry's mimicry of her agent's voice.

Caspar looked upset. 'You should've told me. At least he had no luck.'

Poppy said, 'The guy watching, he wasn't Harry or the chauffeur. I saw Martin before – he's tall and fair, right? The bloke Richard saw had ginger hair and was heavily built. A bruiser, he said.'

'Oh,' Karen laughed, 'we're all getting paranoid. I bet that was a thief. He got himself noticed, then hurried off.'

'They don't usually bother with places looking like ours.' Caspar shrugged. 'There's nothing to steal, anyone can see. Still, I expect you're right. But it bothers me – we're going away and leaving you here. What if Glass did find you, what would happen?'

'He's probably given up. I'll be OK. I'm not going to keep moving on.'

She had to get back to work then. Poppy and Caspar finished their meal. They were leaving in the morning and wouldn't be back until the end of the season. 'See you in September. Come and see the show, if you get the chance.'

'I will. Have a good summer, you two. Caspar's been brilliant – thanks for all your help.'

Karen watched them go, towards the high street and the Angel tube, on their way back to Camden. The café was filling up now, with cinema- and theatre-goers, late shoppers. She was clearing tables when she glanced across and saw, in the tearing white lights of passing cars, Martin standing in the street outside. He was looking straight at her.

She turned and fled, pushing past tables and customers without a word, through to the cloakroom at the back. How long had he been standing there? Perhaps he hadn't recognized her. The cloakroom window was slightly open and she could see through. She was still catching her breath when the street door opened and Harry walked in. People turned to stare. He looked distinguished in his pale Burberry, a white scarf tied like a cravat. Simon was hurrying to attend to him, and Harry gave his charming smile as they began to talk. Celia was hovering, gawping at this sophisticated apparition.

Fear had glued her there, watching. Now she wrenched away, and rushed through the passage. It led into the kitchen, and a steaming smell of food washed over her. Nausea, weakness. Rufus, pouring liquid between steel tubs, looked up. 'Oi,' he said. 'New girl. What gives?' She darted past him, trying to think. A back door – there must be a way out, through to the street. Between sink and stores, she saw the door standing open, a slice of dark night patterned with falling rain, open to freedom. The chef's big hand fell on her shoulder. 'Oi, Sally. What you up to?'

Celia appeared, lit with excitement. 'Hey, your husband's here. Come on.'

'You've got to help me get away from him.'

The chef looked baffled, Celia disbelieving. 'Caspar said . . . But that guy . . . I've seen him on the telly, he's a film star. He couldn't have meant him?'

'He tried to kill me – that's why I've been hiding. Please.'

Rufus said, 'Come on, girl. I show you a way out. And you,' he told the wondering Celia, 'go delay the man, spin him a story and smile sweetly, yeh.'

'OK,' she agreed, with a doubtful look back, vanishing through to the restaurant.

Karen hurried out into the night, the falling rain. She was in a narrow concrete yard, among garbage and barrels of oil. Rufus took her arm. 'Gate's kept padlocked, I don't have the key. The wall, that's your way out. But quick – I left bedlam back there.'

The wall was brick, seven feet high, with broken glass set in the top. Rufus dragged out some rags, threw them over. Clambering on to a bin, she reached up and found a handhold, levered herself to the top of the wall. 'Thanks,' she breathed, looking down on to the empty, narrow street below.

'Good luck, Sally.'

She jumped, landing on the wet, gleaming tarmac. Sounds of traffic hummed from the main road. She glanced that way, and saw Martin walking towards her. 'Hey,' he called out, 'don't act so crazy, come on.' He broke into a run, a great black spider of shadow against the neon, hurtling towards her.

Darting away, she spun up a dark street to the side, towards lights, busy traffic. She emerged near shuttered shops, among people in small, closed groups, and sped across the road, between cars that hooted angrily. Running up a turning, through tall, remote lines of houses, looking round she saw Martin dodging people, lamp-posts, trees. He had grown smaller. She turned off again, gasping for breath, and saw a big black car slide past, slowing. The Jaguar, Harry. Silently screaming, the quiet rain enclosing, she ran into a square, and burrowed among its trees. Bushes, paths, earth. Slithering, scrambling up again, she glanced round, stilled her breathing. No sign of Martin. She crept towards the path, the road beyond. They would search the square, and she needed people, anonymity.

Cautiously, she emerged into an empty street. Yellow brick buildings towered on either side, with black spiked railings, Georgian windows. She walked close to the rails, quickly and soundlessly. She had lost them. Threading through the side-streets, she saw someone walking towards her. Indistinguishable in the night, rain like sparks showering down from the street light on to his hair. Martin.

Turning, she raced back, sped off through a tunnel, a narrow dark alley that echoed, heart thudding and feet pounding, then heard a cry behind her, magnified, close. Emerging into a bright-lit street, friendly houses. Someone walking: Harry, his thickset body encased in silver, moneyed, elegant. Soaked through, and furious. Almost blundering into his arms, she twisted past, splashing through puddles, then fell heavily. She lay, the breath stunned out of her.

'I say, are you all right?' A man had stopped a few yards off, was calling out, but then Harry was closer, his voice pleasant and cultured.

'I'm afraid my wife had a little too much to drink,' he explained, sounding embarrassed. She saw herself as they saw her, splashed with mud, irrational and wild, lying in the gutter.

'Oh, I see,' said the man. He went on.

Harry was leaning down to take her arm, help her up. 'Are you all right, darling? That was a bad tumble. Lean on me.'

Karen stood, trembling and sodden with rain. The Jaguar drew up smoothly beside them. Martin got out and opened the passenger door. She looked at Harry, at his vexed, patient expression. What point was there in trying to resist, in running? She couldn't run and hide for all of her life. Slowly, without a word, she climbed into the warm, soft, leather interior. Harry got in beside her.

The car glided through the night. 'At least you're safe now. But this is all so undignified. Such an abysmal lack of style,' Harry mourned. 'And just look at you, my beloved. Painted hair, like a Jezebel. I can't believe it has all come to this.'

'Don't touch me,' Karen said.

'I'm afraid your little adventure in the slums has done nothing to improve you.'

They drove back in silence to Pipers Wharf and, without a word, straight to the underground parking, into the lift. What had she to lose now?

Harry closed the bedroom door on the two of them. He slid the catch of a new lock across, then went to the phone and ripped the plug from the wall. He thudded a fist into the dressing table, objects leaped and scattered from it. 'I saw him. I saw you with him!' His small eyes were red, pig-like. Didn't Harry know he need never hit her again? He was coming towards her, straight for her.

Karen drew herself up tall, and made her voice harsh. 'What would they think of you? Your smart friends, and your fans?' As he hesitated, she went on, 'I've told people, if anything happens to me then you're to blame. Don't ever hit me again, Harry. If you did, you'd find the media having a field day – with your entire life.'

Harry looked shocked. 'There is no need for this.' He sat down on the bed. 'You must not provoke or deceive me again like that. Never try to leave me – I would seek you out, you know that. So, promise.' She nodded: there would be no point in trying again, she knew now. He took her hand. 'I'll never let you go. I can't live without you, Karen. I love you too much. You have made mincemeat out of me.'

She saw that his eyes were wet with tears, everything he said was true. When Harry leaned against her, she put her arm about him and comforted, rocking them both. Her fear had become mixed with pity. She stroked his hair, until Harry fell asleep that night.

She was thinking, every minute now, about Damien. So much time seemed to have passed. He could have moved on, might even have returned to the States. She couldn't ask them because she longed to say his name. All her feelings would be laid bare, in speaking that one word: then Harry, or Martin, would know how she felt. No one mentioned him. Did that mean he had gone? She could hardly wait until the weekend to find out.

Then, she didn't have to. In the morning Matt Berkley arrived unannounced from France. Either Harry returned with him right away or he was resigning. If he did, it would leave no one in charge, and the production was a shambles. Did Harry care to take over, or was he intending to jeopardise the six films he was making?

'I'll have to go to France,' Harry told her. 'Come with me.'

'But you'll be back very soon,' she argued.

'If I can't get back, then will you join me?' Karen nodded.

Without him, might she go to Sussex? Harry decided, 'Yes, I don't want you staying in town. I think it's best if you spend the summer on the coast.' She looked away so he wouldn't see the expression in her eyes. 'I'm taking on Alice full time from now, so Martin can go with you. I wouldn't want you to be bored there.'

The day crawled past, full of delays, as Harry put his London affairs in order. In the early evening, they took him and Matt to the airport to catch their flight. Then, with Martin, she was on the road south.

Still she didn't ask about Damien, and didn't allow herself even to believe he might be there. She had missed him so much. It seemed to Karen, as they sped along those almost familiar roads, that everything in her life had led up to this. He would be there, and she would be with him – or never again. Which would it be? Darkness had fallen when they reached the lanes. Their headlights swept briefly, caressing every tree and bush, heightening, defining each separate leaf and blade of grass. She was teeming inside, with hope.

If he was still there, then she would have him for her own.

They turned in through the gate, and up the gravel drive to the Keep. She saw that its windows were lit, like a signal of victory. Then the door was flung open. He stood poised there in the light, and came out quickly to meet them. As she saw him her heart turned over. He was the real reason why she had stopped running.

9

Martin said, 'We'll be staying a while. Did you get my message?'

'We could be here all summer, if you can put up with us,' Karen added.

Damien was taking her bag, welcoming them into the light of the hall. 'I got your message – but you didn't say Karen was coming.' He turned to her. 'I thought you'd gone walkabout?'

'But I came back. I'm his wife. Are you taking that upstairs? I must sort out one or two things.'

Karen followed Damien up the stairs, and Martin scowled after her, filling with irritation. They had stopped speaking now. He listened to their footsteps, climbing. When there was silence, he went into the kitchen. From the freezer, he took a pint of milk and a small loaf, then searched among the meals he had frozen. A single portion of chicken supreme or fish pie? He chose the fish, wrapping it separately. With the carrier bag and a torch, he stood listening for a moment in the hall. Too bad if Damien came down and found him gone. Let him wonder where he was.

The garden and the beach below were solidly dark. Martin kept close to the house, only switching on the torch when he reached the jetty, with its worn, treacherous steps. On the cool breeze the strong, salty tang of the sea reached him, but he couldn't see its sliding blackness, he could see nothing and only heard the steady sigh of approach, retreat. The circle of torchlight beamed jerkily across the sand, seaweed, the jutting rocks. He tapped on the window.

Even in the darkness he could read Viv's expression, familiar over years. Her pleasure – which left him angry and moved, burdened with guilt. It wasn't his fault if he couldn't love her as much as she wanted. Her mouth was finding his in a kiss, and she pressed her body against him. Instinctively he shrank away, he couldn't help it. Viv let him go.

He closed the door behind them. 'OK?' he asked. 'Harry's gone to France, and I brought Karen here. Look, some shopping.'

'Aren't you an angel.'

'That's fisherman's pie, kept specially for you.' When he saw just how happy she was, instantly he felt trapped. His discomfort always showed. Viv drew back, becoming casual – it was like closing the airflow on a fire. 'You've made it cosy in here, with those rugs and cushions.'

She began to moan, familiarly. 'That tap's dripping, it drives me crazy.'

'I'll have a look and see if the washer's worn, while I'm here.' She was lighting a cigarette. 'I wish you wouldn't,' he said.

'If I got cancer, wouldn't that be convenient?' She saw his stricken expression. 'Sorry. It's only a matter of time, you know, before he finds me. He walks on the beach every day. Brooding over his sister, I suppose.'

'Damien's had such a life. He's an amazing guy.'

'Yeh. So would you brood, over your sister? I get pissed off, to tell the truth. The things I do for you.' She drew deeply on her cigarette, then looked up at him: she had made a mistake.

'Viv,' he said, letting his voice be warm and caring, 'I'd be the last person to tell you where you should go, or what you must do. I've no right to that.'

'OK,' she said miserably. 'Like a glass of wine? It's outside, cooling.'

He fetched the bottle, and the two blue goblets. 'Cheers, then. You look in good shape.'

'Do I? Cheers, Martin.' She was making an effort. 'So you'll be around, looking after her till Harry gets back?'

'And Damien will be staying,' he said, his voice unconsciously lightening. 'He wants to go fishing with me, further up the coast.'

A shadow crossed her face. 'I'm glad,' Viv lied, 'that you hit it off so well. After all, Damien and I were an item, we've been close.' Martin turned to look at her. She held his gaze, his new attentiveness. 'The things I do for you – well, they're sometimes for me as well.'

She had him now, and they both knew it. He moved nearer to where she sat. Then she held him, her arms around his body. He stroked her skinny shoulders, and she drew him closer. 'Why don't you come to bed?' Viv whispered. 'They won't miss you.'

Damien pointed some distance ahead of them. 'Shall we go as far as that wall, by the tree? We could stop for a while, and the horses could graze.'

Karen's sleek bay mare turned along the path ahead of him. His grey, Pegasus, followed without any urging. As they rode across the empty flatlands, through the stolen, bright afternoon, on every side the marshes were deserted. Nothing moved except the birds, and the slow, plump sheep. On the horizon hovered the pale ghost of the power station.

He was supposed to be running an errand for Martin. Driving into the village, walking out of the post office, he had seen her. They decided on impulse to hire the horses, and ride as far as they could. Here no one knew or cared who they were, how they looked at each other, and the lightness of freedom had overtaken them.

Two days ago, he had thought he might never see Karen again, until she suddenly arrived from London. They were happy in Harry's absence. Even if he came back soon, there were still months ahead and they might spend part of that time together. In this strange, flat landscape of bleak sun with no shadows, it was almost possible to forget other people.

Karen reined in the bay, slid to the ground and began to loosen its girth. She took off her borrowed crash hat, shook her head and released her hair. Its redness glinted like a weapon. If he were to kiss her, there was nobody in this place to see. If he did, they might not be able to part. What would become of them? He knew what had happened to the others – Harry's second wife, and his own mother.

Smiling at him, she sat down on the low stone wall. He sat beside her; they watched the horses greedily tearing at the sparse turf. 'When did you learn to ride?' he asked.

'I only sort of learned,' she corrected. 'My family was far too poor. And you?'

'On vacation, way back – we did some riding, canoeing, a bit of shooting.'

'A bit of shooting? What else?'

'I play guitar. I do a great spaghetti carbonara.'

'Yes?'

'I'll make that for you, some day. Let's see . . . I'm a poker player. I did some racing – cars. Uh-huh. That's about it. And you?'

'I make a fantastic salmon in cream sauce with dill.'

'You do? Hell, I adore salmon in cream sauce.'

'I'll make it for you.'

'Right. What else?'

'I'm a good driver,' she told him, 'but I fall off bikes. Can't stop, for some reason. I was in a TV commercial where I had to cycle down a hill, then pull in outside a shop. There I was, flying past. We did twenty-two takes. A barricade of mattresses, I had to have.'

'Really?'

'Not really.' She laughed, she had been embellishing.

'You've done the classics,' he said. 'Shakespeare.'

'Yes. Ibsen and Chekhov. It all added up to quite a lot. I miss acting.'

They fell silent. Was she thinking about Harry? He glanced at her. 'Why did you run away?'

'I'll tell you, some time.'

'Now,' he insisted. And when she didn't answer, 'Did he ever hit you?'

'Yes. He won't do that again,' she added, maybe seeing the fury that swept through him.

Harry was a bully. Why hadn't he known before? 'Why the hell did you marry him?'

'Because he was protective and I felt safe with him. How wrong I was. Now, I don't want to talk about him any more.' She went on, 'This is such a weird place. You can just imagine the smugglers in these coves at night, with their barrels of brandy. Running the gauntlet of the excisemen.'

'From what I've heard, it was the excisemen who ran the gauntlet. It was open battle.'

She laughed again. 'A lawless place. Good.'

If he reached out a hand, he could touch her. It would be easy. The air was electric between them. He desired her, and she was his stepmother. How could they ever get together? It could never be. Yet he was sure that she did want him, and he was living in a state of tension, of hope. If only it could be enough, just to be around each other like this, and close. But it was not. He wanted to hold and kiss her, to make love.

Damien touched her fingers, and they closed around his. Then she squeezed his hand. 'Damien? We ought to think about turning back.' He nodded, confused. What did she want from him?

Remounting, they set off at a walk back the way they had come. 'You want to do this again? We've got the summer.'

'Yes. Oh, yes. And we could take the boat out, further along the coast. Shall we?'

After that they were happy, and it seemed the simplest thing in the world to have times like this. The lights of the real world, the village and farmhouse, were flickering on distantly, twinkling mirages through the flat dusk, nearer and nearer. It was evening already, they couldn't believe it. They had forgotten how to pretend with each other, he thought with misgiving. The way he felt must show so clearly, if anyone saw them. As if by agreement, they stopped talking as they approached the houses and lights. The only sound was the steady, ringing fall of the horses' hoofs and the cry of a seabird. At the top of the lane to the Keep, he drew in and looked at her. 'Shall I take the horses back?'

Something flashed across her face in the fading light, a moment of mutiny. Did she want everyone to know what was happening, then? Even, almost before they themselves knew? His heart began to beat faster.

She was dismounting. Diminished, in her jeans and blue sweatshirt, as she stood patting the mare. 'Yes,' she said slowly, 'I want to go back alone.' She gave him the reins and the hat. Tossing her head impatiently, she strode away down the lane. He had suggested caution to remind them both, for Harry had a thousand eyes and many of those were nearby, right now. It was a small community and people talked; anyone could have seen them together. She was out of sight by now. This was for her, because he felt responsible. He could make her a focus for malice, and even place her in danger. How could he think of doing that? He must leave her alone.

He took the horses back to the farm, then drove to the Keep. Only Martin was there, preparing an evening meal. 'Sit down, have a drink. What've you been up to?'

'Not much.' He was starving from the ride, and stole from the bowl of carrots on the table. 'Isn't Karen around? You shouldn't bother with this, just for us.'

'Harry would say it's my job. He rang – she wasn't around then, either. Which is bad news, because he'll have my balls if she's taken it into her head to try walking again.'

Damien helped himself to the black Italian olives that Martin was putting out for him. 'I expect she's mooning around somewhere,' he answered, harshly. 'She isn't a lot of use here, is she?'

'Haven't you seen Karen today?'

He tried to avoid answering. 'Mm, these olives are amazing. I saw her earlier – she wanders about. Think she misses him – is it a love-hate thing?'

The phone on the wall rang, and Martin jumped. 'Speak of the devil. That'll be him, again.'

'I'll get it.' He picked up the phone in a surge of nervous energy. His voice sounded angry. 'Hello, Harry.'

His father said, 'Damien. What are you doing with yourself? And where's Karen?'

'Martin and I were just wondering about her. So how's the filming?' Too late, he saw Martin pulling a face: don't ask.

Harry launched into a catalogue of can't-dos. He had just fired the director and, at this late stage, had decided to take over himself. 'This should be a piece of cake. But I've inherited a sow's ear of a muddle and strong-arm tactics are needed. You must learn about the business, Damien. Now stop evading my question. With you and Martin both there, one of you must know – where is Karen?'

'Maybe she's gone for a walk, Harry. She was around earlier, so—'

'A walk in the dark? That's the limit. What are you both doing all day that you can't keep an eye on her and know what she's up to?'

Damien listened as Harry burned on a short fuse. Othello wasn't a patch on this, and it was like looking into a mirror. What other ways did he resemble his father? When there was a brief pause, he jumped in. 'I think she's lonely, maybe she's pining for you.'

There was a silence. The next moment, Damien was cursing himself. 'She must come. I want Karen to join me,' Harry said. 'Martin can bring her and stay. Is he there? Put him on the line.'

Handing over, he listened to Martin's snatched answers. 'If you insist . . . Well, don't go blaming me . . . I'll have to check that out with Alice.' He couldn't bear to listen any more, but went out through the hall – anywhere, to get away from this – and opened the front door. Karen was sitting on the steps, leaning against the whitened stone of the wall. What the hell did she think she was doing, stopping out and arousing Harry's suspicions? Not that it mattered, now. She was going to join him and maybe she would be gone for months.

She looked up, then got to her feet at once. An irrational anger had swamped him. 'Your husband's on the phone.' His voice was cool, hostile. 'You're to join him in France. Martin's going along, to act as your minder.'

'But I don't have to.'

'You must go.'

She turned on her heel, without a word, and went in. He stood there in the absence she'd left behind, then thudded his fist towards the wall. All Harry had to do was make a call, snap his fat fingers, and she must go running.

He paced around the Keep, through the blackness, his feet grinding on the shingle, the breeze chill on his face. Through the spilt light from the house, into the secret dark beyond. Trying to cope with the sudden reversal, to accept it.

When he had calmed down enough to pretend, he went back into the house. The kitchen was filled with the smell of cooking, and Martin was alone. 'There you are,' he said. 'And Karen's come back, so we could have supper. Listen, Damien. Think you could cope with playing nursemaid in France?'

He must have looked shocked. 'Sorry to land you with this,' Martin went on. 'But I spoke to Harry's secretary and her mother's not well. She's going up to York, and I've to hold the fort in London while she's away.'

'You want me to go to France with—'

'But,' interrupted Martin quietly, keeping one eye on the door, 'you don't have to stick around. There'll be people on location that you could leave her with, while you get yourself a sight of Europe.'

'That sounds OK,' Damien answered, coolly. 'How long for?'

'Only a week or so, I'd think. He doesn't want her running again. Harry's got enough problems without that.'

Over supper, as Karen asked for details of their trip, they were careful not to look at each other. 'Alice has booked a morning flight – for Toulouse, and that's a fair drive, I'm afraid,' Martin apologized.

'What a bore.' Karen sighed. 'And where do I stay?'

'Harry's using an old château near Florac. The cast and crew are staying separately. The film's way behind schedule – in about ten days, they move to Paris. You'd better go and pack.'

In the morning, Martin drove them to the airport. Karen went towards Departures, while Damien hung back. 'You'll be in London for a week?'

Martin nodded. 'Give me a call. The place won't be the same without you. Keep a close eye on her.'

'I will,' Damien promised. 'When I get back, we must take in that fishing trip.'

They were free. At first, it was as if some vestige of Harry remained between them, as if Martin might materialize again, deciding to travel after all. They stopped in the middle of the departure hall, and both glanced back towards passport control. Then they looked at each other. 'No Martin,' breathed Karen. There was a gleam in her eyes, a dizziness of relief.

'No Martin,' Damien echoed incredulously, grinning at her. The effort of acting cool and reluctant fell away from them. He began to laugh aloud, from all the feelings he'd pretended not to have – about being with her on the journey, the week ahead – while all around them a plastic, air-conditioned control was descending. Bright-lit shops with aisles of stuff, ludicrously undesirable, patterned nylon carpets, anodyne announcements, tinny patches of music like unwanted thoughts; and people yoked together, already snapping at each other. He took her hand, amazed because among all this dross they were free.

'What is it?' She had partly caught his mood, was still quizzical.

He studied the flecks of amber in her blue eyes, her freckles, the way the vampire lights sucked all the life out of her pale skin. Her mouth, her smiling expression. He wouldn't say what he was thinking, and wouldn't kiss that mouth. The mixture he saw – of happiness with a thread of apprehension – would change its balance. He didn't want to see that change.

They were alone, with no one to notice. The flight could not be long enough. Constant small interruptions, trays of plastic offerings, were transformed in the sharing. She leaned against him, head to head and hand in hand, pointing out the landscapes far below, and cloudscapes to die for in the magical, rolling grasp of heaven. Too soon they were circling over southern France, close above the mountains, then landing in Toulouse.

When they stepped out of the airport building to find their car, the heat hit them, solid, low.

He drove east along the N126, through valleys and hills, past sleepy towns and villages, and farmhouses of pale stone, that lay scattered across the steeply wooded slopes. At first he was concentrating, on the car and the route. Then, as they talked again, he wanted to know everything about her. They had so much to learn; and if he told her about himself, would she lose respect for him?

The sun was fierce, high overhead, and they saw few people. The streets of the towns lay almost empty, each village was deserted, shadowless. They decided to stop, and ate lunch in a small restaurant overlooking a river. Then, asking for the bill, Damien took out a credit card. It was a spare of Harry's, lent him to pay for their trip. Until now, it had been almost possible to forget they were going to rejoin Harry. Damien signed, his mood changing. He was a courier, and had been hired to deliver Karen, hand her over. They couldn't delay on their journey much longer. 'I don't want to go on,' he said.

'It's too hot to drive,' she agreed at once, perhaps misunderstanding. 'Let's go down to the riverbank, and find somewhere cool to rest.'

Across a bridge they found a path, narrow and overhung with trees, and walked a little way. Here the river tumbled singing, and polished stones gleamed through its rippling glass. He would deliver her to Harry but, he knew by now, somehow they would be lovers too. He looked at her and sensed it. Crouching at the river's edge, Damien dipped a hand into the cool, flowing water. 'I want to tell you some things about myself. I guess that I need to.'

'What kind of things?' She had taken off her shoes and, sitting down beside him, dipped feet and ankles into the clear water. Her face, close by and looking round at him, was dappled by shadow.

He had to say something about it all – the past, his own violence – but what might she think? 'When we met, in Sussex, that wasn't the first time I'd seen you.'

173

'Go on,' she prompted, trustingly.

'The first time was in New York.' He saw her surprise, and hurried on. 'Yes, last winter. I'd heard Harry was there, he was publicizing a TV show, right?' She nodded. Damien said flatly, 'Angel had just died. Some years before, my grandfather had given me a handgun . . . It all seemed to fit together. I tracked down Harry, and I followed him and you through the streets.' He shivered in the heat, remembering the sheer force of his own hatred; remembering drawing the gun. 'I had this idea . . .'

He had stopped. 'What?' Karen asked softly, surely guessing. But he couldn't go on. She added, quietly, 'Your sister had just died. And so you were crazy.'

'I was crazy about her,' he said.

Karen sat looking at him for a long time. Like a mermaid emerging, drawing out from the water, she knelt on the bank and opened her arms to him. He felt his heart expand, then grow hot: a powerful force gathering momentum inside. They held each other, until she stirred a little. And at once he desired her. He would not move apart, but felt the fast, strong pulse growing between them. Her breasts, her nipples hardened and pressing, demanding. Then he leaned to kiss her mouth, to feel the hunger in her response. But she pushed apart, restless, and carefully he let her go. 'I want you,' he told her, thinking: She doesn't love him, she shouldn't be with him.

'We shouldn't have done that,' Karen said, at last. She was breathless still, her voice shook.

'Why not?' he demanded, and saw the confusion in her eyes. 'Why the hell not?'

'Oh, I don't mean . . . Now, you listen. There's something that you must know about.' Her face broke into a troubled smile, ironical. She said firmly, 'I don't enjoy sex. I almost never have – not for years. So, you see, it would be no good for us, anyway. And you would be awfully disappointed.'

He laughed, he couldn't help it. His body was still racing inside, his erection felt huge – and her own response, her longing for him, had done this. 'Karen, I don't believe what you're saying.'

'You had better believe it,' she said, serious.

After a minute he asked, 'But why? If you really mean that. Why?'

'Something happened.' She shrugged. 'Years ago. When I was eighteen, I got raped. And—'

'Was it Quentin?' The words were out of his mouth before he had thought them, because in a flash everything had fallen into place. Now she was taking her time to find an answer, but he knew what it would be.

'Yes,' she said slowly. 'How did you know?'

'Because of how you were around him, that weekend. And something he said to me. Anyone carrying a grudge that deep must have done you bad harm. Karen, I'm really sorry. Won't you tell me? Talk to me.'

As they drove slowly, for the rest of their journey, Karen told him things she had never told anyone. She felt as if she would never be alone again. But by early evening they had reached the hills near Florac. Damien unfolded the list of directions. In silence, they turned along a steep, winding road, through tiny villages and hamlets, until a stony track veered off towards a large stone house.

'Not really a château, but how like Harry to call it one.' He lay between them now, a bitterness.

'I'll park by the road,' Damien said shortly. 'You go on and find him.'

'No. You come with me,' she insisted, now. Fiercely she went on, 'He's here to work, remember that. Tomorrow or the next day we'll get away.'

Leaving the hire car near the roadside, like strangers they walked around the house. A massive door of studded wood hung open on to a tiled hallway. Then they heard Harry's laughter, coming from somewhere outside. Following the sound, they came to a paved terrace behind the building where half a dozen people were seated round a large dining table. From across a low parapet, they could see the evening gathering, over a view of wooded valleys, blue hills.

Harry was there, eccentrically dressed in a safari suit. Nomadic and homeless, despite the two homes, with his life crowded by acquaintances and empty of real contact. Karen took a deep breath, trying to feel ready to move forward and greet him, to make all the effort it was going to take.

'Sweetheart.' He had turned and seen her, and was getting up, crossing the uneven paving, unsteadily. 'What a gorgeous vision. Such a long time.'

'Hello, Harry.' She returned his kiss, then added, using all the exasperation that she felt, 'Finally, I'm here.'

'This is my late wife, Karen,' he was introducing her, fondly. 'And my lost boy, Damien, to whom I foolishly entrusted her.'

Karen said hello to the producer, Matt Berkley, and to a harassed-looking assistant, Linda. She missed other names, apologized: they seemed to be in a meeting, surrounded by papers. 'That was a long drive. Yes, you entrusted me to someone with no sense of direction, Harry.'

'The signposting was not brilliant,' Damien said.

'And I had wanted to see some countryside, really. Darling, I must go and freshen up.'

'Sweetheart, don't leave me – not for a moment, when you've only just got here. You shall see plenty of countryside, I promise. You must come with me to our location, first thing – yes?' Harry patted her, then leaned across and thumped imperiously at an old brass gong. The noise of it crashed out across the silent hills for miles. As it faded, Harry laughed. A woman hurried from the house. 'My wife has arrived, and my son, and they'd like drinks. This is Madame Faysse, darling, who's looking after us. We'll dine in half an hour. And I would like a refill – why don't you leave those bottles on the table?'

'Are things going OK?' Damien asked, when the housekeeper had hurried off again.

'We're getting there,' Harry said. 'We've to catch up on schedule – no mean task, eh, Matt? We have to work on script changes every damn night, then get pages to the actors.'

'We've had to cut some locations and change others,' Matt explained. 'A legacy of he-who-got-the-sack.'

'And I've had to get it in one, on occasion,' Harry boomed. 'No easy task. Because, you see, there are the *actors*.'

Everyone laughed dutifully. Madame Faysse was lighting lamps, carrying food. Through a seven-course dinner, Karen tried to play the part. Harry's drunken laughter, his loud, forceful voice, made her want to scream at him. She had banished every ounce of pity and almost crushed her sense of guilt. I am married to him, and he repels me, she thought. I loathe and despise him. Did he have any suspicion of how she felt? Might he be acting, too? She tried not to catch Damien's eye, tried not to look across in his direction at all – because surely everyone would see instantly, the way things were between them? Close to midnight she slipped away, pleading tiredness from the journey. Damien stayed, seemed interested in the script conference beginning. Harry must be crazy, thinking they could work after such an evening, so late between days of filming.

Karen went in through the house to find the bedroom she was sharing with Harry. Its windows overlooked the terrace, the noisy meeting and the softly gathered hills. She had lost all respect for and any belief in Harry. The regime he was setting up looked doomed to failure through excess, but he would be king, whatever the price, as the kingdom tottered and fell. She had seen it before in a director – that loss of judgement, while no one knew what to say without getting fired or punched for daring to disagree.

She stood a while at the darkened window and watched, in the circle of lamplight, Damien's face and his lean body as he moved around. She felt astonished at the strength and power of her longing for him.

Damien was woken just before dawn by someone shaking him. It was Harry. He sat up, head throbbing as his memory returned, edgy and jagged. It was still the middle of the night, he thought. 'What's happened?'

'I've got a job for you. We're setting off and I want Karen with me. She isn't ready so I want you to bring her, then stick around.'

His mind flew into gear. 'I'm the driver. You want me to tow her around each day, that's what I'm here for.'

'She's got maps for getting to the locations. I want her to have a good time. My lucky mascot – you see that she's all right. You do look rough,' Harry said, as a parting shot. 'People your age, they've no stamina.' Then he was gone.

A minute later, a navy Renault Espace was sliding out from its parking space, below Damien's window. Dawn was spreading quickly now, over the slate-blue ridges of the horizon, while wreaths of clouds still encircled the low mountain tops. He showered and shaved, his mood lifting. Downstairs, Karen was having breakfast alone, waited on by the silent Madame Faysse. The housekeeper's English was good, he reminded himself. 'Have they all gone?'

'It looks like it.' They exchanged a small, friendly, sociable smile. OK, he would go with her to find Harry's film unit, and they would hover around him there, being friendly and sociable. Almost, that was amusing. Did she think so, he wondered. She had wanted him, but that was yesterday – and she had spent the night with Harry. Perhaps she had changed her mind, or come to her senses about him. He tried to extinguish hope.

Twenty minutes later, he was reversing the car down the hill. 'So where are we to go?'

'Shall we lose the maps?'

His heart skipped a beat and he stepped on the brake. 'We could get a bust tyre.'

'Or smash the car? Maybe later.' She sounded serious. He stole a fast look at her, and they laughed. A hot tide of recklessness swept over him. He knew that he would do what she wanted: whatever, whenever.

A few miles further on, they found the first location. It was a small Methodist chapel, being dressed by an anxious design team. For a real-life historical story, signs of age and decay had to be covered up, and an overgrown entrance turned into a well-used track. Horses and carts stood by, actors and extras in costumes of the poor, farming community. The scene looked slow and relaxed while, underneath, big tensions seemed to be simmering.

'Get a chair for my wife,' Harry ordered someone, briefly switching his attention to Karen's arrival.

Damien found a tree stump, sat down and watched. From the script conference he knew the story. It was about a death from dishonour, after the young daughter of a poor, Cevenol farmer had been seduced by a Catholic nobleman from the north. Now Harry was the centre for many hurried discussions. Almost no action had been filmed. A group of actors, looking like a deputation, had gone over to where Karen sat on the sidelines. Things between everyone here felt heavy, like before a thunderstorm. He had nothing to do. Was this how Martin felt, waiting on Harry, depersonalized and empty until the next instruction? But Martin didn't love Harry's wife.

She was being asked to intervene, he thought. Then the actors were melting into the background as their director came to investigate what they were up to. The next moment, Harry erupted into one of his rages, famously reported in gossip columns. The film from a camera went flying, awesomely. His direction would be obeyed, his decisions supported, and he would not tolerate dissent. If people conspired behind his back, he would walk out on the lot of them right now. There was truth behind his conspiracy theory, and everyone sank into shamed silence. Harry had reminded them where the power lay, and intimidated with his loss of control. There would be no discussion or any exchange of views. When it became clear that no one was going to expose him, he subsided enough for Karen to take him aside.

She seemed to succeed in calming him down, and later in the morning the cameras began to roll. Now Harry was intent, everything else forgotten. During a break for resetting, Karen went to him again. 'Harry, I'm going back to the château.'

As he turned to her with a vague concern his mind was on the next take. 'Sweetheart, you look pale. It was the heat yesterday, am I right? All that way from the airport. Damien,' he called, 'I want you to give Karen a ride back, and hand her over to the care of Madame Faysse.'

They were several minutes on the road back together, before Karen asked, 'Where are you going?'

He slowed. 'To the house?'

'Oh, no. Whatever for? We've got the whole day to go anywhere we like. Let's take that left fork, and see where it leads.'

He turned, obeying her whim, his mind flooding with conflicted thoughts. She had got rid of Harry pretty fast, but he hadn't been sure if that was for him. What did she intend? Some miles further on, the road led through a small busy town. 'Let's stop,' she suggested. 'It's so pretty. Look, it's market day.'

The town was crammed with visitors, and the jostling, noisy crowds annoyed him. Karen wanted cash, so they queued in the bank, then she towed him round the demented square. He was surprised to see her gabbling in French with the traders. She handled the mounds of fruit, selecting and discarding, and he envied the things she touched and the talk that excluded him. Seeing his expression, she smiled. 'What would you like?' They bought figs and cheese, bread and wine. She seemed amused at him again, as they drove on, out of town. 'What now, Damien?'

For answer, he headed off down a stony, unsurfaced road. It wound beside a river that glittered, hurrying past. The late-morning sun, its intensifying heat, lay over the hills and valleys now, spreading a great arc of solid light. Damien drove slowly, hypnotised by the tumbling threads of the river, following it along until the road began to veer away and climb, steeper and rocky, up thickly wooded slopes. Beside him, Karen had grown silent. The road was becoming a narrowed track, potholed and pitted with boulders, and the dense vegetation grew in from each side, squeezing, brushing the car and spreading before them a path of green.

She said, into the quietness, 'Where are you going?'

'As far as we can into the mountain. We could picnic there.'

'We must be completely lost. Damien? If I asked you to turn back, would you?'

He stopped the car, idling it there, and saw that the screen of trees had fallen away. The valleys lay open below, soft, tamed. 'We could find the way back. You want to?'

She didn't answer. He looked round at her and guessed how, driving deep into this lonely, wilderness place, she had become afraid of him. 'Hey, if you want to go back, we can do that.'

'Let's go on, as far as we can. It's a good place for us. No crowds, no people.'

Soon the track had almost disappeared under a screen of undergrowth. The car pushed over bushes and bracken, foll-owed the patterns of slight hollows where twin wheels had used to pass. It laboured, stopped, and he switched off the engine. 'Looks like this is it, as far as we go.' Silence hung heavily around them, punctured by the song of crickets, a flight of tiny mountain birds, humming bees: underneath, they grew aware of the faint sound of water rushing, crashing like laughter. 'A stream. Or is it a waterfall?'

They got out, and stood in the dense heat. A narrow path led down around the hillside, under beeches and holm oaks. It was shady, cooler, and the scent of wild thyme rose, bruised underfoot. The rushing noise grew loud. Between the trees ahead, they glimpsed the waterfall tumbling white, over rocks into a pool. Beside it, a stone folly or lodge had been built, and left empty long ago. They went close. Karen said, 'It must have been sited here for looking at the waterfall.'

'It's a hunting lodge. This is a long way up, and the track leads almost to it. They'd come here to shoot – deer, wild boar. Maybe there were wolves in the hills.'

'Perhaps there was a house nearby – look, you can see the old terracing, steps cut into the earth for a garden – and this was built as a secret place. An escape, for lovers to meet.' She turned to him and drew him close. He found her mouth and kissed her. His body was on fire as she clung to him. 'Make love to me,' she whispered.

He heard her desperation, and sensed the conflict in her. She was tense as a wire. He tried to still the demands, the turbulent clamours of his own needs. Holding her gently, he stroked her hair. 'I don't know what you really want – because you're scared of me.'

Karen didn't answer. Then, uncertainly, she stepped away. He let her go.

He was burning up, he seemed to have been wanting her for years, for ever. Kicking off his shoes, he took off his shirt and walked down to the edge of the pool, below the waterfall. He stood there a while, staring into that mirror of his own chaotic feelings. Then he waded into the troubled water, its iciness, deep under. Swimming the few yards to the opposite bank, he grasped at the rocks. His hair streamed water and he shook his head, rubbed the wet from his eyes so that he could see. He looked up again, to where Karen stood on the steps of the folly.

With a mixture of longing and dread, she watched him. The sun glistened on his skin, sculpting with light and shadow the taut muscles of his shoulders and chest. He was beautiful, and powerful. She had been afraid of him, driving up the hillside, and she felt afraid now, even as she melted inside, just from looking. They were so alone, in this strange and silent place. It was what she had wanted, but now, with no one around to hear if she called out – or if she screamed – it was all reminding her horribly of Quentin.

She reminded herself: Damien had been gentle – first with the seagull, and with her. He didn't want to hurt her. Still, she knew that when they made love, it would be no good for her. It never had been, not for so many years that she could scarcely remember anything better. Sex was uncomfortable and always hurried because she was afraid of hurt. All of this, she knew, was because of her fear. And she could not change it.

But what had happened once, and long ago, was not going to destroy the rest of her life. Slowly Karen slid off her clothes, her shorts, her top and briefs. She hesitated, before crossing the springy grass to the river. Beneath the waterfall the noise was immense and the air electric, with a sharp, fiery energy. The pool was a pit, a black hole, and the sun missing behind these rocks. She shivered and heard Damien yell something, swallowed by the crashing water. Then she dived in, and surfaced gasping, close under that pounding, icy turbulence. She was right inside its storm, and laughing at her own helplessness – flurried about like a scrunched-up leaf, a twig – reaching out to fend off the sharp, lethal stone.

'Crazy!' he yelled, beside her now. They were treading water like pale, fronded anemones swirling over the depths. She was cold, and struck out strongly towards the bank, hauled herself up, stepped into the sunlight, the heat again. And he followed her there, bringing half the river in a cascade from the jeans that clung, sodden, slowing his progress. She leaned her naked weight against him, this strange amphibian creature: he felt coarse against her tingling, sensitized skin.

'Didn't anyone ever tell you? You're supposed to take off your clothes before a swim, not afterwards.'

'I was not a well-raised boy. You'll have to tell me what to do.'

Sitting him down on the riverbank, she tugged at his buckle and the buttons of his jeans, tried to peel off the wet clothes that stuck to him. They struggled and wrestled, giggling. It was like trying to slough off a skin. He was a snake in the grass: a phallic predator. She shivered, rubbing them dry with her clothes, although the sun was blazing. His cock reared, trembling before her. Damien knelt and they held each other, kissing. Desire swept through her again, battling with fear, almost overcoming the warnings shouting out inside her mind. He began to kiss, to lick and stroke her shimmering skin, the insides of her arms, her breasts, her stomach. It was too much. She was all liquid, boiling pleasure and she couldn't stand it. 'Make love to me,' she whispered, meaning: Let me lie back then fuck me, use me, make yourself come and leave me alone again; that's what I'm used to, I can handle that.

Damien looked at her, quizzically. 'I am, we are – this is – making love. You're beautiful. I guess guys have taken advantage because of that. You've not been treated right, my love.'

He was treating her right. Her body had never been so vibrant, from the tips of her toes to the topmost hairs of her scalp, simmering with electricity. Singing to her, to him. She scarcely dared to touch him now, he was too aroused by her gathering, soft cries, and he took her hands away and gently sucking, nipping her palms, finally placed them around the small of his back, those neat haunches, as a safe place. She felt hot and restless, full of an unbearable yearning. This isn't fair, she thought: this is so selfish, and I must explain . . . 'Damien? Damien . . . I can't have orgasms, I don't come. So you might as well—'

'Is that right?' He smiled, stroking her stomach and the insides of her thighs. She hadn't noticed before, how each was of the softest, deepest velvet.

'Yes. I expect it's because I got so – my body was too traumatized, you know?'

'That was a long time ago,' he reminded.

'But don't you want to be inside me?'

'Not yet – and not this time. We've all the time in the world, as you said. We could picnic or swim, if you're feeling really bored, that is.' He laughed again, at her expression. He began to kiss her stomach, then her flower, nuzzling and suckling greedily. She opened to him, and felt a wave of panic, or pleasure, begin then fade. The sun was moving slowly over the sky, and her heart had begun to ache. She was falling so much in love with this strange and contradictory man, she was as-tonished by his generosity, the pleasure he was taking in her pleasure. That care, his unexpected patience moved her. Almost, she could trust . . . But I can never give us what we both want, she thought, because my body was too scared, was scared to death. And she felt a drawing back, away from them both, remote. Then a strange ripple of tension, a cord of energy drawing her into his touch and into some unfamiliar state. She yelled, shocked at her body's shattering, as a red wall of pleasure rose up deep inside, and swelled and broke, ribboning out.

Lost in its echoes, she felt Damien beside her, and held him close. He moved against her until he came, his body trembling.

Karen rolled over at last, and propped herself on one elbow, to study, then kiss him. He had freed her, and she could want no one else: she loved him, and her body's response to him. The power that she possessed inside her was new and profound.

IO

They drove back to the valley at dusk. Switching off the engine, he let the car glide, carried by its own momentum, silently downward. He could see just enough of that faint, descending track to keep them on course, on a rollercoaster of rushing, hesitation, tumbling down. She was holding her breath beside him, he could feel it, because they might hurtle over the edge. She was trusting him – just about.

By the time they had found their way back to the house, it was too late for dinner, late enough to make everyone wonder. As if he cared. They crossed the lakes of light towards the terrace and he stopped her, gestured to the sound of voices. 'What are we doing? I don't want this.'

'We can't change anything now,' she whispered. 'You must see that? Listen, Damien, just take it easy.'

He followed her to the terrace. Harry was there, with someone. He heard them say, 'But it's just a matter of what could be proved, you understand.'

It was Robert Bellman. What was the lawyer doing here? The next moment, Karen danced up behind Harry's chair and placed her hands over his eyes, prettily. 'Surprise, darling. Guess who? Such a long time apart, what a mistake I made today. I felt better, and wanted to see the south – the real thing. So your son obliged, and I did get to Montpellier.'

Surely Harry would see straight through them, or if he couldn't the lawyer would?

'Sweetheart. Come and sit on my lap. A little kiss? I suppose you got lost. And didn't you have any dinner, either? Serves you right for neglecting me. Robert has come to offer his counsel. Damien, bang the gong.'

Soon they were surrounded by people again. Maybe it would be OK, after all. Damien sat next to Matt, and tried not to watch Harry's possessive display. He was preening and bossing Karen around, pawing at her, and she was being real affectionate. Disgust swept over Damien – he hated Harry and felt like swiping away that smug, stupid, drunken smile. Then, gracefully managing him, she was taking her husband off for the night, to bed. Surely she wouldn't sleep with him, but would make an excuse to avoid him tonight?

He thought: We're not really even lovers. Immediately, he remembered her cries, her face as she came. He had shown her fulfilment then handed her straight back to Harry. He wanted to break down their door, burst in on them and announce she was his. They had been crazy to think secrecy might be possible, even for one night. Anything would be better than this, being shut out, watching her act with him – having to wonder, was she really acting? It was she who wanted the charade to go on. Maybe she did want Harry, and was stringing him along.

From a fractured night of troubled dreams, he woke late. She had gone with Harry to the filming, and he was not expected there. He had to find some calm, to be able to pretend. Without the heart to leave the place, hoping she might get back early and alone, he waited. He tried to read in the orchard, but the print fled before his eyes. When he swam in the river nearby, his mind filled with that first sight of her naked, diving.

In the early evening, he heard the car. Climbing the slope between the fruit trees, he saw Karen go straight into the house. The day's filming had gone well, Harry had decided that Karen was lucky. She was to be with him each day, good luck was her job. 'And you, Damien? Perhaps you should explore France – and decide what to do with your life.'

He knew what he wanted to do, after living for twenty-four hours in this siege of sudden, euphoric hope, the despair of loss, unable to speak with her. When they all went to bed, he signalled to her behind Harry's back. He waited in the silent kitchen for what seemed like hours before Karen appeared.

'You must be mad,' she whispered. 'The house is full of people.'

'Come out to the garden or the orchard.'

'I can't. Harry will be here looking for me at any moment.'

'I can't stay like this – not another day. I'm leaving tomorrow.' He held her close, kissed her. Softly he asked, 'Karen, come with me.'

'You know that's impossible. If he even suspected . . . Harry would find us – what would he do to you? No, I can't.'

He let her go. 'You want to stay with him.'

'I do not. I love you – why can't you believe that?'

'Then why stay? He wouldn't find us, not in the whole world. Come with me.'

She whispered urgently, impassioned, 'Look what's happened to people around him. He'd track us down. You don't know Harry as well as I do. Just wait a little. I don't know how, but we'll be together.'

'What will you do at night? Shut your eyes and think of his money?'

Anger flared between them. It felt better than the loss, emptiness stretching ahead. Karen said nothing, then, 'I won't sleep with him. Don't quarrel with me—' She stopped abruptly, listening as if she had heard a sound. He couldn't hear anything but she went quietly to the kitchen door, looked out. The next moment, she had vanished silently through the hall.

His heart was drumming a sense of danger. Was Harry there? The hall was empty but a thin slice of light shone under the door to the dining room opposite. He hesitated. The door was slightly ajar and he pushed it open.

'Good evening, Damien.' Robert Bellman sat, one leg crossed over the other, in a tall, green leather armchair. His face was almost in darkness, but lamplight glittered on the glass in his hand.

Damien could think of nothing to say. Then, 'I didn't know anyone else was awake.' His words sounded dumb, he felt terrified for her. How much had the lawyer overheard? If he had just looked in and seen them talking, he would surely have understood what they were about. Harry was his client and he would tell him.

Bellman raised his glass. 'Are you in search of the same sustenance?'

Had he come to the kitchen looking for ice? Damien poured himself a Scotch. 'I guess the ice is in the kitchen – you want some?'

'I've never understood the American passion for ice in everything. It spoils the palate. Are you enjoying your holiday?'

Damien shrugged. 'Harry asked me to come over to act as driver, but I'm not really needed.'

Bellman leaned forward and the light shone on his round, bland face. 'She knows which side her bread is buttered on. Don't worry about it.'

His heart skipped a beat. 'What d'you mean?'

The lawyer smiled, inscrutable. 'Don't worry, be happy. Isn't that what they say?' He got up, went to the door. 'It's late and I'm for bed. Good night.'

Damien sat in the darkened living room, playing and replaying the lawyer's conversation in his mind. What had he meant? Had it been some kind of game? Perhaps he suspected nothing, and had been commenting on the lack of a job. If he had heard or seen things, surely he would have shown hostility, out of loyalty to Harry?

There was a soft sound, a footfall in the hall, and he jumped up. She had come back to talk. She had changed her mind and wanted to leave with him, right away.

It was a cat, a small, calico creature with wild eyes, stalking through the sleeping château. Karen was with Harry. As soon as he had gone, she would be safer, with no more fear of discovery.

He packed his bag, left a one-line note to Harry: *Decided to take your advice – I'm out of here.* He drove north through the night, manically as the dawn came up, aiming vaguely towards Paris. This continent was weird: tiny and alien, so complicated. Each time he stopped the tourists, swarming around, swilled a dozen different languages through his head. He put five hundred miles on the clock, reaching a Paris deserted by natives, crowded with visitors, hot. Calling the hire company about the car, he booked into a cheap hotel to get some sleep.

He must stay away from her, but didn't know how. She had somehow got inside him, and changed the fabric of his being. When she wasn't here, he became something empty, rattling aimlessly around to the tune of memories. He took Eurostar then, from Waterloo, walked the miles to Harry's town apartment. He stood a long time looking at the Wharf, then never went in. Martin would be staying, and he didn't want to see Martin yet.

As if she was there, as if she was drawing him back, he found himself travelling to the Sussex coast. The empty shore-line where they had walked was transformed now into holiday seaside. Not far off, the café had opened and an ice-cream van had appeared. Families, little kids, had taken over. The beach ran with their shrieks, excitement drowning the swell of the surf. Oiled bodies lay out, sacrifices.

Now it was like before he had ever seen her, before he had begun to love: a pit of dark, swelling inside, suffocated out the sun. Bright, thin cries were ringing alarm. Mothers called their children away. He was unshaven and his eyes looked wild, his clothes were odd for the beach.

Damien sat on a breakwater, thinking of her. The sea rolled nearer, scarred by tourists, burning his eyes. Until a shadow fell across, blocking the sun, and he looked up to see Viv, of all people, grinning down.

'Hey,' she said. 'I thought it was you. Except you look kind of different. What is it?'

The minute she learned Damien had gone, Karen knew that, whatever the risk, she should have gone with him. She had thought he would relent, stay around, take whatever chance they had to be together. Now she felt frantic, convinced of never seeing him again. He would return to the States because what was there to keep him? Perhaps he would think of her sometimes, just for a while. How could she have been so stupid as to let him go?

Or maybe he did need her, and could be feeling like this too. She was burning up inside, unable to relax by day or sleep at night, living out a state of constant, nervous momentum: a cat on hot bricks. Memories and thoughts of him were the only relief, spreading their balm across the wrongness, the sick, tearing pain of absence and loss. When she thought about him she felt redeemed, brought more alive than at any time in the years since Quentin's poison. It seemed strange that trust might be reborn through Damien, through Harry's son. There was somehow a new life and strength, under all of the bad feelings.

Friends of Harry came to visit the filming, and to stay at the château. Shepherding them around, she was briefly caught up in the local expatriate community. This was rural France, sociable and welcoming, and the last thing she wanted right now. She marvelled that no one could read her mind or see into her heart. Harry, preoccupied with work, was suddenly being sweet to her. She felt guilty then crushed the guilt when he assumed she would stay on the road with him. Paris and Milan, then Sicily, where he was replacing the line producer on his next *Cry Murder* film.

'I don't want to go to Italy,' she started to tell him, beginning to hope and dare to hatch schemes. 'The heat is too much.'

When the filming moved to the outskirts of Paris, she was able to find a phone with no one listening. Might Damien be in Sussex or London? Calling Pipers Wharf, she willed him to answer, but across the Channel the machine clicked on. She left a message to Martin. 'Tell Damien he left something behind in France, which urgently needs his attention. Ask him to get in touch with me.' She repeated for them the Paris hotel number.

Martin played the phone tape, erased Karen's message and decided not to tell Damien about it, for now.

Since returning to Pipers Wharf, Damien had spent several days with him. 'You seem under the weather,' Martin noticed, 'but it's not bad out – shall we go for a drink somewhere? Come on.'

190

They went to a wine bar, overlooking the Yacht Haven at St Katharine's Dock. 'Tell me what's up. Don't keep things to yourself,' Martin urged.

Damien sipped his beer. 'I was thinking about Angel. It would've been her birthday last week.'

Martin leaned towards him, his voice sympathetic. 'You hate him, don't you? Harry.'

'Is that a terrible thing?'

'I used to think Harry was ace. Achieving so much, self-made. Will Vengeance was my hero, as a little kid. It took me a long time to see the man underneath. You want to know what Harry cares about? Just getting his ego polished, diamond hard, on a regular basis.'

'And a lot of us keep doing the job.'

'I had better chances than Harry, you see, in terms of education,' Martin went on. 'Then I got a place at Cambridge. Not bad – I've no lack of brains. But things went wrong. It was all too much, and I was obliged to drop out. That broke my mother's heart, after all she'd done and hoped for.' Looking at Damien, he saw that he wasn't even listening. He was staring across at the yachts, at those sleek, shiny toys of the rich, idly bobbing at their moorings.

Damien turned back to him again. 'When Al Quentin was at the Keep, that weekend . . . Have you spoken to him since?'

Martin looked curious. 'Why?'

'Just wondering. Has he been around?'

'Harry says that Quentin's left Amanda. Gone off somewhere, with another woman. True romance. And how about you?' Martin asked suddenly.

'What do you mean?'

'There must be someone – a woman – isn't there?'

'No – not over here, anyway. Why did you say that? You have a girl somewhere?'

'Not me.' Martin smiled at him. 'You've told me nothing of your trip to France. Did you have a good time?'

Damien shrugged. 'It was not set up to be the greatest trip of all time. It was OK. Let's get back now,' he suggested, restlessly.

Following him out of the wine bar, Martin said, 'I know what you'd like tonight. A nice bouillabaisse. Mm? Listen, Damien. If there's anything you want to talk about . . . We're friends, right?'

'Sure we are, yeah. Where is Harry, now? They must have got to Paris.'

Martin didn't answer for a minute, he was thinking. Casually he said, 'I'm wondering if you could do us another favour.' He glimpsed Damien's sudden attention, that swift, inadvertent turning towards him, as he began to explain, 'Karen's coming back on her own, to stay in Sussex.'

Damien saw Karen among the summer crowds at Arrivals, and hurried forward. Her face broke out of its preoccupied expression, lighting up with astonished pleasure. She darted to him through the people and baggage. 'You! What are you doing here?' Then quickly, 'Is Martin here?'

In answer he kissed her. Her arms went around his neck and she pressed her body against him. They stood a long time, in that milling hall full of reunions. He stroked her cheek. 'Beautiful. We're on our own.'

'How did we get to be so clever? I can't believe it!'

Picking up her bag, so familiar from the journey to France, Damien led Karen to where he had parked. She was still laughing from the surprise of it, eyes dancing, tossing back her hair as they set off. 'I never thought Martin would play the guardian angel to grant our wish – and twice? He's no idea, poor Martin, he'd be mortified. Oh, you can't know how I feel.'

'I know exactly how,' he said, stealing glances across at her.

'I almost gave up when you didn't call back. Did you get my message? Martin must have forgotten to pass it on. I was desperate to hear your voice and so regretted not going with you.'

'If I'd known . . . How long have we got? What did you tell him?'

'We've most of August,' she breathed out, happy. 'I told him I couldn't take the Italian sun, and refused to go along. If you knew what I've been through—'

Damien swerved into a lay-by and braked fiercely. They held each other, unable to let go, rooted in need. 'It's like when you wake after a bad dream,' he said. 'You suddenly realize – everything's fine, life is great after all.'

When they neared the coast, twisting through the familiar lanes, the sea was a strip of metallic grey, flat under ribbons of ragged cloud. With no word between them, she took her head from his shoulder, in case they passed anyone. Subterfuge was a habit already. As Damien swung the MGF through the tall security gates and up the drive to the Keep, they saw the old blue Mini parked to the side.

'The housekeeper.' He swore softly, fervently.

Karen touched his arm. 'Every woman deserves a holiday. I have plans for Christine.'

She came out to welcome them, small in her floral dress, with smiles that were mostly for Damien. 'Martin rang, to let me know your plans. Mrs Glass, you must be tired from coming all that way. I've got both rooms ready, done the shopping, and supper's on the table whenever you want it.'

'How very kind, going to all this trouble. Will you do one more thing for me? I'm used to being called Karen and would be much more comfortable with that. All right?'

She looked flustered. 'I'll try to remember, then.'

'Damien.' Karen turned away from him, her voice edged as if with a slight dislike. 'Perhaps you'd better deal with what we were talking about. Now, Christine, did you mention supper?'

Over the meal, Damien got chatting with her, softening her up. She had a sister living in the Lake District. It must be fantastic there, at this time of year. Did she often visit? Had she taken a vacation yet? Christine seemed immune to hints. 'I want you to take a break while Harry's away,' Karen told her at last. 'When he gets back, you'll be needed much more than now.'

'What would I be doing with a holiday?' the housekeeper protested. 'And how would you manage? No, I couldn't.'

'Christine, we all want to see the roses in your cheeks. Martin was saying so, the other day.'

'Was he, indeed.' For the first time, her stubbornness faltered. 'But even if you managed, the house would still need cleaning. I can't let it go to a ruin.'

'Of course not,' Damien agreed quickly. 'And it would be hard, without you.'

'The house can wait until you get back.' Karen had picked up the phone and was busy dialling. She listened. 'Martin? It's me. You did say Christine will be needed from September? Should she take her time off now? She's right here, d'you want to speak to her? Oh, I see.' She rang off. 'He had a call on the other line. But, yes, we want you to take a couple of weeks' leave now. Although we will miss you. And that was a delicious supper, by the way.'

Christine said she would probably go and stay with Lesley, although it was rather short notice and Lesley might have plans. 'I hope you won't have too difficult a time, fending for yourselves in this awkward place.' She showed them the supplies she had got in, and how to work the new blender; then she set off.

They looked at each other. Karen grabbed his hand and pulled Damien up the stairs, into the bedroom. There they stood at the window—back from it a little, in case the housekeeper looked up—and watched her car putter away along the drive. It paused for the slow opening of the security gates, then turned up the road and out of view.

She hugged him, triumphant and gleeful. 'She went pretty easily – you were brilliant.'

'And you're quite an actress. You never spoke to Martin?'

'Of course not. I knew how much you wanted us to be alone. Me, too. Look how special, how ordinary we are now. A real bed. A house to ourselves.' Karen smoothed the summer duvet. There was no sign, no scrap of Harry visible in the room. Damien drew the curtains closed as she switched on the bedside lamp, in a familiar, completely new ritual. 'Which side of the bed do you like?'

'Whatever side you're on.'

She began to undress him, to slip off his shoes, caressing him. 'Do you snore?'

'Do you want to find out?'

She laughed. He leaned over, picked her up. Now she lay with her pale limbs spread out, across a kingsize expanse of deep blue. He kissed her neck and throat, unfastened the buttons of the black silk top she wore. Karen stirred, beginning to ease out of it. 'Oh, no,' he murmured, 'keep that on.' He stroked her with a gossamer touch, through the fine fabric, sliding it across the swell of her breasts and releasing them, kissing her erect nipples. 'Keep just that on. You look radiant, wicked. Irresistible.'

They were almost naked, tuned to each other, pulsing to the same insistent beat. He delayed, his kisses wandering, grazing over her soft skin, and marvelling. He sensed that if he pushed into her, thrust them towards what he wanted, then she would be hurt, and retreat. And he loved her. He could feel the wetness inside her, under his hand. The life sap, and the springy, tight desire in her flesh: she was longing for him.

Damien rolled on to his back, and stretched out there. 'You can do anything you like, with me.'

She knelt, pleasuring and cherishing him, his maleness and strength, the phallus that reared before her, that was for her. He was close to coming, as she crouched across, and slid his cock inside her. She held him there, warm and good, pleasure trickling and rippling through them both, from the good, the beautiful phallus. Surely, it could always have been like this? Until she moved gently, and with a groan he thrust against her, and instantly she grew tight, rigid with terror. Now, he knew he was a knife inside her, sawing or tearing, monstrously destroying. He was hate, not love and not tenderness, as she cried out with fear and pain.

He spoke her name. 'This is me – Karen, my love.'

She opened her eyes and saw his face, his watching expression. Coming back into present time, she seemed to feel nothing, to be frozen, until tears welled up. 'How can I ever give to you?'

'You want to run before we've even walked,' he chided, warm.

They lay beside each other, holding, stroking. 'But I may never really recover,' she said, in a voice of despair. 'And you deserve the best of loving.'

'I've got that.' He kissed her. 'We've all this time to learn about each other – you'll get to trust me, honey. But when I think about the guy who did that to you . . .'

They were silent, each thinking about Alistair Quentin; now he was in the bed with them. Outside they could hear the sea lapping. From the depths to the shore, it murmured about things that could never be known. Damien went on, 'I called Quentin's wife last week, to check what had happened to him. Amanda told me he's cruising the Med – and she has no contact number for him. He's split.'

'I'm sure he's dead.' Karen sat up. She seemed cold, pulling the edges of the sheet around her. 'I think Harry killed him. Years ago he left Tanya to die, knowing she'd taken an overdose. Before that, your mother's suicide – after he'd left.'

'It's like Harry's culpability has escalated through the years. He's real sick, Karen.' Damien jumped up. He stood beside the bed, and took her hands. 'What happens to us? He'll find out, he's sure to. We must go. Just leave, together, now. We've got to!'

He saw his own horror reflected in her face. She had caught it: they were looking into their future. 'How? Where could we go that he wouldn't find us? We've no money, and couldn't get far. He'd find you – because you're his son. Harry is vengeful and vicious. When I ran away, I knew then that he'd never give up. Damien, we'd be living in fear, in hiding, and I couldn't do that to you. Not that.'

He turned away from her, crossed to the tall window that overlooked the sea. Karen got up and stood behind him, holding his naked body against her own. 'We've got each other. And we'll find a way. Look at the moon, tracking over the ocean. We must forget about Harry, about all of them. Right now, this is our world.'

It became a pact to make up their own world, for as long as they could be together. Harry no longer existed, and no one else could enter this time. They lived each moment vividly, as everything ordinary was heightened by sharing. If she couldn't leave with him, then this was all they had.

The house was theirs. They slept and made love in the giant bed, in the master bedroom, waking to the cries of seabirds, rolling surf, the cool salt air of day beginning. From the quiet kitchen, they took meals out to the terrace, overlooking that changing infinity of sea and sky. Somehow, Damien was never sure if they were alone in the house or garden. There were other people who might have keys, or know the pass code to get in. The local police, including Hargreaves, could walk in if they wanted to.

Wherever they went, people who knew Harry could be watching. Avoiding the beach, the village and lanes, they shopped in supermarkets in the town. After a couple of days, Karen suggested taking the boat along the coast. 'There are quiet beaches, and no one knows us.'

They packed food and drink for the day, and took the dinghy from the boatshed. Damien rowed out between children, beach balls and inflatable beds, through swimmers and pedalos, strayed from the resort. Beyond it all, bobbing on deep water, they looked back at the narrow strand of crowd and heard cries, soft and distant, as if from people who were submerged. The sun bounced off the sea's surface, sharp, polished as a knife.

He started the outboard and took the tiller, cutting through choppy green waves. The gulls, noisily following, abandoned them as they turned in to land. There were low dunes here, backed by water meadows that stretched for miles. The beach, of shingle and sand, appeared quite empty.

The day passed too quickly, as they picnicked and swam. He noticed an empty flagpole and warning signs, unreadably pitted and holed, by stones he supposed. They were hidden among the dunes, sleepy from sun and salt air, lying close together and kissing, when the world exploded.

Four gunshots, close by and deafening, then silence. Instinctively he had rolled over to shield her with his body. Welded together, they heard the silence lengthen, stretching out. He raised his head to listen.

The emptiness that had welcomed them was sinister now. He stood, like a target. They were the only moving creatures, scanning the dunes and the uninhabited sea, the marshlands with their fretwork of ditches.

'There's nobody around,' she said. 'But it sounded so near.'

He was certain, terse. 'That was very close by. Someone was here.'

'I think these are army practice ranges – but they fly a red flag, when there's any danger.'

'That was a shotgun. The army, firing a shotgun here?'

'So, someone went after a rabbit. But these are meant to be wildlife reserves. They've gone, anyway.'

Their mood, the solitude, was broken now. 'Shall we go back?'

Karen shrugged. 'There's no need to. I feel safe with you.'

He turned sharply towards her. 'How can you feel safe with an ex-junkie? An ex-prisoner?'

'Easily.' She traced his frown, his eyebrows drawn in disbelief. 'People change. I know who you are now, whatever the past.'

After a minute, he asked, 'Did Harry tell you? The things I did, back then?'

Karen nodded. 'You stole. Went to jail, and got paroled.'

She had said it so matter-of-factly. 'I pulled a gun on a guy, at a liquor store.'

'Was the gun loaded?'

'The guy thought it was – he thought he was dead.' He saw the punk fall to his knees, face wide with terror. Kneeling there, pissing himself as he begged for his life. He felt shame. 'I robbed a gas station and got pulled in later. That saved me. Heroin was costing hundreds of dollars each day. I'd have done anything. Anything.'

'You never harmed anyone,' she reminded him.

'Who's to say I wouldn't have? Karen, I don't know, so how can you?'

'We can't always do what's right. Look at the life you'd had. I trust you,' she said.

He felt a fierce pleasure, a pride mingling with despair – because he couldn't trust, didn't know himself any more. The life he had grown up in seemed bleakly distant to him now. She had lit things up in a new way: he looked back at shadows, a lack of the real and the warm, and those things he had done. 'Of course I harmed people.'

They motored back to the Keep. It was evening, cool, and the beach had been deserted by its visitors. Waves lapped at the shore, washing a million footprints from the sand. They tied the boat at the jetty then went through the garden to a house that lay in gloom, almost dark, and he flooded the rooms with light, drew curtains against the night outside. She put on a CD and began to dance with him in the kitchen, her head on his shoulder as they moved, slow. Seconds ticked loudly, in a pause in the music, from the clock on the wall.

'Whatever happens,' she said, 'it has been worth everything.'

Drawing him up the stairs, in the big blue bed, she seemed insatiable in pleasing him: as if time was counting against them but could be slowed down, and evil warded off, from inside a circle of lovemaking. Perhaps she was right. Through the dark hours, nothing existed beyond his senses. The scent of her skin and hair, mossy and warm, animal, and the heat between her thighs as he went into her, that melted and re-formed, fired him. The stretch of her body, an arc of pleasure taut against him, moving inside his own enclosing limbs, while her tongue touched his core, sparked and fused them into one. Her soft sounds of pleasure, from deep in her throat, rose and paused then quickened, sang in their own rhythms. She wanted him inside her again: he lay over her, stretched out her arms and wound their bodies so close, they were one body, her legs wrapped around his thighs, his shaft pushed tight against her swollen bud. He needed this, to inhabit and possess, thrusting and digging, becoming a cave-man, a tunnelling explorer. Rocking them, sliding into the hot, seeping volcano, they were swimming inside. Through the night, slaves to their ten senses. She came twice. He was counting.

In the morning, he left her sleeping late, and went down to the kitchen to make coffee. Filling the kettle, turning off the tap, he heard the front door opening.

Damien cracked down the kettle, strode into the hall. Light was flooding in from the opened door. Silhouetted there – stopped dead, maybe from surprise at seeing him – stood a tall, burly guy. He was ginger-haired and unshaven, older than himself, wore a leather jerkin, jeans and cap-sleeved vest; his forearms were covered in tattoos. A brute, an animal of worked muscles and heavy, almost idiot jaw: there was something slightly familiar.

'You must be Damien Glass.'

'Who the hell are you, just walking in?'

'Force of habit. Should've thought to ring the bell – my apologies. My name's Joe Taylor, I came by to do the collection. Maintenance, servicing – the antique weapons, you know.'

'You're Christine Taylor's son?'

'That's right, mate. Shall I go ahead, then?'

He remembered the snapshot on Christine's mantelpiece. It had been taken some years ago, and her son was heavier now. Damien felt tension drain out of his body: his hands had been fisted, his jaw and shoulders clamped. 'Right. I don't know Harry's arrangements.'

'I help out Mother, as a favour to old Harry, really. Because she's got the arthur–itis, plus she don't like guns and stuff. But I give 'em a rub. Oil 'em up. You know.' He gave a wink, and turned to close the front door. He wore a shotgun, slung over his back.

Damien paced forward, his voice rough with violence. 'What's that for?'

'What – this?' Joe Taylor's voice was silvery with innocence. 'Oh, you know. Take out a few rabbits, a pigeon for the pot. From among the bushes.'

Harry's Brigsea mafia. He stared, right up close, into those little eyes, that thug face. 'Yesterday. Were you out shooting?'

'Yesterday? I believe in yesterday. I might've. Look, watch it,' he complained suddenly. 'There's no need for that, getting difficult with me. Harry and me, we got enough of an

200

understanding, and there's such a thing as loyalty. People around here, they've got respect for Harry.' He paused, and a long look passed between them. 'So, do I work down the cellars today, or not?'

Christine Taylor's son – well in with Harry, and all the local people – must have been at the army range yesterday, must have seen them together. Or had he? Watching his expression, hawk-like, Damien began to ask, 'Did you know – my father's wife, she's staying here—?'

'That's not my business, is it?' Joe interrupted. His face was bland as an eggshell, his voice had gone flat. 'I can mind my own – if I take a liking to people, that is. It depends.' He was polite, and friendly suddenly. 'Not sure what I call you – Mr Glass? Junior?'

'Damien. She wasn't – we weren't – expecting anyone.'

'Damien, that's nice,' Joe said, deferentially. 'I can see it's not convenient, so I won't disturb you today, then. Like I said, I should've rung but forgot. I forgot you were both here. Mother's up at the Lakes or she would've reminded me. Cheerio, then, Damien. See you around.'

He went out. From the front steps, Damien watched him walk down the drive, pausing at the gate, turning off along by the sea. Had it been him, firing the shots? If it had been – even if he had seen them, lying there together, kissing – he didn't seem about to tell anyone. He had seemed OK.

Going back upstairs, Damien saw Karen was still asleep. Perhaps he wouldn't tell her, wouldn't worry her about it, not unless she mentioned the gunshots again. Watching her, he felt a tenderness that opened up inside him, welling through his chest, his throat. He had swallowed a sea of bitterness, right the way through his life. She, the alchemist, had started turning it all into something sweet.

It was a temporary, fragile world, Karen knew that. Some day, not far off, Harry would come back and everything would end. That was unthinkable, unreal. But it took an effort now, not to allow Harry to creep into her mind and get a hold. It was late, towards the end of August.

Day on day, she had felt trust growing, pushing through. Damien seemed different, and peaceful, no longer at war with the world. She could not imagine life without him. As he filled her consciousness, she learned how to glory in her physicality and strength, to become her own senses and live in that luxury. He had unlocked her heart, casually, along with her sexuality.

There had been a number of phone calls. Martin rang frequently, and people wanting Harry, expecting him to be there. DCI Hargreaves' wife, Joan, had left a couple of neighbourly messages. One morning, about to leave for a drive up the coast, they heard the phone switch itself to record. Joan Hargreaves' voice sounded across the hall, and Karen started towards the machine. 'I have to get that.'

Damien was half-way out of the door. 'Why? Leave it.'

'She'd wonder too much.' Picking up the phone, she was exchanging greetings, like remembering how to speak a foreign language.

'You're so isolated there, we've been worrying about you,' Joan said. 'Is all well?'

'Not too bad.' Karen turned her back on Damien, to try to find the right downbeat tone. 'Of course, it's a bit lonely,' she added, without thinking.

'I'll come right over, and we'll have elevenses,' the detective's wife decided. 'No, I won't hear another word. We're so close by car, really. I'll bring something that you asked for.'

Karen put down the phone, and met Damien's eye. 'It would look peculiar to keep avoiding the neighbours. She'll be here in fifteen minutes. What'll we do?' If Joan saw them together she would know at once, they were crazy about each other. It was too late for pretending. 'You must go out somewhere. And don't come back till you see her car's gone.'

Distractedly, she rushed around the ground floor, the bathroom and kitchen, checking there were no giveaways. Thinking up things to say, ordinary small talk as an alibi, she caught sight of herself in the mirror. She was too vibrant: Joan Hargreaves would only have to take one look. She had to tame and restrain herself.

Flying upstairs, Karen burrowed through clothes in her wardrobe, looking for something drab in which to hide herself. She stopped in surprise. Among the few frocks, jeans and shirts, was the black silk top she had worn travelling from France, and making love here for the first time. She had left it in the laundry box, surely. As she drew it from the wardrobe, she saw it had been slashed to ribbons.

She went cold with fear. The silk bore none of her old scent, it was clean and pressed. Someone – *but who and how?* – had come here and laundered the blouse she had worn, making love with Damien. *But why, how did they know?* They had pressed it carefully, before cutting it to shreds, with something like a razor.

Karen sank down on the edge of the bed. Who could have done that? Was it to frighten her off? There had been the anonymous calls, from a woman, then a man. But who could have got in? Christine Taylor? Martin, perhaps? Had someone been spying on them, from that first night? This was a warning, like the phone calls had been. Someone knew.

The front doorbell rang. She sprang into reflex action, stuffing the torn silk into a deepest corner of the wardrobe. Pulling on a baggy T-shirt, she ran downstairs and opened the door. Joan's kindly face looked up at her. 'I let myself in at the gate to save you the trouble. Look, I've brought some cuttings from the scarlet Busy Lizzie.'

She must have looked blank, before remembering. She had admired the Hargreaves' pot plants, months ago, a lifetime ago. 'That's kind. You must tell me again how to root them.' They went through to the kitchen. 'Would you like coffee?'

'I'd prefer tea, if that's no bother. I've brought some Rich Tea biscuits, just in case you're low. So is Harry still abroad?'

'For a bit longer, yes. Do sit down.' She busied herself with teacups and milk jug, and tried to recover her old identity. 'How's Colin?'

'He's been off duty with flu. In this hot weather – imagine. I haven't had it. How are you keeping? You look rather peaky, if I dare say so. Missing Harry?'

'It does seem a long time.' Karen smiled, putting the biscuits on a plate. 'But poor Colin. I expect you're busy looking after him?'

'He can be rather a baby, when he gets ill. But don't ever say that I said so. He does get under my feet.' Karen made a sympathetic sound. 'I'm sure I saw Harry's son at the petrol station the other day. He didn't see me. He was filling up a snazzy-looking car. Harry gave him that, I think.'

'That's right,' she said, heart thudding with danger. 'He's around sometimes.'

'He's a very attractive boy, isn't he? I thought Harry said he was studying in America. He seems to have been in Brigsea all summer.'

'They do seem to get a lot of time off. Do you take milk and sugar, Joan? Are you enjoying the sun?'

She listened to her neighbour's gentle complaints, and traded a few, but that was difficult. It was still new, this sense of power in her own body, a strength inside herself. She could scarcely remember how it had been – those old feelings of weakness and victimhood. Listening to Joan, she thought how quickly she could learn again to deny her sexuality, her life's energy. By suppressing herself, woman could repress the world, other women and men. For exploring her own eroticism, for being fulfilled, she would be condemned and isolated.

As soon as Damien came back, Karen insisted they get out. She felt close to screaming. 'Let's go as far away as possible, somewhere anonymous.'

They drove to Brighton, and spent the rest of the day among the crowds, on the seafront and wandering through The Lanes. Walking near the Royal Pavilion, Karen thought she saw Harry's car, the sleek and elegant lines of the black XJ12 slipping past them and away. It was heading east. She never saw who the driver was, and didn't have time to look at the registration.

'That was not him,' Damien told her. She wasn't so sure, but he insisted, 'Each time we've visited, I've seen Jags in this town. That was just another of them.'

Of course it couldn't be Harry. He was safely in Italy. Relaxing again, they decided to stay and have dinner before driving back.

It was late evening and had been dark for a couple of hours when they sped along the road home. Turning up the lane towards the Keep, ahead they saw the lamp tower, then the squat form of the house. Its windows were lit.

Damien stopped, a little distance before the gates. 'Did we leave the timer system on?'

'No. I don't think we did.'

Damien got out, walked up to the gates and looked through. He stood there a while, before coming back, swearing softly. His face was white and harsh. 'Harry's car – it's in the driveway.'

11

Harry. Flown in like a vulture, blotting out the summer, just waiting to pick them apart. She got out of the car. Damien took hold of her arm, still in its T-shirt sleeve, voluminous, virgin white: how appropriate. 'Come on. We must go.'

But if they left – the two of them – or went in together, then Harry would kill his son. 'No. Just think for a minute. It might be only Martin.'

'Martin would've called first. We've got to tough it out.'

'Can't you see? Everything has to change, now. He mustn't suspect anything – you know that, you know why.' She felt in despair. 'So just let me go.'

His jaw jutted, stubborn. 'I won't let you go in alone.'

Harry might come out of the house. He could even be close by and hear them. Her eyes raked the dark gardens ahead, and the lane where they stood. A rustling sound – the breeze, maybe, in the long grass, or a sigh of the sea over rocks – and she stepped nearer again, to Damien. 'If we go in together, they'll know at once, they'll see. What do we do then, ever to be safe again? Harry must not guess. Listen, Martin won't let anything happen. If you're not around, no one can suspect. Nobody's seen your car. If they ask, I'll say you've been out seeing the sights. It's the only way.'

'I can't do that.' In the headlights, he looked bled of life or warmth.

'I'm not giving you any option,' she argued crisply, making her voice cold. 'You're not to come in the house. That would be

206

the worst thing for us – the worst for me,' she added, with emphasis. 'Get your car out of sight – to the other side of the village, at least. We'll meet tomorrow, below the jetty. I'll find Martin and say I've just been for a walk. Get your car out of here, fast.'

'Harry won't know anything.' He was giving in to her reasoning. 'And Martin's there.' Was it said to comfort or convince them both? He started to turn away, and she caught him up in one last, hurried kiss, a hug. 'Tomorrow, then. But I'll be around –'

'Don't hang about. Go now.'

He vanished into the dark. She went through the gate and stood waiting, listening. The powerful engine of the MGF growled quietly, reversing, drifting away in a mist of sound up the road, its friendly lights tiny, extinguished. Then she was alone. There was no sound from the house as she began to walk up the drive, footsteps soft as she could make them, rehearsing her story. A stroll along the beach, then watching the sun go down, chatting with the group of fishermen a bit further along as it got dark and they cast their lines. Hooked their bait. Would Harry swallow that? Would Martin? If she said Damien had been away, Martin would know that she was lying. She must be vague, say he went this morning, maybe say they still couldn't get along? Could that sound true? She must seem ordinary, everyday. Could she seem pleased to see him?

The Jaguar, metallic jaws and glittering body, crouched close to the front steps, dwarfing her as she slipped past. Its engine was cool. How many hours could they have been back? Without Damien, without transport, how far could she say she had walked – for, maybe, up to seven hours? Perhaps she had called in on Joan? But Harry might check. Why didn't Martin warn us? she thought irrationally.

She let herself in, and at once sensed something different, something indefinable about the place. Harry's bags, familiar matching cream leather, were waiting near the foot of the stairs. And the heavy tapestry-weave rug that ran across the tiles of the hall was pulled crooked, rucked at one side. But it wasn't that.

The house was too silent. Lit and empty: waiting or listening. For her.

She stood still. Harry's luggage . . . Why hadn't Martin taken it straight upstairs, as he always did? But, then, if he had . . .

Karen took the stairs two at a time, quietly up to the bedroom. Damien's things, his clothes were on the floor, on Harry's bedside chair. Bundling them up under her arm, punching at the pillow where his head had lain, she cast frantically about the room. A paperback, a US thriller. A glass of water, half full, on the wrong side of the bed. How could they have become so careless, and sure of themselves, of privacy? At the bedroom door she waited, listening, then swiftly, silently, crossed the landing, stuffed his clothes into a corner of the guest room, out of sight to anyone just glancing in. She was dizzy with fear, sick with it. What now? She must think of a reason why Damien's clothes – and his night things – had been in Harry's bedroom, along with hers. She nearly laughed aloud, almost hysterical. What could she possibly say?

But Martin hadn't brought the bags up yet. He hadn't seen. And, quite likely, Harry hadn't come upstairs either, not yet. So, get calm. Down the stairs, as if she had just walked in, casual. They would be in the kitchen or the living room with music on or watching the news. There was a red light on the answerphone. She switched it on. Martin's voice, suddenly too loud in the hall, so ordinary, except . . .

'Hello there. Martin. It's just after noon on Friday. Thought I'd let you know, Harry's in from Italy and is on his way down. He's taking in a meeting, and I have to stay and look after things in the office –'

She never heard the rest of the message. Harry was here, and she was alone with him. He could have – he probably had – gone into the bedroom and seen . . . The click of the machine reversing itself echoed like a shot through the hall, through her mind. Why had they assumed Martin would be here? Harry had been to a meeting, or was in one, and had been too busy to go upstairs. He suspected nothing. But she couldn't bear this waiting, this silence. Where was he?

She took a deep breath and called, 'Harry! Where are you? I'm back.'

There was no answering voice, he didn't appear. Slowly, she crossed to the living room, its door wide open. The dimmer lights were on, and something moving caught her eye. The TV, with its sound turned down. Harry had been working in here, then. She went over to the alcove where he kept his desk. The drawer in the middle was open, and two brandy balloons, used and empty, were nearby. He'd had a visitor. Might they still be around, and Harry be friendly and charming when he saw her? Her hopes lifted. Absently, she picked up the two glasses, and went to turn off the TV. A familiar face, being interviewed: it was O. J. Simpson, talking about his innocence. She switched off.

It was late, almost eleven by now – she could see the kitchen clock. The teacups still stood by the dishwasher, from Joan's morning visit. Martin had rung around noon so Harry might have arrived here before two. What could she say she had been doing for such a long time?

He was nearby, she could feel that. His car was still here, and Harry never walked anywhere. Could he have gone for a run in the dark? It seemed the only explanation. Then, what if he had seen her drive up with Damien – and Damien leaving? They had kissed. What could she say? Or perhaps Harry's guest had taken him for a meal somewhere. He would be back, and all might be well. But she could feel his presence, disturbing, close. The house felt odd, eerie, with some difference.

'Harry!' she called again, suddenly angry now. 'Where are you?' Her own voice mocked her. Right, she thought. He'll turn up when he does, and I'll deal with it. A weariness began to seep over her. She checked through the rooms again, living room, kitchen; then the utility room, the downstairs cloakroom. No Harry. She would go and freshen up, and change perhaps, but she wouldn't go to bed. Upstairs to the bathroom. The door open, she washed her face and hands, splashing the cool, cleansing water over her neck and throat.

There was a footstep behind her. She whirled round. Harry

looked dishevelled, as if he had been running in day clothes. His face was lined with fatigue, glistening with sweat and the silver hair, always carefully groomed, was uncombed. He had a strange, alert expression, with a strained smile. 'I wondered where you were,' he said, lightly. 'Do I get a little kiss?'

Revulsion tightened her throat, as she touched her lips to a cheek that felt cold, slimy over-pampered leather. This was so false. He smelled of the distinctive soap he used – and of some vestige of basic emotion. Was it fear?

'Where have you been?' she asked quickly in turn, to deflect him. Her voice sounded too abrupt. She tried to smile back at him, but caught her own grimace in the bathroom mirror. She looked white and sharp, poised for something.

'Out for a bit. I've had a day of travelling.'

'You had a meeting, too? It must've been important. You must be wiped out, Harry. It's late, and I think we should get straight to bed.'

She edged past him, nervously, remembering past times. On the landing, freer, she glanced back, and saw him sway like a drugged bull. He had been drinking. What should she do? Get him to sleep, somehow. Don't undress, she thought. Don't get trapped. Her anxiety sparked, fused with guilt. Keep him talking, get him to bed, to sleep. 'You've had a few brandies. I wonder how many? Come on, Harry, get undressed. Or why not just lie down? You know, Martin said you shouldn't drink . . .' Prattling on, defensiveness making an odd aggression in her voice. She stopped, drew a breath. His eyes looked fixed. Might Harry be ill?

'Don't ever attempt to patronise me, Karen.' His tone was cold, ugly now.

'But you look awful. And, at your age, you shouldn't strain your heart. Just get to bed, come on. Did you fly from Corsica?' She tried to be conversational, light.

'From Sicily. Si–ci–ly, Karen, is where I've been working. How your thoughts must've dwelt on me, obviously. Now I come to think about it, how extremely well you're looking. Unusually – glowing, almost. During my absence, you've been enjoying yourself – indulging yourself, I take it?'

'I've been – taking care of things here.'

'Taking care of what, Karen? If all I hear is true, I know very well why you came back. What you came here – without me – for.'

For a precious couple of seconds, she couldn't answer. Moments passing rapidly between them, when he must have seen her guilt. 'I don't know what you mean,' she said coolly. 'I'm sorry if you've had a summer of strain while I've been on the beach, like everyone here.' But she knew exactly what he meant. Harry had found out, or someone had told him. Why else would he turn up here, unexpectedly early and unannounced? Or maybe he had guessed but wasn't quite sure – that's why he was being so strange with her. He seemed like a clockwork toy, trying to go through the same old routine. He seemed old suddenly, or perhaps she had just forgotten the way he was. She had grown used to Damien. Harry's bullying tone, that had used to cow her – she could not, would not tolerate it now, that egocentric whine underneath, violence waiting to erupt. He might try to kill her, but she felt strong, and heady with recklessness.

Harry had taken a step towards her. Karen glanced quickly around. Lying on the chest, by the bedroom door, was his spare mobile phone.

'I can see it in your face,' he said.

'What, Harry? What do you want to see, that would satisfy you?'

'I've been betrayed –'

She cut his words short, with a flood, a great release of pent-up hatred. 'You are unbearable. A self-deluding, ugly old pig, miserable to be with. You think you can buy people, then abuse them. I'm sick of your bullying! The threats, all this controlling stuff you do. How lonely to be Harry Glass – but I don't pity you, I despise you. I'm not for sale, I never was. And, yes, you've frightened me, like you frighten everyone – when you're not busy charming us all instead. You're sick, Harry, you don't know how to be with people.'

'I have done rather well,' he said. He was smiling at her, perfectly lucid, suddenly sober. 'And now, you common little guttersnipe, remember yourself and shut up.'

She took a deep breath. 'I'm leaving you.'

His odd smile was wiped away. 'I think not. Because of a tiff? Why ever would you want to do that? When you have everything.'

'I don't love you. You're evil, a monster, Harry. You don't know what love is. I'm leaving. So divorce me. I don't want any—'

'I would never give you that satisfaction. I never break my word — haven't you learned that by now? I said before, I will never let you go. Not ever. Although I have picked the world's worst wife, God help me. Did she ever give one ounce of support?'

'You've never begun to let me be myself—'

'Yourself? Don't make me laugh. A cauldron, a hell of faults and shortcomings, bad habits. I did try to help—'

'It won't work now, Harry. All that scrutinising, criticising, trying to reduce me – I'm immune. I woke up. So let me go.'

'So keen to leave,' he mused. 'One can't help but wonder why.' An edge crept into his voice. 'What's the new attraction, Karen?'

She bit back more words. 'It's over between us.'

'How self-deluding! It will never be over. Such a pretty little – whore. Dirty bitch.'

Karen backed off, towards the dressing table. 'I'm tired of your jealousy – it's too loud, it goes on too much, it doesn't ring true.' She heard herself ask, 'What've you been doing, that you're hiding?' So unwisely, she was challenging him. 'You're hiding something from me. Or is it someone?' He had stopped in his tracks. She snatched up the hand mirror. It was silver-framed, ornate and heavy, and she grasped it tight behind her back. 'Don't come any nearer, Harry.'

'I'll come as near as I like – and you will do what I say. Come on, haven't you had enough? I thought you'd learned a little, improved slightly.'

She could smell his brandy breath, see the red veins standing out in his eyes. If he touched her, she would strike.

Harry reached out a finger, pointed. 'What is that, on your neck? Those small bruises. Don't lie to me.'

He waited for her to speak. She said nothing. He recoiled slightly, then unfurled his arm, his fist and weight, to punch like a piston at her stomach. She ducked to the side, and his knuckles glanced off her ribs. Screaming with rage, she raised the mirror and brought it down, the silver case striking his skull: it seemed to bounce off, Harry staggered slightly and she darted past, grabbed the mobile and ran out to the landing. Something was plucking at her back – Harry's hand, seeming nerveless – and she caught a glimpse of his shocked face. Pushing him off like something inert, into the bathroom, slamming, she shot home the bolt. Strong brass, best quality, nothing but the best. Would it hold? He was shoving, rattling the door against its hinges. The phone slid out of her shaking hands, on to the tiles. She crouched, listened, got the dialling tone. She punched out 999.

'Are you trying to make me break the bloody door down?' he shouted. 'You're mad! You want certifying! What're you up to?'

'Police,' she told the emergency operator. She improvised, 'My husband tried to kill me. Harry Glass, at the Keep, Sea Lane in Brigsea. Quickly, quickly, please.'

Behind the door, Harry had grown quiet. He must have heard her making the call. She could almost hear him thinking, as the silence went on. Then he knocked at the door. 'Come along – come on out of there.' Then, less certainly, 'What have you done? You stupid little fool.'

Silence. Was he waiting for her to open the door? She began to think that he must have crept away. She sat down, on the carved oak shelf that ran around the bath, and stared at the dizzying patterns of tiles. Ten minutes passed before she heard voices from the drive outside.

It must be the police, arriving without any siren. Cautiously, she unlocked the door and went downstairs. She saw, with relief, the two police officers, a man and a woman. Harry had shown them into the living room as if they were guests, and he turned to greet her courteously. He was playing the charm card – the distinguished, ill-used citizen – and he seemed completely sober.

'Here's Karen, she's decided to join us. May I introduce Sergeant Bill Waits and Constable Ann Fielding. Perhaps you'd like a drink, darling? I'd offer you both something, but . . .'

'We're on duty, sir.'

'Tea, perhaps. Darling, could you—'

'My husband attacked me,' she said, ignoring Harry. 'He's done it before. He tried to kill me.'

There was a pause, uncomfortable. 'Sounds a little melodramatic, doesn't it?' Harry said. 'Dear Karen, I must find her a new acting role before too long. We had an argument, I must confess. My wife started screaming blue murder, and locked herself in the bathroom.'

'Harry punched me.'

'Do you have an injury?' Fielding asked, embarrassed, apologetic towards Harry.

Karen rolled up her T-shirt, to show a mark spreading across her ribs. Harry peered over the WPC's shoulder. 'I can't see anything – but then, you did barge into that dressing table.'

'She seems to be all right,' the sergeant agreed with him, easily. 'Well, you know, couples will always have the odd row.'

'I've just arrived, all the way from Italy,' Harry said in a vexed, weary tone. 'I expected a welcome, at my own house. Instead, she flew at me in a terrible rage. Such a temper! Karen hit me with a mirror – it had glass in.' He pulled up his right sleeve. Along his forearm there stretched a two-inch scratch, oozing blood.

'That might be deep. Is there glass in it?' Waits asked, concerned.

'We can see who's been attacked here,' Fielding added.

Three accusing pairs of eyes turned on her. Karen stared back in confusion. 'Are you sure . . . Did I do that?' She tried to remember if the mirror had broken. She had no memory of flying glass, but it had all happened quickly, and she had been in a panic.

'I won't hold it against her,' Harry told them, affable, magnanimous. 'These things, as you said, do happen. And we have to let bygones be bygones,' he added, with a glance at Karen.

'Yes,' approved Waits. 'We get these calls all the time, sir. We calm things down, let tempers cool. Make sure there'll be no more trouble.'

'Quite. We have our differences, but so does everyone. Remember that, sweetheart.'

The sergeant added, in a deferential tone, 'I saw you on ITV last month, sir.'

Harry glowed a little. 'And did you enjoy the film?'

'Very much. And my brother—'

The front doorbell rang. 'I'd better get that. It seems late for a visitor. Excuse me,' Harry said, and went out.

Harry looked at the two police officers. Waits was taking in the furnishings, Harry's shelves of leather-bound books, the antique chairs with their rich upholstery. 'A nice place,' he said admiringly. 'I've always wondered what it was like inside.'

'I like the fireplace. Does that make a lot of work?' Fielding asked. 'But then, you have Christine Taylor to look after things.'

'Listen,' she tried, without much hope. 'Harry did attack me. And it's not the first time—'

'But you provoked him, didn't you?' the WPC said, slightly coolly. 'In my experience, trouble can usually be avoided, if you want to avoid it. He's an important man around here. I'm sure he wouldn't —'

'Yes, I can see that he is.'

Karen gave up. Unsurprised by now, she heard Colin Hargreaves' voice from the hall. The Chief Inspector came in with Harry. 'I heard that Harry had a spot of bother. But it seems all is well, after all.'

Harry reassured him. 'Nothing to worry about, Colin. I'm sorry you were troubled.'

'Just checking to see you were all right.'

'I must apologise, this call was unnecessary. Taking your officers away from their work, when we all know how hard

215

pressed you are, and the terrific job you do in the community.'

Colin Hargreaves nodded. Waits began moving towards the hall, and Fielding followed. 'All seems OK, so we'll get back to the station. We can see ourselves out,' the sergeant added. 'Good night. Good night, sir.'

'Thank you,' said Harry, pleasantly. 'Good night.' As they went out, he turned to the senior officer. 'Colin, my friend, it's almost one in the morning. I've just travelled from southern Italy, you know. And your night's sleep has been disturbed. I do appreciate your concern. A nightcap?'

'A small one, perhaps. Thanks, Harry, and then I'll be on my way. Joan woke, too.'

Harry went out. Karen, forgotten, saw Hargreaves' attention turn back to her. She decided to try, for one last time, telling the truth.

'Mr Hargreaves,' she said, and went to where he had sat down by the empty fireplace. 'Chief Inspector. My husband tried to kill me.' He said nothing, watching her closely, and she thought she could read scepticism gathering in his expression. 'It happened before. This is the third time he's attacked me. If you don't believe that, then you must have some idea, surely – that he was responsible for Tanya's death?'

Then she saw how angry he was, and just how coldly he felt towards her. 'I would advise you to be very careful what you allege,' Hargreaves answered, quietly. 'That death was most carefully investigated. I can only wonder at your own motives in saying these things. Shut up,' he hissed, as Karen opened her mouth to argue. He leaned forward. 'You have been seen with someone, a man. There are those . . .' he gestured vaguely, distastefully towards his own throat '. . . those marks, on your neck. You're not worthy of Harry, not by a long chalk. And may we all forgive you, for shaming your husband. You're a disgrace to womanhood, and to this community.'

Karen drew herself up, and looked him straight in the eye. 'How dare you say that to me. How ignorant – and archaic – you are.'

★

216

Towards two in the morning Colin Hargreaves left. Now she was alone with Harry, and fear turned into disgust. He was being fond and reasonable.

'We've missed each other, being apart. I admit it. Darling, come to bed. I ask for nothing, only your kindness. So unkind, what I've been put through. I cannot help it, can't help myself. You're the world to me – don't you know that, sweetheart?'

Her one thought was to get him to sleep because every word he said, every sight of him, grated on her and left her rigid with hatred. He lay on his side, his arms a straitjacket around her body. His breathing deepened, and he began to snore. When his grip around her slackened, she eased out from his bed and he didn't stir. Karen sat on the edge of the mattress, breathing deeply.

Had she injured Harry, or had he faked it to get sympathy from the police? The hand mirror was nowhere to be seen. It must have fallen, after she had struck him and run, but there were no fragments of glass either. Harry must have hidden it, a cherished antique, rather than breaking it himself. He had injured himself to get the police on his side.

He was snoring now. That familiar noise of his sleeping soundly, his easy conscience.

Karen padded downstairs, and poured herself a tumbler of whisky. Its heat spread through her, melting away the terrors of the night. She drained the glass and refilled it, then climbed the stairs. She wanted to watch Harry sleeping. Sitting down in the window seat, she stared at him for a long time, in the faint moonlight, her shadow raking over his grey, fallen face. Now and then he stirred, and once he muttered in some dream.

The strange thought came to her that she should simply kill him. Fetch a knife from the kitchen, or one of the weapons from the cellar. Just put it through his heart, where his heart ought to be. It would be so easy to do.

In her mind, she went through the reasons and provocations, the humiliations and pain, the months of terror she had endured in his home. And then the other lives he had damaged, the premature deaths. Carla, Tanya and Angel: those were the women she had heard about, the ones she knew were dead. Then Quentin. Harry was a murderer, but he would never be caught, never be brought to justice. He would always be on the side of the angels, coming up roses, a favourite, the star. He had no morality, and infected the people with whom he came into contact. Perhaps there was another, natural seeming justice. Why not?

Downstairs in the kitchen, she placed her empty whisky glass carefully by the dishwasher, then took a knife from the rack above the marble chopping block. She went back to the bedroom, to Harry.

He was lying on his back now, breath sighing in, then rasping out. A fish, a great shark, gasping. She thought of his body, his muscular blubber on her, pounding into her and intent on his satisfaction, oblivious to her fear and pain. She turned over the knife she was holding in her two hands. It had a narrow, six-inch, finely serrated blade, sharpened and pointed, riveted into a wooden handle. A chef's knife from France, and the best. It was wet. Tears had been coursing down her face. She wiped them off on her sleeve.

Harry deserved to be dead, like his victims. She thought of other battered wives – news reports she had seen, a book she had read – and of what they had done in the end. A stabbing, a setting fire to the bed, where he lay in a brandied sleep. An end to it all: so simply done. I must be in delayed shock, she thought. But it seemed the most rational thing she could ever do, just to get rid of him, stop him. Nothing and nobody else would. She had the power and could find the strength. Her mind tumbled with reasons, justifications. A life for a life – a good thing to do. She ought to do that, make the choice, and save the world from Harry Glass. So easy, a few seconds, and he would probably never know. Except, she might miss wherever his heart did live. He might feel the same terror that she had felt. There would be blood, it would become real violence. Her mind began to shy away.

But the people, the lives that he had damaged. Damien's life.

And how things could be, right now and in the future, if Harry just didn't exist.

Her mind had turned away from it somehow, from the physical act, blood, and screams. The night was dragging on, and she no longer felt sure what was right, what to do. So as the dawn dulled up, bringing into flatness the land, the sea, she carried the knife stealthily to the kitchen, replacing it exactly as it had been. She would ask Damien what they should do. She crept back to bed, lay on the edge as far from Harry as possible, and slept a little.

In the day's full light, she felt calmer. Unused to drinking, her head throbbed from the whisky. The idea persisted. Did Harry really deserve to go on living? She could not see one redeeming feature, not one genuine, human trait in him. Seeming to have forgotten last night, intent on business, he spent most of the morning talking on the phone. It was easy to slip away without being noticed.

The day had turned into silver and gold, glittering and dazzling, and the sea became a mirror of perfect, unbroken glass. This world could be heaven, she remembered with a jolt, as she went through the garden to the jetty. Down the wooden steps, missing the seventh, the broken one, and her feet stumbled a bit, finding the innocent sand. She rocked from such ordinary beauty, a child calling, groups of bathers further on. An Alsatian dog bounding, barking, up to her and then away. Sheer, pure energy. Light and warmth.

She stepped from the shadow of the jetty. The tide was out, and Damien was sitting on a rock by the shore. Her heart lurched, and she began to run towards him. They had broken all the rules, had transgressed so very far, they were beyond acceptance now. But, inside, she was laughing from certainty. She would have him, whatever the cost, and whatever she had to do.

Some instinct made Damien look up, after all the waiting, and see her running across the sand towards him. He ran to meet her and they held each other. He buried his hands in her hair, her clothes. Seconds later, Karen was pulling away from him.

'I think everyone might know,' she said.

'How? Are you sure?' He looked about them, at the sand, the sea. No one but visitors was around, but here they were almost within sight of the Keep. 'Come back, underneath the jetty.' If it was too late, then he would deal with that, and would almost be glad. If people knew, then she would have to run away with him, there would be nothing else to do. As they reached the shade, leaning together against the greened, barnacled struts of the jetty, he saw how she was looking really sick – and something else, too. Such a wildness, he couldn't recognize her expression.

'What is it? Karen, you're sick, your head's burning.'

'Harry and I, we had a fight.'

He gripped her arms, tight. 'Are you OK?' She nodded. How could he have let that happen to her? But he had thought . . . 'Where was Martin?'

Karen gave a little shrug. 'It's all right. The police came, I called them. They sorted it.'

'I heard a car going by. But I had no idea.'

'Listen,' she said. 'I think we ought to kill Harry. To just get rid of him.'

His mind spun, spiralled out to somewhere. What had she said? She couldn't mean it. 'Say that again.'

'He tried to beat me up.' She sat down suddenly, on the sand. Damien knelt beside her and took her hand, mutely questioning. 'He punched me, and I knew he was going to kill me. And he'd get away with it.' She gave a little laugh. 'Damien, we don't have any choice. Help me.'

But it was him who didn't have any choice, who had to deal with this. Slowly, he got up. 'I want you to wait here for me. Will you?'

'What're you doing?' She stood up and caught at him. 'Don't. We have to think it out. And not be caught.'

'You don't understand, Karen.' He looked at her. She looked like he had been, after Angel's death. 'I have to tell Harry. To warn him – if he ever touches you again, then he'll have me to reckon with.'

'Don't you see that's what he wants? To have us bring it into the open, to give him that excuse? He probably isn't quite sure, not yet. But if you go to him then he'll know for certain.'

He stood still. Reached out a hand, and stroked her hair back from her face. 'Then just come away with me.'

She took his hands in her own. 'Yes – but not yet. Because where could we go, and without any money, that Harry couldn't find us?' Then she seemed suddenly calm, strong. 'We will leave, I promise you. But we have to think how. I've got to go back now or he'll notice I've gone. Damien, promise me you won't come near. Promise.'

He wasn't going to say yes. He nodded.

'It could only be disastrous, you know that. Now his card has been marked with the police here, Harry won't do anything else – not to me. But you must stay out of sight.'

'Then you've got to be real careful and handle him right. Be a mealy-mouth. Yeah?' He gave her a little shake.

'I'll humour him. Where are you sleeping?'

'The boatshed. And if you need me, I'll be here. But –'

Karen put a finger over his lips. 'We'll meet tomorrow. I'll try to come around the same time. I've got to go, now.' She held him tight, then she was gone, feet clattering up to the jetty and overhead.

Then silence. He missed her already, with a dull ache. The night without her, the morning: twenty-four more hours to go.

He had slept on the beach under the stars, with the sea in his dreams. Towards morning it had begun to rain. Chilled, he had broken into the boatshed, twisting off the padlock and splitting the wooden doorframe. Inside were canvas sheets, and shelter, but the concrete floor was cold and that kept him awake, with thoughts of her. Tonight, after dark, he must drag the dinghy up the slipway and into the boatshed, and sleep inside that.

He missed her so much: the hours would drag by, so slowly. It was crazy that they were apart like this – then just a few snatched minutes together. How long could he tolerate it? When he thought about Karen, remembered her touch and her smile, he grew hard, wanting her.

Now he had to think about what she had suggested.

Maybe he owed it, and everything was leading up to this. Maybe it was right, what she said before: that they could never be together or free of fear so long as Harry was still alive. What if Harry attacked her again, or even . . .?

He could not pursue it, his ultimate fear. He groaned at his own futility. What else could he do – except kill Harry for her so that she would finally be safe? The guy deserved it, that was for sure. He had known so before and had tried, had meant to do it then.

But murder his own father? Even to protect her life? Harry had become real to him, and they had got some relationship. He couldn't begin to unravel his thoughts, what he really felt underneath it all. He had stolen the love of his father's wife. Did that make him guilty? Or did he want to yell it out to the whole world? Some pride, a triumph. The guy almost deserved pity. Except for the people he had destroyed.

When he looked at that – and when he thought about Karen, getting hit by Harry last night – it was easy to see the rightness of what she had asked. Harry would only deserve what was coming to him. But there was blood and flesh between them, shared genetics – they were tied, by some profound bond. There had to be another way, any other way. He had recognized his own craziness – just how off balance he had got after finding Angel dead. He couldn't go back to that now. It was through Karen, by loving her, that he had learned to value life, to respect his own and other people's rights. How could he possibly end Harry's life?

And, the more he thought about it, how could he not?

Karen walked back through the garden towards the house. Her steps slowed, then faltered as she got nearer. She sat down on a bench, and stared at the gravel path. Small weeds were sprouting.

There were many ways that people could die suddenly, so many accidents. The human body was so vulnerable. Harry could fall from a high window, from the lamp tower, or their bedroom balcony. Or out running he could have an accident, with no one to see it, on the road. He could drink a household poison accidentally, or let off a gun that was being cleaned. He could drown on a boating trip.

There were a dozen ways that Harry could die, and nobody would suspect her. But every idea – each specific, violent thought – brought with it an image of suffering and destruction, a real sense of horror. The bile rose to her throat.

Then she saw Harry. He was standing on the front steps, looking out, and probably wondering where she had gone.

Harry knew about them. Damien would never be safe again, not unless she . . . Perhaps it was all her fault, for coming between a father and son. Because in a way, surely, she had betrayed them both by preventing their relationship. Watching his suave figure, expensively dressed, beautifully groomed once again, she reminded herself that Harry had destroyed Damien's family. He was dangerous, especially now.

He saw her then. Karen got up at once, but he came quickly along the path to her and she stopped, not wanting to be close. He looked oddly gentle, tender towards her. It seemed genuine.

'I've been neglecting you, darling, and I didn't mean to. So much to sort out, I don't want to bore you with all that. Can I ask one thing? If you would. My neck and shoulders are hurting, too much tension in them. I can scarcely move my head. Could you give just a little rub to my neck?'

She nodded unwillingly, and Harry sat down on the bench before her. Bracing herself, Karen touched his neck. It felt like corrugated iron, under the loose skin. She felt disturbed by his vulnerability, because it seemed real, but she could not feel sorry for him. 'Ah, that's bliss,' he purred. 'What a sweet angel you are. That's much better already. It's past lunchtime, and I spotted a roast chicken in the fridge. Also, some Dayville's ice cream in the freezer. Shall we take a tray to the terrace?'

Harry ate hungrily. She tried to banish the image of the chicken, trussed and gutted, and tried to take a mouthful of flesh.

'My son seems to have decided to leave us to ourselves. I wonder why. Have you seen him, Karen?'

The mouthful turned into sand. She shook her head, not looking at him, and tried to swallow. Harry knew. He was playing with her, and was planning some terrible revenge against them both. If he guessed the worst thing he could do to her, then would he harm his son? Of course he would. She must think, act quickly. It was unbearable, waiting for the blow to fall. She had almost been taken in by his softness and must guard against that.

At around five, Harry announced he was driving into the village. She ached to run down to the beach and look for Damien, but there would be too little time. Suppose Harry was setting a trap, just waiting secretly for her to go to him, so he could follow. That staged discovery would give him the excuse he needed for a sudden loss of control, predictable violence. This time it would be aimed at Damien, she was sure of that. So she stayed in the house, thinking about him. She imagined Damien watching the tide, walking maybe. When the phone rang, she picked it up absently. 'Hello.'

'Karen? What a long time, my dear, since we've spoken. This is Nora.' Her mind went blank, she couldn't think who Nora was. 'I'm just about to leave for Montreal,' the woman's voice went on, 'but I got Harry's message. Is he there?'

It was Harry's sister, calling from Canada. How could she have forgotten that Harry had a sister? 'I'm afraid he isn't, but he'll be back in ten minutes. How are you, Nora?' she responded automatically.

'I'm well, but too busy. And yourself? I'll have to try him again, when I can. Is Harry all right? I've been concerned about him, with all these business worries. I hope they're getting resolved. You must give Harry my love.'

They talked for a few minutes, before ringing off. Karen felt shaken by the call. Harry hadn't mentioned to his sister anything wrong between them. What were his business problems? So far as she knew, the *Cry Murder* filming had been completed, and editing was under way. He had never confided in her – did he feel that he couldn't, that she had been uninterested? Or was he shielding her, even, from his worries? Perhaps she had been the world's worst wife.

You must give Harry my love. Harry was a person. His sister loved him, and so did other people. Could they all be mistaken about him? Or might she be wrong?

Harry returned and the evening dragged past. She felt sucked into a mire of guilt, of her own creation. When they went to bed he held her, and her body felt like a tightly coiled steel spring. 'You seem awfully cross with me still,' he said, in a sad voice. 'Will you tell me what's wrong?'

'Nothing's wrong. Go to sleep, Harry.'

'I had no option but to work in France and Italy, you know. You were lonely, perhaps, and in need of other company. I've told Martin to come down tomorrow. Although I'm afraid he didn't look after you properly, at all, before.'

He fell asleep, and Karen lay awake, her thoughts circling endlessly. Then she must have slept: she woke sobbing, in Harry's arms.

'It's all right,' he comforted. 'How badly you're sleeping, these nights, my darling. Have you such a guilty conscience? Sweetheart,' he smiled, gentle. 'That was half a joke. Remember jokes? How nervy you are.' Surely Harry was seeing straight into the blackness of her heart, the thoughts she was having. Wistfully he added, 'Perhaps you'd feel better if you told me who he is. The one you shine for?'

A surprised hope touched her. Was it possible that he really didn't know about Damien? Perhaps she had only imagined that he knew. Or else Harry was busy disarming her. He wanted them to be unsuspecting and lulled into a false sense of security.

The next day, all the ideas she had constructed about Harry suddenly collapsed.

He had stayed close to her, that morning: if she said she was going for a walk, he could too easily follow. Karen's frustration grew, with her craving to find Damien, to be with him. He would wonder what was happening – and they had arranged no other time. She could scarcely bear Harry's nearness, the way that he seemed to be following her around. They were still together, sitting on the terrace, when she offered to go in and make drinks for them. She had to get away from him, if only for a few minutes.

Busy in the kitchen, she heard the phone ring then switch itself to answer. A familiar voice floated through the hall. 'Harry. Not there? It's Al Quentin, call me on the mobile.'

Recognising his voice, she was too shocked at first to move. Then, hurriedly snatching up the receiver, she got the dialling tone.

Alistair Quentin was alive.

She had been so certain, when Harry returned alone from their sailing trip: he had killed Quentin, in a rage, from jealousy. She had watched that happen in her mind. Perhaps – could it be true – everything else had only happened in her imagination?

Or had Harry been the caller, mimicking Quentin? But Harry was still on the bench, in the garden. Taking out the coffee tray, she was filled with confusion, and relief. Perhaps Harry was not any kind of a killer. She had exaggerated his violence because it had been aimed against her. Quentin was alive, after all, and there was no proof of anything else. Harry was asking, 'Did I hear the phone?'

'It was Al Quentin.'

Harry started getting up. She explained, 'He rang off, you're to call his mobile.'

'All right. He's living on his yacht at present, with this new woman. Thank you, darling.'

She sat down. 'I didn't know you were still dealing with him.'

'Oh, yes. Al did almost let me down, on a business commitment – but he's shaping up nicely now. Sweetheart, you look as if you've seen a ghost. Or is it your period?'

She smiled wanly, and shuddered at what she could have done as the full horror of it burst upon her. She must be mad, or amoral. For one long, tormented day and two nights, her sense of what was right had deserted her. She had been so certain he was purely evil, she had almost turned into a killer herself.

'Poor little Karen.' He smiled, fondly.

'Aren't you going to call him back?'

'Was it very urgent?' She shrugged, in answer. Harry went on, 'Our time together feels precious to me. I haven't always treated you as you wanted, but believe me, I've tried not to complain too often.'

He was guilt-tripping her, of course, but had she ever been able, or willing, to give him what he wanted? So many times she had avoided sex with Harry, and had never let him know why. She had been very angry, from before they ever met. He had just been himself: arrogant and controlling, then sometimes out of control when he drank. They had been lovers – his flesh linked with her own – and then, she had even thought of murdering him. She must be an absolute monster, and totally unlovable.

It was half past two before Harry called Quentin back. Karen slipped out through the garden, and ran down the jetty steps. She scoured the beach, and thought she glimpsed Damien by the rocks. Then, as she got closer, she saw that it wasn't him but a stranger. Where could he have gone? Suppose something had happened to him? She ran across the sand, searching for him. As she walked back, by the rocks and along the path, she looked over towards the jetty again. He was waiting there, just outside the boatshed. They had only missed each other, and that was all.

12

When she had seen him, Damien went back into the boatshed to wait for Karen. In here there was no sound but the sea. Sun rayed through the small high windows, lighting the dust, the pools of diesel oil. He had slept on a mound of canvas sheets, inside the boat wedged against the wall. He stood back from the door now, waiting and counting seconds, like a man in jail. In this idyllic stretch of a foreign shore, he had found the perfect prison.

A rattling sounded on the boards outside, then the door opened. She was peering into the gloom, not seeing him at first after the brightness outside. 'Karen,' he said. She let the door bang shut.

Then she was with him, warm and real in his arms, and seeming somehow frantic. 'Hours, I've been trying to get away. Let me look at you. I thought you'd gone, or something – that I'd never see you again. And you must've felt . . .'

'I came to find you. Then I saw you in the garden with him.' He had seen them there, chatting on the bench outside the house. Something lurched inside him, remembering that: a new softness and a new capacity for suffering. 'I thought about what you'd said. Hey, what? It's OK.'

She was between laughter and grief, some kind of desperation that was knocking her sideways. 'Make me human again.' He wiped the tears off her face, and she touched, then brushed the stubble over his chin. 'It's like fur, strong fur. And you smell of the sea's brine, and of yourself – like an animal.' She breathed his scent deeply, pressing her body against his body, and she was like fire. 'Fuck me,' she whispered. 'Just fuck me to death.'

He picked her up off the ground then stumbled in the half dark to the boat and climbed inside. He slid her down on his prison bed, where he had lain awake, thinking about her in the night. Kneeling over her now, he pushed a thigh between her thighs. His hand dragged up her shirt, and found her breasts naked, full. Her face, close beneath his in the sifting light, was sharp with need. A sense of power flooded through him and mingled with the tenderness as he stroked her, seeing that longing. She was his father's wife, and within his power. That was the crazy, anachronistic truth: she was kind of possessed – by the man who had spawned then disowned him for so many years, by the man he could destroy. He knew such a darkness inside his own heart, poisoning it. He kissed her, hungry for the magic that could drive out the pain and the evil. She could do that, always, for him. Now she was grasping, aggressively taking, as if he was life. Tearing open the buckle of his belt, and his zip, she released him, then took his prick between her lips, into her throat. He groaned, and after a minute pushed her down on to the bed of oilcloths. She wanted fucking, she'd get fucked. He pulled down her jeans and briefs, felt her wetness, opening under his hand, and thrust his swollen shaft into her. Crying out, grasping his hair, she was possessed by him, now – and trusting or not, he didn't know. He glimpsed her face, wild, beyond human, and taking her wrists, pinioned them in his fist, against the gunwale of the boat. 'Babe,' he whispered, then, 'Christ,' thrusting into her. She came with a long, high snarl, her body convulsing, aftershocks flowing. He let go, hammering inside her, and thought he had died. I have died and gone to heaven: the Chinese people said that. He laughed. I can never let her go, he thought.

They were quiet, pulses slowing. He had melted into her warmth, soothed. Other senses, outside things, returned them to the here and now. Reality, what could be touched: the sides of the boat, the salt-stiffened canvas they lay on. Scents and sounds of the sea, the outboard engine and a bumble bee, trapped against the window, trying to get out. She was lying with her eyes closed, and he wanted to see her looking at him. When he stretched, then kissed the insides of her elbows, that tender skin, she opened her eyes and looked sated, drugged. Whatever had been driving her, it was over now. She hugged him to her. Damien whispered, 'Hey, we rocked the boat.'

Karen began to laugh. 'Crazy – we're crazy. I go around like a zombie, because I'm off with you, wherever you are. And in a boat? I've never had much time for them. But I will, now.'

Taking in what she meant, he drew away a bit. 'We've got to decide what to do.'

'Yes.' She struggled to sit up. 'Listen, I only slipped out for a minute. We shouldn't have —'

'You're not going straight back?'

'I'm sorry. He only went to make a phone call, and I —'

'The hell with that! Stay.'

'No. We're too close to the house.' She was straightening her clothes again.

'I don't believe it.'

'Damien.' She knelt, kissing him. 'If there was any way —'

'Just don't go back. What could Harry do to us both, really?'

'You don't understand.' Then she had pulled away from his grasp, she was out of the boat and crossing towards the door. He fumbled, fastening his jeans, going after her. 'We'll meet tomorrow, whatever happens.'

'And then what?' He stared down at her in the shadows, at her stubbornness. 'If I found somewhere for us, then would you stay with me?'

She opened the door, and light swept in. 'You know – I've said why not.'

He was trying anything to stop her leaving: they had to talk this out, at least. 'If you go now, when can we ever have time, or be together?' Angry, insistent, he blocked her way outside the door. Could she really turn her back on him again?

'Tomorrow.' Her voice was still stubborn, and edged with upset.

Then he looked round, scenting something different under

the ozone smells of sea and beach. It was cigarette smoke. Someone was standing only a few yards from the jetty. Damien whirled abruptly and pushed Karen back inside. 'Someone's coming, stay there.' Softly closing the door he turned back to see.

It was Martin, leaning against the fence. He was looking straight at him, and the boatshed door was in his view. Unless he had only just walked up, he had seen them coming out, and how close they were. Damien's mind stalled, searching for false explanations. He couldn't find one, but must go greet Martin, anyhow. 'Hi,' he called out, and strolled over.

'Hello.' Martin gave him a small smile. 'We can't go on meeting like this, can we?' He drew on his cigarette.

Damien laughed at the joke. It sounded all wrong. Martin, the faithful Man Friday, would report everything he had seen and heard to Harry. If there had been any secrecy left, it was going to be all over. 'I didn't know you were back.'

'Alice returned to the London office, so here I am. How are things? You look a bit – rough. Harry thinks you left.'

Martin was looking him up and down, with an odd expression Damien couldn't read. He had got to find out what he was thinking. 'I look like a real bum, you mean. I've been sleeping out, while summer lasts. Under the stars. You ever done that, Martin?'

'Sounds fun, if you've got the right company.' Martin dropped his cigarette stub, and ground it out, underfoot, in the gravel. It seemed a slovenly, un-Martin thing. Next, he started ambling away, alongside the fence.

Damien began to follow along the other side and came to the gate. Remembering the code numbers, he pressed them and went through. 'It's been a long time. You're looking good.' Martin did look good, he noticed as he said it. He looked fit, and cheerful. The blue jeans and white shirt he wore were new and more like his own, not Harry's hand-me-downs. And why did he seem OK, almost friendly, when he must have seen them? Martin was walking on slowly, and he kept pace. 'I didn't know you smoked. You never did, before.'

'Terrible, isn't it? Taken it up again, and swore I wouldn't.' Martin put his hands in his pockets. 'I need the sea air in my lungs. We were going to do a fishing trip, remember?'

'Yeah, of course. Name your day.'

'We could take the boat,' Martin suggested, straight-faced, and too innocently.

'Listen, Martin. You probably saw, just now—'

'Shut up.' It was said quietly, under his breath, and Damien looked at him in surprise. Then Martin called out, 'I'm just taking a breather, after that drive.'

Harry's voice drifted, in a stage-whisper, across the grass. 'I didn't expect to be seeing you again.'

Damien stood still. They had been walking through the garden and Harry was there on the path ahead, barring the way. Maybe he had been searching for Karen. Looking at his father, he knew they needed to have it all out – everything – but, then, whatever he said could rebound against her, especially if she wouldn't leave with him. How could he stay around and see she was OK? He had never even known about last night, until afterwards. He took a careful step forward, about to speak. Harry held up a hand, palm forwards as if to ward him off.

They were like two cats in a stand-off, bristling with the charge of mutual hostility, but Harry's voice was mild, controlled in a jibe. 'Have you come looking for the sports car I bought? Did you really think it would be here, after the way you've treated me?'

'Yeah, what way is that?' Poised between a guilty shame and total triumph, he waited for the accusation. Could Harry even smell the sex and her on him? He had got to know, he was not any fool.

'You have used – not to mention abused – my name and good nature, and hospitality. My money.'

Just who was kidding whom? 'Hey, come on—' he began.

Martin interrupted, 'Damien's been sleeping rough.'

'Be quiet,' Harry ordered him, coolly. 'And get lost.'

'Don't talk to me like that,' Martin retorted, folding his arms.

Harry ignored him, turning back. 'I gave you a chance to

shape up, to decide how to make something of yourself. And what did you do?'

'Go ahead. Spell it out, Harry.'

There was a tense silence. 'You've neglected me. And shown me up.'

'Bullshit. Listen, I heard the police called here, in the night. You going to tell me why?'

A faint purple mottle was creeping into Harry's cheeks. 'And what business is that of yours?' He went on, fast, 'Aren't you wondering what's happened to the car, the MGF?' He paused, flicking some imaginary speck from the sleeve of his navy blue jacket, before looking up again. 'I decided to give it to a friend, who was more deserving. I'm more than slightly disappointed in you.'

Damien was silenced, by the taunt and by the *non sequitur*. Harry really did not want to talk about Kåren.

'That was a gift,' Martin reminded, disapproving.

'You could never amount to anything,' Harry went on, ignoring Martin. 'I was deluded, persuaded into giving you a chance. Now your bag has been packed and is waiting in the cupboard, inside the front door. Martin will fetch it.'

'That's real kind,' Damien put in, resorting to sarcasm.

'I've taken back the other gifts, as well. I don't think that you can have expected to keep them, in the circumstances.'

'Tell me, Harry – the circumstances.'

'You've let me down. You're probably not even my son, and never bore my name. Just her bastard. And a complete loser. You'll never achieve anything.'

This is for all of us, Damien thought, and he launched himself at Harry. His fists connected, but Harry had ducked sideways and grabbed at him. For a second, it was an embrace, the only embrace, ever. Then they were grappling, and Harry had lost all dignity, skidding and tumbling in the gravel. He would not have tried to hit him again – not when he was sprawled there, defeated, ungainly – but Martin pushed between them. He was warning him away, and hauling up the spluttering Harry.

'Martin, call the police,' Harry said.

'You don't want that.'

Darting him a look Harry pulled himself up tall and turned to Damien. 'I will call them myself, now, unless you clear off my land. Get out! You are never to return, and I wish no further contact nor sight of you.'

Damien answered, 'Right. There can't be many fathers get to throw their sons out twice. At birth, and a quarter-century later. But then, you're such a doubly generous man, Harry. You're real famous for it.'

Damien stormed off, down the driveway, to the big iron gate on to Sea Lane. He never looked back. The gate clicked behind him. Stumbling away towards the stretch of the beach, he sat down below a dune and buried his head in his hands, blotting out the brightness. His father despised him, believed he was worthless. The long summer, the attempt at a reconciliation, was ended.

It was all way too late, for him and Harry. It had already been too late when he turned up here. The man who had it all had never wanted his own kids. Perhaps they had made him feel old, fettered and responsible. Or they had just never measured up, somehow, to his expectations.

That first day of meeting his father, he had felt hope begin, a hope that the past could get cancelled out. But maybe he had really come here to repay the pain, and the damage. Perhaps I wanted to hurt you, he thought, but I haven't even the power to do that: you don't love Karen, the loss of her couldn't touch you. In your mind, I'm only someone who's been enjoying your toys.

But suppose Harry took out his temper on Karen – what could he do? And how would they get to see each other again? The full weight of their situation, and its hopelessness, crept over him. He stared at the distant tide and the long, rippled wet sand. Someone sat down beside him. It was Martin. 'I've brought your sports bag.'

'Great. Thanks.'

'Those things Harry said – so harsh. Don't take them to heart. Try not to.'

Impossible not to. A bratpack of footballers, running along the beach, was drawing level with them. Two teams, yelling, cheering and taunting. 'Karen,' said Damien. 'Is she OK?'

'She's fine. I can keep an eye on Harry, now I'm around. I could see that he doesn't get out of hand.'

Damien studied him: that seraphic expression, as he idly searched through the pebbles at their feet. 'You know, Martin. Hell, of course you do.'

A small smile twitched at the corners of Martin's mouth, then it was gone. 'Of course I do,' he agreed, quiet.

'For how long?' Damien went on, slowly. 'I begin to think, since before we did, ourselves.'

Martin laughed, flashed him a look. Then he sounded almost angry. 'You will wear your heart on your sleeve. Didn't you think it a bit too easy, the way you were sent off together? To France? Then here, alone together, for all of August?' He chose a pebble and aimed it out towards the sea. It fell short by a long way. 'You seemed miserable. I wanted to – do what I could.'

Damien was staring at him. Had Martin really been trying to help him and Karen, all these weeks? And wanting to deceive his boss? He and Harry had been together for about a hundred years. It didn't make any sense. 'You and Harry – aren't you close?'

'Don't worry,' said Martin, with something like irony in his voice. 'I don't think Harry actually knows—'

'Sure he does. You were there just now.'

Martin shook his head. 'I don't think so. I'd be surprised. And you don't need to worry on my account. Close? A lot of things have changed, in that direction. OK, I'm taking a chance.'

'But why?'

'Why not?' He shrugged. 'Maybe I've a sense of fairness, or maybe I just had enough, too. What are you going to do now?'

'I'm between the devil and the deep blue sea.'

'You certainly are.'

'Karen doesn't want to leave with me. Martin, if you knew how I've felt—'

'Ever contrary, mm? I mean – women.'

'She thinks Harry could destroy us if we ran off together with nowhere to hide. And – he could hurt her.'

'What you need is time to think.' Martin paused. 'Perhaps I can help. There's a beach chalet, further along. You must've noticed it, on the edge of Harry's land?'

'Up by the rocks, that path? Yes.'

'It's half civilized, and more important, it's empty. Well, someone's there at the moment, but she can just clear out a bit early. My sister. You met her, you told me. In London.'

'That's right. Yeah, and on this beach, a month back.' He saw Martin's eyes narrow in surprise. Of course, Martin didn't know that he and Viv had been close, once. That seemed a lifetime ago. 'I ran into her, we talked. Friendly, you know.'

'She never mentioned that. Anyway, Viv can stay somewhere else. She'll be going back to town soon. Would that fit the bill? And you could stay around – so long as Harry doesn't set eyes on you. That café, near the road, stays open till mid September. And there's electricity, and—'

'Hey. This is brilliant, so great of you, Martin, you know.'

'What friends are for. Come on, I'll show you the place. Let's go.'

Shouldering his bag, Damien followed Martin along the beach. Suddenly, with him on their side, things didn't look so bleak. It would be easier to arrange to meet, and they would have the time they needed to sort out a way ahead.

He remembered the beach chalet, one of several tiny holiday homes scattered above the rocky promontory. He and Karen had sheltered in it from the rain, during Quentin's weekend visit. So Harry owned that, and never used it. Set back from the path, the hut could be reached by a trail through gorse bushes, sloping down towards the shore. 'Actually,' Martin was saying, 'that café's a greasy spoon, chips with everything. But there's a cooker. And I'll be around, any time you need anything. To talk or whatever.' He opened the small blue door and tutted. 'She's left it unlocked, as usual. It's not five star, I'm afraid.'

Compared to the boatshed, it was five star. Damien looked around the small home that Viv had made. His first thought was that Karen could come to him here, and it would be safer, further from the house. 'There are two rooms,' he pointed out, slightly unwillingly. 'There's no need to ask Viv to go.'

'Oh, she won't mind. It's OK, then? Wait here a minute, Damien.'

Martin disappeared abruptly, out of the chalet door. Taking a mug from beside the tiny sink, Damien ran the single tap. The water looked clear, and he drank thirstily, then went out to the front deck. The view was breathtaking, so close to the ocean. If Martin took a message straight to Karen – who must be out of her head, by now, wondering what had happened – then she might be able to come here soon. Like tonight.

Where was Martin? Minutes had passed. Damien went back round the chalet, and saw him in the distance, on the path. He was with Viv, who had a shopping bag, and they were talking intently, or arguing. He decided to go and meet them and began to climb the path. They went quiet, they had seen him coming. Then Martin greeted him, sounding very cheerful. 'That's all right, then. Let's go back. Hungry, Damien? Viv, you could make an early dinner. She's staying around a little while,' he added. 'Don't mind, do you?'

'Viv. Great to see you.' But she was avoiding looking at him. What was going on? 'Hey, if it's not OK for me to—'

'Hello,' she said in a polite voice, as if they were strangers.

'It's OK,' Martin reassured him. 'Did I see a bottle of Chardonnay in this bag? Stay out here on the verandah, Damien, give Viv some space. To do the food.'

He nearly asked Martin what was wrong, but the partition walls were thin as card. They sat out on the deck, and Martin talked. Damien scarcely listened. It was early evening. Where was she now? All he wanted was news of her, and to know when they would meet. Then Viv appeared, with a couple of bowls of tomato soup. She handed him one, and turned to Martin. For an instant, Damien thought she was going to throw the soup over him. Perhaps Martin thought so too. He had got up, fast, from his deckchair.

'Do you want soup?' she asked, setting it down on the table.

'That's for you, both. Viv,' he said, warningly, 'I've got to get back to the house now.' She turned towards him, with a wounded expression, and Martin kissed her swiftly on the cheek. 'You'll be company for each other.' There was a look of appeal in his eyes. Viv disappeared off, inside the chalet.

'What's up?' Damien asked, in a low voice. 'She's really mad.'

'She's just in a cross mood. Ignore her, if she's difficult. She'll get used to things, to sharing. Anything you want, just let me know.'

Damien followed him to the path. 'Will you give a message to Karen? Ask her to come here – tomorrow or tonight. Any time at all.'

Martin nodded. 'Fair enough, I'll do that. And I'll see you very soon, OK? Don't show any light, by the way.'

It was early dusk, as he went back to the chalet. Its blinds had been drawn. Viv must have done that, the minute he stepped out. She had vanished again, into the tiny bedroom he supposed. He drank his bowl of cold soup, then went through and rummaged in his bag. It had been neatly packed with all his old clothes, the stuff he had brought over, from back home. He shaved, and took a shower in the cramped booth, banging knees and elbows on hollow, plastic walls.

If Martin had gone straight back, given the message to Karen right away, then she could turn up here any time from now. The thought sent his pulses racing, and gave a solid purpose to everything he did. He sat through the evening, waiting and watching for any sign of her on the beach or the path. When it was late, he unfolded the camp bed and found a blanket, switched off the light.

'Good night,' he called softly through the partition. Viv didn't answer. She must be asleep, or just not wanting to speak to him. He frowned, puzzling a bit over her new hostility. He had never thought of her as being possessive about places before. This chalet was the perfect base, temporarily, for staying close to Karen, and all he needed was a corner of its living area. He tried to shrug it off. Viv was her brother's problem, not his. He fell asleep, thinking about Karen being so nearby, and feeling confident.

During the night he woke, hearing someone moving around. Quietly, on a wave of hope, he spoke her name. There was no answer. It was pitch black, and he fumbled for the light switch, not remembering where it was. Then he found the door and lifted the latch.

It was dawn outside, a slate grey light. Someone was sitting on the steps to the deck, and smoking a cigarette.

'Viv. What is it?' Damien sat down beside her, but she didn't look at him. 'Can't you sleep? You want me to go. Listen, Karen and I, we just need somewhere —'

'It wouldn't make any difference, not really. If you left.' She was biting her lip, staring straight ahead.

'But you're hating it, me being here. Martin said you wouldn't mind, he was sure—'

'Well, he would be, wouldn't he?' She blew out smoke, then turned to look at him. 'What a fool you are, Damien. That you haven't even noticed. Can't you see Martin's in love with you?'

His mind reeled, seeking escape or explanation. Surely Viv was joking? But no, she didn't seem to be. His memory leaped back, hooked up to images, little things he had scarcely been aware of these past months. Martin. Friendly, he had thought. A good friend. Being real nice to him . . . Could it be true? And if it was, that still didn't explain the way Viv had suddenly changed towards him. 'I don't understand,' he managed to say. 'Martin's not gay. Is he?' Then he saw there were tears in her eyes, tough little Viv. 'And if he was, why would that be such a big deal for you?'

Viv could scarcely believe how stupid Damien was being. 'As if it was that simple,' she answered. She sniffed, then almost laughed at his expression of astonished disbelief, comical. She had watched Martin's focus, all of his attention, hurtle straight towards Damien every time he was around. So why couldn't Damien himself see it? 'Believe me, there's nothing simple about my lover. Nothing. You didn't really think we were brother and sister?'

He was just staring at her, clearly trying to take it all in. 'But if you're not, why did you pretend?'

'Because it was what Martin wanted – like everything else. And he'd never forgive me for telling you this. He'd stop tolerating me . . . Martin got me a job with Harry, years back, that was when it started. He didn't want Harry to know he had a girl. Perhaps he's always been ashamed of me. Anyway, it stuck, as a way of passing me off. At first, I found it almost erotic. Then it became just another rejection.' Viv looked up. 'Martin hates me, right now, for not just shoving off. Not leaving him with a clear field.'

Damien looked horrified. 'But Martin can't think . . . I love Karen. I've never been interested—'

'Doesn't stop him hoping, though, does it – that you'll turn out to be like him? Bisexual men, they're a curse. Because no one's enough for them, and no one's really loved. I can't tell you how much he's hurt, humiliated . . .' She was crying and had lost all pride. It was such a relief to talk to someone, and Damien was giving her a hug. He was on her side, not Martin's. Not so far, anyway. 'The thing is, he half wants me. He keeps me hanging on – with being fantastic, and full of promises. Then he falls for a guy again. I count for nothing, every time.'

But how could she really explain it in words, all the years since she'd turned eighteen and met Martin? He was the only man she had ever loved. At different times he'd promised they would live together, and he'd meant it, for a little while. Once they were close, if she dared to start hoping he really did care for her this time, then he'd meet another man. Abruptly, Martin would start to look at her as if she was a stranger, rejecting their past, denying his knowledge of her and her needs. Because she was inconvenient: even as a pretend sister, she must seem like a hindrance then. How he could hurt her. Why did Martin have to keep chasing after his own prick in other men's pants? 'When Narcissus gazed into the pool, it wasn't his face he was looking at.' Laughing at her own joke, she heard her bitterness. It was the sound she lived with, tasted constantly.

'Viv. If you're this unhappy, why don't you just leave him?'

'Yeh – of course I should. I did, a couple of times. Thing is, without Martin there's no point to living. I really tried – but then he promised me again. He does sort of need me, you see. I'm the only person who's stayed. I've done everything for him.'

They were quiet for a while, as she let it sink in. Viv could feel Damien thinking things out beside her. The sun was poking feebly over the horizon, and washy colours were beginning. He asked her, at last, 'When you and I . . . When we first met?'

She nodded. It was best he knew everything now. Or almost everything. 'It took Martin all of two minutes to work out who you were. He wanted a look. Then, wham, bang, thank you, ma'am – I fancy him. So I had to get his attention back. Sorry, if that's not too good for your ego, but—'

'And what else – these things you've done?' Damien interrupted.

'Recently? Well, now, let's see. Martin didn't want Karen around so I tried to frighten her off, OK? A few anonymous phone calls, that sort of thing. And I ripped up something that she'd been wearing. Anyway, it didn't seem to scare her off.'

'You're telling me a lot.' Suddenly he sounded angry. 'Why – and why now?'

'Desperation, maybe? Because I've had it.' Viv shrugged, and flashed him a false smile. 'To make friends with the enemy. The funny thing is, they always do look just like you. Tall, with dark hair.' She parted the tufts of her own hair, and bowed her head, to show him the ginger roots. 'I dyed it black, hoping Martin would like me better – or like me for a bit longer. Didn't work, hey? And there's one respect where I can't compete.' She thought how undesirable and unloved she had felt, how foolish and unfeminine, powerless, inadequate, shamed, and offensive. Strung along and excluded, she was all wrong. His fear of her femaleness affected her and then she would mutilate herself. Why wasn't she enough? Why wasn't Martin man enough, for himself?

'I want to show you something,' she said, very quickly so there was no time to change her mind. She pushed up her sleeve. There was the lattice of old and new cuts, white scars, red weals. Old, faded words: fat, reject, bad. And the new razor cut, the secret that wasn't a secret any more: fag-hag. She saw the revulsion on Damien's face, then the pity starting. She wanted that pity, because it could – it just might – change things for her.

'When it all gets too bad,' she explained, matter-of-factly now, 'I do that instead of killing myself. It sort of relieves the pressure, helps a bit. You're the only person who's ever seen my cuts. Except for Martin, of course.'

'How can Martin be so cruel?'

Viv flew to protect him. 'He's not! He doesn't mean to be, he just can't help it. Sometimes, when it's only us, he can be the most brilliant lover that anyone could ever want. You don't understand. Martin is great.'

Martin was refilling Harry's breakfast cup, the green French one with the gold rim. Strong arabica coffee, freshly ground and filtered. Two sweeteners, no milk. Then he took it through because Harry had already gone into the living room and was at the computer. His study alcove was spreading out, at an alarming rate, into a real muddle. Harry had always been efficient and methodical, a man with an almost clear desk. It certainly wasn't clear now, and the space was limited.

'Top up,' he said. 'Mind you don't knock it over, with all these heaps of stuff.' Harry, intent at the keyboard, didn't answer, so he went on, 'Honestly, what a mess.' He rescued a stack of paper, about to topple, and an audio-cassette sliding off the top. 'You want me to file these, put things –?'

'Leave them,' Harry snapped. 'I don't want you touching anything here. I can communicate with Alice perfectly well.'

'There's no need to be like that. And how d'you expect to ever find anything among this?' Martin felt offended. Harry no longer used him or valued him properly. When had things gone wrong? While he was in Italy, perhaps. Or before that, in France.

'I want you to look after Karen,' Harry said, slightly more civil now, 'and make sure she's not bored. Keep her in your sight this time, please.'

'Fine. I'll play nanny then, today.' He went out quickly, before Harry could remonstrate any more. Maybe he did suspect something. But more likely, Harry was getting tetchy because of business. Where had it all headed, he wondered with some curiosity, after Harry had forged the guarantees for the bank loans? He was almost certain that he had forged them, to try to get himself out of trouble. There was serious money involved – and was Harry in, or out of, financial crisis now? He no longer knew what was happening, because Harry had been keeping secrets from him.

He didn't much care about that, he thought with surprise, going back to the kitchen. He had picked up Damien's attitudes, his view of his father. After all, where had it got him, all these years of willing slavery? Harry was selfishness personified. He was ungrateful.

Martin closed the kitchen door quietly behind him and refilled Karen's coffee cup. How dull she was, and abstracted, with nothing to say for herself. He couldn't believe Damien really wanted that. She was a pretty girl, but alien, or arid in some way. Where was the attraction? It wouldn't last, for sure. 'You seem very thoughtful this morning,' he said.

She glanced up, and he sat down at the head of the oak table, next to her. 'A penny for them.'

Karen seemed to hesitate. 'Tell me something.'

'That depends,' he began, teasing, 'what it is.'

'When did you last see Alistair Quentin?'

It wasn't what he had expected, and he felt nonplussed. 'Why?' She shrugged, her eyes on his face. He thought back. 'Not long ago, must've been the end of last month. I seem to remember he and Harry had a meeting.' He pursued, 'I don't think Al's the one who's on your mind.' She stared at him with a

243

new attention. 'I think you're wondering where Damien is.'

There was a silence between them, and Martin smiled. He wasn't going to help her out. 'I have wondered. Why? Do you know?'

Martin picked up the milk jug, noticing it was empty. 'As it happens – yes, I do.'

She said in a rush, 'There was some quarrel, wasn't there, yesterday? Harry seemed—'

'There was a disagreement.' He nodded, drily. 'But Damien's still nearby.'

She was all sudden friendliness and gratitude. 'Where is he, Martin?'

'He's staying in Harry's beach chalet – the first one, along by the rocks.' He watched her face changing, suffused with life, fresh energy. She couldn't pretend, and he felt a pang of sympathy. 'He wants to see you there, as soon as possible.'

'Martin.' She had taken his hand, and he looked down at it in surprise. 'You're our friend, aren't you? I can trust you?'

He nodded, again. 'Yes. I'm taking a risk, with Harry. But then, I'm a sucker for romance, you see.'

'Tell him . . .' Karen dropped Martin's hand and jumped up from the table. 'Tell Damien I'll come tonight. During the evening – will you? And . . . Martin, wait.' She hurried out of the kitchen. Martin began to clear the breakfast things. A message would give him every excuse to call by, this morning or lunchtime at the latest. He felt a scramble of mixed feelings inside. Then Karen was back, pushing a soft carrier bag into his arms. 'Give him this. And tell him, this evening.'

'It's the Mayor's Charity Supper, tonight,' Martin remembered.

'I'll get out of it.'

'How?'

'I don't know – make an excuse, pretend to be ill. Go,' she said. 'Can't you go now?'

Martin shook his head. 'Be a bit cautious,' he reproved. 'When you're safely with Harry – lunch or elevenses. Then I'll

244

go.' She seemed about to argue, then changed her mind. A bossy cow, she was turning out to be.

'Thank you. Thank you, Martin.' And she kissed him on the cheek, something he didn't want.

The morning passed slowly, and he got through it by thinking, imagining. Damien had woken up this morning to that beautiful stretch of beach view. A pity the day had turned cloudy. What would he be doing right now? Settling in, probably. He could take him a book to read, he knew what he liked. There wasn't much to do around the chalet, and his visit would be welcome. The hours, minutes, were crawling by. When Damien wasn't around, the whole world seemed dark and depressed, slowed down. Sending him off to France, then the Keep, to be with Karen – that was one of the hardest things that he had ever done.

At last, while Harry and Karen were having their lunch, he was able to set off. The beach was empty, it was threatening rain but he scarcely noticed. Nearing the chalet, he was inside his own light and warmth, striding across the rocks and along the path, swinging the two bags he carried. One was from him, two novels he had picked out with care and a pack of beer. The other, hers, he had looked inside. It held one of her nightshirts, crumpled from wear. He could almost smell her on it, and wrinkled his nose at the memory.

He stepped round the side of the chalet – and there was Damien, in the red chair. His step missed the ground: he had looked forward to the sight so much, for hours. 'Hey. You look busy.'

'Martin.' Damien got up quickly and stood at the verandah rail, frowning.

At once, Martin sensed that something had changed. 'That's my name,' he said, going forward after a moment. 'Have a good night's rest? I brought you something to read and something to drink.'

Damien didn't answer, he stepped back a pace. Then Viv appeared in the chalet doorway, and Martin stared. He couldn't remember the last time Viv had put on a skirt. It had been years ago, and the sight was unnerving – as if this wasn't really her but someone pretending. 'Hi,' she said, cheerfully. 'You're just in time for lunch.'

Then Martin understood. The bitch had told him everything. He could sense it in Damien, in that new coolness. Viv had told him all of their secrets when she had promised that she never would. He felt a rage inside at her obstructiveness, and the betrayal. She would do anything to destroy, to spoil it. He hated her.

Damien said, 'Hello, Martin. You made it, then. Did you get to tell Karen? What did she say?'

How easy it would be to lie, Martin thought: how easy to tell them both the wrong things and to push them apart. Then he would feel gutted, but I would be around. Reluctantly, he said, 'Yes. She said to tell you she'll be here this evening.' He saw Damien's face light up, warm towards him. 'Hey, Martin. Thanks.'

Damien persuaded Martin to stay ten minutes, then walked back with him, along the top path between the gorse bushes. He felt sorry for Martin, but uneasy in his presence, and was being careful not to encourage him. Mostly he pitied Viv, for getting hooked and then led on, time and again. He'd had no idea, none at all. And why had she suddenly told him all that? What was he supposed to do, to help her?

He said goodbye and stood watching Martin go into the Keep to rejoin Karen and Harry. Disconsolately, he turned along a fork in the path towards the café, not wanting to go back to the chalet or Viv, that claustrophobia. He couldn't forget those scars on Viv's arms. They were alike, he and she, and the knowledge filled him with wretchedness. Going into the café, all steamy with frying fat, he ordered a pasty, which came with chips and a cup of translucent tea. He sat at a Formica table, among the last straggle of chilled holidaymakers. Outside it had begun to rain. Harry would never dream of coming to a gig like this, not in a million years.

Later he walked back across the deserted shore, through a

rawly salt, driven wind. Interminable rain, empty space. Red seaweed lay like streams of glistening blood. Gulls hovered, then hurtled on invisible strings, and the long low wailing tore at him.

Then there were only a few more hours to wait. She had sent him something she had worn, a nightshirt, and he buried his face in the fabric, breathing its faint scent. He flooded with hot memories, feeling her energy surge through him at the contact. His mood lifted again. This was the hardest time, these days of being apart, but she would be here soon, this evening. Then they could talk about what to do.

Evening came early. A wet dusk blotted the barren sea and darkness fisted around the chalet. He sat on the deck, wrapped in an oilskin, waiting and watching for her to appear. It was after eight thirty when he saw a shape loom from the path. He jumped up and ran to meet her.

It wasn't Karen, it was Martin.

'What's happened?'

'He made her go with him. To a charity function in town. I'm sorry, Damien.'

He tried to absorb the disappointment. For some reason, he wasn't very surprised – he had almost expected her not to make it. 'Did she say when she would come?'

'I haven't been able to get close. Harry's keeping her on a short rein. Is there anything else I can do?'

The full impact reached him then. How would he ever see her? Harry could spirit Karen back to the city any time. 'What?'

'Is there anything I can do?'

'No,' he said savagely, and saw Martin recoil. 'I just need to be alone.'

He walked along the shore in the wet night until it was past midnight. Then he stood sheltered by the rocks, staring up at the tower of the Keep. The lights of a car torched through the sky, approaching. They had come back from the charity function. The beam went out, and the house lights appeared. They were going to bed, Karen with Harry. Over his head the rocks sheered dizzily, peppered with gulls and seamed. An old man, a god's features were lowering down at him, malevolent. He would always be dominated by Harry. There was no escape. He walked slowly to the edge of the sea, and felt a precariousness, a closeness to shattering apart. A white net of broken waves pulled at his feet, frothing and bleeding the pale sand dark. The ocean was alive with phosphorescence, beckoning, attracting.

Reluctantly dragging back to the chalet, Damien found Viv waiting for him. 'You're soaked through to the skin,' she exclaimed, scolding. 'That's not going to do any good at all, if you go and catch pneumonia.' She began to pull off his wet clothes, and he just let her.

'Listen,' Viv went on, then, 'I've thought of a way out. Harry has loot, right? And loot is what it all comes down to – loot is all that you need.'

13

Damien looked at Viv, at the planes of her face, hardened and flat in the greyly electric light. 'What are you thinking?'

'He owes you, Harry does. And with him it's all about money. Don't you see?'

'He tried to buy me off. I'd never accept anything again.'

Viv laughed. 'Not likely to offer, is he? Not now. But I've been around both his pads with Martin, plenty of times. Harry Glass has got more stuff crammed into those places than he'd ever notice. If it went missing, I mean. He's so rich—'

'No.' Damien stopped her right away.

'You're his son. You deserve it – as a right.'

'I won't get into that again.'

'For God's sake!' She sounded exasperated. 'The man's a walking horror show. Look what he's done to the people around him, your family. Karen's there with him – you should worry.'

'Quit this. I'm not going to hear it any more.'

'But don't you see it's the only way for you both? I was just trying to help. OK, forget it.'

Damien rubbed himself with a towel and found a dry T-shirt. The damp air was sharp and cold. Viv had stomped off crossly behind the partition. She was crazy, it was an insane idea. For one thing, they would never get away with it. He unfolded his bed, switched off the light and lay under his blanket, listened to the clattering rain on the chalet roof, the mean wind, the angry tide.

The only place worth breaking into, where he knew what was

valuable and small enough to carry, was the cellar of the Keep. Those antique weapons and the safe.

The safe held jewellery, worth thousands. One or two pieces belonged to Karen: Harry had taken things back, and locked them away. The other stuff, which Martin had shown him, had belonged to Tanya – and possibly, first, to his own mother. It was Harry's equivalent of hoarding under the mattress. He kept cash in the safe.

'We'd never get away with it,' Damien said softly, into the darkness.

There was an instant's silence. Viv's voice hurled exultantly across the partition. 'Don't you believe it, mate. It would be dead simple.' He heard the curtain drawn back, then the light snaked on again. Viv sat cross-legged on the floorboards, staring into him. Her eyes were intent, watchful.

Damien propped himself up on one arm. 'The security's too tight. If we went for the cellar? It's Fort Knox.'

'The cellar? That opens with one bloody key! Talk about old-fashioned.' She laughed. 'Just because it looks good – in period.'

'But that's a steel door, we'd need to have the key. And code numbers, for getting in the gate, then the house. There are always people about. And it could never look like a break-in—'

'Exactly. There's always people – trade, maintenance, cleaning – who know the security codes. An inside job, that's OK. It's a piece of cake.'

'I'm not so sure. It depends what we do after.' But Viv was right, this was the only way. He could get Karen home to the States, they could hide, and even buy new identities. Harry wouldn't know where to start looking. There was a perfect justice to the idea, and maybe Viv was a genius. If Harry judged their love affair as a property crime, he was about to drive them into something else, something more accurate. 'Martin showed me those small weapons, the daggers – and the jewellery in the safe. But where would we sell them?'

'There's a guy I know. He'd look after all of that.'

'You're full of surprises.' How long had she been thinking of doing this, he wondered briefly. Was it really for him and

Karen? Of course not. Viv had never met Karen and, only yesterday, she had wished him at the bottom of the sea. 'So what do you want, Viv? A life of luxury, is that it?'

'And Martin. We bring in Martin.'

'Uh-huh.' Damien got up from the bed, took one of Viv's Death cigarettes and lit it for himself, thoughtfully. 'Come on. You know Martin, he'd never rob his boss. And how would that help you with him, anyway?'

'Martin and me, we were always going to live together.' Viv was remembering, dreamily. 'We did this holiday, touring in his old Ford transit, when we'd been together a year. All round the coasts of Ireland, the south and west. Martin promised – he suggested it – we'd take a cottage there. Back in London he met a man called Derek.' Her face grew pinched. 'The next few years were hell. And, meanwhile, Harry was getting his hooks in.'

'You think Martin would rob Harry, then move to Ireland with you?'

'No – but he would with *us*,' she emphasised, and went on quickly, 'Yeh, money could buy us love. Martin wouldn't be bothering now, with Harry or that job, if he didn't need a wage.'

'I wouldn't be coming with you,' Damien pointed out. Her ambition with Martin sounded impossible, but then only Viv could look after her side of things. Money would buy freedom, a future. It would give Karen and him the means, the power to leave Harry behind for good. 'Everything that's really worth taking is in the safe. It's got a combination lock – would that be a separate set of numbers?'

Viv nodded, and blew out smoke. 'Karen would know that code, and the house access.'

'But so does Martin.' He began to argue, to lay down what he would agree to. 'If he'll come in, then there's no reason to involve Karen in any way. Look at her situation, stuck with Harry. She's really vulnerable. No one must ever suspect her.'

'Doesn't she sort of have some legal right to what's his?' Viv asked calmly. 'Why would Harry's own wife need to thieve from him? He might find it too awkward, publicly pointing the finger at Karen.'

'Her jewellery's in that safe. We'd be taking what's hers. But I won't let her get involved – and not afterwards, either.'

'I've got an idea,' Viv said, suddenly. 'There's someone goes into that cellar on a regular basis. Martin told me. Some guy who cleans the guns and stuff.'

'You mean Joe Taylor?'

'Whatever his name is, yeh. Harry will accuse him, won't he? The police will go for him, if we play it right.' She added, 'There's no need for Karen to help, if Martin will.'

'She's not even to know what we're planning,' he insisted.

Viv said slowly, 'Then you'll have to create a rift, a fall-out with her. Or a pretend one. That's the only way to get Martin.'

'Look, Viv,' he told her reluctantly, 'I don't think Martin is going to agree to this. And what if he told Harry, or alerted him somehow?'

'You don't understand. Martin hates his boss, these days – partly because of what's happened to you. He'll listen all right, and he'll come in – if it's you that asks him nicely. You will, won't you? Because he wouldn't do anything for me. And you've got to let him dream a bit, Damien. You know, just be friendly, like you were before I told you.'

'You mean, let him think it's over with Karen. How can I do that?'

'It's the only way,' Viv repeated, easily. 'You've got to be practical to get results, OK. And now I'm for bed, I'm knackered. Don't worry, it's going to be easy. We'll be rich – and out of this stinking way of life. We'll be happy then.'

Viv had woven a web around him. She had baited it, made it hard to retreat or extract himself. Now it was up to him to get Martin to agree, because without his help they would have to involve Karen. Still, he felt uneasy about tricking Martin and getting his co-operation that way. He would have to think about it more, because it seemed wrong. But Martin had access to the cellar key, and the safe's combination number. They needed him, at whatever cost.

The drumming rain seemed cheering now. Damien slept deeply, as if a sense of purpose had permeated, changed him already. When he woke in the morning, as soon as he remembered everything, it seemed clear. His commitment was to Karen and getting her away to safety, making a future. The means would justify the end, for all of them.

Viv was expecting Martin to come by before the morning was over. 'And we had best get some word to your fancy girlfriend fast, hadn't we? Where could you meet with her, that Martin couldn't know?'

'On the marshes?' Damien suggested quickly. 'At the shore-line, past the first Martello tower. I could go by boat. Is there a way you could get a note to her?'

Viv looked thoughtful. 'If Karen's there, she could have it now. Keep it basic, though.'

She went off with his note, seeming confident that no one at the Keep would challenge her. Half an hour later, she was back. She had handed over the letter at the front door, where Karen had read it and said yes, that would be all right. She had been warned not to talk about him to Martin. They would be meeting: he would see her this afternoon.

During the morning, as he waited for Martin, Damien raked over their plan. The scam was simple enough – provided that Martin would come in with them. It would be no more than Harry deserved. But some of the things he would have to do, or go along with, were still troubling him. Like deceiving Martin. He had decided to do that because it was necessary, but he felt bad about it. Still, this way Martin would finish up with Viv. Surely that would be for the best? She was crazy about him, and this would settle things. He felt sorry for Viv, and her life lay in his hands, it seemed.

By the time Martin arrived, soon after midday, Damien had almost silenced his scruples. The rain and wind had died away. Sitting on the rocks nearby, they ate baguettes filled with bacon and lettuce. 'How are things with himself?' Viv asked. 'Is he giving you a better deal?'

Martin began to complain: Harry was getting worse, no longer confiding in him or using his skills, just treating him like a household skivvy. 'He thinks I'll put up with anything.'

'You should get out,' Damien suggested.

'What would I do, without a job?'

Viv leaned towards him. 'Day and night, you've been at Harry's beck and call for years. What's he given you? A mean, lousy little wage.'

'I'd like to leave,' Martin told Damien. 'Truly, after the way he chucked you out. Disinherited you, when he's so loaded.'

'Almost, Harry deserves to mislay a slice of wealth. Don't you think?' He saw that Martin was looking quizzical. 'If Harry got robbed, if he was burgled one night, that wouldn't bother you. Would it?'

'I'd be laughing. What are you suggesting?'

'Taking a few things from the safe. And the weapons collection, that would be real easy. What is it, Martin? You'd be too scared?'

'It isn't that. I don't want to end up in jail.'

Viv put in, 'Someone else will take the rap. And Damien won't mind if that's Karen. They've split. Tell him,' she urged.

Damien wiped his hands roughly on a piece of towel. It seemed to be tearing apart, into shreds. 'I met with her, during the night,' he lied, gruffly. He glanced at Martin and saw his eyes widen with surprise, then soften in sympathy as he began to explain. He was being believed. 'It seems she's had enough of me. It's over.'

Martin said, 'She was distant this morning. So that's why. But I expect you'll make it up with her.'

'There's no way I'd take her back. It took me a while to believe it – what Karen wanted with Harry. Now he's disowned me she's not interested. She's got his money and was only amusing herself.'

He threw pieces of bread for the gulls. Martin said, 'I'm sorry. But you're well out of it, Damien. To tell you the truth, I never trusted her.'

'As things turned out, it was only an affair.' Damien shrugged, smiling at him and feeling like a Judas.

Packing up the remains of their picnic, Viv asked, 'What about Damien's plan? What d'you think?'

254

'Harry's been hanging around a lot. I don't see when we'd get any chance.'

'He's sure to go to London some time. We need to be ready,' Damien suggested.

Martin looked along the beach. He stood up. 'Like to take a walk?'

'OK. You coming, Viv?'

'I've got some things to do. You two go.'

'We won't be too long,' Martin told her.

They walked along the edge of the sea. The tide was in, with waves the deep green of glass bottles. Around them, the day seemed calm and purposeful now, as if it was waiting for action. Further on, they stopped and cast around for flat pebbles, sending them hopping over the long rollers. Martin turned to look at Damien. 'You must be angry with Karen.'

He nodded: he was feeling bad, all right. 'Look where she is right now,' he said, bitterly. 'She was just playing with me. Harry holds all the cards.'

'You want to get even, and you need me to help? If we did – relieve Harry of a bit of surplus, what then? I'd have to go on working for him.'

'He'd blame you in some way, I guess. Then you could give notice, or just leave.' Damien began to walk on, saying in a careless voice, 'We'll need to stick together, the three of us. Viv thought we could stay in Ireland.'

'And would you?'

'I've always wanted to go there. Did I tell you I'm quarter Irish? My grandmother Bridie, who raised us, she used to tell me about her home country.'

'It should be easy, hiding away. There are remote places – perhaps we'd rent a farmhouse. And you'd let Karen take the rap?'

'Someone has to.'

'A lot of people, locally, never did take to her. They never trusted Harry's choice.'

'Like you, Martin?'

'Me? I just have a suspicious mind.'

★

Karen had been waiting all day to see Damien. At three in the afternoon she saddled the bay mare from Friar Farm and set off alone across the marshes. So much had happened in the past few weeks, since they had ridden this way together. Now she was filled with impatience, bursting with questions, and the bleak, flat landscape seemed interminable. Arriving early at the shore, she loosened the mare's girth then tethered her, and sat down to wait. The sea was almost empty, except for a couple of ferries, a few small sailing boats. Soon she saw the motor dinghy, with its steady approach.

When the boat puttered in to shore, Damien jumped out and they embraced right there, in the surf. He seemed tense, or distant even. Together, they dragged the dinghy part way up the beach. 'What's happening? Why couldn't I come to the chalet?' She sat down near to him, on a fallen post, and put her arm around him. She could not get close enough, while he was abstracted and still. 'Who was that woman who brought your note?'

'She's just an old friend. You mustn't come near me—and not to the chalet, any more. At least you were able to get away, and here all right.'

Karen frowned at him. Then she laughed a little, remembering. 'Harry's been staying awfully close to me. But you know how terrified he is of horses? That was a good way to shake him off.'

He didn't even smile. 'It's the last time. No more of this.'

'What's happened?' Karen had been desperate to see him, and now he was acting so strangely.

'Listen, don't try to contact me again. If Martin asks, you must tell him that we quarrelled. It was just an affair and it's over.'

'But why?' She was searching his face for answers.

Damien said, carefully, 'I've found a way to get us money. A lot of money, and soon. We'll go back to the States. Harry will never find us there, he wouldn't have any clue where to start looking.'

She tried to take it in. What was he planning? 'Tell me. You must tell me.'

'I daren't. You must keep Harry unsuspecting, just be as usual with him—'

'And why on earth pretend to Martin? When he's the only friend we've got.'

'There are things you don't know about. I can't involve you because that would put you at risk. Just get ready to run with me. Have your documents around. We won't be able to meet up again.'

'If you told me, I could help.' He shook his head, impatient. 'You're treating me like a child,' she accused, angrily. He was treating her like Harry did, as someone unequal, not valid.

Damien grasped her wrist, pulling her close again. 'The only reason is for safety. And I promise, we'll be on that flight together soon. Trust me. We're going to make a new life.' He kissed, then hugged her. 'You must go now, to get home before dusk.'

She breathed in the scent of his body, tried to memorize the feeling of him against her. 'Damien, don't do anything where you could get hurt.'

'No one will get hurt. And soon we'll be together all the time. Go, now.'

Leaving him there, Karen rode away slowly. Once she turned to look back. He was still watching her go and raised a hand in goodbye. Then a turn in the bridlepath had hidden him, and the beach, from her sight. Feeling suddenly too solitary, and like a target on these miles of exposed, empty grazing land, she urged the mare into a canter. What was Damien planning? After so many years, she had rediscovered trust and it was precious: she would do as he asked, and try to quieten the clamour of guesses in her mind. She must pretend to know or suspect nothing, and must be exactly as usual with Harry.

Perhaps it was the desolation of these marshes that filled her with unease, and almost with a sense of foreboding. It had been such a brief meeting – and Damien wanted it to be their last. Whatever he was planning, she had been excluded. He was doing it for them, so that they could be together. A new life, in the States. She tried to picture it, and to believe in it. Perhaps, if she knew more, then it might all seem more real to her.

At the farm, she rubbed down the bay, watered and turned her out in the field. As she walked back through the village and along the lanes to the Keep, it was early evening, almost dusk. Coming up the drive, she was surprised to see Christine's Mini still parked at the side. The housekeeper was in the kitchen, replacing things on shelves.

'Christine, you're working late,' Karen greeted her. 'Did you have a good holiday?'

'Quite nice. Although it wasn't as warm at the Lakes as down here. Been riding, I see. Didn't Damien go with you? His luggage seems to be missing from the spare room.'

'He's not been staying recently. I'm making a cup of tea. Would you like one?'

'No, thank you. It's past time for our evening meal, I must get home and put it on. Mr Glass wants to see you. He's in the living room with my Joe. I've had a fair old day, catching up and getting things back to rights.' She was pulling on her coat. 'It's none of my business, of course, but I hope we'll see him again.'

'I really don't know, Christine. I don't see why not,' she lied.

The housekeeper gave her a beady look. 'So long as there's nothing wrong. He was so interested in reading about his father, combing through all my cuttings, and I brought a new one for him.'

A small square of newsprint lay on the kitchen table, next to Christine's handbag and keys. 'May I see?'

'It's only a tiny one but it mentions Mr Glass. He was so keen to read about his father, it's a shame.'

Karen picked up the news cutting, headlined *Tycoon Last Seen Near Brigsea*. It was very short. Local readers were told that Alistair Quentin, a business and entertainment entrepreneur, whose family and colleagues had not heard from him for a week, had last been seen visiting a famous Brigsea resident, film actor and producer Harry Glass. After sailing in Mr Quentin's private yacht to the Isle of Wight, they had parted at Brighton Railway Station.

'Alistair Quentin turned up again,' she said, folding the piece of paper. 'That's why there was no big hunt for him. He'd left his wife, and was staying with another woman.'

Christine took the cutting from her. 'We all know who causes that sort of trouble,' she exclaimed. 'Young women who display themselves.'

Karen recoiled from the housekeeper's covert hostility. Christine must believe that men were incapable of free choice, and that was untrue. She crossed the hall to the living room, where Harry was standing in front of the fireplace. The man with him was built like an oversized bulldog, with muscular arms that bulged from a leather jerkin, a bullet head spiked with orange stubble. He was looking her over, quickly and interestedly.

'There you are, darling. Did you have a nice ride? I want you to meet Joe Taylor. He's our new security guard.'

Her dismay must have shown in her expression. 'But, Harry—'

'I know you've become very used to Martin,' Harry interrupted drily, with some hint of amusement. 'And that's part of the trouble. Joe is going to look after us, and has been thoroughly briefed. He's done some work for me here before, and knows his way around. All right, Joe.'

'See you tomorrow then, at nine, Mr Glass. Mrs Glass.' Joe Taylor gave a little nodding bow that managed to be somewhere between obsequious and insolent. Before he went out he smiled briefly at her. His voice was slightly familiar, she had heard it before, but could not remember when.

'Better not to offend him, darling,' Harry said softly. 'Joe's main brief is to look after you.'

'But I don't need looking after. Why?' And why now, she wondered. Did Harry have a sixth sense?

'Suppose someone tried to do you harm? After all, you're the wife of a wealthy man. Joe Taylor will protect you – he's been around.'

'He looks as if he's been inside. Has he? I don't want to be guarded, Harry. That's ridiculous, and so old-fashioned.'

'Allow me to know your best interests, Karen. It has all been decided and arranged.'

She sat down on a sofa, determined to look as if it didn't matter. 'Is he supposed to work with Martin?' Damien would have to be really careful now, with Christine's thug son hanging around. They would both have to watch out. Damn Harry – and for pretending he gave a damn about her. All he wanted was to keep his possessions under lock and key. Was that what Damien had been talking about, perhaps? Might he be planning something here?

'What a crosspatch you are. And I still care about you.' Harry had turned away from her; he was pouring drinks. 'Martin's turned out a disappointment to me. I shall get rid of him, when he deigns to show up. Or, come to think of it, we won't say anything to him until tomorrow morning, as that's when Joe starts.' He laughed, in a way that sounded friendly. 'Don't look so terribly panicked, Karen. Joe is here to protect you. Truly.'

'Yes, of course.'

As he handed her a glass, their eyes met unexpectedly. 'I've to visit New York on business, the day after tomorrow,' Harry said quietly. 'I'm sorry you can't come – it'll be just a day or two, a short trip. But will you miss me a little, anyway? I wonder. Karen, might you always think well of me, perhaps? After all, I changed your life.'

Puzzled, she stared into his face, and had no idea how to answer. No, she could not think well of him – he was a bully and a woman abuser, at best – but why was he asking? It was almost as if . . . A sudden hope crept into her. Might it be that he was thinking of letting her go? She might even begin to forgive his violence, if, after everything, they could simply divorce. 'You certainly did change my life,' she said, slowly. 'Harry? I'd like to talk to you, about our future.'

Harry kissed Karen lightly on the cheek. 'When I get ·back, darling. Then we'll talk about the future,' he promised. He saw the lifting in her expression, her hope. There were things about

Karen that he was going to miss. Her youthfulness, with that capacity for hoping. Also, she was so pretty. He sighed.

'What is it, Harry? This business trip – d'you want to talk to me about it?'

He suppressed a slight smile. He could never tell anyone about his present troubles – and, certainly, he would not confide in her. Although, if she knew that side of things, Karen would surely thank him. As it was, he must simply act to protect himself.

But through the evening, and as they went to bed, he watched her. Their time together was almost over. He had chosen her, had tried to elevate her in the world, and to give her a better life, everything that a girl might want. Somehow, it had not worked out. She had a way of setting off rage in him. He could trace all his misfortunes in business to her arrival in his life, when she had distracted, spoiled his judgement. She had never seemed content with him, or their being together. Somehow she had failed to recognize him as an exceptional man. Instead, she had flirted with boys. His mind shied away, and he fell asleep.

In the morning, over toast and marmalade, he sacked Martin. 'I've decided that our association is at an end. To be perfectly frank, I no longer feel I can trust in your loyalty. There has been cause for disquiet.'

Martin was looking astonished. 'I'd like you to explain that.'

Harry sliced his toast in half, into triangles, and replaced his knife. 'You've become too prone to question. Instead of doing what I say.'

'If you were dissatisfied—'

'It's too late, Martin. I've decided. I want you to leave. You can finish breakfast first, if you like.'

Martin pushed away his half-eaten toast. 'You can't treat human beings like this. But then, you always did. Why did I ever put up with it?' He stood. 'I won't come back this time, you know. In five minutes, you'll be begging as usual.'

'I rather doubt that.' Harry took a sip of coffee. Martin did make an excellent cup of coffee, and he was a good assistant, but it couldn't be helped.

'Could this be part of the financial straits, maybe?' Martin asked him, mockingly. 'Or is it because of her dropping her knickers?'

'Get out,' said Harry, calmly and succinctly. 'Out of my house. Now. Your wages are on the sideboard, in that brown envelope.' He watched Martin struggle briefly with himself before taking up the pay packet and pulling out its contents. The month's wages. No more, and no less.

'You'll be completely lost, Harry. You'll be sorry about it.'

'Your replacement arrives at nine.' He consulted his wrist-watch. 'In five minutes.' Why was Martin still standing there and not leaving? He was looking puzzled. 'Joe. Joe Taylor,' he explained, 'is taking over the job of looking after us here.'

When Harry looked up again, Martin had gone, had simply melted quietly away into the hall. He hoped there wasn't going to be a scene, but if there was then Joe could handle it. Joe could handle anything, in the physical universe.

In some ways it was a pity, losing Martin. But he knew, or suspected, too much. And his loyalty was in question, which was not to be tolerated, not for a moment now.

Harry frowned. He was, he knew, surrounded by enemies.

Viv had arranged to be at the fairground, a few miles further up the coast, for six o'clock that evening. But then, he was always late.

It was chill and overcast, threatening to rain. The fairground was closing for the autumn, and men were busy dismantling the rides. She waited near the shooting stalls, which were shuttered and padlocked, and looked towards the empty stretch of road. The men were loading fairground horses, riveted to bright, striped poles, into an old truck. 'Got the time?' she called.

'Gone six ten, love.'

Joe must have left the Keep by now. She'd be glad when she didn't have to hang around waiting for him any more. She heard the motorbike before she saw it, with its throaty exhaust – something he'd done to make it noisier or faster. It streaked up close, then braked abruptly.

'Wotcha, Viv.'

'Hi. You're late.'

He parked the bike; they sat on the low wall by the shooting gallery. She lit up for them both as he took off his leather gauntlets. 'Martin staying with you, now?'

'With us, yeh. And Harry's off to New York in the morning?'

'That's right. I'm driving him in his Jag to the airport. He's only going for a day or two, you know.'

'Damien wants to do the job tomorrow night.' She glanced at Joe when he didn't answer. 'What d'you think? And – hey, you're not trucking, these days. So how're you going to find the right kind of freight, and—?'

'That's my problem, not yours. I'll get the major stuff out of the UK, but I've a fence or two here – and that's all you need to know.'

'So we use the cave, Martin and me? If we do go tomorrow night, then we'll have to hide the stuff, right?'

'All of it,' he said, looking at her.

Viv complained. 'How long've we been planning this? You don't think —'

'Just checking.' Joe grinned at her. 'Hey, little cousin, a treasure chest, and in our favourite smugglers' cave.'

She smiled slightly, reminded by him of their childhood game. 'Listen. You think Harry might change the combination for getting into the safe, now?'

'If he does, I can change it back. Mother will be my alibi.' Joe dropped his cigarette end, pulling on his gauntlets. 'Harry's lad – is he still sweet and keen?'

'Both. New love's a wonderful thing, Joe.' Viv shrugged, as they walked towards the bike. 'Suspicion's got to fall somewhere, and I've waited far too many years for those misty mornings. I'm not going to share my man.'

Joe wheeled his motorbike to the road with her. He would wait within sight until someone stopped, and she could hitch a ride back to join the others. They could hardly risk being seen together, not now. 'I can scarcely believe it's going to happen, after all this time,' said Viv. 'Tomorrow night it is, then. And you be sure to stay well clear.'

Damien and Martin, sharing a beer at the chalet window, had watched the progress of the tide, rolling in up the shore. The sky, darkening early, had lowered already to meet and merge.

'When I started with Harry,' Martin said, 'I hated the coast. Really, till this summer. Now I like it. I'd miss the sea.'

'Ireland has a lot of ocean,' Damien answered, absently. 'Where did Viv go?'

'I don't know. We'll find a house to rent by the coast, then. That'll be easy, especially at this time of year. I'd be poor now, if it wasn't for your idea. Harry's the meanest person I ever knew.'

'Yeah, you're free. You won't have to face him in the morning, the day after tomorrow – or when he gets back from the States.'

Martin shifted uneasily. 'This rushing it forward, the timing – it could look like a grudge thing.'

'But there'll be nothing to connect you with the job. It's too safe an opportunity, him being away – we can't miss it. Here she is.' He almost heard Martin groan with annoyance as Viv came looming through the misty dark.

'Hi,' she said. 'Hasn't anyone got supper on?'

'Martin's promised to do a pasta. And, now you've said that, I'm an appetite on legs.'

'Pasta, that's great. We won't be in this crummy dive much longer. So are we going for it – tomorrow night, then?'

Martin was looking through their bag of supplies. 'I need that carton of cream. Look, I'm still worried about what Harry will make of it.'

'I'll get the cream, it's in the cold store,' Damien told him. He went out quickly, pulling Viv after him, out of earshot. There was the sand pit among the rocks, where things were kept chilled, although it wasn't needed now autumn had come.

'What?' hissed Viv.

'It's got to be tomorrow, as soon as possible. Otherwise those code numbers are more likely to get changed. Then we'd have to ask Karen, and she'd be involved. I won't let her take the rap.'

'OK, OK. I see what you're saying. Because Martin got the sack—'

'And we have to warn Karen to stay upstairs – to keep away, no matter what.'

Viv shrugged, in the near darkness. 'You think that's necessary? I suppose I could get a warning to her. She'd trust me, I expect.'

'The other thing – Harry's new guard.' Viv was looking blank. 'Harry's taken on Joe Taylor, Christine's son. Martin told me.'

'Oh. Right.'

'We need to make sure he's out of the house tomorrow night.'

Martin stuck his head out from the chalet door, calling, 'Damien, where's that cream got to?'

'We'll think of something,' Viv whispered. 'He may not even be sleeping in. But listen, I'll handle that too, somehow.'

The evening passed in a blur, as the reality hit him. They were going to do it. Damien felt the beginning of a gathering tension, or excitement. He slept patchily, waking constantly through the night, as if there was something he had to deal with, to argue out. In the early morning, creeping from the chalet, he left Viv and Martin still sleeping. Outside, disorientation took hold, as he walked across white, virgin sand like a moonscape, under a lifting dawn. The sea had retreated, narrowly binding up the world's edge, studded with toy ferries. The waves only whispered distantly, too weak to roar.

Crouching hidden among the dunes, he watched the driveway to the Keep. At half past nine, the Jaguar slid out from the gates. He craned to see – glimpsing one person in the back, just the driver in front – before Harry's car had rounded the corner into the lane, then gathered speed and disappeared. Harry, with Joe Taylor, had left for the airport. Kneeling a while, and staring towards the house, he thought of Karen alone inside, behind the tall, automatic gates. He waited and watched in the slight hope of seeing her. When Christine's car appeared up the lane, he wanted to run out from his hiding place, to try to draw on the housekeeper's friendliness, her old approval, to get to see Karen. That wasn't possible, or wise. Christine was loyal to Harry, and could have been turned against him. The Mini rolled in between the gates, and they drew gently, firmly shut.

Now time crawled again, passing them through a grey, sunless day that never seemed to happen. At noon, Viv went off to the Keep with a note for Karen, kept secret from Martin. She came back to report that there was no sign of Harry's car returning, nor of Joe Taylor. The housekeeper seemed to be still around. Karen had read his warning note, she told Damien. Then they heard Martin, coming back from buying a torch battery.

'We could go in as soon as Christine's left for the day. At five,' Martin suggested. 'If we just see where Mrs Harry Glass III is first.' Then he must have seen Damien's reaction. 'Or as soon as it's got dark?'

'During the night will be safer for everyone. And not before midnight. People could call by, and we've quite a lot of stuff to shift. We'll be in the cellar a while, so the hall and drive must both be guaranteed deserted.'

'After midnight,' Viv agreed, outvoting Martin.

They assembled a rucksack and a knapsack, to carry things in. They would take Viv's torch, and would wear gloves and hoods, with scarves across the lower halves of their faces. Martin had a black balaclava, and had cut holes for his eyes and mouth. In this mask he looked suddenly sinister, as if he was capable of doing harm. Damien was surprised by his own nervousness, at the pragmatic, theatrical, small preparations they were making.

At nine in the evening, they ate soup. He made himself swallow, never registering any taste. He tried to think only of the future beyond tonight, and to imagine being with her.

Karen had never felt more alone. The house, with its rambling, chill stone, seemed vast around her as the darkness of evening drew in.

Harry had been gone since this morning. The new aide, Joe Taylor, had called at eight: his mother was ill, it might be just something she had eaten, but he ought to stay with her tonight. Would that be OK?

'Of course,' Karen answered, automatically. 'Tell Christine she shouldn't come in tomorrow. And – I need to call Harry, d'you know his hotel?'

There was a brief pause from Joe. 'Should be in the green file, over the desk. Harry shoves everything in there.'

'I'll have a look. There's really no need for you to stay here while he's away.'

Then, putting down the phone, Karen was less sure. She knew – she had guessed – that something might be planned for tonight. As soon as that woman had appeared at the door again – with Damien's note telling her to remain upstairs, to keep clear – everything had fallen into place. But who was the woman? Why was she supposed to pretend, to Martin, that there had been a break-up?

She no longer knew who they could trust, she and Damien. Something was nagging at her, an instinct, telling her things weren't right. It was something about the way Harry had been, perhaps. She wanted to check, and make certain the place really was clear, in case Damien did come in, maybe tonight.

There was a booking memo in the green file, just as Joe had said, and it carried the hotel address and phone number. Karen checked the time in New York. Harry would have landed at JFK several hours ago. She pressed out the hotel's number, and got through at once. 'I'd like to speak to one of your guests, Mr Harry Glass.'

Again she was put straight through to Harry's suite. A simple, 'Hi, there.' A woman's voice, intimate and sensuous.

Whatever she had expected, it wasn't this. But why not? Surprise had taken her breath away. When she spoke, her own voice sounded secretarial, ruthlessly practical. 'Hello. I'd like to speak to Harry Glass.'

'Harry's not here.' Then, sharply, 'Who's that calling?'

She knew that voice, surely? It was months since she had heard it, but . . . 'D'you mean he's gone out?' she asked crisply. 'When should I call back?'

'No, I mean Harry couldn't make it. He's not in town. Who is that?'

'He never got into New York? This is Harry's wife, Karen. Hello, Raima.'

There was a tense silence, no reply. Then the phone cracked down. The line hummed, empty, in her ear. She had embarrassed Raima, she thought with satisfaction.

Harry had flown to New York for business talks. He had told her, told everyone that. If he wasn't there, if he had never arrived, then where was he?

Damien would come to the house tonight, she felt sure of that. Her unease lay heavy, deepening into a solid fear. The night was so silent, dark. It was too still.

Karen walked slowly to the top of the stairs, to a high vantage-point where she couldn't be seen. From here, she could look down from the tall landing window of the tower, see the sweep of the drive and part of the garden. She would hear if anyone moved around the house. What time would Damien come, and who would be with him?

She settled against the stone wall, at the edge of the banister rail, to wait and watch.

Just after midnight, they left the chalet. The night had cleared a little, a three-quarter moon riding high between clouds. They slid down through the rocks, and crossed the beach to climb the jetty steps. The small gate, by the boatshed, would be less conspicuous, especially if there was any problem.

Viv whispered, 'Fingers crossed that code still works.' Martin pressed out numbers on the panel. After a moment, the gate swung open.

Damien laughed softly, briefly. 'It's going to be OK.' He glimpsed the faces of the others half hidden, not recognizable.

Now they had to circle through the garden, keeping to the path away from the house. As they approached the front, the security light flooded on: they were among the bushes then darting, from nerves, up to the steps. The light could be set off by anything, a cat or a fox. Martin was fumbling at the door, getting the sequence wrong, maybe, as nothing happened.

'Try again,' said Viv, sharp.

The door swung open into Harry's house, into a great, yawning, breathing darkness. She had done as he had said, switched off the lights and gone to bed: kept out of it. Relief filled Damien as they scurried like shadows across the hall, chasing the crooked, leaping beam of Viv's torch. Martin had his key copies out, was nervous still, dropping the improvised wire ring with a small, sharp clank on the floor. He swore under his breath. With Viv, Damien moved the brass stand full of swordsticks carefully to one side. Martin unlocked the cellar door.

Quickly inside, on the curve of stone stairs down, they let the heavy door swing closed. Viv switched on the light, unbelievably bright, white and shadowless. As they stepped down, the rooms below unfolded, Harry's private museum, with neatly ordered ranks of displays, glittering trophies. The strange, biting, sea-filled draught swept through, on a faint undersmell of something rotting. A trapped rat, perhaps, or a seabird.

'Here we go,' Martin said, eyes glittering behind the balaclava. 'Viv knows what to take.' He thrust the keys into her hand, and she started towards the display cases. Damien unrolled the rucksack.

Looking back, he saw the shiny breastplate lifted down, clear of the wall. Something was tugging, nagging at Damien's memory, but he couldn't think what it was.

Martin was at the safe, working its combination lock. If that didn't open it, they wouldn't have enough money. Not to get away together, not back to the States. Not anything.

Then the heavy steel door of the safe swung slowly, silently open, yielding. And, as it did, Damien remembered what he had forgotten, until now.

He had promised his sister, promised Angel, the year before she died, *I've kicked crime. I'll never do another job, I swear to you.*

But it was too late, remembering that now.

Karen stood poised at the top of the stairs, straining to hear, to see. Her hair was prickling on her scalp. They had come, as she expected. Soon after midnight she had seen the security light outside, washing over the drive and garden, over empty space. A minute later, they had come in through the front. She had heard muffled sounds, a key turning in a lock – the cellar, opening.

Then silence again. The outside light went off. Everything was as usual.

How many people were in the cellar? Martin must be part of this. And maybe the woman. She wanted to warn Damien that Harry was not in New York. But Damien had told her to keep away, stay clear. *If Martin asks, you must tell him we quarrelled, our affair is over* . . . If she went to warn him, to find out what was happening, then she might blow everything and send all his plans sky high. So she waited, watching and listening.

When it happened, she knew that this was what she had been watching for.

The security light flashed on again, flooding the grass, bushes and gravel with an eerie, false moonshine. A man was walking quietly up the drive, dark clothes, soft shoes, so it took her a moment to recognize Harry, who never walked anywhere. He was crossing the circle of light, to the front door.

She flew down the stairs.

14

As Karen reached the dark hall the front door swung open. He stepped in, and she rushed to bar his way. 'Harry. What's happened? Why aren't you in New York?'

She moved close to kiss, to distract him, but Harry pushed her aside. He seemed furious. 'Not asleep, Karen? In the middle of the night?'

'I called New York.'

For a moment, his attention swung towards her. Then he was staring straight at the cellar – the steps down, the steel door. Too late, she saw that the brass stand of sticks had been moved to one side and a sharp slice of light showed.

'Who's in the cellar? Why is the light on?'

As he shot out the words, she scattered into a fall of wasted response. 'Is the light on? Someone must've forgotten to switch it off – perhaps Joe did. I'll see to that, Harry. You go and —'

In the faint light, she saw that his face had grown vicious. Harry strode down the steps, grabbing a walking stick. A long glittering blade hissed out of its sheath. In an instant, she was between him and the cellar door.

'No, Harry. Leave it! Let me—'

'Get out of my way.'

Karen stood her ground. Harry grasped at her sweatshirt, and pushed her backwards, on to the steps. As she fell, she twisted round and saw him turning the handle: the door swung open, unlocked. Then he was on the stairs down, and she scrambled up, following. Into the chill of stone, the gaseous smell of the cellars, air rushing, as the heavy steel door swung shut on them. Beyond Harry and his silent, menacing descent, she glimpsed the brilliant, striplit caverns below. The dark figures at work, hooded, masked with scarves. There was Damien. He was entombed . . . Harry, swordstick raised. In that merciless light.

If Harry couldn't see, then surely they could still be safe. Where was the light, the switch?

It was so silent, deep in the cellars. A secret ceremony, a sacrificial violation: the tabernacle of the safe. Gold. Diamonds, pearls and emeralds, spilling out, ripe like a heart. They were stuffing the glittering spoils into an ancient, faded knapsack. Paper documents and rolls of banknotes, envelopes, a cashbox, all went in. No time to be ceremonious.

Viv had felt a draught whining through the cellars, but she hadn't really noticed.

'Look out!' The girl's warning scream pierced through them. They turned, and froze there.

Harry Glass. He was on the bottom stair, face blazing with rage. He was holding a long sword, shouting, lunging forward. Abruptly the light went out. Total darkness and confusion. Someone crashing into her. Martin. 'Stay close,' Viv yelled.

The girl screamed again, 'Damien, come this way!'

Viv grasped the knapsack tightly. She crashed into a corner – something hard, a display case, a shelf. Then, soft drapes, a curtain or flag. Lost people, stray limbs, cries, milling in a panic in the dark. Anyone could be a friend. One of them could kill. Find the tunnel into the rocks, the cave . . .

Find the torch. In her pocket, Viv worked it up through the lining, found the button. Its sudden beam flashed out a nightmare gleam of weapons, a dungeon grid of iron; some face, caught in a scream, she didn't recognize. The torch slid from her sweating hand, was gone, cracked out. Darkness. Martin, taking hold of her, grappling towards the floor for it. Viv fumbled at her lighter, flicked on its tiny flame. Then she was getting her bearings, towards the wall panel, her fingers finding the lever to work it.

'Come on,' she yelled to Martin. The steel panel slid open, the dank tunnel wafted towards her. Looking back, in the flame's flicker, she saw a shape – Damien – hurtling across the cellar towards her. Instinctively, she threw the lighter at him. She only glimpsed it falling, way short, into the shelf of cleaning fluids. Its flame burning, then sparks beginning, as Damien stood frozen. Someone had begun to scream.

Viv pushed Martin before her into the narrow stone passageway. She stumbled through after him. The panel slid shut automatically, sealing them off.

Scrambling helter-skelter along the narrow tunnel, they heard and felt the boom of explosion.

From nothing, from the seed of a spark, the dark exploded, deafening. The fireball leaped raging, molten, alive. It was hell's demon: Damien felt it clawing at his face, his eyes. The heat and a searing pain knocked him backwards, helpless. The last thing he saw was the creature climbing hungrily up the hangings along the wall, higher and higher, cackling in triumph.

Something fell, sharp and singeing, close by with a crash, nudging him out from unconsciousness. He kicked away from its burning, choking from thick, scorching smoke. They were broiling alive, and pain flashed through him, he couldn't breathe, sank back again. Fire forced a stormy red sea through his head, melting him. Until his face was buried, tears and scalds soaked in something solid, fabric ... He couldn't breathe, smoke cooked his lungs, his chest and throat were stabbing out coughs. Wanting to lie still, to die: being propelled, torn sideways, half dragged, he sensed her there, agitating at death, saying no, screaming it out into the tide of fire. Crawling, wriggling through flame, under smoke, snakes stricken beneath the beast's belly.

He could not. The weakness of death, the release of it, waved over and spread through him.

She would not let go. No words would come: he groaned. She was plucking, then pulling, dragging at his deadened limbs, one by one. Rolling him over. She had no mercy.

The smell of the creature, acrid and sharp, mineral. A

ravenous cackling, applause gone mad. The clatter of falling prey. The dissolving, cutting tongue of it, knowing it was winning. Crouching, leaping over. A lick and a kiss, an abrupt roar and pounce, that rending. He sensed all around the fire that was stalking, killing them. His mind's eye, impressed with it, held the fire. He could not breathe, and ached with pain. He could not go on.

She was forcing him on, grabbing and pulling, through the tumbling, roaring seafire. Had rolled, shoved him against hard stone, a wall: they were crouched, crammed together inside some narrow space. It was different, the heat less and the noise behind them. The scarf fell from his mouth and nose, and he breathed real air, chill. They were racked by coughing, his eyes and nose streaming, he was gasping for oxygen, his chest in paroxysms of contraction. It felt like a file, a rasp, inside.

The blissful breath. Life. They were sheltered in cool rock, somehow further out from it all. She was here, they were alive. Long minutes were passing, he didn't know what was happening. He could hear, then, that the fire was lessening, and he felt its heart weakening. It was burning itself out.

When he could, he whispered hoarsely to her, beside him, 'Where's Harry?'

'I don't know. He seemed to disappear when the chemicals exploded. Are you OK?' He didn't answer her, because he knew that something was wrong. 'It's dying down, now,' Karen went on. 'Are you all right?'

Damien tried to shift sideways. Cramped, he tried to glimpse the red, leaping light. He could hear it behind them, and could even see it, vivid in his mind. So why was everything dark? He tried to form the words, asking at last, 'Can you see the fire?' Karen didn't answer, and he could feel her look at him. He shouted, 'Can you see the fire?'

'Of course I can see it.'

Then he understood. The flames had beaten him, burning themselves into him. He was living in a world of darkness now.

★

The torchlight was playing their shadows, huge and distorted, over the walls of the cave. 'While it's still dark,' Viv was saying, 'we've got to get away. That big bang – whatever that was – suppose someone heard it?'

'We'll wait,' Martin insisted, 'for Damien.' There had been a big explosion behind them, but he didn't want to think about it, what it could mean. 'He'll come. Damien knows where we are.' He needed to be busy, to distract himself. Viv was still digging the sand, at the back, and there was only one spade. Martin rifled through the knapsack, sorting loot like jumble. Precious stones. Documents.

'That'll do it,' Viv said. 'We'll bury everything in the bin liners. What're you doing? What are these?'

He shrugged her off, irritated. He wanted to listen for Damien, under the pounding of the tide. To hear his voice, calling a greeting. Viv was taking an audio-cassette from among the papers, peering at it, getting out her Walkman. He tried to ignore her.

'He won't come,' she said. 'Damien isn't going to turn up again. You want to know why? Because he's with her. He was thieving for her. Damien lied to you. And it'll be daylight soon.'

'Shut up,' Martin told her. 'I'm going to wait.'

'For ever? Listen, this tape is mad. All it says is, "Harry. Not there? It's Al Quentin, call me on the mobile." Why was that in the safe?'

'That's one of his answerphone tapes. I don't know why,' he answered vaguely. His attention was all on the papers, the evidence. Harry's scams were bigger and more intricate than he had thought, with a few added noughts. And, yes, Al Quentin had been right in it, up to his neck with Harry. Funny, that. Artemis Productions turned out to be an aborted company, long dead between them. Quentin not signing after Harry had over-committed, precipitately. Harry had forged more than just bank-loan guarantees, and the sums involved looked staggering, even by his standards. And he had been transferring everything.

'What're you doing with those mouldy old papers?' Viv demanded. 'Come on, all these into the rubbish-bin liners – but not that rubbish.'

Martin slid the wad of documents into his inside breast pocket, just in case they might ever be useful. The shiny black plastic sacks were stuffed with old daggers, pistols and jewels. Joe would be picking up those tomorrow. Now the sand had to be shovelled back over them. Buried treasure. Helping Viv, Martin glanced up, startled by their shadows leaping mammoth over the cave walls.

If only Damien would come. He knew in his heart that he could wait for ever, and would still be alone. But it was hard, giving up. They smoothed the sand, lightly, innocent. Viv stood, shouldering the knapsack. 'Listen, he fooled you.' When he didn't move, just kneeling there, she reminded him, 'I've got the cash here. What're you going to do? Martin, if you don't come now, I'm leaving anyway.'

He heard that she meant it, knew she would leave. Damien had deceived him: somehow, on some level, he had known. He could only go with her again. Filled with resentment as he was, Martin found himself slowly getting to his feet, and following Viv.

Damien stared into the dark. 'I don't know where we are.'

'We're inside one of the air shafts, that lead out to the ventilation grilles. I went towards where the draughts were coming from. Damien, why do you need to ask?'

'I can't see.' He felt the horror of it, as he forced out the words. 'I can't see anything, since the explosion.'

He felt her stiffen. When she spoke, it sounded careful, controlled. 'That'll be temporary, because of the brilliance. A fire blindness. But we must get out of here. The fire's dying down, and there are patches of stone floor. We can tread round the fire now.'

Darkness had never held terror like this before. Leaving the narrow stone shaft, he heard the fire shift, restless at their coming, with a crack and sigh of something half destroyed.

Here the heat was intense and the smoke gritty, thick with flying bits. Pulling the scarf round his face again, he held on to her, as she picked a path through. Something brushed past his neck, brought a stabbing pain. He was ablaze. Crying out, maddened, he tried to beat the invisible flames from himself. He felt her tearing at his jacket. Her voice, 'Get this off, quickly.' Wrestling clumsily, rending stitching, he hurled the leather jacket from him. Blundered into her. 'Something's caught overhead – hold on to me and run.'

Not running, but stumbling over unseen obstacles, arms wrapped around each other, falling against her, dragging her down. He heard Karen cry out, then she was hauling him up again. 'Mind your head. Up the stairs.' The journey endless, until his feet found steps. On hands and knees now, up those last few debris-thickened stairs. As they pushed out into the hall, he thought too late that Harry could be waiting for them.

'OK?' Karen's voice was calm. If Harry appeared, he wouldn't be able to see, there was nothing he could do. Damien crouched on the floor, breathing in the unfamiliar air, cool and clean. She said, 'Wait here. I'm going to call an ambulance.'

'No.' He held on to her. 'Don't be crazy. Because of my eyes? But they'll come right. It's only temporary – you said so.'

'We can't know that. I don't know anything about it. You must see a doctor,' she insisted. 'I'll get you to Casualty.'

'No,' he argued. 'Look, we've been set up. We're the scapegoats for this – burglary, arson – and Viv's run with the lot. It'll look like us. It's the one thing I never wanted, that you should take the rap.'

'But your eyes, your sight.' She shook him, her voice urgent. 'That's worth more than anything, any of this.'

He felt exhausted, weakening. He was still determined. 'Hell, Karen, we'd die in separate jails. And this will wear off.'

'There must be something . . . Let me call Dr Greene.'

'Harry's doctor? That would be comic. Are you all right?' he asked, anxious. If she'd got barbecued, he had no way of telling.

'I've got a few burns. So have you. Would we really look like pyromaniacs and burglars? I'm not so sure.'

'I want to bathe my eyes,' he said, to distract her. 'And we need to put something on these burns.'

She guided him through the silent house. Then she was turning on taps. The pain in his eyes felt like needles. He choked back cries. There had been chemicals on that shelf, they had exploded in his face. Had they caused this blindness, and not just the brightness of the explosion? Panic brought a cold sweat, he was shivering. He could not live without his sight.

'What is it, Damien? Please, let me—'

'It's just shock, I guess.'

She sat him down on something, a chair. Something heavy went round his shoulders: it was a coat maybe. He clasped her hand so she couldn't move off again. He was still trembling violently. 'We always wanted to be alone together.' He forced a smile.

Karen put her arms around him, and stayed there. 'Where did they go? Martin and – that woman?'

'They disappeared – right into the wall. It seemed to open up, then close behind them.'

'There are secret passages – a smuggler baron built this house. Where they go to, I don't know.'

'Neat, huh? If you get to know about them. We were going to split the loot, I thought.'

Karen asked, 'Who was the woman?'

'Just someone I'd met before. She turned out to be Martin's girl. We were all in it together, I thought . . . Jesus. Karen, I've dropped us both right in it.'

'I called your name, Harry will have heard that.'

'He knows anyway, for sure. But if I'd just gone to you . . .' If he had simply gone to her when she had called, he would still have his sight. It was useless to think that way but he couldn't help it. The shivering was less now. But he felt scared and bitter, helpless to take care of them, in this house that was way too empty. 'Harry would know about the passage, you think?'

'I think he just got out. And left us all to fry.'

'Why was he around? He was meant to be in New York.'

Karen didn't answer, and they were silent. Harry lay between them now. He was in the air. At any minute they would hear his approach, his voice. Karen would jump up . . . A tap was dripping, steadily. The wall clock ticked out seconds.

At last her voice came. 'I want to go and look around for him. We need to know where Harry is.'

'No. If we stick together . . .' They could stick together, but there was nothing he could do. He heard someone groan. It was himself.

'Oh, love. You look so . . . What battered people we are. Listen, we must forget him, forget everything for tonight. You need to rest, sleep. And tomorrow we'll think what to do.'

He would never sleep, he thought, but allowed her to guide him through the strange spaces of the silent, waiting house. There was a creaking, somewhere. 'What was that?'

Pausing, she said, 'It's just the wind. Or the house. It creaks – old houses do – but you only notice at night. It's OK. Mind the chest by the banisters. Turn right, here. We'll have a cool bath – we're like a couple of chimney sweeps. And then we'll sleep.'

She ran the taps and helped him to undress. 'There's a trail of soot, leading from the cellar, and I ought to make things look like before.'

He was holding on to her, stepping into water he couldn't see. 'Leave it until the morning. Won't you?'

'All right. I told Christine not to come in tomorrow. This water is soup already. This is almost funny, really. Except, these poor burns . . .'

She was chatting, keeping up a stream of talk for him, he knew. It was to soothe, to remind him how close they were. She was touching, soaping him. After all they had been through, he desired her still. It was a peculiar world, the pitch dark: without touch, without sound and smell, he became lost at once, as if he had got buried alive. She took him in her arms, laid her head on his chest. He couldn't tell if the wetness on her cheeks might be tears.

'We have our lives, and we have all this,' she was saying, in a soft voice from out of the dark.

He remembered again, then. 'I promised Angel, my sister. Before she died.'

'Promised what?'

'I'd never do another crime. Not anything. But then, I forgot.'

'That doesn't matter. You will see again, you will.'

Washing soot from his face, she had seen the small burns, like claw marks. His poor eyes were reddened, the swollen lids closing. She had cried, silently. She could not imagine him a blind man, and dared not think about that future, for Damien. She bathed him, finding burns on his neck and his leg, the right hand. Her own burns were worst on both hands, and on her scalp, where her hair had caught fire.

She found an antiseptic salve, dressings and aspirin, and took a bottle of brandy from Harry's store. They would sleep in the guest room behind a locked door.

Damien slept, and she lay listening beside him, in case Harry came. It didn't make any sense, the way Harry had appeared – on foot, so late, and unannounced – and interrupted the burglary. The way he had vanished, into the dark, as soon as the fire broke out. Why? Where could he be hiding? Perhaps he was just waiting, to catch them unawares.

She woke early, startled by a sound. It must have been the wind, rising in strange gusts around the gables, the tower. Or had it been Harry, walking past their door, trying the handle? She listened, heard nothing from inside the house. Damien was still sleeping, his breath deep, his face peaceful. When he opened his eyes, he might be waking to darkness and she must be there. But Joe had to be told not to come in today.

At eight, she crept from the bed, and softly turned the key. No one was around, on the landing or stairs. Harry's bed had not been slept in, there was no sign of him. She padded silently from room to room, her skin prickling. Harry could be close, he could be waiting for her.

But he was nowhere in the house, and swiftly she returned to the hall, dialled the Taylors. When Joe answered, her own voice sounded shockingly loud, cracked like a bell. 'It's Karen Glass. I hope I didn't wake you, Joe?'

'Just got my breakfast, was going to get the bike out. Is everything all right, Mrs Glass?'

'Yes, of course. Everything's fine. But I'm concerned about Christine. How is she?'

'Mother's sleeping in. A bit tired, is all. She had your message.'

'Joe, I want you to stay home and look after her today.'

He agreed, surprisingly easily. Relieved, she put down the phone. Now they had time, a day to decide what to do and what to tell people. If only Harry stayed away.

She made coffee, took it upstairs and watched Damien waking. She felt a moment of hope, because it seemed that he looked at her. Moving closer, she saw that his eyes, bloodshot from the smoke and flames, were unfocused and fixed. 'Can you see? Anything at all?'

After a minute, he shook his head slightly. She took his hand. 'We must go to a specialist. We could go to London today. Look, we have to.'

Damien said nothing. She felt a great wailing inside, a mourning for him. How could she persuade him to see sense, get to a doctor? 'There must be something they could do, to save your eyes.' Her voice was breaking, she couldn't control it. He reached out, trying to find her, and they held each other.

She became his sight, found his clothes, and guided him down through the house to the kitchen. Eating breakfast, neither of them mentioned Harry. Toast and boiled eggs. So ordinary, she thought, on a wave of hysteria. When Harry appeared, would he be wielding the Victorian sword, or something else from his pillaged collection?

'We'll be accused of theft,' Damien said, 'and of setting fire to Harry's place. I must go to the cops, turn myself in. But when would we ever be together again? Once people hear about this . . . There's got to be a better way.'

'Perhaps it could look as if we were both tackling the burglars.'

'No one broke in,' he reminded her. 'No smashed windows, or . . . that cellar door could never be smashed.'

'There's the secret passage, wherever it leads. Local people must know about it, surely? And the air shafts, with ventilation grilles. Or it'll look like who it was. Martin, who'd just got sacked. And he's run for it.'

'If he has. If he doesn't come back, exuding innocence. People around here, they'd find it hard to suspect Martin. While you and me – we got burned. We got to be kind of talked about. Harry will come back, and he'll testify.'

'We should go and have a look right now. Maybe we could remove a ventilation grille, from the outside. And make the safe look damaged.'

'We'd have to report it fast, this morning. Let's go and take a look. You'll have to do that, and figure it out.'

She found a storm torch, from the cloakroom shelf, and led him through the hall. Opening the cellar door, she was swamped by dread, remembering danger, her heart racing. Then, the cellar lay still, dark below them. Smoke clouded up the stairs, a smell of destruction. The cooling embers of the room were wreathed in sudden breaths of heat, fire stirring, glowing, flickering up from the corners, unexpectedly.

'Is it all burned out?' he asked, uncertainly. 'It still feels like an oven.'

'It'll be cooler down the steps. Yes, the fire's out. There's the odd flare-up, the draught going through.' She trained the powerful torch into the pit below, where its beam lit through the curls of smoke, fallen debris. She shivered. 'You must wait, sit here.'

'Keep talking to me. I want to know you're OK. You're going to find where they escaped to?'

'I'll look for that first. They went from the far corner.' Coughing, she pulled out a sleeve, held it over her nose and mouth. She must keep on talking. 'You would not believe this place. How did we survive? Everything inside is burned out. The walls are black – it looks like Hades. Just all charred. Shapes in ash, not solid.'

'Be careful,' he called out. 'I can smell things burning still. That isn't just smoke.'

It was a strong draught, fanning at something glowing. New young flames were creeping, wriggling. Something fallen from the ceiling, part of a beam. Tears were streaming from her eyes; she tried to wipe them away. A sudden vision caught her, of the fire that had died, springing into life again. Red, hellish. 'It's OK, just some stray wood,' she called. 'There's nothing else to catch. It's giving me more light.' She shook her head and stared. 'You won't believe this,' she called, laughing, beginning to cough again. 'There's a fire extinguisher hanging on this wall.'

'Carry it with you. Karen?'

'I want to find the passageway. But it was in the corner, behind where the new fire is. I could—'

'No, leave it. We can come back. Karen? I don't want you to stay down there any longer.'

'My eyes are watering, it's hard to see. I just want to look at the ventilation shafts, that's all.' Then she saw it. As if it had tumbled out from the second air shaft.

At first, the torch beam gliding casually over, she thought it was charred wood, somehow formed into the shape of a human. Curled, legs drawn up to the chest, foetal. The arms were outstretched. The head was skinless, shrunk too small, with snarling teeth instead of a mouth. It had no eyes . . .

Karen reeled backwards against the wall, gasping. Retching. The cellar whirled, zipped around her. She couldn't scream.

Forcing herself to look back at the thing, at Harry, she saw that his hands, those claws were raised to ward off the flames that had rushed and killed him. She glimpsed patches, less burned on the side of his jacket. A charred, grey cloth that she recognized.

'What is it? What's happening?'

Damien's voice. She found her feet, and lurched back across the ravaged room to him.

'I found Harry,' she wailed, teeth chattering.

'But how? Is he dead, do you mean?'

'I have to get out of here.' She stumbled with him, up the steps and out through the hall, the front door of the Keep. It was cold and windy. As she took great draughts of air, the nausea began to pass.

'OK,' he asked. 'What was it? Tell me.'

'Damien, it's horrible. He got burned up. I hated him, and yet—'

'But how did it happen?'

'He must've got trapped in the explosion. He was by the second air shaft, trying to escape.'

They were quiet. The immediate shock was fading, and her mind had begun to race. Harry – the batterer, the indestructible – was dead. And accidentally. She began to laugh. Damien grasped her shoulders, gave her a shake. 'We always wanted to be alone together,' he said softly, intent.

Yes, but not with the price of blindness. Not with the police about to close in, to start questioning. 'We got framed – and he died during the burglary. Everyone knows that we're lovers. You see? It'll look like we murdered Harry.'

'Yeah – and we could've done.'

'But we can't let it happen, not after everything. Damien, we could hide the body.'

'How? And how explain his absence?'

'People go missing,' she said, stubborn. 'If we just report him missing eventually.'

'Honey, everyone would suspect us.'

'If they did, they couldn't prove anything.'

'I won't stay away from you or wait for things to go quiet.'

She would rather be dead herself than in jail and not seeing him. But there had to be some way. Harry was gone: there was no more need to fear. They were free, now, to be together. If only . . . 'We'll get rid of the body. We'll take it out in the boat to bury at sea.'

'What about the cellar? Do we lock that up, throw away the key? How long would it be before the cops decided to break in? And find out everything.'

'We'll have to think. I don't know. But if they did, right now, then you and I would be up for murder. We must get rid of the body.'

'We could still get charged –'

'But they could never prove he was dead. Damien, it's our only chance. There's a high tide tonight. We'll use the boat, well after dark.' She tried not to think too much about what it would mean: that she would have to face the thing, and get it moved. She felt sick again. 'You do see, it's the only way?'

'You'd have to steer the boat. And, you would have to—'

'I know. OK. Look, I'm going to check the boatshed. We'll need something . . . Some kind of sheet and a rope. A weight.'

'The anchor? We'll need the outboard to get far enough out and back.'

'You go in,' she told him, 'and I'll be back in about half an hour.'

There was nothing to fear, Karen reminded herself. There was no Harry. As she crossed the garden, the wind snatched at her, sudden and spiteful. She hunched against it, and pulled up the hood of her sweatshirt. First, she wanted to check the beach chalet where Damien had stayed. Martin and his girlfriend might have gone there, or have left some clue behind.

The chalet had been locked, but the key was easy to find, hanging from a hook above the lintel. It grated rustily in the lock. Then, inside, it looked as if no one had ever been there, not for years. Clean and tidy, it had been swept bare, the furniture neatly stacked away. Karen checked through the few drawers, the shelves. Nothing. If Damien had left things here, they had vanished now, like Martin himself.

She retraced her steps, back over the rocks and beach, up to the jetty. Inside the boatshed, she switched on the light. There was the boat they had made love in: that seemed so long ago. She found the anchor. It would be traceable, of course. But then, if the sea ever yielded up its secret, that would be the end for them, anyway. Carrying a large plastic sheet, with a couple of ropes, she walked back through the garden.

A car, a navy saloon, was parking in the driveway in front of the house. Karen dropped the ropes and sheet behind a bush.

Someone, a man was getting out from the car, and she recognized the tall, stick-like figure of Colin Hargreaves. He must have let himself in through the security gates. Why had he come?

Striding up the path towards him, she pulled her hood close to cover the singed hair, then thrust her hands into her pockets. 'Good morning,' she called, and saw him turn towards her: in another moment, he would have rung the doorbell. Suppose he had seen Damien, his burns, his blindness? She spoke coolly, remembering their last encounter. 'Were you looking for Harry?'

Chief Inspector Hargreaves was taking his time, looking her over from head to toe. 'Good morning. That is correct.'

She tried to sound casual. 'I'm afraid he's away in New York, on business.'

'I didn't know he was going. When did he leave?'

'The day before yesterday, Joe Taylor took him . . .' She had to stop herself: Don't say too much, don't sound anxious.

'What a shame.' Hargreaves seemed to be deliberating. 'I wanted to ask him something. When does he get back?'

'He didn't say. I expect when he's got the deal that he's been chasing. Can I give Harry a message if he calls?'

'No, thank you. I'll be in touch. I'll be back.' He looked at her carefully, then nodded, and got back into his car.

Karen watched the detective drive off, all the way along the curve of gravel, through the gates and out of sight. He would be back.

In the afternoon, they had to wrap the body. She was Damien's vision, reluctant. Training her torch at an angle, propping it up, so its beam only slightly illuminated what she did not want to see, she unrolled the plastic over a patch of floor. From the corner of her eye, the thing seemed small and alien, wrong somehow. Metal staves, fallen from shelves, could act as levers pushed under its side. She gritted her teeth, then gave the order. 'Push, now.'

The body shifted in the half dark, as if it might spring up. It moved crookedly, because of their uneven weight, and she tried to push it straight again. The sheet underneath was dragged sideways, and something fell on to her feet. It was charred fabric, or skin. She was crying now, from a hatred of the task, and for the poor, burned thing. Rolling it on to the plastic sheet, they folded it over and over, out of sight. Damien put the ropes around, knotted them. It had become an opaque chrysalis, a sleeping lava, for returning to the sea. 'Are you OK?' he asked.

'We must drag it to the door now. There's debris everywhere.' She talked them through. Like worker ants, they dragged it in a trail between the wreckage. Hauled it through obstructions, up the steps, and left it there behind a locked door. She needed to wash off the past, obliterate a sense of guilt. When she was in his arms, Karen cried herself out: from the horror, which wasn't quite over yet, and from shock and pity, perhaps, at mortality.

The long day was ending. Dusk began to fall around the Keep. The high wind moaned, sending black clouds racing overhead. It was stirring at the incoming tide as she led Damien through the garden to the boatshed. There he fitted the outboard motor, stowed the anchor and chain, the oars. It was almost dark by the time they dragged the boat out, down the slipway. They moored it and went back to the house.

The body was heavier, as if it had grown. As it bumped stiffly down over the steps and through the bushes, the plastic glistened, white. It rustled eerily. What was this like for Damien, the darkness, the sounds magnified, and touch . . . ? She tried not to think, to concentrate: talk him through the shrubbery of acanthus, and silver thistle, right for this harsh climate. Concentrate. They got through the gate, closed it and at the top of the slipway, stopped to catch their breath. The angry roars of the sea were deafening.

Now it was so dark, moonless and starless, that she needed the beam of the torch to find their way down. A shallow step, and the ridges on the slipway, preventing sliding. There was a tearing sound. 'What was that?'

'We'll have to lift it, carry it.' He couldn't see, she had to keep reminding herself. She took his wrist. 'I'll go in front. Remember the slope. We'll go very slowly.' No way of holding the torch now, not until they had reached the boat. Here, in the open, the gale buffeted them to and fro. Her arms, her back ached, then she lost the ground and her feet slid into descending space. They were felled together, tumbling under the weight of the corpse, splashing into and under the icy sea. She swallowed salt water and gasped, surfacing, reaching out. Her hands closed over the jetty's substructure. 'Damien, Damien.'

His voice answered faintly, drowned by the roar of the waves. Hauling herself, hand over hand towards the sound, she blundered into something floating, a slippery gleam of white. Damien, his arms clasped around it, was treading water as they swirled, tossed together against the jetty. She forced words through her chattering teeth. 'Hold on. I'm going to pull the boat alongside.'

She worked her way round to the plunging boat, struggled to free it from the mooring. It had pulled too tight, the knot was solid from salt and wet, and her blistered fingers were numbed by cold. Finding a foothold, she hauled herself up, skating on seaweed over solid planks. At the jetty end, the knot unravelled. The boat bucked, like a frightened horse, as she towed it closer. She heard a cry from Damien. Pulling the torch from a sodden pocket, she pushed the switch. It wouldn't work. She yelled to him again, 'Hold on,' and felt the boat bump into something soft. Into him or the body. Winding the rope around her arm, she jumped.

The waves closed over her, swallowing hungrily, rollers hurling her, feet scraping shingle. Her arm was breaking, until she was tossed up on the crest of a wave, thrown against the gunwale. Stunned, she tried to reach out, saw the dark shape sucked away from her. Then hurtling back, close. She grabbed at the boat, threw her arms over the side, hung there. Now she could see the thing gleaming, white and sluggish, and Damien was grappling his weight against it. He cried out to her, and she shouted again. Washed closer, she caught his hand, and guided him to the boat's side. They hung there like dead fish, pegged out. She saw it floating, half submerged, away from them. 'What happened? This is hopeless!' he yelled, furious.

'Get in the boat! I'm going after it.' She pushed off from the side, diving in and swimming sideways against the current, pursuing the translucent gleam, its beckoning promise. When she got close, her hands rubbed over its slippery side, then found the handhold of a rope. He had played his last card, and they were still alive. She pedalled close, then grabbed at the boat's side.

They were in a pocket of calm, sheltered by rocks. Moving, too close to the rocks. 'I've got it,' she shouted. 'Give me the anchor chain – we'll tow it out.' She wound the chain around the body, sliding the end through its own loop. The thing floated out, a giant egg, from the anchor. 'I've got it fixed. I'm coming aboard – brace yourself against the side.' She was in with him, the boat rocking. It grated, vibrating, over something hard. 'Start the motor. I'll steer.'

The small boat throbbed out from the shore, jumping over and into the swell of waves. The lights of land, strung in clusters, were soon washed out. Now there were lights in the water, steady, blinking or moving, in white and green and red. They were on a road to the open sea. Behind, their strange cargo swam in pursuit, leaped and furrowed, sowing a trail of wake.

Far out in the bitter night, they cut the engine. Damien stood and lifted the anchor. He threw it from the boat.

A swirl of white cut through the black, rollicking world below. Then there was no sign of him. Harry had gone. She could hardly believe he was gone for ever.

They were warm and dry, beginning to recover now. She had made coffee with chocolate in it, and added measures of whisky. They had come through. For now, tasting the sweetness of safety, she didn't want to think what they would do next. It was enough, just being together: it was so much, with no Harry, no threats. Glancing at Damien, she saw that he was reaching out a hand in front of him. 'What is it?'

He answered, slowly at first, 'I can see . . .' Then excitedly, 'Patches of lightness, there! There's something . . . in that corner of the room?'

'Yes,' she breathed, scarcely daring to hope, and willing him to see it all.

'You've put the lamp on. In the corner, in front of the mirror?'

'Yes, oh yes. Anything more?'

'I can see the dark outline of the curtain.'

'You're going to be all right, you are.'

They sat together for a while, taking it in and laughing, like children, just from happiness. 'We mustn't hope too much,' he cautioned, sobering. 'In case it doesn't . . .' Then he laughed again. 'I can see lightness!'

'It will all come back, I'm sure it will.'

The wind was howling outside in the dark, all around the Keep. Soon the sky would be lightening into dawn, another day. She said, 'We must decide what to do.'

'We'll just leave now. We'll go to London and disappear into the city. Perhaps you could get money from Harry's account. Or we could sell something.'

'Then we must go soon, before Joe or Christine arrives.'

Karen packed her clothes into a bag. Going round the house, she chose a few small ornaments, then added the silverware. That would sell easily, and so would her wedding ring.

She cleaned the trail of soot from the cellar, deciding to lock it and to replace things as they normally were, to give them some time. But then, with the key in her hand, she felt too curious just to leave. She needed to have a quick look. 'I've got to know. What did happen to Martin? And that secret passage, does it exist?'

'We need to go, honey. Take a real fast look, then.'

Leaving the bags in the hall, Karen unlocked the cellar. It was chilled now, with the bitter smell of old fire. It seemed more blackened, and darker, under the small bobbing ray of the hand torch. Damien came to the top of the steps. 'Don't take long, OK?' She stepped down, through the shifting sigh of ashes that floated, trembled in the air she made.

Although the light was weaker, this time she found it, or

thought that she had. It was in the far corner, where Martin had vanished: a steel wall panel, tall and narrow, set into a recess. She fumbled all around the edges, and found a metal bar set into the rock. It was a lever of some kind, and she tried to push or pull it, in every direction, but it wouldn't work. They had left this way, but she couldn't see how.

'I've found the door,' she called. 'It must lead to the passage, but I can't open it.'

'They've gone, wherever it leads. Come on.'

'OK.' She was stepping back carefully, with the torch trained on debris underfoot, when she saw something else. A pair of broken spectacles, the colour of gunmetal. She knelt, and picked them up, to make sure.

They were Quentin's glasses, lying there, where Harry's body had fallen from the air shaft. Except, she realized now, that had not been Harry.

'What're you doing? What's going on?'

She whispered very softly to herself, 'Harry killed Quentin, after all.'

Harry had phoned the house, from his mobile, pretending to be Quentin. And in a flash, she saw: it had happened the day he returned from Italy, there must have been a meeting, a quarrel. Harry had acted so strangely – and she had called the police that night, to protect herself. She had given him an alibi, then got rid of the body, destroyed the evidence.

She sat back on her heels. The world had become dizzy, and dark.

If Harry was still alive, where was he now?

From Harry's balcony the views were perfect. Miles of white sand lay fringed with tall palms, and the luxurious deep blue of sea and sky. The apartment was everything he had wanted. The servants were obedient and well trained.

He had acted only to protect himself and what was his. Threatened with ruin, he had disposed of his enemy to survive. Now there was nothing to do except enjoy his money and the sweet life.

They would spend mornings at the beach, usually choosing Copacabana. In the afternoons, while she was still resting, he might go to his club or a bar. Sometimes he would have his driver take them out, into the mountains perhaps, in search of new sights, fresh places. Then, many restaurants in town were excellent, and the night life was international.

He was safe here: but then, he was nobody. Having everything, it was difficult to admit to being bored and missing the past. But he did not love Raima – particularly not, with the disfigurement of her pregnancy. When he looked at her body, which was now elephantine, his lip would curl in distaste.

Sometimes, then, Harry would think of Karen. He would catch himself wondering exactly where she might be. Was it only idle daydreaming, to imagine that he might see her again one day?

She would take the Underground home each night, from the café where she worked.

It was a winter of blizzards, bitter cold. She walked through the mean streets, in the dark, from pool of lamplight to pool of lamplight, over the stained sludge of snow. Around her, people were spilling out from the pubs, laughing in oblivion or complaining at the spiteful wind. Her steps were heavy, pushing onward, slowed by tiredness.

Sometimes she would pause, quickly glancing behind her, just to make sure that he wasn't there.

At the last corner, outside the tenement block, Karen stamped her feet and, with numb fingers, fumbled for the keys. Inside, as she dragged herself up four flights of vinyl-covered stairs, from behind the closed doors of the other flats there came sounds of television and people talking.

She unlocked their door. He wasn't there, but only the heaps of text-books, his study sheets and folders. A torn-off scrap of paper lay on the table, with a message. *I love you.*

Karen smiled. She turned up the heater to maximum then, crossing to the window, drew the curtains against the night.

It was almost midnight before she heard his key in the lock.

Damien came in from working at the hospital, his drawn face creasing up with a sudden lightness as he saw her. Arms outstretched in pleasure, she welcomed him. Now they could both forget whatever might lie outside.